DEATH'S G
WHISPER

A Meg Harris
Mystery

R.J. Harlick

RENDEZVOUS
PRESS

Cover photo by R.J. Harlick. Photo illustration by Christopher Chuckry

Le Conseil des Arts | The Canada Council
du Canada | for the arts
depuis 1957 | since 1957

We acknowledge the support of the Canada Council for the Arts for our publishing program.

Napoleon Publishing/RendezVous Press
Toronto, Ontario, Canada

Printed in Canada

08 07 06 05 04   5 4 3 2 1

National Library of Canada Cataloguing in Publication

Harlick, R. J., date-
       Death's golden whisper / R.J. Harlick.

(A Meg Harris mystery)
ISBN 1-894917-11-1

       I. Title. II. Series: Harlick, R. J., date- Meg Harris mystery.

PS8615.A74D42 2004   C813'.6   C2004-903226-7

To my Mother, Jean McLeod, my first fan.
I only wish she were here to enjoy the book
that she avidly read in its beginnings.

ACKNOWLEDGEMENTS

A first novel is always a labour of love. It starts with a simple desire to write and ends with the thrill of finally seeing the hard fought words firmly encased in a book binding. But the journey to this destination is long and arduous and cannot be done alone.

Many people have supported me on this journey. I would like to express my gratitude to them: authors, Nino Ricci and Lyn Hamilton, both of whom read my first writings and inspired me to keep going; the many critiquers—Dominique Benoit, Alex Brett, Barbara Fradkin, Judy Nasby, Madona Skaff and Jane Tun—who offered valuable advice; Line Bastrash who perfected my French; Pauline Decontie, Annette Smith and the Kitigan Zibi website, who gave me insight into the Algonquin First Nation community; and, of course, my publisher Sylvia McConnell and editor, Allister Thompson, who have worked so diligently with me to bring my words to these pages. And I must not forget my family: my father, Penn McLeod, my two sisters, Sally McLeod-Miller and Susan McLeod-O'Reilly and, of course, my husband, Jim, who have been sources of continuing support throughout the lengthy process. And lastly, DeMontigny, my black standard poodle, whose constant presence helped to cheer me up during the inevitable low moments every author faces.

ONE

They arrived without warning on a perfect Indian Summer day. Marie and I were outside enjoying the rare autumn heat, the last before our northeast corner of the Outaouais was locked into winter. We were planting daffodil bulbs. Or more correctly, Marie was planting while I pretended, my interests slanting more towards soaking up the sun's rays than doing actual work.

We were partway down the steep rocky slope that dropped into Echo Lake when they swooped over the forest canopy. Perhaps Marie heard them coming. I didn't. One moment I was daydreaming, the next I was running for cover.

The first roar startled me into thinking we were under attack. By the time I realized it was only a floatplane swooping down to land on Echo Lake, a second plane was clipping the tops of the pine trees. At least, that's what I thought when a shower of dead needles rained down upon Marie and me.

"Get the hell away from my trees!" I shouted from behind a particularly solid wall of rock. These pines had survived forest fires and logging frenzies. The last thing I wanted was to have them destroyed by a couple of kamikaze pilots.

The second plane zoomed down close on the tail of the other, so close I feared they would collide. But neither attempted a landing. Instead, one behind the other, they raced above the flat water, then with deep howls arched back up in time to clear the giant trees of Whispers Island at the far end

1

of the lake. The roar of their engines reverberated through the hills. A flock of ducks burst from behind the island.

With their wing tips shimmering in the autumn sun, the planes circled over the gold-drenched hills and back down towards the lake like giant ospreys, talons extended, zeroing in for the kill. Each landed this time, one after another, and skidded along the glass surface, sending a jet of spray into the air. They coasted past the empty shore of Whispers Island and disappeared behind the cliffs of Indian Point into a neighbouring bay.

Within seconds, several motor boats appeared from the north, from the direction of my neighbour, the Forgotten Bay Fishing Camp. They swerved past us and headed west across the half mile distance to Indian Point, to the bay where the planes had gone.

Unfazed by the planes, Marie remained on the exposed rock close to where I'd been planting. "See, only fishermen," she said, laughing. "You think the trickster come to get you, eh?"

Her black eyes twinkled as she climbed to where I'd fled and offered her hand.

However, feeling like an idiot for overreacting, I declined her help and scrambled to my feet unaided.

She was right. The planes had to be bringing fishermen. It was the noise of their sudden and unexpected arrival that made me think it was something more threatening.

Marie brushed the long, brittle needles from her shoulders and arms. Several pierced her treasured red scarf, the one she always wore. She called it her dream kerchief, because it kept her dreams from flying away. I delicately plucked out the needles.

I moved her thick braids aside and swept the needles from her back. Some remained entangled in the loose weave of her sweater. I debated leaving them, but knowing Marie's penchant for neatness, I eased them out carefully, so they wouldn't pull on the worn threads. As for myself, I just shook like a dog, and with a few brisk swipes over my purple sweats, considered myself clean.

"No time to stop, lots work left to do," said Marie in the brusque tone she assumed when goading me into doing more work.

I rubbed my aching back, did a few deep knee bends and reluctantly returned to the rock ledge.

A third plane thundered overhead, but this one missed the pines and landed without fuss on the lake.

"Sure is a big fishing party." I watched the plane taxi through the still water to join the other two planes behind Indian Point. "Must be in a hurry, if they can't handle the two hour drive from Ottawa."

"White man always in a hurry," muttered Marie, obviously not wanting to miss an opportunity to add more ammunition to her side of our ongoing debate over the advantages of country living versus city. A debate she was winning, since I usually agreed.

She handed me my basket, more full than empty of daffodil bulbs. Although we'd been planting for much of the afternoon, we were barely past the mid-point of the steep incline that defined the edge of the Point. This massive mound of granite with its fringe of old growth pine extended like a giant finger into Echo Lake. My great-grandfather had christened it Three Deer Point. Although no one knew the origins of the name, I suspected—if the Harris family tales of Great-grandpa Joe were anything to go by—that it was to immortalize a successful hunt, not a romantic sighting of three deer.

This morning I'd had the great idea of banishing winter's blahs with a cascade of spring yellow. Now, I was thinking a rivulet would do just fine.

We were following the stairs that led down to the dock. I was planting on one side of them, Marie, the other. I found it painstaking work and hard on a back not fully conditioned to manual labour. My knees hurt from kneeling on uncushioned rock. My bottom was sore from losing my balance on the uneven slope. Still, I was kind of proud of the number of scattered pockets of earth I'd populated with bulbs, even if I had been concentrating on my tan.

Marie, more used to physical work, crouched several rock ledges further down the hill. Despite her weight, she moved effortlessly over the steep, uneven slope. The shimmer from the lake cast her in a fiery halo, making her look almost ethereal.

I thought, as I often did, how lucky I was to have found Marie Whiteduck, or more correctly, to have been found by her. Shortly after I'd moved into Three Deer Point, she'd stood on my doorstep, a squat, solid mass of denim, ready to help make my great-aunt's long vacant cottage livable. I couldn't say no to the beseeching but determined look on her deeply lined face. Besides, I owed it to her mother, Whispering Pine, who'd spent a lifetime helping Aunt Aggie, my great-aunt.

However, as close as Marie and I had become, I couldn't convince her to call me Meg, Margaret or even Ms. Harris. Instead Marie insisted on using "Missie", and when she was feeling less sure of our relationship, "Miz Agatta Ojimisan".

Although I was proud to be known as Agatha Harris' Ojimisan, meaning grandniece, the name made me uncomfortable. I didn't like being reminded of the gulf that separated us; Marie, an Algonquin Indian who'd spent most of her fifty-plus years on a reserve, and me, a Torontonian, just shy of forty, who was still adjusting to wilderness living.

Looking for an excuse to stop, I said, "You must be very proud of Tommy now that he has his law degree?"

"You bet. My boy's gonna be a good lawyer," Marie replied, but didn't stop working. She continued tapping the earth with her trowel, then dug a new hole for the next bulb.

Realizing my ploy hadn't worked, I inched down to another patch and began preparing it for the bulbs. "Has he found an articling job yet?"

"Yeah. Maybe. But he don't tell me much these days."

"That's a change. I thought he was pretty open with you?"

"Yeah, used to be. But now he clam up. He get mad when I ask about the job. He away lots too and don't say where he goes."

"Sounds like his father."

Marie stopped. "Louis's a good man," she said, lifting hurt eyes towards me, then she dropped her head and resumed digging.

I'd done it again. I should know better than to make any disparaging comment about her man. A month ago, I'd suggested partly as a joke that she should hide her money from him, since Louis seemed to be drinking it up faster than she could earn it. She wasn't amused, hadn't talked to me for the rest of the day.

A distant echo of engines caught my attention. I looked up to see a convoy of boats emerge from behind Indian Point. I watched them head towards Whispers Island and beach on the island's only flat section of shoreline, a narrow spit of land that jutted out from the northern tip. Tiny figures, more like black dots from this distance, swarmed out of the boats. The wind brought the cough of dying motors and the smell of pine mixed with gasoline.

"Still think they're fishermen?" I pointed to the no longer empty shore of Whispers Island.

Marie narrowed her eyes towards the island. "Where? I don't see nothing."

"It might help if you wore your glasses."

Marie glared at me, then smiled weakly.

I suppose we all have our quirks of vanity. With Marie, it was her glasses. Said they made her look like a raccoon who'd been scared by a bear, which might have been apt, but who was I to confirm her worst fears. With me, it was my hair. Lately, I'd taken to brightening up its greying brilliance with Flame by Clairol.

I watched the figures disappear into the shadow of the giant pines. Other than the ones on my property, they were the last of the ancient white pine that once covered every hill in sight. They extended along the backbone of Whispers Island, making it look like a sleeping porcupine, its tail the spit of land where the boats were beached.

"It looks like they're checking it out," I continued.

"What they do that for?"

"I don't know, maybe they want to have a picnic?"

"Forbidden. Ancestors get mad. Go tell them to leave, Missie." Marie stood up.

"But Marie, I can't do that. It's reserve land. Besides, they must have the chief's permission, they're using his boats."

"No, Miz Agatta Ojimisan. You tell them." She started walking down the stairs towards the dock.

"Don't be silly, Marie. I've got nothing to do with Whispers Island," I shouted at her retreating back.

"Hurry!" Marie yelled up as she stepped onto the dock.

Before I had a chance to respond, Sergei, my on-again, off-again watchdog, suddenly erupted into a fit of barking. I scrambled up the stairs to see what had got my large but wimpy black poodle into such a state and was promptly greeted by the small, wiry figure of Louis limping towards me. He ignored the dog snapping at his legs.

He thrust his weather-eroded face into mine and demanded in his thick Quebecois accent, "Where my woman?" Without waiting for an answer, he brushed past me and down the stairs, leaving me in a wake of alcoholic fumes. I made a grab for the dog but decided to let him snap at Louis. Sergei was a good judge of character.

It wasn't more than a couple of minutes before Louis reappeared over the brow of the hill with a subdued Marie in tow. Head bowed, she never gave me a glance as she shuffled to the rusted metal box Louis called a truck.

An all too familiar feeling of dread washed over me. I didn't move. I didn't speak.

With a final challenge from his startling blue eyes, he slammed the door, rammed the gear into place and rumbled down the drive.

I whispered "Bastard" at the retreating car.

TWO

I returned to the planting, determined to finish what Marie and I had started, but I couldn't. My heart was no longer in it.

Annoyed with my cowardice, I stomped up the stairs to my cottage, which stared back at me with unblinking opacity from its perch on top of the Point. One of the turrets seemed to cast judgment when the windows suddenly flared with reflected sun and as suddenly returned to the shadows. I stopped and stared back at this brazen hussy that dared to call itself a cottage.

It was a folly that more properly belonged in one of those turn-of-the-century summer playgrounds like the Charlevois or Bar Harbor. Instead, Great-grandpa Joe had it built in the middle of nowhere with the only neighbour being the reserve of the Fishhook Algonquin or Migiskan Anishinabeg as they preferred to call themselves. A hundred years later, it was still a folly, and while the reserve now boasted a general store and hockey rink, it was still a hundred miles from nowhere.

I loved this cottage, always had from the first moment I began spending summers with Aunt Aggie. There was something about its rambling Victorian quirkiness, the turrets and arches and wrap-around verandah, all fashioned out of squared timbers, cedar shake and stone, that seemed to shout "I don't give a damn".

I sure wished some of that thick-skinned nonchalance could rub off on me. Instead, I was feeling depressed and mad at myself for letting Louis just take Marie away without making so much as a whimper. It wasn't as if I didn't know what was probably happening right now. I'd seen that look Louis had worn enough times myself to know the kind of mood he was in.

Gareth.

Gareth used to wear that look. And, like today, whenever I'd seen that look, I'd done nothing. As if in punishment, my arm started throbbing. I rubbed it, as I always did, and headed into the kitchen for the only thing that could wipe out Gareth —vodka, lemon vodka to be exact.

Fortified with a three-finger-full tumbler, I retreated to the deep recess of the verandah, away from the reach of the late afternoon sun. It was the kind of sprawling verandah, complete with fretwork and a whimsical roofline, that modern architects decreed superfluous. It was the place where I spent much of my time, when the weather wasn't brutally cold.

I sat, where I normally sat, in Aunt Aggie's old rocker, and took a searing swig of vodka. My fingers, toes tingled.

With a groan, Sergei eased his large curly-haired body onto the wooden floor by my feet. He placed his long, black, pointed snout on his neatly trimmed paws, paws which made him look more like a citified dandy than the dirt-grovelling country dog he had become. I supposed it was unrealistic of me to think I could keep him in the same elegant clip he'd worn in Toronto. But, if he didn't mind the tugging, I didn't mind the daily brushings to remove burrs, twigs and whatever else was entangled in his thick coat.

I rocked back and forth, back and forth. Took another swig of vodka. Gradually, the pace slowed as the tonic coursed through my veins. It was a good tonic. It worked every time, a blend of numbing vodka, unrelenting wilderness and syncopated rocking. My arm stopped throbbing.

When I'd first moved in, I'd tried placing the rocker in several different locations, but for one reason or another I was never satisfied, until finally I'd placed it under one of the turreted roofs where a bulge in the verandah extended over the cliff wall. It wasn't until several months later that I remembered this was the spot where Aunt Aggie used to sit hour by hour. It had a clear view of Whispers Island.

Right now, that clear view of the beached boats showed that the men were still on the island. Who were these guys? Certainly didn't fit the profile of fishermen. For one, there were too many. Must be at least fifteen or twenty.

Maybe there were plenty of prime fishing spots on Echo Lake, but even Eric Odjik, Band Chief of the Migiskan and operator of the Forgotten Bay Fishing Camp, never had more than four or five boats on the lake at the same time. "Spoils the image," he'd say in that soft, measured drawl of his. "Our customers want to feel they've got this wilderness all to themselves, they don't want to be staring eyeball to eyeball." So Eric trucks the overflow fishermen to other lakes scattered throughout the thirty-five square miles of the Migiskan Reserve.

And fishermen didn't tramp over land looking for fish. In fact, nobody tramped over Whispers Island.

A year ago, shortly after I'd moved in, I'd watched Eric's silver boat skim across the water to kick out some campers who'd pitched their tent on the same spit of land where the Fishing Camp boats were now laid out in military precision. It had been a warm Indian Summer day, like today. The small sandy beach, with its silver birches and overarching pine, was a perfect spot for camping. Eric hadn't cared. He soon had the couple back in their canoe searching for another location. A difficult task, since the entire northern shore of Echo Lake belonged to the Migiskan Reserve.

I'd watched through my binoculars to see what this forlorn looking couple would do. When it looked as if they were paddling my way, to one of the few beaches on the Three Deer Point shoreline, I'd decided I would play Bob Cratchit to Eric's Scrooge and let them camp. They'd veered left instead and had landed on the only land where they wouldn't need to ask permission, the uninhabited crown-owned shore to the south of the island.

Now these men, who looked considerably more threatening than a couple of campers, were wandering all over the rocks of Whispers Island, obviously with Eric's full permission. I sure hoped he wasn't planning on expanding his Fishing Camp operation. He often said the island would be a perfect spot for a resort, like one of those condo/resort combinations which were consuming the Laurentians to the south. But he always said it with a glint in his eye which made me think he only wanted to pull my chain, which he invariably did.

I didn't mind his Fishing Camp, out-of-sight at the far end of neighbouring Forgotten Bay. In fact, I often dropped by when seeking more voluble company than my own. With its limited number of rooms, there were never enough people to erode the stillness I'd come to treasure. However, a full-blown lodge with hundreds of rooms within full view and hearing of my cottage would be a disaster. As far as I was concerned, I'd left the teeming masses behind when I fled Toronto. I didn't want them back.

Deciding now was the time to start voicing my opposition before plans moved too far along, I phoned him. However, he wasn't at the Fishing Camp nor at the band council hall. I left a voice message.

I'd no sooner hung up when the phone rang. Convinced it was Eric, who'd listened in while I was leaving my message, I answered, "Eric Odjik, you'd better keep your grubby paws off Whispers Island."

"Eric? Eric who?"

"Hey, wait a minute. Who's this?" I was confused. This wasn't Eric, but the voice was familiar, too familiar.

"You mean you've forgotten me already? Who's this Eric guy?"

And then, with slow creeping dread, I realized who it was. How could I fail to recognize the deep timbre of a voice which once had the power to send a tingle of pleasure up my spine and now brought only dread?

Gareth.

"Ah…hi," I said. The first words I'd spoken to him since we'd sat with our lawyers more than a lifetime ago.

"I hope you don't mind my calling out of the blue like this?"

I mumbled something, as I desperately tried to control my spiking nerves.

"I see it didn't take you long to replace me," he said.

"What do you want?"

"Can't a man call up his former wife and say hello?"

"Look Gareth, you never did anything without wanting something in return. Now tell me what you want."

"To say how much I've missed you."

"Those words don't work on me any more. I've got nothing to say to you."

I slammed the phone down so hard that it almost collapsed the fragile antique table. My hand shook.

The phone began ringing before I'd reached Aunt Aggie's rocker. I sat down, drained the remains of the vodka and rocked back and forth.

Damn Gareth, why did he have to re-enter my life just when I finally had him out of it?

After four rings, the phone stopped when the message system swung into action. Five minutes later, the phone rang again. I ignored it. It stopped after four rings. I rocked back and forth and tried to focus my thoughts on the men on the island.

Why now, after three years of silence?

The phone rang again. Gareth was never one to admit defeat. One of the reasons why I invariably gave in. That and other reasons. The ringing stopped. I rocked and waited for it to resume. It didn't. The tension eased from my grip on the arms of the rocker.

Maybe one of these calls was from Eric? I returned to the living room to check the messages.

"Megs, I'd like to talk to you."

Megs. It had been a long time since Gareth had called me that.

"I'll call one more time. If you don't answer, I won't bother you again. Megs, I've missed you."

It was the "Megs". It used to make me feel sort of squishy inside.

The phone rang again. I hesitated. It rang twice. I wasn't sure. A third time. Gathering up my courage, I grabbed it before the end of the fourth ring.

"You've got to the count of ten to tell me why you're calling, otherwise I hang up," I said, with more bravado than I felt.

"Christ, give a man a chance."

"Two."

"Okay. I want to see you."

"Four."

"My life's empty without you."

"What about Janice?"

"You know you're the only woman who's ever meant anything to me."

"Still counting," I replied. "Seven."

"Christ, what do you want me to say?"

"You tell me."

"I'm sorry, Megs. Is that what you want to hear? I was never sorrier than the day the divorce went through."

"You haven't told me what happened to Janice?"

"I got rid of her."

"Fine." I walked back to the verandah, the portable phone clamped to my ear. "But what's it got to do with me?"

"I want you back in my life."

"Oh." I sat down on the rocker and began rocking. I strained to hear his voice above my thumping heart.

"Is that all you have to say, 'Oh'? I'm serious. I want to come see you. I know we can't go back to where we were, but surely we can be friends again."

Why had I let myself get into this impossible position?

I watched the island. The black dots were converging on the beach. One after another, the boats slid into the water. Soon the whine of their motors drifted over the flat water.

"Megs? You still there? Say something."

"I don't know, Gareth. I think I've said all I have to say. Besides, I'm busy."

"Busy? In the fucking wilds!" he shot back. Then, as if suddenly remembering the reason for the call, he changed his tack and continued. "Look, I'm sorry. I didn't mean to shout at you. I guess I'm nervous."

"That's a first."

"I mean it. My life hasn't been the same since we separated."

"Yeah, sure."

"You have every right to be angry. Just give me a chance. You did once before. Remember?"

How could I forget? That was the first time he left me for someone else. But he did come back. And stayed until Janice turned up.

"Besides, I've decided it's only fair you have the Chaki," he added.

"Pardon?" I must've misunderstood.

"I said, I'll give you the damn painting."

That magnificent landscape. I'd coaxed him into helping me purchase it for our tenth wedding anniversary. In a fit of spite during our battle over marriage assets, he'd argued the oil painting was his because he'd paid the greater portion. The judge had agreed.

"So what's your answer?"

I hesitated. I really wanted the picture. Besides, it had been three years since I'd seen Gareth. It'd be kind of nice to look once more on the man who'd held me enthralled for more years than I cared to count. But how close did I want to be? Perhaps if I could get him to hand over the painting without getting out of the car, he'd just drive away.

"All right," I finally answered.

Gareth said he could bring it next Saturday. I agreed. The sooner the painting was in my hands, the better. I didn't trust him.

I loosened my grip on the phone and placed it back on the cradle. My fingers were still tense, so was every other muscle in my body. The throbbing in my arm seemed to take on a life of its own. Hell, what had I done?

A sudden roar of engines exploded from behind the distant point. One after another, the three planes skimmed across the water and lifted into the air. They narrowly missed the tops of my trees as they veered up and over Three Deer Point. The droning continued until it was smothered by the silence of the forest. But the silence was short-lived.

The boats revved their engines and, like mosquitoes honing in on the scent of blood, sped towards Three Deer Point. With an ear-piercing buzz, they swerved past my shoreline and headed back to the Fishing Camp. They left a reminder of their passing, an oscillating hum on the wind.

The phone started ringing again.

THREE

Eric bounded up the stairs two at a time. On the phone, he'd said it would take him less time to drive here from the Band Council Hall than it would take a hawk to fly. He was right. But then, he had an unfair advantage, a Harley Davidson Road King.

"Meg, you've got to help me with Whispers Island," he said.

He collapsed his firm, middle-aged body into a large wicker chair next to the verandah railing and shoved his mane of mostly black hair behind his ears. Next he did what he always did when he visited Three Deer Point, ran his soft grey eyes over my magnificent view of the lake and surrounding hills. A sudden burst from the sinking sun ignited a neighbouring hill into a patchwork of exploding red and gold. He smiled.

Then he scowled. "Into that already?" He nodded towards the refilled tumbler of vodka.

I ignored him. I was tired of having him on my case about my drinking. Besides, I needed it after what I'd just been through. I took another sip.

"You've got to be kidding. Last thing I want on Whispers Island is a resort," I said.

"How about a gold mine?"

"Eric, I'm warning you, I'll fight you all the way."

He grabbed the glass from my hand. "Meg, I said gold mine."

17

"Gold mine? Me support you with a gold mine? You've got to be out of your mind." I reached for the glass.

He jerked it away. "Slow down, I'm on your side. I've got nothing to do with the mine."

"Like hell. Who else allowed those men on the island?"

"The Ministry."

"You serious?"

"Very." But he didn't really need to answer. Although he wasn't inclined to show emotion—I put it down to a man or an Indian thing—I could always tell when something was bothering him. The puckered scar above his right eye would turn white. Now it seemed to glow in the growing dusk.

"Please, give me back my drink. And I'll pour you one. I think we both need it." I headed to the kitchen.

"Okay, shoot," I said, returning with two filled glasses, one of lemon vodka, the other single malt.

During his days as a professional hockey player, Eric had developed a liking for some of the finer things in life, such as single malt whiskey. With his increased responsibilities as band chief, he'd decided it was no longer appropriate. He had to set an example for the reserve's youth. However, he couldn't quite give it up. So he kept a bottle at my place.

"It's very simple, a motherlode of gold has been discovered."

"Impossible. People have been living around here too long for something like that not to have been discovered long ago."

"Well, believe it or not, it's true." Eric took a long, slow sip of the scotch.

"How do you know?"

"One of my guys got wind of something early this afternoon when he was renting boats to some guys connected to those planes. Said they were with some mining company, said the band would be in fat city with this new mine.

18

Bullshit." He took another deep swallow. "All we'll get is dead land and dead water. It'll kill the Fishing Camp."

"And anything else on Echo Lake," I added. Visions of smoke stacks spewing out who knows what chemicals swirled through my mind. "What is the ministry going to do about it?"

"Nothing."

"Nothing? How can they?" I still couldn't quite believe it, a gold mine plunk in the middle of my nirvana.

"Jobs, the jerk at Indian Affairs said. Give me a break. Miners don't hire Indians, they think we're just a bunch of lay-abouts and drunkards."

"But Eric, doesn't the company have to get the band's permission to use the land?"

"Yup. So I wasn't all that worried when I first talked to the Ministry this afternoon. But they came back later saying they don't need our permission, the island doesn't belong to my people." No longer able to sit still, Eric began pacing back and forth like a caged bear along one side of the verandah.

"Of course, it does," I said.

"That's what I tried to tell this jerk. But he said the records show it isn't part of the Migiskan Band lands."

"Who's supposed to own it?"

"They do, the government."

"Can't you fight it?"

"Sure, with a land claim. But that'll take years to go through the courts. Meanwhile, the mine goes ahead."

"They're government. Aren't they suppose to make sure the mine doesn't destroy this place?" I saw mountains of mine tailings spilling into the lake, dead fish floating.

"Jerk didn't seem too worried about that aspect. Nope, I'd say it's about regional development and all that bullshit. As if the Fishing Camp and other band enterprises don't provide enough." Eric wheeled around in front of me and started walking back along the railing.

"Eric, sit down, you're making me dizzy. How do we stop it?"

"With the land." He returned to the wicker chair. The last of the setting sun etched every worry line on a face that had seen more of the sky than the inside of an office.

"How? I thought you said it didn't belong to you guys."

"Maybe it doesn't, but I'm not convinced it belongs to the crown either. Between you and me, I've never been entirely sure whether it was part of Migiskan lands. My grandfather used to say Minitig Kà-ishpàkweyàg was ours to watch over, not to use."

"You referring to Whispers Island?"

"Minitig Kà-ishpàkweyàg is what the ancients called it, means Island Where the Tall Trees Stand," he replied and took a long slow sip of his scotch.

"Fitting, but if you guys don't own it and the government doesn't, who does?"

"You."

"Me? Where did you ever get that stupid idea?"

"My grandfather again. Once when he was talking about the island he said 'We do this for Miss Agatta'."

"But that doesn't mean Aunt Aggie owned it."

"No, it doesn't, but it could."

"Eric, Aunt Aggie didn't own it, I should know. All her property passed to me when she died, and it sure didn't include Whispers Island."

"Why don't you check?" he asked.

"Aunt Aggie hated that island. As far as I know, she never set foot on it in the sixty years she lived here. Hardly the actions of an owner."

"Maybe it belonged to your great-grandfather?"

"Believe me, Eric, no Harris has ever owned Whispers Island."

"Look, I know it's not much to go on, but couldn't you at least check it out? It's all we've got right now." He looked at me with all the hopefulness of a young boy.

Then, almost as a foreboding, a loon's haunting laugh echoed from across the lake. It sent shivers up my spine. "All right, I'll check. But we'd better come up with a surer way to stop this mine. Do you know who's behind it?"

"CanacGold."

If I wasn't alarmed before, I certainly was now. Any idiot who could read the newspapers would know that this multinational mining company was bad news. Their name had been splashed all over the front pages these past months. One of their gold mines had caused a major environmental disaster in some South American country. A dam had burst, spilling out millions of gallons of cyanide. Countless fish and other wildlife had been killed, and whole villages forced to move. Last thing I wanted was the same thing to happen here. Echo Lake was my home now. I didn't want it destroyed.

Eric had no sooner started up his bike than I was on the phone to François Gauthier, my notary. He would know if Aunt Aggie had owned Whispers Island, since his father had handled Aunt Aggie's property long before I was born. But he only confirmed what I already knew. Whispers Island was not included in the fifteen hundred acre property of Three Deer Point, nor had Aunt Aggie owned it separately and sold or bequeathed it to someone else.

François did, however, offer a ray of hope.

"There is a mistake, madame," he said in that slow stilted manner he used when speaking English. Unfortunately, my

21

French was limited to a halting high school vocabulary and not up to discussing anything as important as land. "I know much about the properties in your region, and this is the first I learn this island belongs to the government. The records for these lands are very old and sometimes confusing. I suggest my clerk check the municipal records."

I hoped he was right, and the property owner would turn out to be someone other than the government. He promised to let me know by Friday, four days from now.

I could think of only two other places to check. My mother, who sometimes knew more than she let on. But she wasn't home when I phoned, so I left a message.

And the attic.

When I'd moved in, I'd found it locked with the key missing. Although I'd finally found the key hidden away in the back of a drawer, I still kept it locked. I had better things to do with my time than wade through the collection of junk that filled it from floor to ceiling.

I suspected there was a lot of Aunt Aggie's past buried in there. I debated beginning the search after dinner that night, but figured since her junk wasn't going anywhere, there was no reason why the search couldn't wait until tomorrow when Marie would be there to help me.

I returned to Aunt Aggie's rocker in time to see the thin red line of day collapse into night. I rocked back and forth, fortified myself with vodka and worried about the damn gold mine, and Gareth.

A faint sound made me look towards the trees near the salt lick. With ears cocked, Sergei sniffed the air. I placed a firm hand on his back as a dark shape silently emerged from the shadows, placing first one long graceful leg and then another into the fading twilight. A head heavy with antlers reached down to lick the salt.

Sergei stood up. I pressed harder. The stag's head jerked up. As if transfixed in a photograph, he stared at us, ears forward, head alert. A hoof slowly hammered the ground. I too was transfixed, locked into the majesty of the moment. And then with a bound, the deer was gone.

FOUR

Marie arrived earlier than expected. I was out for a hike, chasing the rising sun as it lit up the turning leaves. I'd wanted to recharge myself with fresh air and sun before spending the rest of the day in a dark, dusty attic. I returned to the cottage, expecting to have at least another hour before Marie arrived. I didn't. She was sitting on the porch, her still form all but lost in shadow, with Sergei's muzzle nestled in her lap.

Usually, she was full of energy, impatient to start work. This morning she wasn't. She sat in silence, hunched over her coffee. Her fingers played with the leather pouch she always wore around her neck.

She didn't move when I approached. No sound, not even her usual greeting of "Mornin', Missie. You lookin' good today. Great mornin' for work, eh?"

Only when my footsteps echoed on the wooden floor did she look up. Although she tried to keep her face in shadow, when she turned towards me, I discovered the reason for her silence. The left side of her face was swollen red, her eye puffy with the beginning of a dark purple bruise.

"Bastard," I whispered. I should have been prepared. But with the news of the gold mine and Gareth's phone call, I'd forgotten about Louis.

Marie shrugged her shoulders in mute acceptance and

continued the slow nursing of her coffee.

Damn the bastard, why couldn't he leave her alone? Twice before I'd seen her this way. Each time just before Louis headed back into the bush, almost as if he had to remind her who was boss before leaving her on her own.

"Has he gone?" I asked.

She nodded yes.

"Let me take you to the doctor."

She shook her head. She'd refused my help those other times too.

"Then let me top up your coffee, and we'll just sit here and enjoy the morning sun."

I also brought out a cold pack to help with the swelling. There was nothing else I could do. The only solution was for her to leave him, and she wouldn't do that.

But who was I to talk? It had taken more than a Janice to force me to finally admit to the truth about Gareth. But although I could admit it, I still couldn't face up to it. I returned to the kitchen to retrieve the vodka.

"You need some of this," I said, holding the opened bottle over Marie's cup. She pushed it away and watched silently while I poured a good measure into my own coffee cup.

"Don't worry, Missie," she said. "*Kije manido* says gonna be okay."

"Pardon?" I asked, not sure what she meant.

Instead of answering, she smiled and patted my hand as if consoling a distressed child. Then she resumed nursing her coffee.

*   *   *

By the time both of us were smiling, the sun had disappeared

25

behind a layer of cloud. We retreated to the attic as the rain began to fall.

My pulse quickened at the sight of a lifetime of stuff crammed into every inch of space in the large room. Surely buried somewhere in here was something that would tell me whether Aunt Aggie ever owned Whispers Island.

Trunks filled one side of the room from the floor to the steeply slanted ceiling. Wooden boxes, newspapers and who knew what else were piled one on top of another. Furniture spread from one end of the room to the other. A thick blanket of dust mixed with cobwebs, dead insects and mouse droppings coated everything.

The smell of old wood and dead air made us cough. I opened the closest window and flooded the room with a fresh scent of pine, while from outside came the sound of rain tapping on metal.

I looked across the lake to Whispers Island, a dark hump against the backdrop of golden hills. Something moved. Another group of dots, this time yellow, were scrambling over the rocks. Once again a line of boats littered the northern spit of land. They reminded me of yesterday's strange demand.

"Marie, why did you want me to tell those men to leave the island?"

She shrugged her shoulders.

"But you were so insistent."

"For ancestors." Marie clutched the amulet hanging from her neck by a thin leather thong. Although it was probably once a fine example of Algonquin workmanship, its deerskin had worn down to a fragile thinness, and its decoration was missing too many coloured beads to be a recognizable design.

"Yes, but why me? I've got nothing to do with your ancestors."

Marie pulled her amulet so hard I thought the thong would

break. She stared out the window, then back at me and said, "You got the boat."

It seemed a plausible enough reason, but I didn't believe her. She knew how to operate the motor boat as well as I did.

However, realizing from past experience that it would be a tough battle to move her once she'd dug her heels in, I decided to ask her another question. "What do you know of Aunt Aggie's connection to Whispers Island?"

"Who tell you that?"

"Eric."

"He blowing in the wind."

"Are you saying that Aunt Aggie had nothing to do with the island?"

"I know nothing. You want help, let's get started. I got lots other work to do." She picked up some empty metal tins lying on the floor.

"Marie, if you know something, tell me. It could stop a gold mine."

"Know nothing."

"Tell Eric then, if you don't want to tell me."

My answer was a loud clatter as she threw the tins into one of the boxes we'd brought up.

I gave up. Marie had a stubborn streak in her. I'd discovered the best approach was to leave her alone and hope she'd loosen up as her attention became caught up in her work. Sometimes she would relent as the day progressed.

I looked around, wondering where to begin. "What a mess. You'd think Aunt Aggie would've gotten rid of this junk long ago."

Marie continued to ignore me. She touched the swollen side of her face. And then she answered, "Mooti told me Miz Agatta never come up here."

There was that strange word "Mooti". When I'd first heard

it, I'd assumed it was Algonquin for "mother". I'd since learned from Eric that it wasn't, just a special name Marie's family used.

"Miz Agatta keep Mooti away too," she added, which reminded me of the time when Aunt Aggie had caught me sneaking in here.

I must have been about twelve or thirteen. I'd found a key labelled "attic" and couldn't resist the temptation to go exploring. She was very upset and lectured me for what seemed like hours on sticking my nose where it didn't belong. Next day she changed the lock.

"Mooti said she scared of something," Marie continued.

"Maybe scared of getting hurt. Look at how wobbly some of this stuff is." As if to prove my point, the stack of boxes I'd been leaning against toppled over, leaving us sputtering in the cloud of dust.

Then I noticed a likely possibility. "Don't you think that if Aunt Aggie had squirrelled anything away, it would be in those trunks over there?"

There were five of them shoved against the wall, looking as if they were waiting to be loaded onto a steamship. Even the Cunard stickers plastered on the wooden sides and tops seemed to support this. But the thick layer of grime suggested it was more likely they'd missed the boat a very long time ago.

I was surprised at the discovery. I'd always assumed my great-aunt had never gone beyond the edge of the great Canadian Shield. She had a phobia about leaving Three Deer Point. The only time she left it was to make her annual trip to the village of Somerset, about twenty miles away.

"Marie, did your mother ever mention anything about Aunt Aggie taking a sea voyage?" I asked.

She shrugged her shoulders in response. Maybe the

contents would provide the answer.

We pulled and shoved the smallest into the centre of the floor, away from the sloped ceiling. Although the brass lock was rusted shut, Marie soon had it open after a few sharp whacks with a broken chair leg.

Inside we found the answer, at least partially. On top lay some old menus from the HMS Lusitania, with a variety of dates ranging from July 8 to 16, 1913. While they did confirm the sea voyage, there was nothing to indicate Aunt Aggie was the traveller. The dates, though, did suggest the possibility. She would have been seventeen, old enough for a grand tour of Europe.

A faint whiff of lavender and cedar stirred the air when I removed the next item in the trunk, a richly embroidered Kashmir shawl. Underneath lay more magic.

We lifted out layer after layer of delicate fabrics; laces, silks and sheer muslin, which transformed into a mélange of elegant dresses, flowing ball gowns and other wonderful outfits. They looked Edwardian in style, which would place them in the same time period as the menus. I thought of sumptuous garden parties, glittering balls and romantic moonlight strolls.

"Aren't these wonderful, Marie?" I pulled another feather-soft Kashmir shawl from the trunk and draped it over my shoulders.

"I never seen nothing like this, that's for sure." She held a cloud of pale yellow silk to her short sturdy body while she sashayed in front of a tarnished mirror propped against the wall. The simple Edwardian elegance of the dress seemed to complement rather than clash with her red scarf and long braids.

"Hard to believe, but do you think these could have belonged to Aunt Aggie?"

"I don' know, Missie. They real pretty. I never seen Miz Agatta in this kind of dress."

I hadn't either. I'd only seen her wear plain, tired-looking dresses. However, I had to assume they belonged to her. My great-grandmother had died when Victorian overindulgence was still in style. She'd left only one daughter, Agatha. My grandfather was the other child, but he didn't marry until after the war. Still, it was very difficult to imagine my great-aunt wearing such beautiful gowns. They spoke of another Agatha Harris, one I never knew.

The remaining four trunks were filled with the same luxurious ladies' clothes. In none of them did we find anything that hinted at Whispers Island or even Aunt Aggie's life at Three Deer Point. But we did confirm the trunks and the clothing belonged to Aunt Aggie, with the discovery of a passenger list for HMS Lusitania for the same 1913 dates as the menus. Agatha Harris, together with her brother, my grandfather, John Harris, and their father, my Great-grandpa Joe, were listed among the first class passengers.

When we moved aside a stack of hatboxes, we found another much smaller trunk. However, unlike the other trunks, this one was locked. After we jiggled and whacked the latch several times with no success, Marie came up with the idea of using a skewer from the kitchen. She quickly had it open after a few well placed prods.

At first, I thought it was empty, but moving the light closer revealed that the contents had shrunk to the bottom. When I removed the top layer of tissue, out fell the dried remains of a flower with one paper-thin petal still intact. It looked like a rose petal.

I reached in and pulled out what turned out to be the most exciting discovery thus far, an exquisite lace gown. Once it had been white; now it was a dull, slightly stained ivory. Beneath the lace was the satin under-dress, so soft it slid through my fingers like a breath of summer air. But this was no ordinary gown, for attached was a long lace train which would spread out into a magnificent fan on the floor.

"Wow, isn't this fabulous, Marie?" I carefully held it up to my front. Like the other ones, it would never fit me. It belonged to a much smaller woman, one Aunt Aggie's size. "What do you think? Is this a wedding dress or what? Sure looks like one to me."

"Looks like a dress I seen in a picture." Marie spread the long train on the floor.

"Surely, this couldn't have belonged to Aunt Aggie? She never got married."

"I don' know, Miz Agatta Ojimisan."

But the surprise didn't stop with the dress. Under the gown, separated by another layer of tissue, lay what looked to be a man's suit, the only male attire we'd uncovered in this entire collection of clothes.

Amazed, I looked at Marie. Responding to my raised eyebrows, she shrugged her shoulders. She didn't know either.

I pulled the man's clothing from the trunk, item by item, and laid it upon the floor; a black morning coat with matching vest, a pair of trousers, and a white cotton shirt with a wing collar attached. A man's gold pocket watch complete with fob and chain lay in a small box I found in the pocket of the vest. Wrapped in fine linen was a sash of red silk, the sort of sash dignitaries wore on formal occasions.

I sat back on my heels and tried to fathom what this was telling me. It seemed there was more to Aunt Aggie's life than she had cared to tell. At no time had she ever hinted that her life had been anything other than that of a spinster living alone in the Quebec woods.

However, we weren't completely finished with the surprises. There was one more at the bottom of the trunk, and while it answered one question, it brought with it many more.

Wrapped in the folds of a beautiful piece of finely crafted lace was a framed photograph of a man and a woman. They were clad in the clothes of the trunk: he standing, the sash draped across his chest; she seated with the delicate lace veil pushed away from her face. The gown's lace train filled the bottom of the picture. And pinned to the young woman's dress was a diamond brooch in the shape of a butterfly, the one now lying in my jewel box, the one I had inherited from Aunt Aggie.

This woman could only be my great-aunt at a very young age. Although thinner than when I knew her, her frizzy hair darker, and her stance more upright, the eyes were the same, a pale clear gaze that looked directly at the camera with no apologies. My father always said I looked like her, and with this picture, I could see some resemblance. But from what little I could see of the man, for part of his face was disfigured by a spot of dirt, he was a stranger.

It was a wedding picture. What else could it be?

"Marie, do you know anything about this?" I asked, holding the photo towards her.

"What you mean, Miz Agatta Ojimisan?" She ignored the picture and continued concentrating on refolding the wedding gown back into its former creases.

"Was Aunt Aggie ever married?"

"I don' know. Maybe? Don' know." She stopped the refolding and glanced at the photo. "I remember picture."

"What, you've seen this before?"

"When I was little. Mooti was looking at it. Next time I come, it was gone."

"Do you know who the man is?"

She glanced at the picture again, then returned to the refolding of the gown. "Nope."

She was being evasive again.

"Are you sure?" I asked.

There was a long pause, then she answered. "Yup."

I decided not to push her further. Obviously, she was hiding something, but she wasn't ready to tell me. I'd try to find out next time she came.

I was stunned by the revelation of this marriage. Aunt Aggie had never breathed a word of this, not even a veiled hint. I was positive my father hadn't known. He'd often kidded her about needing a man in her life and even chided her for her obstinate old maid ways.

Judging by her youth and the style of clothes, the marriage would have taken place over eighty years ago. Why would she have kept it such a secret, especially in her last years, when time surely would have blunted whatever had caused her to hide it in the first place? And what had happened to this man, her husband, whoever he was?

So many questions, and no one to ask. It was a year since my father had died and more than likely that my mother, who had never cared for Aunt Aggie, didn't know. And there were no other living Harrises. Well, I couldn't leave this alone. The answer had to lie somewhere.

I returned the wedding clothes to the trunk and took the picture downstairs. Deciding it was time this banished couple looked on something other than darkness, I placed it on the mantel beside the paisley china cat that Sergei had taken to growling at.

The discovery of Aunt Aggie's marriage pushed everything else from my mind. By the time I remembered to question Marie again about Aunt Aggie and Whispers Island, she'd gone.

I did, however, know one further thing about my great-aunt. She was good at keeping secrets.

FIVE

I'd almost given in to Gareth when I found myself hugging a pillow instead. Frantic, I looked around my bedroom searching for his glistening male body. I didn't find it. I heaved a sigh of relief. My body didn't. It continued to tingle in anticipation of the rest of the dream.

It was another second before I realized the phone was ringing. I scrambled to answer and knocked it off the table. A disembodied voice called out from the receiver lying on the floor.

"Hello. Megs, you there?"

My heart stopped when I heard Gareth's voice. I almost slammed the receiver back on the cradle. Instead, with the feel of his naked body still rousing my senses, I shot back, "What do you want, calling me at this hour of the morning?"

"Something's come up. I can't make it Saturday."

I relaxed. "That's okay. I don't really want the painting."

"I'm bringing it, but it'll have to be Sunday."

I hesitated. I should end this now.

"Okay with you?" Gareth continued.

I tried to shake away the dream of our lovemaking—the one place that had always brought us both pleasure—and failed.

"Yeah, I guess so," I replied. Today was Wednesday. Five days should provide enough time to prepare myself for his visit.

"Good, I'll be at your place sometime late afternoon."

"No, wait, come in the morning." But he'd hung up.

I cursed. I knew what was going to happen. Pleading it was too late to return to Ottawa, he'd want to stay the night.

I dialled his home number. It was busy. I tried again. Still busy. Next time, I got the answering machine. I left a message telling him to come early Sunday morning.

I decided to leave another message at his office and was surprised to be informed that the number was no longer in service. Surely, he hadn't given up his law practice? He'd always said he'd never share the spoils with a partner. I wondered who'd managed to come up with the right price.

My head pounded from another night of drinking myself to sleep. With my day starting so dismally, I grabbed a hot coffee and a warm blanket and retreated to the verandah and Aunt Aggie's chair.

I sat down just as the rising sun burst over the lake. I watched the glow streak across to Whispers Island, which seemed to hover like some mythical kingdom above the flat water. Mist rose from the lake in the cold morning air, while the lonely putt-putt of a boat echoed off the surrounding hills.

The island's yellowing birch trees glimmered like molten gold, almost as if they were beckoning. I decided I'd banish my headache and Gareth with a canoe paddle and explore Whispers Island while I was at it. I might by chance find some connection to Aunt Aggie. And I'd look for the gold. I was curious to see where the discovery was located.

*   *   *

I pointed my canoe towards Whispers Island. It had become one of those glorious fall mornings that seem to occur only in the Canadian Shield, one filled with the crystal brilliance that makes everything sparkle in sharp relief. I paddled slowly across the wide mouth of Forgotten Bay to the Migiskan Reserve side of the lake. The canoe cut a knife edge through a mirror shimmering with the reflected neon of autumn. I drifted along the uninhabited shore towards the cliffs of Indian Point.

I surprised a stray flock of merganser ducks, long overdue on their flight south. Feeling somewhat devilish, I decided to chase after them, to see how close I could get before they fled into the air. I dug the paddle into the water. The canoe picked up speed. The ducks raced splashing across the water towards Whispers Island, their large crested heads stretched far out in front. I began to gain on them. I was almost upon them, when suddenly, one after another, they spread their wings, and up into the blue they fled.

I found myself exactly where I wanted to be, at the spit of land where the boats had beached the other day. And it seemed I wasn't the only one paying a visit to Whispers Island.

A battered aluminum boat lay on the sand, half in, half out of the water, its motor raised, its propeller still dripping. I dragged my canoe onto the beach and overturned it beside the motorboat, which looked to be one from the Fishing Camp. I noticed a red tackle box jammed under the stern seat and recognized it as belonging to Eric.

Thinking he couldn't have gone far, I shouted, "Eric! Wait for me."

I'd tag along with him. He knew the island. I didn't. Aunt Aggie had scared me away with her warning of bears, which was another reason for not believing Eric. If Aunt Aggie did own this land, why would she want to keep her family away from its rocky shores?

I called again, but the only answer was a blue jay

squawking his annoyance at my presence. I followed a path through the dense thickets that separated the spit from the rest of the island, and within thirty metres found myself on a slab of lichen-covered granite in a grove of silver birch. Three trails led from the clearing; one followed the shoreline, one pointed uphill towards the forest of old growth pine, and the other disappeared into a tangle of scrub.

It was impossible to tell which trail Eric had taken. I called again without success. It looked as if I'd have to search for this gold on my own. Just one small glitch, though. I had no idea what a gold discovery looked like.

My only knowledge of gold strikes had been gleaned from photographs of panhandlers sifting for gold nuggets during the Klondike Gold Rush. But I was certain if nuggets ever existed on the island, I and everyone else around here would have been out panhandling. That meant the gold was buried under the surface of the island's Precambrian rock. Without the faintest idea of the type of geological formation to look for, I could only hope that I'd stumble across markers left by CanacGold, or eventually find Eric.

Right now, I had to decide which trail to take. I tried to remember where I'd seen the CanacGold men, but only had an image of them scrambling out of their boats. A jay flew from a birch and disappeared in a fury of blue and outraged squawks down the shoreline trail. I let him decide.

Within a few feet, I came across a dirty Styrofoam cup tossed into the underbrush. While it annoyed me that others could be so careless, it at least told me someone had used this path. Further along, I spied two fresh boot prints embedded in a small patch of wet mud.

I'd found Eric. "It's me. Meg," I called out. "Wait up."

No response, but the freshening wind made it difficult to

hear anything above the restless trees. Hoping he was just beyond the next bend, I picked up my pace and followed the trail over the shore's uneven and rocky terrain. Although I encountered another footprint, I didn't see Eric. The path rose as the shoreline rose until a wall of rock forced me to turn inland. I headed deeper into the forest. I'd just reached the top of a steep incline when I was startled by a sudden noise, sharp and distinct, like the sound of a branch breaking.

"Eric, that you?"

Another sharp crack was my answer. Wondering why Eric would go off the trail, I wove my way through the densely packed trees towards the sound. A squirrel started chattering like the nervous twanging of a guitar stuck on high "C" and was quickly joined by another.

"Eric, you there?"

I peered through the dense foliage. A sudden gust of wind sent the overhead canopy into an uproar as a shower of dead needles dropped like tiny missiles onto my bare head. For a second I thought I saw a flash of yellow, but it vanished so quickly that I put it down to an overactive imagination.

I gave up and returned to the trail. I heard another brittle snap, then a dull thump on the ground. I decided it was most likely a deer and not Eric. Still, in case it was one of Aunt Aggie's bears, I walked faster.

I soon reached another decision point, where one fork of the trail disappeared further into the gloom of the forest and the other headed towards daylight. I felt nervous. I turned to the light.

Within minutes, I stood at the edge of a steep drop-off and looked across a wide channel to the uninhabited western shore of Echo Lake. Below me curved a narrow beach littered with deadfall and a few scraggly pine. Cut off from the rest of the island by the shear granite wall, it had a feeling of forgotten loneliness. An enormous dead pine severed it into two almost equal sections. Its weathered trunk stretched far into the still water of the cove, while the massive root ball seemed to be propping up the cliff wall.

I hesitated. It was a fair drop to the beach, maybe ten feet or so. At least it was closer at this end than the far one, which was probably double the drop. Then I thought, why not, it would get me out of the forest. I edged myself slowly over the ledge and jumped down onto the hard packed sand.

I landed almost directly over a set of footprints. Eric's? I called out.

But again the only answer was the moaning forest. I followed the footprints until they stopped at the dead pine's root ball, which hovered like an octopus frozen in motion. I was about to turn away when I noticed a gap where some lower roots had been broken-off. Beyond it yawned a large hole in the rock face.

I crouched down and stuck my head inside. The air smelt dank, with a whiff of decay. I held my breath and crawled inside, crunching over bits of twigs and dead leaves. Much of this debris was shoved to the sides of the cave as if something had been dragged through it.

"Eric? You in there?" I whispered, despite thinking it was unlikely he would remain in such an uninviting place.

The hair bristled on the back of my neck. I didn't like it. Too dark. Too still. An eerie sense of anticipation seemed to hang in the damp air. A slow, steady drip echoed from deep within the cave.

I backed out, my legs and hands pushing the debris further up the cave wall. I was about to stand up when a strange fleck of colour caught my attention. Curious, I reached into the shrivelled leaves and brought out a piece of brilliant fuchsia nylon. I chuckled. It was the shade I was thinking of painting my kitchen chairs. I zipped it into the pocket of my fleece jacket.

Scattered elsewhere amongst the debris were cigarette butts and, amazingly, a used condom. I laughed. The cave was a secret hideaway for clandestine lovers. Mind you, they'd have to be pretty desperate.

However, aside from this lovers' cave, it was evident this beach wasn't going to offer anything. It was clear Eric wasn't here, if he ever had been. And it certainly didn't look to be the kind of place where gold would be found.

SIX

I returned to where I'd jumped down onto the long narrow beach and searched for a ledge, a crack, anything to help me climb the rock wall to the forest above. Nothing. It was glacier smooth and, to make matters worse, the wall was leaning towards me, not away. Climbing out was going to be a lot more difficult then jumping in.

I looked further along the wall and saw a ledge with potential, but I couldn't reach it. I tried to drag a boulder closer to the wall to stand on, but it was too heavy. Standing on the tips of my toes, I could just reach a branch dangling over the edge. It broke with my weight. I began to worry.

I looked across the water and saw only the dense empty bush of the facing shore. When I finally wanted some fishermen, there wasn't a single one in sight. No wonder people used this as a hideaway.

"You stupid idiot," I muttered.

I could almost hear Gareth saying these words. And he'd finish with his favourite expression, "I told you so."

The words sure fit now. How could I have been so dumb as not to check for a way out before I'd blithely jumped down?

I quickly dismissed the idea of swimming out. The water was too cold. Besides, I wasn't desperate enough, at least not yet, to reveal my middle-aged body with its non-conforming bulges to just anybody. Walking along the shoreline was a non-starter, for the cliff at either end of the beach dropped straight into the lake.

I paced back and forth along the edge of the water. I kicked what I thought was a small stone and almost broke my toe on a buried boulder.

To hell with the gold. They could destroy the whole damn island for all I cared.

"Eric, where the hell are you?" I yelled in frustration. He had to be somewhere nearby.

I threw a stone into the water and another. And then it finally sunk in. Although Eric was no longer on this beach, his footprints still were. They would show me where he'd climbed out.

I returned to the tracks and followed them once more to the cave. From there they continued beside the dead pine until they stopped at a boulder. I climbed over the trunk and found them on the other side. Except this time, I saw not one set of tracks, but two.

I easily recognized Eric's footprints by their large size. A deeply ridged tread with an elongated "y" trademark of a popular brand of running shoe. I was surprised. I'd never seen Eric wear running shoes. But then again, maybe Eric hadn't made these prints. Still, that was his aluminum boat. I was almost certain of it. And these tracks did look fresh.

The other set, however, surprised me even more. They were from a small foot, smaller than my own. Did this mean Eric had been here with a woman? Had they used the cave? I started to get angry, but immediately quashed it. We were just friends, after all.

I lost the tracks in a tangle of deadfall, then picked them up again a few feet away. But I found myself following only one set of footprints, the running shoes, to the water's edge, where I swore. He had escaped by boat.

A wedge-shaped indentation gouged the sand where the

bow had been dragged ashore. Although I could see where he had climbed in, I couldn't find any signs of the woman boarding. But she was gone, so either her tracks had been erased by the water or he had carried her into the boat.

Then I reminded myself Eric's boat was actually lying beached on the other end of the island. So this man couldn't have been Eric. Unless, of course, the woman had come separately in her own boat, which would make sense if she were married.

Unfortunately, this escape route wasn't going to work for me. I turned back to the cliff, determined to check one last time, and groaned. The top was considerably higher at this end of the beach than where I'd jumped down. However, to avoid swimming in the icy water, I'd climb Mt. Everest. I searched the smooth granite wall inch by inch for a firm foothold but saw nothing promising.

Out of the corner of my eye, I noticed a splotch of brilliant yellow near one of the fir trees lining the top edge of the cliff. It abruptly disappeared, then flashed again at a different spot.

Convinced it was someone, I shouted, "Hey! Can you help me?"

The yellow remained for another second, then vanished.

"Don't go away! I need help!"

I waited for a face to appear over the edge. But none appeared. I was mistaken. Probably a yellow plastic bag caught on a branch.

Discouraged, I sat down on a log and scanned the empty lake for life. It could be hours, if not days before a boat came to this side of the island. With growing dread, I realized swimming was the only way out.

A raven croaked once, twice, and then twice more. I looked up to find him perched at the top of a spindly pine growing at the base of the cliff. For a few moments we stared at each other, then he unfolded his long black wings and floated upwards. I watched him ride an air current high into the sky and wished I could do the same. I looked at the pine, which somehow was surviving on this barren beach, and wondered how long it would take before I looked as starved. Then I noticed two objects close to the pine that seemed at odds with the natural litter on the beach. Curious, I went to investigate.

At first glance, they appeared to be nothing more than the bleached remnants of old deadfall, but the nailed crossbars made me realize I was staring at two crosses jammed into the sand. Along the length of each crosspiece ran a line of irregular indentations, which had probably once spelled out the names of the dead.

It seemed a lonely and forgotten place for a burial. Maybe these were the ancestors Marie had mentioned. Though they looked as if they belonged more to the modern Christian world than to the ancient one inhabited by her ancestors. Most likely they were loggers, long since faded from local memory, who'd died before this area had cemeteries.

Then I noticed how carefully tended the burial site was and realized they weren't forgotten. The sand around the crosses had been swept clean of broken branches, while the crosses themselves stood firmly upright, not slanted as they should be after years of frost upheaval. In front of each was a small cavity filled with a curl of birch bark containing leaves of translucent mica and several raven feathers.

And to add to the mystery, I found the footprints of Eric's woman beside one of the crosses and two round indentations where she'd knelt as if in prayer.

Suddenly, above my head, a loud crack rang out. I looked up to see a tree hurtling towards me. I lunged out of the way as the tree crashed into my legs, slamming me into the sand.

The ground shook. Branches snapped. I flung my arms over my head. Wood clattered against wood and thumped my back. A branch pierced the ground beside my cheek. I waited, body tense, face down on the sand. I heard what sounded like a stream of dirt landing on the ground.

I waited until the sound stopped, then looked up. An arm's length away lay a dead spruce bristling with sharp branches, some broken, some buried deep in the sand. I breathed deeply, letting the tension slowly drain out. I mentally checked every part of my body, but felt no stabbing pain. My legs were pinned, but I could move them. I carefully eased them from under the broken trunk.

I slowly stood up. Everything seemed okay. My jacket was ripped, but that was minor. My cheek hurt. Blood dribbled from my chin. My legs hurt. Everything hurt. But I could move. I could walk. I silently thanked the gods, any gods, I wasn't skewered to the ground.

More dirt rained down from the top. I looked up in time to see a head jerk back. I leapt far out of range.

"What the hell are you doing? You could have killed me," I shouted.

I backed further away to get a better view of the cliff top. I saw another flash of brilliant yellow deeper into the trees.

"Who are you?"

I waited several minutes for an answer that never came. And then I began to shake. I could be lying in the sand with a broken leg. I could have a thousand branches sticking out of me. I could be dead.

The sound of a boat's engine cut through my whirling thoughts. I jerked around to see Eric coming towards me.

SEVEN

I didn't wait for Eric to land on the beach. I didn't care how cold it was, I wasn't staying on that beach a second longer. I splashed through the freezing water and clambered over the side into the bow, shipping almost as much water into the boat as there was in the lake.

"Watch it! You'll get me wet," Eric yelled. He rammed a paddle into the water to stop the rocking. "Christ, what's got into you?"

"Get me out of here," I yelled back.

"Slow down, you'd think a pack of wolves was after you."

"Just go."

Eric scanned the empty beach and raised his eyebrows in puzzlement. The bristling spruce looked as innocent as the rest of the deadfall on the beach.

"If you say so," he said and veered the boat away from shore.

I shook my feet, squeezed the bottom of my jeans and tried to get the circulation going. It was damn cold.

"So what's up? You're bleeding like a stuck pig." He threw me a small towel.

"I feel like one." I held the towel to my cheek. "Where's your lady friend?"

"Huh?" He stared back at me with confusion.

"You were just on this beach, weren't you?" I asked, with growing doubt.

"Me? What're you talking about?"

Either he was a good actor, or I really had made a mistake. His grey eyes looked back at me with their usual open honesty. I looked under the stern bench by his feet and saw no red tackle box. I checked the rest of the boat. It wasn't here.

"Where's your tackle box?"

"At the Fishing Camp. What's that got to do with this?"

So I told him about finding the boat on the north end of the island, following the trail to the beach and discovering the footprints. When I reached the part about the tree, the flash of yellow and the guy, he swerved the boat back towards the beach.

"What're you doing? My canoe's the other way."

"I want to find out what happened."

"Stop! At this point, I don't care. I'm freezing. Just drop me off at my canoe, so I can go home." I rubbed the backs of my legs, which felt like they'd been squeezed through a wringer washer, and wiggled my numb toes.

"If someone did push that tree over, now's the time to catch him," Eric persisted.

My teeth were chattering so much I could barely get out the words. "I doubt he'd stick around. But if you're so keen, you can probably catch him when he returns to the boat on the other side of the island. It's probably his."

With a look of grudging consent, Eric turned his boat in the direction of my canoe. He took off his heavy lumberjack shirt and threw it to me. "This'll warm you up."

Thankful, I burrowed into Eric's warm shirt. It smelt good, of balsam and male sweat.

"Why would someone want to kill me? All I was doing was exploring," I asked.

"Are you sure the tree wasn't toppled by a strong gust of wind?"

"It was pushed. I know what I saw. Besides, it's in the lee of the island."

"Could've been an accident?"

"If so, why run away?"

"I doubt he wanted to kill you. Probably just wanted to scare you away?"

"By skewering me with a tree? Hardly. Besides, why would he want to scare me? I wasn't doing anything wrong."

"Could be someone from CanacGold guarding the claim?"

"All he had to do was tell me to get off the island."

"Gold can do funny things to people," he replied.

The boat's motor sputtered and died. Eric fiddled with some buttons, banged the casing a few times and got it going again.

"Yup, can make a man crazy," he continued in a thoughtful tone. "Sure can."

I hesitated, wondering if he was talking about himself. As much as I hated to admit it, this mine might do the reserve some good. "Are you sure you don't have anything to do with this mine?" I asked.

His gaze turned to anger. "Believe me, Meg, last thing in the world I want to see is a mine on this lake. If I catch the guy, will you believe me?"

"Of course, I will. Look, I'm sorry. I didn't mean to—"

"Meg, stop it. It's okay. You're shaken up."

He was right. My nerves were still jumping. The sooner I got home, the better.

I didn't know what to think. I was fairly confident the yellow came from an article of clothing. But if it were a simple case of trespassing, why wouldn't he have warned me to get off the island when I'd first encountered him on the trail? Instead, he'd remained hidden and followed me to the beach. Still, if protecting the gold discovery was his main motivation, then perhaps he had wanted to conceal his presence. Unless, of course, I got too close to the claim, then he would want to discourage me. Perhaps as Eric said, the tree was simply a warning for me to stay away.

I watched the shoreline fly by while I tried to settle my nerves.

"Who do you think might have left those footprints on the beach?" I asked.

"Probably a pair of love-sick teenagers." Eric's hidden dimples suddenly erupted on either side of his face.

"Sure it wasn't you?"

Eric's eyes twinkled. He was just pulling my chain.

"By the way, Eric, thanks. I'm very lucky you happened by when you did."

"I was checking the shoreline for claim markers to see if this gold discovery was legit."

"And?"

"I saw a couple of stakes at the south end, but nothing to indicate where the find is located. I want to check inland next. I've an idea where it could be."

I raised my eyebrows in question.

"Come with me, and you'll find out."

"Not now, Eric. I want to get out of these wet clothes." My teeth were chattering, my body shaking. "Aren't you worried about running into the CanacGold men?"

"It's a big island," he replied.

We were almost at the beach. I could see the vivid green hull of my canoe. But that was the only unnatural blip on the beach. The aluminum boat was gone.

Surprised that my attacker had reached it so quickly, I scanned the lake. He couldn't have travelled far, for it would have taken him almost as long to hike from the other end of the island as it did for us to come around by boat. But the lake was empty, except for a fishing boat trawling past Three Deer Point, a half mile away. A little too far and too innocent to be the guy in yellow.

As if reading my own thoughts, Eric said, "I'll check at the Fishing Camp when I get back."

Eric didn't want me paddling across the lake in the condition I was in. I didn't want to either, so he tied my canoe to the stern of his boat. On the way to Three Deer Point, we decided to return to Whispers Island next day to continue the search for the gold discovery. He promised to bring some of his men in case we ran into trouble.

Once at my place, he hauled my canoe onto the dock. As he climbed back into his boat, Eric chuckled and said, "So you thought I was with a woman, eh?"

I ignored him and sloshed up the stairs. Behind me, his laugh rose above the putt-putt of his engine.

EIGHT

The first thing I did when I got inside was light a fire in the living-room fireplace, a massive floor-to-ceiling stone structure. Then I removed my sopping shoes, jeans, socks and the rest of my clothes, fixed the cut on my face and took a hot shower. By the time I'd towelled myself dry and put on a thick terrycloth bathrobe, I'd stopped shivering, but my nerves were still ragged. I sat down in my favourite wing chair next to the stone hearth and tried to blot out the image of the hurtling tree. I still couldn't believe I'd actually escaped with only a few scratches. Sergei nestled against my legs. I gave him a reassuring pat and felt a bit safer.

Flames were licking the top of the stone firebox. Within seconds, my toes tingled with warmth. It spread upwards through my body until my face glowed. I felt almost human. I finally started to relax. On tomorrow's trip to Whispers Island, I'd stay close to Eric. Let him deal with the guys in yellow.

I dozed off and slept until the brilliance of the late afternoon sun on my face woke me. The red message light on my phone flashed, no doubt from a call made when I was on the island that morning.

I played the message. "Hello, hello. You there, Missie? Oh, dear. Gotta say somethin'." The click of the caller's phone abruptly terminated the monologue.

Having encountered this reaction on previous occasions, I'd come to realize that Marie became flustered when suddenly faced with the challenge of leaving a voice message. Once her courage was mustered, she invariably called back.

"It's Marie," began the next message. "I want you to look at something I got. I think it what you want. Mooti give me before she die. Meet me at General Store after work."

A quick glance at the clock told me it was four thirty, the time Marie usually finished work. If I didn't leave now, I would miss her, which could be a big mistake. What she was prepared to tell me today might be refused tomorrow.

*   *   *

Very curious to know what she wanted, I drove as fast as I dared along the dirt road to Migiskan Village. Bumps were the problem. Teeth-jarring waves of corduroy bumps, which reduced the life span of my seen-better-days pickup to yesterday.

It took me fifteen minutes to reach the Migiskan Village. Although the twelve hundred band members were scattered over the southern third of the expansive reserve, most lived in or near the Village, which sprawled along the western shore of Lake Migiskan. The store was situated in the centre of town, where any bustling commercial establishment should be.

I turned right on to the main road, which took me past the new cedar strip building of the Band Council Hall and the equally new rec centre, where a group of kids were setting up the boards for their outdoor hockey rink. A little further along I waved to Eric talking to someone outside the Algonquin Cultural Centre, the centre he had established to re-introduce the Algonquin culture and its language to the band's youth.

Over the years, because of the educational system and other outside influences, English had become the operating language of the reserve. Today only the old spoke Algonquin and remembered the traditional ways. Eric wanted to change that.

Another minute, and I was driving into the parking lot beside the General Store. Located across the street from the church, the clapboard building looked as if it couldn't make up its mind to be a house or a store. While the back still bore the original bungalow structure, the front with the flat roof, enlarged windows and neon sign proclaimed it to be a going business concern.

The parking lot was packed. The only store for twenty miles around, it was the centre not only for supplies but also news. I felt the charge in the air the moment I opened the door. While one or two people were lined up at the check-out, the rest crowded around the coffee counter that the manager, Hélène Tenasco, had set up at the back of the store when she'd realized customers sometimes just like to sit and talk. They were certainly talking now. They were talking so loudly, it drowned out the country music Hélène blasted from the radio, day and night.

I searched through the crowd for Marie but didn't see her red scarf. I checked the aisle with the movie mags. If she was waiting anywhere, she was bound to be there, quenching her thirst for famous people's troubles. But no Marie. The other aisles didn't produce her either. I was early.

I squeezed my way through the raised voices and firmly planted bodies to where Hélène propped herself on her bar stool behind the counter. A long drink of water, that's what Aunt Aggie would've called her, and she looked like one today, with her tall, slender body clad in stone-washed jeans and a pale blue sweatshirt. The usual cigarette dangled from her thin lips.

Today's sweatshirt glittered "J'aime Paris" in purple sequins. This shirt wasn't quite as gaudy as her favourite, "Las Vegas or Bust", with a holographic design of a female bust that only served to emphasize her own shortcomings. While she seemed to have an unlimited supply of souvenir sweatshirts, I wasn't sure how she'd acquired them, since as far as I knew, Hélène had never been beyond Somerset, the closest town to the reserve, twenty miles away.

I shouted above the noise, "Hi, Hélène. Has—"

The talking stopped. A dozen pairs of eyes stared at me from under the multi-coloured brims of baseball caps.

"Marie been in yet?" I finished in a whisper. I tried to tuck my bare red head into my shoulders.

"What's with you guys? You know Meg, eh? She lives over on Echo Lake," Hélène offered.

The talking, this time a low murmur, started back up.

"What do you wanta know?" she asked.

"Have you seen Marie?"

Hélène sucked deeply on her cigarette and blew the smoke out in a slow thin stream.

"Got lots of Maries around here. Which one?"

"Whiteduck."

"Got lots of them, too."

"Come on, Hélène. You know Marie Whiteduck works for me. Has she been in yet?"

"Nope." She took another deep draw, chewed on the smoke then let it out. "Not likely to either, not government day, eh?"

After moving to the area last year, it hadn't taken me long to learn what "government day" meant. It was the day many band members received their government benefits.

"I'll wait," I said. "I'll have a coffee and one of those chocolate doughnuts."

Hélène slopped the coffee into a Styrofoam cup and slid it along the counter. It left a trail of black liquid, which she erased with the swipe of a wet cloth. I wiped my cup with a napkin, grabbed my doughnut and retreated to an empty chair on the edge of the group.

I wondered what was eating her. Although many people on the reserve still treated me with distrust, Hélène was usually friendly. But then, maybe her sociability had more to do with keeping a good customer.

I looked the crowd over. They were all men, dressed in an assortment of windbreakers, lumberjack shirts and one greasy buckskin jacket. Thankfully, none of them wore bright yellow. I hadn't quite decided what I'd do if I did come across someone wearing yellow.

The buckskin belonged to one of Hélène's regulars. Frosty they called him, not because of his white hair, but because he'd lost a couple of fingers to frostbite. We often ruminated on the hit and miss state of the fishing on Echo Lake whenever I dropped in for a cup of coffee and other people's company. He nodded his head in hello. I nodded back.

I didn't know the others. Their ages ranged from late teens to early thirties. Under their baseball caps, they sported various hairstyles from braids to brush cuts. A couple of orange and black hockey jackets identified the wearers as members of Eric's hockey team. They emitted a strong sense of fully charged testosterone.

"Charlie wants the gold mine, that's for sure," expounded one young man with the design of an eagle shaved into his brushcut and a bone choker around his neck. "Says it means jobs and money, lots of it." He pounded his fists on the counter.

Several baseball caps nodded in agreement with loud thumps on the counter and a few hollow stomps on the wooden floor.

I sure didn't like the sound of this.

"He say how much they gonna pay us?" piped up one skinny guy with a nervous twitch to his top lip.

"Nope, but hell, it's a gold mine. We can dig our own money," the guy with the shaved eagle replied.

A few chomped on their doughnuts while they mulled this over.

"Yeah, but what's this gonna do to Echo Lake?" joined in another with what I could only call sudden insight.

"Charlie says why should we care about a few acres of ruined land? This mine's not gonna be near the rez. The only people it'll hurt are the whites on Echo Lake, and what do we care about them, eh?"

The dozen pair of eyes swivelled back in my direction. I concentrated on my coffee cup. This was making me nervous. It meant Eric didn't have the band completely on side.

"Guys, enough. Meg's good people," Frosty interjected. "Look here, Eric says mines use lots of equipment. Whadda we know about equipment? Nothing. Besides, who wants to work miles underground. Not us! It's not our peoples' way. We're the Migiskan Anishinabeg."

A few nods and thumps in agreement.

"And who knows what it'll do to our water?" another voice supplied. "Look what happened to the Kiwatin Band at Great Owl Lake. Eric says some kinda mining chemical got into the water. Almost wiped them out. Hell, no way we want that."

Several "Yeah, no way", "Not here" responses.

"Cut the crap, eh?" butted in Charlie's mouthpiece. "You know that's just talk Eric's using to get us against the mine."

"Yeah, that's right," chimed in another. "Charlie says watch out for Eric. He gonna do whatever he can to make sure Charlie don't win, that's for sure."

"You sayin' Eric's lyin'?" came a challenge from the end of the counter.

"You bet he's lying," wheezed a gravelly voice behind me. I

jerked around to see a large, heavy-set man striding towards me. He reminded me of a bull moose in rut, with his stomach and low-slung face thrust out in front and his black eyes signalling a challenge. The only missing item was antlers. I shrank into my chair, but he stopped directly in front of me and stared down. I smelt stale smoke with a hint of wintergreen on his breath. A long black and white feather tied to his braid fell to his shoulder.

I slid out of my chair and stood up, well out of range of the breath. "Hi, I'm Meg Harris. To whom do I have the pleasure of speaking?" I said in my best city manners, not sure what else to do.

"Yeah, figured," was the response. He brushed past me and continued on to the counter. The men opened a path, then closed behind him. For a second, his fringed jacket looked almost yellow under the bright fluorescent lights, then it faded to the soft gold of new buckskin. Thinking this guy wouldn't be above pushing a tree onto someone, I checked the colour again, but was forced to admit the yellow I saw on Whispers Island was a brilliant artificial yellow, not this natural colour.

"Hi doll, gimme some of your best." He punctuated this with a coarse brittle laugh.

"Sure, Charlie," Hélène replied. "Whatever you want."

So that was Charlie. Now that I saw him, I liked him even less. I guessed my friend Frosty wasn't too keen on him either. He tossed Hélène some coins and, with a final nod to me, left the store. A few of the other men, including the hockey players, followed. The rest crowded around Charlie.

I decided to check out Marie's movie mags. Anything would be better than having to endure the barbs coming from the coffee counter. I'd be glad when people finally accepted my white face.

It was 5:15 pm. I was surprised Marie hadn't yet arrived, but then maybe I shouldn't be. If she was working at one of the houses on the other side of Three Deer Point, it could take her almost an hour to walk here. Particularly since Louis was in the bush and couldn't drive her. I decided to wait another half-hour. If she hadn't come by then, I'd drive to her place.

The drone continued from the back of the store. Although I couldn't make out actual words, I was certain the main speaker was Charlie, with his distinctive raspy voice.

After about ten minutes, the group slammed their chairs on the floor and shuffled out of the store, but not before Charlie hissed from the door, "Lady, you and that traitor Eric better not screw up this deal."

I stood rooted to the floor, staring at his retreating back. As the full force of his threatening tone sunk in, that too familiar shiver of dread washed over me, leaving me with an icy pit in my stomach.

"Hey, Meg, you forgot to pay for your coffee." Hélène's voice jolted me back to the present.

What was I doing? Get a hold of yourself. He's not Gareth. Don't let him treat you like that.

I raced out of the store after Charlie, with Hélène shouting behind me. He was climbing into an enormous red Yukon that glimmered new in the store lights. I ran towards him. He slammed the door and started the engine. By the time I reached the spot where the truck had been, it was peeling onto the main road. I was left in a cloud of sputtering dust and the memory of Charlie's moose grin leering at me through the window.

"You owe me two bucks," Hélène said close behind me. I turned around to find her towering over me. I don't consider myself short, but whenever I stood next to Hélène I felt like a midget.

"He got you going, eh? Pay him no mind. All bellow, no action," she continued. "You want me to put it on your tab?"

"Yeah, sure," I replied and started for my pickup, but stopped when I remembered Marie. I peered through the growing darkness. But without streetlights, it was impossible to tell if she was nearby. The bouncing lights of Charlie's truck lit up a group of people walking towards the Rec Centre. I could hear voices coming from the church cemetery across the street, but they sounded more male than female.

Determined to wait, I returned to the now empty coffee bar and grabbed a stool by the counter. Hélène positioned herself back on her perch. While the harsh overhead light cast her sequined sweatshirt in a glittering glow, it only emphasized the acne ruin of her face. It was a shame. Otherwise, with her model-like figure, she'd be an attractive woman. Though I didn't think the scars were the cause of her unmarried state. More likely it was because she had little time to spare for romance. As far as I could tell, she spent every waking hour at the store.

"That's some nasty cut on your face. What happened?" Hélène asked.

I touched it and shivered. "I fell." I didn't want to go into my near-death experience. I did, however, wonder if she could help me find the culprit. "You know most people around here," I said. "Know anyone who wears a yellow jacket?"

"Yellow jacket? Why you asking?"

I did my best to come up with a quick answer. "Some guy wearing a yellow jacket almost drove me off the road."

"Yeah, lots of bad drivers around here." Hélène laughed hoarsely. "I seen some yellow jackets, but can't offhand remember who was in them."

"Could you let me know if you remember?"

"Sure." She swirled coffee into a china mug with the words

Harrods printed in red and handed it to me. It looked as if I was back in her good books to be given the special mug.

"Marie won't show," she said.

"She told me she'd be here, she'll be here. By the way, who's Charlie?" I asked.

"Charlie Cardinal."

"What's he got against me?"

"Simple. You're a friend of Eric's."

"He doesn't seem to have much regard for Eric, does he?"

Hélène snorted, took a deep drag on her cigarette and pushed it back out in a cloud. "Can't say as I blame him."

"What did Eric do to him?"

"Took his job." Hélène began leafing through a well-thumbed travel magazine that was lying on the counter.

"As band chief?"

"Yup, by rights it's Charlie's. Will you look at this?" She held up a picture of some fabulous looking tropical island.

"Maybe we could dye Echo Lake turquoise," I suggested, then asked, "Was he running against Eric?"

"Yeah, but that don't mean nothing. Charlie's our traditional chief. He's Bear Clan. They been chiefs going way back, eh? Eric's clan is fisher. Never been a chief of that clan till Eric come along."

"I'm sure Eric won the election fair and square." I didn't know what else to say. I knew how the government had forced the bands into electing chiefs back in the twenties because it believed inherited chief rights was undemocratic. Whether this was good or bad, I didn't know, I just wanted to avoid a confrontation with Hélène.

She snorted again. "Yup, Eric made a big fuss over Charlie passing out booze for votes. Don't know why, we always done that. But Eric made such a stink about running an honest election that the band voted him in."

"Well, from the newness of his big truck, I'd say Charlie's not hurting."

Hélène looked up from her magazine and directly into my eyes. "He got lucky. Went away after the election and made some good contacts."

She continued leafing through the magazine. She snorted every now and then when she turned to a particularly captivating island picture.

I sipped my coffee and watched the time. I was surprised Marie hadn't yet arrived. Although I was beginning to wonder if she'd forgotten, I decided to wait until six o'clock.

I thought over the implications of Charlie's shiny new truck in sharp contrast to the rusted-out wrecks of most band members. "Looks like Charlie has some connection to this mine, if he doesn't want Eric to screw the deal," I suggested.

Hélène continued turning the pages of her magazine.

"Any idea what it is?" I asked.

She turned another page, stared at the glossy picture, then looked up. She spewed out some smoke, shrugged her shoulders and said, "Charlie only wants the mine 'cause Eric don't."

"Maybe he's working for this mining company, CanacGold?"

Hélène snorted and almost choked on her smoke. "Charlie work for someone, you gotta be kidding." She pointed to a photograph of a white sandy beach lined with palms and turquoise waves. "Boy, what I wouldn't give to go to some place like this. You been to one of these places, eh?"

Realizing I wasn't going to learn any more about Charlie, I told her about my one and only trip to the Caribbean, a lifetime ago, when Gareth was still the man I married. And then he discovered ambition.

When the clock reached six o'clock, I gave up on Marie and

left with Hélène's "I told you so" ringing in my ears. Annoyed that Marie hadn't bothered to come, I headed home. If she really had something for me, she could come to my place. I wasn't going to drive around on these miserable roads in the dark looking for her.

Partway home, I changed my mind. It wasn't like Marie not to live up to her promise. Maybe something had prevented her, like Louis, who might have returned early from his traplines. I headed to her place on the edge of the reserve. I watched for her along the way, but my truck's lights only lit up the eyes of a raccoon sneaking into the underbrush.

When I reached the lane to her place, I fully expected to see light filtering through the trees. Instead there was only darkness. However, I still thought she was home, just hadn't turned on a front light.

I turned in and followed the narrow track through the woods until I almost collided with a pile of firewood that some stupid fool, probably Louis, had dumped smack in the middle. I jumped out, picked my way on foot around the logs and stopped at the sight of her darkened house, with not even a glow of light from the back to say she was home.

"Marie! You there?" I shouted.

Silence.

I called again.

I debated going right up to the door but decided against it. The thought of continuing through the rustling night was more than I could manage. I was afraid of the dark. Had been since I was a child. And with today's near escape still fresh in my mind, I was even more on edge.

I walked back towards the security of the halo behind the woodpile. So I was being a chicken, but it was obvious Marie wasn't home. And I didn't have to worry about Louis. No sign of his truck meant he was still miles away in the bush.

Wondering where Marie could be, I finally remembered that tonight was bingo night, Marie's addiction and the one thing that could make her forget her meeting with me. I thought of driving to the Rec Centre to ensure she was there, but I was annoyed. I'd go home instead.

NINE

I followed the ribbon of light through the dark to Three Deer Point. My annoyance with Marie waxed and waned with each jarring bump along the main road and up the lane to my cottage. One moment I was trying to excuse her no-show with "bingo", one of the few joys in her hard life. Next moment, I was deciding it was intentional. She was angry with me for pestering her about Aunt Aggie and Whispers Island.

Whatever her reason, I would go back to her place first thing tomorrow morning before she left for work and ensure that this time she told me what she refused to share with me yesterday. I hoped it could be used to help us fight the gold mine. From what I'd learned at the store, Eric and I were going to need all the help we could get to fight Charlie Cardinal and his groupies.

When I reached the looming shape of my cottage, I swore even harder. Except for the faint blemish from the timer light in the front room, the building had been all but consumed by the moonless night. In my haste to meet Marie, I'd forgotten to turn on the outside flood lights. Keeping them lit in the dark hours was a habit I'd adopted after I'd managed to survive my first traumatic night all alone at Three Deer Point, a terrifying night with no city lights to banish the darkness. I'd since managed to overcome my fears through pigheaded determination not to give in to such childish behaviour and by leaving on a few lights. Still, there were those moments when my imagination suddenly shifted into overdrive, and I'd sit up wide-eyed with the sound of adrenaline throbbing in my ears.

Like now. Images of lurking yellow were convincing me my attacker was here waiting for my return. I stayed in the truck and tried to bring the waves of panic under control by counting slowly to twenty and telling myself this was ridiculous. I strained to see through the darkness, ears, eyes alert for anything that didn't belong. From inside the house, Sergei barked. But it was his high pitched greeting yelp, not his deep warning woof. I relaxed a bit and waited.

Finally, I gathered up my nerve and raced up the stairs into the house. I locked the door, switched on the hall light and giggled. What a ninny I was. Of course, there was no one in the house. Why would there be? Sergei seemed to agree. With his usual jubilance, he greeted me as if I'd been away a month, then after a few pats returned nonchalantly to his sofa. He wasn't concerned about unknown visitors.

Still, I immediately turned on all the outside lights. If anyone intended to sneak up on me, I wanted plenty of warning. Unfortunately, while the immediate woods were flooded with light, anything beyond was blotted out of existence. But I did have my early warning system in place, Sergei.

After double-checking all the outside doors to ensure they were locked, I stoked the fire and filled the silence with the Gypsy Kings, the liveliest CD I owned. I started to pour myself the usual calming tonic but remembered Eric's admonishment. Maybe he was right. Maybe I was drinking too much. So I shoved the bottle aside, sank into the chesterfield in front of the fire and tried to relax on my own.

It was ridiculous, all these precautions. Just my nerves

taking over. There was no reason for the guy in yellow to come here. As Eric said, this guy was only protecting his interests on Whispers Island. As long as I didn't interfere with the claim, he'd leave me alone.

Gradually, I calmed down as the heat of the fire wrapped me in a cocoon of soothing warmth. I sank deeper into the cushions, while the Gypsy Kings' dancing guitars swirled around me.

As I contemplated the flickering orange, my eyes wandered to the mantel, to Aunt Aggie's amazing wedding photograph perched beside Sergei's china cat. She and her unknown husband appeared just like any other newly married couple, shy with each other, but with a hopeful earnestness in their smiles.

I found it a very sad picture. This happy looking Agatha Harris was not the Agatha I knew. Although Aunt Aggie had seemed content with her life, she never smiled. It used to bother me so much that I used to crack jokes, make funny faces to get her to laugh or at least raise the corners of her mouth, but it never worked. She just grunted and told me to stop such foolish nonsense.

Wondering if I could learn more from this photo, I removed it from the mantel.

They looked comfortable together; she, seated with an unfamiliar elegance, a serene smile on her lips, her eyes sparkling, hands clasped firmly on her lap; he, towering behind her with one hand resting on her shoulder, as if proclaiming "she's mine".

This young Agatha Harris was slightly slimmer than her older version. While Aunt Aggie's mind might have suffered from old age, her body hadn't. Perhaps it was the active life she'd led during her years alone at Three Deer Point that had kept her from becoming stooped and unsteady. She, with the help of Marie's mother, Whispering Pine, had performed all the heavy work; chopping firewood, tending a flourishing maple sugar operation, maintaining a large vegetable garden and keeping Three Deer Point in good repair, not an easy task, as I was discovering.

Her hair was dark in this picture, not the grey of her later years. No doubt it was the deep auburn I remembered from my childhood. A colour I used to wish I had, not the fiery red I was born with. But it was the smoothness of the skin on her hands and her arms in the photo that I noticed most. With not a blemish to mar the milky whiteness, it was in sharp contrast to the disfigured hands and arms I knew. I'd once asked Aunt Aggie about the angry scars she hid beneath long sleeves. She'd replied they were from a fire a long time ago and then, more as an afterthought, had added, in another life.

I'd assumed she meant when she was a child. I'd even thought the scars had kept her from marrying, but clearly this photo showed that the accident had occurred after the marriage. Perhaps her husband was the kind of man who couldn't bear disfigurement and had left her.

But then I was assuming it was he who'd left. Maybe it was Aunt Aggie who, unlike me, had had the smarts to call a halt to a relationship that was growing worse by the day. And then again, maybe death had intervened. Death, however, seemed unlikely, for I doubted Aunt Aggie would have hidden her widowhood. In her day, being a widow would have carried a certain cachet, unlike the stigma of shame that would have been associated with a failed marriage.

And who was this ramrod-stiff stranger with dark hair, neatly clipped mustache and pince-nez clamped on the end of his nose? His pale eyes and the shape of his brow seemed familiar, but I couldn't recall from where. I tried removing the spot of dirt to get a better view of his face but discovered it was under the glass.

The photograph itself didn't provide any clues. I assumed it had been taken sometime around World War I. My aunt's gown was of that period. And the setting of the photograph was no different from any I'd seen from that time; the standard chair, this one intricately carved, a small spindly table with a large bouquet of flowers in a Chinese vase, an oriental carpet on the floor and heavy tasseled drapes in the background. Clearly this wasn't a poor man's wedding, unless the photographer had provided these props. But then, my great-aunt wasn't poor nor, judging from his confident demeanor, was the bridegroom.

I tried to remove the picture from the silver frame to see if there was anything written on the back, but the clasps were tarnished shut, and I was reluctant to force them open in case I damaged the photo.

Since this photograph wasn't going to tell me anything further, I decided to phone my mother, who still hadn't returned my earlier call regarding Whispers Island. This time I reached her.

"Are you calling to tell me you've finally come to your senses?" were Mother's opening words, before I had a chance to say more than hello.

"Forget it, Mother, we're not getting into that now. Just tell me if Aunt Aggie ever owned Whispers Island."

"How should I know? I don't even know where Whispers Island is."

So I told her about the gold mine and the threat it posed to Echo Lake.

"Thank God, now you'll return to where you belong."

"Mother, stop it, I am where I belong." I should've known

she wouldn't be sympathetic. She hated Three Deer Point and anything to do with Aunt Aggie.

"Just like Agatha Harris to waste her money on a slab of useless rock. But if there's gold on it, you'll be rich, dear."

I ignored her last comment, as I did with most of her asides, but perked up my ears at the inference. "Then you think she owned it?"

"Heavens, how would I know that?"

"Family records, something she said, anything."

"Of course not, first I've heard of it."

"Okay, what about her marriage?"

"Married? Agatha Harris? What a ridiculous idea. I told you living alone would make you go queer, just like it did Agatha. Why don't you—"

I interrupted her with a description of the picture and the wedding clothes.

"But, dear, that can't be. She never married him."

"Never married who, mother?"

"That dreadful man."

"What dreadful man?"

"Why, the one who wouldn't marry her."

"Stop! Start from the beginning."

It turned out that Aunt Aggie hadn't led such a spinsterish life, at least in her youth. The daughter of a wealthy man, she had been pursued by a variety of suitors, including a few fortune hunters. It hadn't taken long for one of these men to capture the heart of Agatha Harris.

Unfortunately, as far as Great-grandpa Joe was concerned, this potential suitor had three marks against him: he was more handsome than John Barrymore, he could charm the bloomers off a nun—Great-grandpa Joe's words, not my mother's, so she said—and although he seemed to have money, refused to divulge its source. Great-grandpa Joe forbade him to court his daughter. The upshot was a planned elopement, which was only prevented by a last-minute betrayal by Agatha's maid, who'd decided her employment was more certain with Harris senior than with this would-be husband.

Mother then told me what I'd already discovered. Great-grandpa Joe had taken Agatha on a grand tour of Europe, in part to take her mind off her troubles and, more specifically, to introduce her to eligible suitors. But it seemed he wasn't very successful, and this was the point where Mother's story became a bit hazy.

"I don't know for certain, dear," Mother said, "but there was something about a wedding. I think it was meant to take place shortly after Agatha returned home. But the man never turned up at the church. At least, that's what your grandfather told me. 'Left her in the lurch,' were his words. Your Great-grandpa Joe refused to talk about it. And of course, I didn't dare ask Agatha."

"What a terrible thing to happen to Aunt Aggie. I don't blame her for keeping it a secret," I said. "But Mother, this picture suggests the marriage did take place. Maybe he left her in the lurch after the wedding. Any idea who the man was?"

"I'm not certain, but I think it was the man she'd tried to elope with."

"Do you know anything more about him? His name? Where he came from?"

"How could I? You know how the Harrises were. Hide anything unpleasant. You're no different. Just like your father, never telling me anything."

"Forget the commentary. Just tell me what more you know, if anything."

"It was only by accident that I found out about the earlier

scandal. I came across an old letter from Great-grandpa Joe to your grandfather. Poor Agatha, I suppose I shouldn't have been so hard on her, but she was such a difficult person to like. And I know it comes from living alone all those years. Margaret, I don't—"

"Now that you mention old letters, what about those boxes of Harris family papers father kept in his study? Why don't you search through those? Maybe you'll discover more dirt about Aunt Aggie. You'd love that. And while you're at it, look for anything that might connect her to Whispers Island."

"Come to think of it, it was a short name," Mother continued as if she hadn't heard me. "English name. Started with a 'w' I believe. Yes, a 'w'. Winter, Waters, something like that."

"Sounds like a good starting point. Let me know the minute you find anything."

"She went crazy, you know. Tried to drown herself in the lake, but was saved by one of those Indians. She spent several years in an asylum, so your grandfather said. She had another spell, shortly after you were born. This time that Indian woman looked after her."

"You mean, Whispering Pine?"

"Whistling Tree, whatever, one of those silly Indian names."

"Enough, Mother."

"I'll never understand how Agatha put up with that miserable woman. Why, she never said boo."

"You know full well Aunt Aggie couldn't have survived without Whispering Pine."

"You're just like Agatha. Care more about those wretched Indians than your own flesh and blood. Why Agatha treated—"

"I said, enough."

"You're just lucky you got Agatha's money, not—"

"Stop it. I suggest we end this call now."

It was all I could do not to slam the phone down. But I guess she was used to it. It was a frequent ending to our conversations.

My heart went out to poor Aunt Aggie. Little wonder she was so sad. I should've guessed a man had been the cause.

As I placed the photo back on the mantel, Sergei suddenly barked. I dropped it, and it smashed on the stone hearth, sending shards of glass in every direction. I tensed, waiting for Sergei to bark again. He didn't, so I retrieved the damaged photo from the ground. As I lifted it from the frame, something other than glass floated to the ground.

Sergei barked again, this time with real warning. Visions of stalking yellow pushed everything else from my mind. Sergei leapt to the window. For a moment, I hesitated, not sure if I wanted to know what was out there. Then, deciding I wouldn't relax until I knew, I moved to the wall and poked my head around the window sash, careful to keep my body away from the window. The last thing I wanted to do was present a full frontal to this guy.

I didn't see anything, not even a hint of yellow. Sergei continued yelping at the door, so someone was out there. And then I saw a small dark shadow lumber slowly towards a tree on the edge of the light.

"Damn you, Sergei! You didn't have to scare me like that!" I threw a cushion at him. He continued barking, desperate to chase after the raccoon. I was afraid to let him out. Wait a minute, this was crazy. There was no one out there, except that stupid raccoon.

I opened the door just enough to let Sergei get through and

slammed it shut. He streaked across the driveway as the raccoon scurried up the trunk twitching his tail.

This was absurd, letting my fears get the better of me. If I kept this up, I'd be packing my bags by the end of the week. I refused to let that happen. I would shove all thought of yellow from my mind and close my ears to strange sounds. I breathed deeply, counted slowly to twenty and let the air out. I felt better. I was going to conquer this fear of darkness for once and all.

I swept up the splinters scattered over the floor and the carpet. I cut my finger on one and accidentally ground a few others into the hard maple flooring. This was obviously not one of my good nights. The sooner I retreated to bed, the better.

After ensuring the doors were locked and the lights on, I started towards the bedroom. Then I remembered the object, which had escaped from the frame. I searched the hearth, where I thought it had landed, but found nothing. Nor did I find it on the floor. Deciding it was just a piece of backing that had become unstuck, I gave up and went to bed.

TEN

Next morning, I woke up to a hundred woodpeckers pounding my head, while my mouth tasted as if it had become the pit of Aunt Aggie's old privy. I gingerly raised one heavy eyelid and snapped it shut when the morning sun flooded in. I was disgusted with myself. I'd given in. After lying wide-eyed awake for an hour the night before, jumping at every squeak and rustle, I'd run to my tonic and poured myself a hefty glassful, in fact several. At least, the vodka had done its job. It had put me to sleep, a state I'd just as soon return to right now.

Why not? I had nothing planned for the morning. Eric and I weren't going to Whispers Island until the afternoon. I rolled over and groaned. Not only was my head pounding, but my body, after yesterday's encounter, felt as if a herd of caribou had trampled me.

However, within seconds I was sitting up, staring at my clock. I'd forgotten Marie. Seven o'clock. If I didn't go now, I wouldn't find out what she wanted until the end of the day.

So once again I found myself bumping along the dusty tree-lined road to Marie's homestead. This time I drove more slowly, and not just with the interests of my truck in mind. The last thing my head or body needed was more pounding.

And once again, the pile of wood in the middle of her lane

prevented me from driving right to her cabin. I climbed out of my truck and walked along the strip of gravel between the logs and the bordering trees. On the other side of the wood pile, the sun was starting to melt a veneer of frost that coated each roughly sawed log. Flies, sparked by the warmth, buzzed in and out of the gaps. They swirled up as my shadow passed over, then settled back down again.

I was amazed that Louis would be cutting firewood this late in the season. Even I, the city slicker, knew freshly cut wood required a summer to dry out, otherwise it would produce more smoke than heat. I supposed this only confirmed Eric's low opinion of Louis. Just as leaving the wood in the middle of the road did.

According to Eric—for Marie would never tell me—Louis wasn't up to much. Other than tending his traplines in the bush or taking on the odd job as a hunting guide, Louis spent most of his time collapsed on the sofa with a bottle of *piquette*, the Quebecois version of moonshine. He preferred to live off the money Marie earned as a housekeeper or the benefits she could receive as a registered band member. Although Louis appeared to have some Indian blood, he wasn't registered as one, and therefore was not entitled to band-specific social assistance.

Eric acknowledged that she had at least had the smarts not to give up her status by marrying Louis. And even though the Indian Act had subsequently changed, she still hadn't married him. On the other hand, Eric couldn't understand why she stuck with him. Unfortunately, I could. I knew too well the vice-grip of a love-hate relation with a man who worked on all your insecurities to keep you grovelling at his feet.

The front yard looked as if it suffered from the same lack of energy. That is, if you could call it a yard. It was really just a patch of dried weeds and dirt that had been hacked out of the surrounding bush. The rusted remains of several cars and a snowmobile were scattered amongst rotting tree stumps. At the far end, a canvas canoe with a gaping hole in its side was propped against a battered oil drum.

Underneath the front windows of her log cabin, Marie had created a small strip of garden with the daisies and phlox I'd given her. I remembered the sparkle of life it had provided in the summer. Now it was faded to a few scraggly blooms and shrivelled stems that rustled in the faint autumn breeze.

As I silently approached, the small, square cabin stared back at me, equally silent. No smoke rose from the blackened chimney. Under the weight of its rust-streaked metal roof, the cabin carried a look of defeat. Strips of bark were peeling from the cedar log walls. Not a single speck of paint graced the weathered exterior. But a spark of defiance at this surrender seemed to leap out from the two front windows that shimmered with a reflected sheen that only came from frequent polishing. Marie wasn't going to give in.

Not wanting to get splinters from the door's rough wood, I knocked on its small pane of glass. I peered through the tiny window, expecting to see Marie's surprised face, and saw only a dark empty room. I knocked again and called out. I turned the doorknob and found it locked.

I was surprised she wasn't home. It couldn't be much beyond seven-thirty, a full hour before she usually left for work. I knocked again, but the empty silence continued. I began to wonder if she'd spent the night elsewhere.

I peered through the front windows. The room looked much as it always did, empty but for a few items of basic furniture; a threadbare sofa, three spindly metal chairs and an Arborite table. In the corner stood an ancient television set. Since Louis had never gotten around to having the electricity hooked up, it served no purpose other than as a place to display family photos. In the opposite corner, the wood stove looked cold and forlorn.

The room may not have offered much comfort, but it was immaculate in the same way as the windows were immaculate. I didn't expect any less from Marie. But it was too clean. There was no empty coffee cup, no sweater draped over a chair. There was nothing to suggest that Marie had been here earlier this morning.

"What are you doing here?" spoke a voice suddenly from behind me. I jerked around to see Tommy walking up the drive. Feeling like a child caught with her hand in the cookie jar, I backed away from the window.

"I'm looking for your mother," I replied.

"What for? She's at work." He looked at me suspiciously, through those startling blue eyes that I could never quite reconcile with the rest of his dark features. For Marie's sake, I hoped that was all he'd inherited from his father.

He was dressed in a dark suit with a white shirt and very bland tie. He reached up and pulled hard on the knot to loosen the stricture around his neck. His body seemed tense, as if unused to such conforming attire. I imagined it wasn't. A recent law school grad, he probably preferred the pro forma uniform of jeans and sweatshirt.

"Was she here last night?" I asked.

"I assume so, but I've been away. Just getting back now." He unlocked the door, swung it open and stepped inside, sports bag in hand.

Not sure if I should follow, I waited on the doorstep. I didn't feel the warmth of an occupied house or smell the smoke of a recent fire.

"I don't think she stayed here last night," I shouted to his retreating back.

"You'd better come here," answered his voice from another room in a tone that only intensified my concern.

"Where are you?" I called out.

"In the kitchen."

He was lighting the kerosene lamp as I entered.

"Look." He held the lamp high to light up the dark room.

My heart sank at the sight of cupboard doors gaping open, dishes scattered on the counter, drawers lying upside-down with their contents spilled over the floor. Tommy's feet crunched over splattered coffee grounds. He bent down to pick up the overturned coffee tin and stopped when he spied something else. He pulled up a piece of material, filthy with coffee. He shook it. With dread, I realized it was Marie's red dream scarf.

Without saying a word, he looked up at me. We both knew what the mess pointed to. Seeing Marie's scarf without Marie confirmed it. She was in trouble.

"Where's your father, Tommy?" I asked, very worried that Louis had beaten her up in a drunken rage.

"Supposed to be in the bush."

"Not any more. No one else would do this."

With his young face a mask of stone, his fists clenched, Tommy brushed past me into the main room.

"Dorothy," he said, walking out the front door. "Dorothy will know."

I ran after him.

By the time I reached my truck on the other side of the woodpile, Tommy was backing his mud-spattered Honda Civic down the drive. He rolled down his window and shouted, "I'll take it from here."

But he wasn't going to get rid of me that easily. I had just as much right as he to make sure Marie was all right. In fact, I was feeling guilty I hadn't ensured she was okay the night before.

I tried to keep up with him, but he soon left my truck in a whirl of dust. At least I knew Marie's friend, Dorothy Tremblay, lived in Eric's Acres, as the band jokingly called Eric's improved housing initiative.

I manoeuvered my truck around the potholes of the one and only street of this miniature replica of faceless suburbia and headed towards the last square bungalow on the street. While they wouldn't win any awards for innovative design, they were a considerable improvement over the older form of reserve housing.

Dorothy had tried to give her bungalow a bit of flair with a coat of pale yellow paint and dark green trim. A small flower garden wound its way along a brick path leading to the front door. Next to the house stood one of the village's few garages, which I attributed to her status as a teacher at the school.

The front door was closing as I stopped behind Tommy's car. I raced up the walkway, as Dorothy swung the door back open.

"Meg Harris!" she exclaimed, clearly surprised by my presence. Tommy glared at me from over her shoulder. "What brings you here at this hour?" She turned around to Tommy. "Both of you?"

A few years older than my early forties, Dorothy was tall, with a certain feline elegance to her walk. She was dressed in a simple earth-tone skirt and turtleneck sweater. Her thick hair flowed over her shoulders and down her back like a shawl of ebony satin.

I didn't know her well, but what I'd learned from Marie I liked. I had the impression Marie confided much of her troubled life into Dorothy's care and saw her as a sanctuary when things became just a little too unbearable.

"You're lucky. I was about to leave for school," she said. Her warm brown eyes arched in worry. "It has to do with Marie, doesn't it?"

She led us into the front room.

While the outside of her house was sedately suburban, inside was an exotic world. The walls were a riot of rainbow coloured creatures. Some I recognized as paintings by the native artist Norval Morrisseau. Others were less familiar, but equally dramatic. Sprinkled amongst the cavorting creatures were other staring faces with empty eyes peering through cornhusk masks, their tongues sticking out in mock derision.

In the window hung a dream catcher. The circle of delicate webbing with seven long slender feathers flirted gently with the sun. Dorothy had hung it where Marie had told me to hang mine, in a spot where the morning sun could turn the bad dreams trapped overnight by the web into dew. It had worked. I was no longer bothered by nightmares.

"I want you to tell Meg to leave, Auntie," said Tommy. "This has nothing to do with her."

Before I had a chance to state my case, Dorothy replied, "Meg's presence says it does. Quit your complaining and tell me what's happened."

Dorothy gestured us to sit in the two wing-backed chairs, one on either side of the fireplace, dark but for the faint glow of a few dying embers. I took one of the chairs, while Tommy remained standing, arms crossed in front, an angry scowl on his face.

"Mooti's not at home. I'm hoping you know where she is," Tommy said.

"What has Louis done now?" Dorothy said in a voice that suggested more resignation than surprise.

"Hell, how should I know? Probably nothing, but it looked like there was some kind of argument or fight. Thought she might've come here."

"God, the number of times I've prayed he'd just disappear into the bush and never come back." Dorothy shook her head. "Sorry, Tommy, but your father should have been locked up years ago."

"I'd just as soon not get into that now, if it's okay by you." Tommy's blue eyes flashed quickly in my direction, then back to Dorothy.

Insulted by his inference, I shot back, "Tommy, I'm not sure what you're trying to hide from me. It doesn't take too much brainpower to figure out what your father was doing to her. Besides, don't think you Indians have cornered the market on abuse."

"Okay, okay, just tell me where she is, *Noshenj*, and I'll be on my way."

"Relax, Tommy, you're not going anywhere until we all know." Dorothy sat down on the velvet sofa across from me and motioned Tommy to sit too. "Where's your father?"

Tommy remained standing. He glanced at me, then turned back to Dorothy. "Thought he was in the bush. Not sure now."

Dorothy continued. "I don't know where your mother is this moment, but she was here Tuesday after work, two nights ago. She was okay then. Do you know when this fight took place?"

"Tuesday night, last night, what does it matter?" Tommy wrenched his tie from his neck and tossed it with his jacket onto the chair.

"It matters a lot," I retorted. "Say the fight happened after she left here. Say your father injured her badly. That would mean for the past two days, your mother has been lying hurt and unattended, possibly outside in this cold."

"Okay, I get the point," he replied.

"But you're lucky," I continued. "The fight probably happened yesterday between the time she phoned me and the time I was supposed to meet her at the store. Still, one night outside in these near freezing temperatures wouldn't do her any good."

Dorothy added, "I can't believe Louis would hurt her that badly. He always seems to stop just short of doing her serious harm."

Without a word, Tommy pulled Marie's dream scarf from his pants pocket.

Dorothy's shoulders fell. "Are we sure it was Louis? Maybe something else happened?"

"Perhaps, but what? Louis beating her up is the only explanation that makes sense," I replied. "But before we go too far, I think we should at least check to see if by some miracle there wasn't a fight, and she's working this very moment blissfully ignorant of our fears."

"I'll check," replied Tommy as he headed down the hall to the kitchen.

"And yesterday too," I yelled at his retreating back.

"God, it's all my fault," Dorothy groaned. "I should have made her stay. I knew something was up. She was so upset, wouldn't sit still, kept fidgeting with her amulet. At one point, she even took it off. I thought after all these years she was finally going to show me what it contained. But she changed her mind and put it back on again."

"Did she say what was bothering her?" I asked.

"Louis, who else." Dorothy played with the gold band on her finger. "I'll never forgive myself if something has happened to her. "

"Please, don't blame yourself, Dorothy. There's no way you could have anticipated this."

"If you only knew the number of times I've blamed myself for not interfering."

I nodded in sympathy, thinking of Monday afternoon, when I hadn't interfered either. I'd let Louis drag her off without a whimper of protest, knowing full well what would probably happen, and it had.

"Did she say why she was upset with Louis?" I asked.

"Not really, but she was very upset about the gold mine, kept asking me all sorts of crazy questions, as if I would know anything about it. She wanted to know who CanacGold was. How'd they know where to find the gold? Who told them? Questions like that. She never stopped. You know, from the way she was talking, it was almost as if she knew the gold was there before talk of this mine started."

"Is it possible?" I asked, wondering if this was the information she had refused to tell me.

A low murmur, punctuated by the sound of a fridge opening and closing, drifted in from the direction of the kitchen.

"I don't see how. The first any of us learned about it was a few days ago, when those planes came in. Except now that you mention it, she did mutter something about Louis and a lot of money. She seemed to be accusing him of something."

"What's that about Papa and money?" joined in Tommy walking into the living room. He carried a bottle of beer.

Before he had a chance to take a slurp, Dorothy grabbed it from his hand. "I don't care whether you're white enough to be a lawyer or not, you're not drinking in my house at this hour of the day."

Tommy stopped, plainly startled by the force of Dorothy's response. For a moment, I thought he was going to grab the bottle back from her, but he kicked the chair instead.

"Is she at work?" I asked, anxious to know the answer.

But Tommy ignored my question and turned to Dorothy.

"What were you saying about Mooti and a gold mine?"

"Nothing to do with you," she replied impatiently. "Just tell us if your mother is at work today?"

He shrugged his shoulders, as if to say "have it your way." "No, she's not there, and she wasn't at Betty Braun's yesterday."

ELEVEN

I wasn't happy with the way Tommy wanted to proceed. Neither was Dorothy. He insisted we keep our busybody noses out of it. Marie was his mother, after all. The Migiskan First Nations Police would take it from there. I argued we shouldn't wait for them, but begin the search for her right away. He refused to consider it, saying the cops were better equipped. We ladies would only get in the way.

But he wasn't going to get rid of me that easily. There was no way I was going to sit back and let a police investigation take its slow course. I decided to pursue a couple of ideas of my own. And it seemed Dorothy thought likewise. Before I stepped out her door, she was on the phone asking someone if they'd seen Marie.

Although I was certain Marie had made the call yesterday morning while I was battling my own demons on Whispers Island, I thought it would help narrow the search if we knew the exact time she'd made the call. And knowing the phone number she'd called from would narrow it even further. With no phone of her own, Marie would have used someone else's. Fortunately, I wouldn't have to search far to get the time or the number. The information attached to her voice message would tell me.

However, my heart sank when, back at home, I discovered the actual time. Instead of the day before, she'd called two days ago on the Tuesday at 8:02 pm, right after she'd left Dorothy's, and while I was at home. Where else would I be? I didn't exactly have a thriving social life.

But I couldn't remember the phone ringing. And I knew I'd been at home, because that was the day Marie and I learned about Aunt Aggie's secret marriage. It was also the day Marie refused to tell me what she knew about Whispers Island.

While I tried to come up with excuses, like I was outside getting firewood or taking out the garbage, I knew there was only one reason why I hadn't heard the phone ring. I was passed out on the couch, a state I seemed to be in a lot lately. I didn't remember much, just waking up around midnight or so, shivering and stumbling off to bed feeling like roadkill.

It was my fault she was in trouble. If I'd been sober, I'd have been there for Marie. I could have talked to her, found out what was wrong, made her come to my place instead of going home. She'd be safe. Now I really had to do all I could to find her.

I quickly dialled the number she'd called from and wasn't the least surprised when I heard Hélène's voice. The country music blasting in the background of Marie's message had tipped me off.

With no patience for pleasantries, I immediately jumped in with, "Where did Marie go after she left your store the other night?"

"Pardon? Who's this?" Hélène replied in confusion.

"Sorry. Meg Harris. I need to know where Marie went after she made the phone call the other night."

"How should I know? Why don't you ask her?"

"Can't. She's missing."

"Missing? When?"

"Two nights ago. She used your phone. Remember?"

"Jeez, a lot of people use my phone. What night you say?"

"Tuesday, around eight o'clock."

Behind Hélène's heavy breathing, Shania Twain belted out one of her latest hits. "Yeah, I remember she was here all right. Seemed kinda upset."

"Did she say anything to you?"

"Nope, not that I remember. Just came in, used the phone and left."

"Any idea where she went, even the direction she took?"

"Hmmm, let me think. It was kinda busy." She expelled a rush of air into the phone. "Nope, don't know.'

"Well, thanks for your—"

"Don't hang up! I remember something. Louis's old heap went by about that time. He probably picked her up. Ask him."

"You're sure? He was supposed to be in the bush."

"Yup, can't miss that blue pickup of his."

I hung up, feeling sick. It was confirmed. Louis had been there. And he'd been with Marie. No doubt drunk, he'd taken her home and beaten her up. What happened afterwards, I could only guess. I just knew she hadn't gone to work the next day and wasn't home the previous night when I'd gone looking for her.

If only I'd heard the damn phone. Eric was right. I had to cut back on my drinking.

I decided to return to their cabin and search the grounds. Maybe she really was lying hurt somewhere on their property. No doubt Tommy would be obnoxious when I turned up again, but I didn't care. This time I fully intended to interfere.

However, before I had chance to climb into my truck, Tommy's dirty Honda rumbled to a halt at my doorstep in a swirl of dust and amber leaves. Tommy looked considerably more amenable than he had less than an hour ago.

He rolled down his window and shouted, "I've found Mooti!"

"Thank God. Please tell me she's okay?" I asked, hoping she hadn't been lying injured outside in the cold all this time.

"I assume so," he answered. "She's with Papa at his hunting camp near Lac des Bois. Left a note in the bedroom."

I felt my antenna go up. "You haven't talked to her then?"

"No, but I'm sure she's all right."

I wasn't convinced. "How do you explain the mess in the kitchen?"

"Papa did it. Mooti probably didn't have time to clean up before they left."

"Yeah, I suppose, but what about her dream scarf? You know she would never leave it behind."

He stopped smiling. "She does have other ones, you know. Probably put one of those on."

I supposed it was possible, except that I'd never seen her wear anything other than the red one.

"Seems kind of sudden, this trip. At least, she didn't mention anything to me," I said.

Tommy stiffened. "You may be her boss, but that doesn't mean you have to know everything."

"Hey, don't get defensive. I just want to ensure your mother's okay."

"Ms. Harris, let's get one thing straight. You Harrises may be white, and you may be rich, but you don't own us. Not any more. So back off."

And I did. I was so startled by his attack that I stepped back and almost fell into the bushes behind me.

How dare he? After all my family had done for his. And not only his family, but the entire Migiskan Band. Why, it was Great-grandpa Joe who had kept them from starving. Not only had he established the Fishing Camp to give them jobs, he had convinced all his friends to use it. And Aunt Aggie had started the Migiskan school, which Indian Affairs eventually took over. She had provided all the money and even devoted time to teaching them how to survive in our world. Who did Tommy think he was to talk to me like that?

Hey, wait a minute. What was I thinking? I was sounding like some nineteenth century mogul. Maybe Tommy did have a point.

By the time I was ready to respond, his car was disappearing behind a bend in the driveway. I remained rooted to the ground, confused. Surely I didn't treat Marie as if I owned her?

I was still standing in the drive thinking, when Eric bounded up the stairs from the lake.

"Ready for Whispers Island?" he called out.

But I wasn't thinking about finding gold. Instead I asked, "Eric, what am I doing here? I don't belong. My mother's right, I should go back to Toronto."

"Wait a minute. What's brought all this on?"

Sergei, who was asleep under a nearby tree, woke up, sauntered over and stuck his muzzle into Eric's waiting hand.

"Something Tommy said," I replied and told him the gist of our exchange.

"What do you think?" he asked when I finished. He scratched Sergei under the chin while the dog moaned in ecstasy.

"I don't know. Maybe I do come across as patronizing. But shit, I don't mean to."

"If it's any consolation, you don't. But don't forget your family, particularly your aunt, has been the single greatest force in the lives of Tommy and his mother. In fact, Tommy wouldn't be a lawyer without your aunt's money. Bound to be some kind of resentment."

"What money?"

"You don't know?"

I shook my head. First I'd heard of it.

Eric continued. "Your aunt set up a small trust fund for Whispering Pine, which was passed on to Marie when she died."

Mother was wrong. Aunt Aggie had given Marie some money. Good for her.

"But what did Marie do with the money? Look at how she lives. No electricity, no indoor plumbing, and a shack that probably leaks like a sieve."

"Louis. He drank some of it and squandered the rest on various hair-brained schemes. Before it was completely used up, Marie came to the band council and asked them to take it over." He gave the dog a particularly vigorous pat, who in turned nudged his arm for more.

"This has nothing to do with me. No reason for Tommy to lash out at me."

"Because of Louis, he tends to be somewhat protective of his mother," Eric replied. "Maybe he thought you were interfering too much."

"I was only pushing him because I'm really worried about Marie."

"And he's very worried too. Told me as much. That's why he's decided to go to Louis's hunting camp to make sure she's okay."

"He's going? Why didn't he tell me that? I thought he didn't care. That's why I kept asking all those questions."

"You can relax now. Nothing you can do until Tommy gets back in a couple of days time. It takes that long to hike in to the isolated camp and back out again."

"I hope to God Louis hasn't done anything to her. But

you're right, it's in Tommy's hands now." I replied, not completely comfortable with the situation, but there really was nothing I could do other than wait for Tommy's return.

I started walking towards the verandah stairs. "Come on in the house, while I put on some other clothes."

"Meg, please don't take Tommy's words seriously. For what it's worth, I think you belong here. I wouldn't want to see you leave."

Not sure I'd heard right, I turned around and looked into soft grey eyes with a hint of something that wasn't the sarcasm I'd expected.

TWELVE

I quickly changed into a clean pair of jeans and turtleneck. In my haste to get to Marie's that morning, I'd picked up the first thing that had caught my eye, the previous day's clothes lying in a heap on the floor.

When I returned to the living room, Eric was bending over the coffee table, peering at Aunt Aggie's wedding photograph, which I'd removed from the broken frame the evening before. Sergei, still glued to his side, looked at him longingly.

"I see you've acquired a new friend," I said, glad the dog, who could be a pest at times, was looking elsewhere for attention.

Eric laughed and gave Sergei another vigorous pat.

"Before I forget, Meg," he said, becoming serious. "Looks as if your man in yellow didn't dock at the Fishing Camp yesterday."

"Where could he have landed then?"

"One of my guys found a Fishing Camp boat abandoned on band lands, close to Indian Point. Probably his."

I was surprised at the answer. I'd never considered that it could be a member of the band. It also meant there might be another reason for the attack other than keeping me away from the gold.

"I know some of your people would prefer I hightail it back to Toronto," I said. "But I never thought any of them would try to drive me away."

"I don't like it either. Leave it to me. I'll get to the bottom of this and make sure it doesn't happen again."

I wanted to ask him if he had any suspects, but the closed look on his face convinced me not to. I turned to leave.

"A moment, Meg," Eric called out. He held Aunt Aggie's photo in his hand. "I never knew your great-aunt had been married."

"Neither did I."

"Any idea who the husband was? Sure had a bad scar."

"Scar? What scar?" I grabbed the photo from Eric's hand. Where the smudge of dirt had covered part of the man's face, a long ugly scar ran from his right eye to the tip of his mouth.

"I'm surprised he still has an eye. Wonder how he got it?" I said.

"Given the age of this picture, it could be a war wound, maybe from a bayonet. Or possibly a sword."

"Bayonet, maybe, sword hardly likely. This injury may have happened a long time ago, but it certainly wasn't when people fought with swords."

"Seriously, it could be. I've seen pictures of men with scars like that. Prussians. They used to have dueling clubs where they'd fight with bare sabres until blood was drawn. A scar like this was considered the ultimate badge of manhood."

"You mean like yours?"

He looked at me in surprise, then reached up and touched the small scar under his eye and laughed. "Yeah, I suppose you could say that. You know Meg, this guy looks vaguely familiar. It's that scar. I'm sure I've seen it before," he continued.

"Where?" I asked in surprise. The last place I'd expected to find an answer to the identity of this secret husband was from our area.

"Nothing immediately comes to mind, but the more I look at this guy the more I'm convinced I've seen his face somewhere else."

"What about a name like Winter, Waters, something like that? Sound familiar?"

He thought for a few minutes, then shook his head. "Nope, doesn't." He continued studying the picture then placed it back on the table. "We better go, or my men will start looking for the gold without us."

*　　*　　*

Eric's aluminum boat hammered through the chop towards Whispers Island, directly into the eye of a strong west wind. Each plunge whipped more spray into the air. I huddled in the seat in front of Eric with the hood of my GoreTex jacket snug around my head and attempted to keep my back to the cold, drenching spray. I rubbed the back of my legs, bruised and sore from yesterday's encounter. I moved closer to Eric. Once on the island, I intended to stay glued to his side and let him handle any confrontations with men in yellow.

Trouble, however, seemed to be far from Eric's mind. With the tiller firmly clenched in his hand, he was smiling broadly into the wind, ignoring the spray. His mane of hair streamed behind him like a triumphant flag. He was in his element, meeting the challenges this northern land flung at him.

His gaze turned towards me. "That's a nasty cut. You should have the nurse look at it."

I touched it. It hurt. But not wanting to dwell on it, I said, "I can't stop worrying about Marie. What if Louis did hurt her, and she can't walk out on her own?"

"If he needs help, Tommy can use the satellite phone I gave him. But I don't believe she's hurt. Remember, she hiked in with Louis."

"Yeah, you're right. What if Louis's drunk? How's Tommy

going to deal with him?" I stuck my freezing hands into my sleeves.

"Don't worry. Tommy knows how to handle his father." He looked at me with the kind of look people should only give sick puppies. "Meg, everything's going to be okay. Trust me."

Although I nodded in acceptance, I wasn't completely convinced. Eric hadn't seen the kitchen. Marie would never have left that mess willingly nor, despite what Tommy had said, would she have left her dream scarf behind.

To take my mind off Marie, I watched the cliffs of Three Deer Point merge with the vibrant colours of the surrounding hills. Although the maples still wore their autumn splendour, patches of bare branches were beginning to eat into the gold. A "V" line of Canada geese, fleeing south, was fast disappearing beyond the furthest ridge.

I could just make out what looked to be someone wearing purple at the edge of the Lookout, a granite outcrop high in the hills behind Three Deer Point. I was surprised to see someone using my favourite retreat. But I supposed, even if it was my land, there was no reason why others couldn't take advantage of the marvelous view. Still, I was surprised. I'd never seen anyone there before.

Eric beached his boat on the north point in the lee of a clump of birch and young pine. His guys had waited, four of them. They stood in a group stamping their feet and flapping their arms against their bodies to keep warm.

I recognized John-Joe, the bartender at the Fishing Camp. You couldn't miss the orange baseball cap clamped low over his forehead. I wasn't sure whether he wore it low to avoid noticing customers' requests or to hide behind. Although with his sculpted cheek bones and cougar eyes, I wasn't sure why he would want to hide. His looks would make any girl's heart flutter. They did this one, even if he was a bit too young.

Eric quickly introduced the other guys: Pete, in a black and orange Migiskan hockey jacket; Gerry, who obviously liked his beer; and Jacques, whom I remembered seeing at the General Store yesterday. He'd followed Frosty out the door when Charlie Cardinal had arrived.

"Eric, take a look at this." John-Joe walked to the end of the narrow point and kicked at a wooden stake hammered into the loose pebbles. A brass plate with a series of numbers was screwed into the end.

"It's a claim stake with a registration number," answered Eric. "I found a couple yesterday on the other end of the island. There's probably at least one other at this end. Needs to be four to make it official."

More concerned about the looming threat, I cut in, "What are we going to do if we run into the guy that came after me yesterday?"

"Kick him off the island, eh guys?" Eric grinned.

"You bet," came back the replies.

But Gerry answered, "It's our gold, no way they can take it," which made me nervous. I'd been naïve enough to assume that if we proved this wasn't crown land, there would be no gold mine. Gerry's reply was suggesting otherwise.

"Men, I want you to head up to that large clearing in the ancients' forest. You should see some long streaks of white rock embedded in the granite. I have a feeling that's where we'll find the actual discovery. Meg and I will catch up to you later."

As they headed off on the trail leading away from the point, I turned to Eric and asked, "What gives?"

"I want to go check out your favourite beach."

"You've got to be kidding. What's there to see other than deadfall and sand?"

"Never can tell. Might be something."

"Count me out, I'm not going back."

"Why not?"

"You have to ask?" I searched his face for some hint that he was joking and realized he really didn't appreciate how frightened I'd been yesterday. "Forget it, I'm going with John-Joe."

Before he had a chance to answer, I was running along the path the guys had taken. I stopped when I reached the same clearing as yesterday, with the three diverging trails. John-Joe and friends were nowhere in sight.

Unsure of their direction, I shouted, "John-Joe, wait up." But the wind overruled any answer.

Close behind me, Eric said, "They're too far ahead to hear you. If you want, you can try that trail." He indicated the middle path, which disappeared into a tangle of dense forest. "Or you can come with me."

I looked into the gloom of the endless trees and quickly decided. "Okay, you win." I turned to walk back to the point.

"Where're you going?" Eric asked.

"To your boat. Only way we can get in and out of that place."

"No need. We can climb out."

I looked at him in disbelief.

"Trust me," he said. "If I remember correctly, there's an old hunter's track at one end of the beach."

"And what happens if there's not?"

"Then we'll be stuck. Might have to come up with something to pass the time until we're rescued, eh?" His dimples erupted.

"You can go on the beach. I'm staying on top." I headed towards the trail I'd taken yesterday. Eric's chuckles followed behind.

We reached the drop-off in considerably less time than it

had taken me the day before. Maybe Eric was no longer a physically fit hockey player, but his walking pace was equivalent to my running. I arrived panting. Eric was barely breathing. Below our feet stretched the narrow beach, split in two by the giant pine. Except for the addition of the dead spruce, the beach looked as desolate and forgotten as it had the day before when I'd stood on this same spot.

"That the tree?" Eric asked.

"Yeah."

From this height, the spear-like branches that bristled the length of the shattered trunk from the roots to the tip made the tree look even more life-threatening.

"Christ, you were lucky, Meg. That could've done serious damage."

I shivered in response. For a heartbeat, he gripped my shoulder, then he turned and started walking along the top of the cliff. I stood, unable to move. My shoulder tingled.

"Come on, let's find the spot where the tree fell," he said.

I shoved back the feeling that was rising unbidden and ran to catch up.

It wasn't difficult to discover where the tree had clung to the edge of the cliff. But it was impossible to tell whether the dead roots had been forced to release their hold in the thin soil or whether they'd surrendered to the laws of nature.

A search of the adjacent ground revealed no footprints or other clues that would suggest someone had stood there, only the day before, and watched me below.

We retraced our steps to where I'd jumped yesterday. Without another thought, Eric dropped the ten feet to the beach and turned around, hands raised to help me down.

"I told you, I'm not going down there."

"Meg, trust me, we can climb out at the far end of this beach."

"How do you know?"

"We used to do it as kids. Considered it one of the tests for becoming a warrior."

"It's straight up. I can't climb that."

"Meg, you can. Quit the whining and jump down."

And I jumped, but away from Eric's waiting arms. The memory of his first touch was too unsettling. I glanced to where I'd seen the footprints yesterday, but they'd merged with the other indentations in the sand.

"Whew, what a smell," he said as he walked towards the giant pine.

"Yeah, I noticed it yesterday. It's worse today, coming from that cave over there." I pointed to the dark opening in the rock wall behind the pine's tangled root ball.

"Could be an animal den? Bear, maybe wolf?"

"Lover's cave is more like it," I replied.

But as if to prove his point, we saw animal tracks spreading out from the cave opening, none clear enough to identify. "Wolf, coyote, possibly lynx" was his calm observation, accompanied by a broad smirk.

With a sudden desire to get this over with, I clambered over the pine and ran to the spruce tree. Eric chuckled. He seemed to be doing a lot of that lately.

I peered through the web of branches bleached smooth by years of harsh weather. Many were broken, but a few were still as pointed and sharp as yesterday.

A strange fluttering object dangling from a branch caught my eye. I bent down to investigate. At that moment, something burst from the tangle. I jumped back and thrust out my arms to ward off another attack. Eric laughed. I looked up in time to see a raven land where I'd seen one yesterday on the twisted crown of the pine. He let out a hoarse guttural croak and ruffled his feathers as if settling in for a long vigil.

"Afraid he might peck your nose?" Eric grinned.

I ignored him and turned back to the object I'd seen.

"Curious," Eric continued. "I wonder what he's doing here."

"Using the facilities." I pointed to the bird droppings smeared over several branches.

"Don't joke. The raven is special. My people call him the trickster. Usually, he just causes trouble, but sometimes he can be a messenger from the spirits." The raven emitted several loud crackles. "What do you think he's trying to tell us?"

"Maybe he just wants this back." Though I doubted it belonged to the raven, unless he'd fallen into some bleach. I reached down to pick up a large black and white feather.

"Don't!" Eric yelled.

My fingers stopped inches from the feather.

"Sorry, but you can't touch it."

"Why ever not?" I stared at him in amazement.

"It's an eagle feather, one of our people's most sacred objects. I didn't mean to yell at you like that, but no one can touch it but the owner."

"The bird?" I was confused.

He glared at me in disgust. "The elder or honoured person it belongs to, who else? You'll anger the spirits if you touch it."

"What? Just because I'm white?"

"Meg, you should know better than to say that."

He placed his hands on the feather, closed his eyes and mumbled. Then he gently picked it up and held it by the tip with the vane pointing skyward.

"*Kije manido*, the Creator, chose the eagle as the leader because it, of all creatures, flies the highest into the heavens, up where the thunder and lightning roam. The eagle feather unites us with our spirit world. When a person becomes a keeper of an eagle feather, we conduct a special ceremony to notify *kije manido*. Once that is done, the spirits are appeased."

"I thought you didn't believe?"

"Well, I do, and I don't. As the leader of my people, I feel I should. And, I guess you could say, there is a touch of superstition in me that makes me not want to tempt the anger of *kije manido*."

"Then why are you holding it?" I wasn't inclined to anger the gods either. I figured every little bit helped to keep things moving along on an even keel.

"Don't worry. I think *kije manido* wanted us to find the feather. That was the raven's message."

"This feather belongs to the person who pushed the spruce tree over, doesn't it?" I asked as the implications finally sank in.

"Yup." Instead of smiling, Eric was strangely subdued.

"This means it really was one of your people?"

"Looks like it."

"Why would he want to harm me?"

"No idea, but I'll soon find out. I'll make sure the person without his feather tells me."

THIRTEEN

I glanced up at the raven, now perched on the tip of the pine's highest branch. As if sensing my eyes, he unwrapped his wings, and with a final croak floated into the air. For a second he blotted out the sun as he drifted over our heads and upward into the sky. I shivered, and not from the cold.

"Any idea who it is?" I asked, thinking there couldn't be that many owners of eagle feathers in a band of a thousand members.

"I do," Eric replied grimly, "but I'd rather not say right now."

I didn't blame him. A false accusation would be worse than none at all.

I ran my eyes over the cliff wall, which looked no more climbable than yesterday and asked, "Where's this ancient hunter's track suppose to be?"

Eric pointed to a rock fall behind the raven's pine, which just happened to be on the other side of the dead spruce. Without another word, he started smashing a gap through the bristling branches, while I tossed the broken ones out of the way.

We had almost created a passable gap when I noticed a flat straight-edged piece of wood lying under the trunk. Suddenly remembering, I wrenched it free and held it up. "Eric, do you know anything about this cross?"

For a moment Eric looked blank, was about to say "No",

then his face lit up. "Amazing, it's still here. There should be another one."

I nodded yes and asked whose crosses they were.

Eric replied, "Two Face Sky and Summer Wind, people of the Migiskan Anishinabeg. At least Summer Wind was. Two Face Sky came from elsewhere."

"Seems strange they weren't buried in the Migiskan Reserve cemetery."

"They were, but these crosses were put here as a memorial."

"That must mean they died on this beach. Do you know what happened?

"It's a long story."

"Tell me, I love a good story."

"I will, but let's get out of here first. I don't want to leave my men too much longer on their own. No telling what kind of trouble they're getting into."

Eric walked behind the pine and pointed to what looked to be a ladder of rock ledges climbing to the top of the cliff. Although it was much higher at this end, the wall sloped backwards making the climb seem more like a walk on a badly groomed trail.

If only I'd known yesterday, I could have saved myself a lot of grief. But then again, maybe it was just as well. I would've found myself face-to-face with the guy in yellow, and I would have been a lot easier to push off the cliff than a dead tree.

Within minutes, we were walking towards the interior of the island. It was a slow, steady climb through a relatively new forest of spruce, birch, poplar and the occasional young pine. Each step forward brought us closer to the whisperings of the old growth pines high on the backbone of the island.

While I struggled to keep pace, Eric told me the story of Two Face Sky and Summer Wind.

"I don't know how much is true—you know how things get embellished and twisted over time, but this is essentially the story I was told by the elders when I was a child.

"One very harsh winter, many, many years ago, a mighty warrior named Two Face Sky came out of the north. He arrived after the Great Rain locked the land in ice. Because my people were unable to hunt for food, they were slowly dying. He saved them. Apparently, so the story goes, *kije manido* had given him a pair of magic snowshoes that floated above the ice. With these snowshoes he was able to search far and wide for the game trapped by the ice, and so he saved my people.

"In the spring after the snow melted, he left, but he didn't leave alone. He stole the very young and beautiful Summer Wind from the arms of her lover. He carried her away in a silver canoe to his lodge hidden deep within the ancients' forest on this island. And here she remained entrapped under the spell of Two Face Sky until killed by the fiery wrath of the angry spirits."

"What a sadly romantic tale. I didn't know you had such a Byronic streak in you. But seriously, how much of it actually happened?"

"Apparently, that's the way it more or less happened. Summer Wind was betrothed to the chief's son. Several times the chief forced her back to the village, but each time she escaped and returned to Two Face Sky. And then, one winter, there was a great fire on the island, and in the spring, my people found their charred remains amongst the ruins."

"How tragic, but I imagine back then it wasn't all that unusual to be accidentally killed in a house fire."

"Maybe not, but over the years there have been persistent rumours that it wasn't an accident. Apparently, some years after the fire, hunters discovered bullets embedded in the burnt timbers of the lodge. Some people said they were left by a hunting party, others said Two Face Sky and Summer Wind had been murdered."

"Anyone ever try to find out?"

"No. My people weren't interested. Summer Wind had brought dishonour to the Migiskan. She and Two Face Sky had angered the spirits. It didn't matter how they died. It only mattered that the harmony of the circle had been restored."

"Intriguing. Strange name, Two Face Sky."

"Not really. You know how descriptive Indian names can be. Look at mine." Eric suddenly stopped walking. He looked back the way we'd come, then turned his gaze back to me.

"What's up?" I asked. "Think someone's out there?"

I peered around the surrounding trees, which seemed to be taking on a life of their own in the rising wind. A large branch knocked intermittently against another. Although gold leaves swirled around us, nothing resembling a person flashed into view.

"No. It's nothing," He quickly answered and continued walking.

We soon reached a steep rock incline that looked as if Eric's *kije manido* had overturned a bowl of giant boulders. It marked the end of the second growth forest. Beyond, the ancients' forest rumbled in the wind.

"So what's your Algonquin name?"

"Angry Scar Man."

I laughed. I wasn't the only one who had noticed.

Grinning, he shrugged his shoulders and said, "Not my choice, I can tell you, but then your Indian name never is. Three guesses as to what your name would be, and the first two don't count."

"Forget it, I don't want to know." But I knew it would have something to do with my flaming hair.

Eric chuckled.

We began the final climb to the top of the island. Eric climbed easily over the giant boulders, while I slipped several times on the moss covered rocks and almost twisted my ankle when a mat of pine needles turned out to be obscuring a hole.

I stopped to catch my breath and took the opportunity to ask another question. "Eric, Summer Wind must be related to some family on the reserve. Any idea who?"

"Why do you ask?"

"It looked as if someone had recently made some kind of offering to these crosses."

Eric looked down at me through a curtain of hair. He shoved it behind his ears. "Interesting. I thought they were long forgotten."

"By whom?"

Without answering, he turned around and scrambled effortlessly up the final layer of rocks to the top of the ridge. I clawed my way behind him.

When I finally reached the top, I asked him again whose relatives they were. But he replied that it wasn't his place to say and walked away, leaving me wondering about his sudden lack of openness. Surely, it had nothing to do with my being white.

I watched him disappear behind a massive trunk and reappear again, rounding another. I followed. After the unforgiving hardness of the climb, the forest floor was like a soft springy carpet, one created by centuries of discarded pine needles. Eric stopped beside one particularly large specimen of pine, whose trunk would have taken the outstretched arms of four large men to completely encircle it. He stretched his eyes along its length. I did likewise.

"My people call this one *kokòmis mitig*, meaning grandmother tree," he said.

I supposed that if any of these monsters were to be the

parent of all the others, it could be this one. Its enormous trunk continued straight up through the foliage of the surrounding trees, its crown hidden far from view. Several trunk-sized branches gnarled and denuded with age interlaced with the green fringed branches of its neighbours.

"The ancients called this island Kà-ishpàkweyàg, Where the Big Trees Stand, because of these trees. My people have always revered and protected them. In fact, in the late 1800s, when this area was logged out, we were able to prevent the loggers from destroying this part of the forest."

"How'd you manage that?"

"Essentially a camp-in. My people set up camp and refused to move. I guess you could call them the first environmentalists, and successful ones at that, since the loggers decided not to challenge us. But we were only able to save this stretch of trees. As you know, they cleared the rest of the island and all the surrounding hills."

The memory of one of Aunt Aggie's old photos came to mind. It showed a stump-studded view of Echo Lake's southern shore. It looked like the aftermath of a nuclear war.

I nodded sadly in agreement. "The pines on Three Deer Point were only saved because spring break-up came early that year. The loggers had to follow the already cut timber down the flooded rivers to the mills. The next winter they moved on to another area."

We continued walking in silence. High above our heads, the forest canopy roared, almost as if the ancient pines were trumpeting their survival in the face of man's greed.

For some reason, these trees seemed larger than the pines of Three Deer Point. But that was probably my imagination, for both forests should be about the same age, three hundred years and more. I knew, because I'd painstakingly counted all 316 rings of a dying giant that someone from the reserve had cut down when Aunt Aggie was afraid it would fall on the cottage.

Without warning, the giants suddenly stopped, and we found ourselves at the edge of the backbone of the island, a massive granite knoll, which cleaved the ancients' forest in two. At the far end of the crest stood John-Joe and the others. They were frantically waving.

FOURTEEN

W e've found the gold!" John-Joe shouted. He beamed and so did the other three standing next to him. "You were right Eric, it's here, really is. Christ, it's been here all along, and we didn't know."

"Slow down, John-Joe," Eric said. "Show me what you've found."

I could feel my heart quickening. Holy shit, there really was gold. Right here on Whispers Island. Real live gold. Almost at my doorstep. Maybe there was even some at Three Deer Point. Wait a minute, what was I thinking? I didn't want there to be gold.

But what I was thinking was clearly revealed on the faces of the others, even Eric's. His eyes gleamed, almost as if he were touching the gold.

"Remember, guys," I said, "even if there is a deposit here, we don't want it mined, okay?"

They looked at Eric. He nodded slowly. "Meg's right. And you know damn well if it does get mined, our people won't see a penny of it. So John-Joe, where is it?"

John-Joe stopped beaming, as did the others. He clamped his orange cap down further over his eyes, then pointed to a wide band of puckered white etched into the nubby surface of the greyish-pink granite. It looked as if some giant hand had drawn a line through the rock with a thick white marker.

"Why, that's just a seam of quartz," I said, feeling let down.

"We see that all the time around here. What makes you think this has anything to do with gold?"

I bent down, hoping to see glints of gold, but saw only dull opaque quartz.

John-Joe gave me an angry look and said, "Because of these." He walked over to where several blotches of orange fluorescent paint marked the white rock. "And these metal stakes!" His foot tapped the dulled end of one, which had been hammered in with such force that the surrounding ground was littered with quartz chips.

"The gold's here, eh?" John-Joe said, turning towards Eric. Gerry, with the beer belly, smirked, while Pete and Jacques just stared blankly back at me.

Eric grimly nodded. "They're new, all right." He walked along the rock face, following the line of white. "See, here's another stake. Spread out everyone. Let's see how big this sucker is."

As we walked along the ridge we discovered more stakes and orange markings. They followed the length of the granite backbone. On either side, the ancient trees grumbled and sent showers of dead needles rasping across the rock.

I spied another seam of quartz and started following it as it descended the ridge into the ancients' forest. Next moment, I was lying on the ground. I lay there, unsure of what had happened. My ankle felt like someone had jabbed it with a hot poker.

"You okay?" Eric helped me to my feet and brushed the dirt from my clothes. My ankle ached, but I could stand on it.

"You should pay more attention to where you're walking." Eric indicated a small round hole in the rock by my feet. There were several others close by, perfectly cylindrical holes filled with dead needles and other debris.

"Curious, what do you think these are?" I asked, sticking my toe into one of them. "Don't look natural."

Eric poked a long thin branch into another hole and dug out some of the debris. "Could be a drill hole? But these weren't made by CanacGold, too old. See how eroded the edges are." He jabbed the stick further into the hole. "Not sure if there's a bottom to this." He pulled out more debris and inserted the stick to its end.

"Same thing here," called out John-Joe as he poked a stick into another hole. "Looks like someone else thought there was gold here. Wonder why they didn't mine it?"

"Maybe, oh joy of joys, they didn't find any?" I hazarded hopefully.

"Or maybe they struck water, not gold," Eric replied with a chuckle as a splash of water from too hard a jab soaked his pant leg.

We spread out again and resumed our slow search. I continued along the edge of the ancients' forest and discovered more markers. Gradually a sense of doom crept over me as the reality of the location sunk in.

I noticed a sudden twinkle in the rock. I crouched down to investigate and found a narrow, yard-long trench littered with needles. I brushed aside the needles and saw a dark thread cutting through the translucent quartz. At first I thought it was black, then the sun caught an angle, and gold gleamed back at me.

"Come here, quick!" I screamed. "I see it."

"Look at that, will you", "There really is gold here", "Who would've believed it" came the murmurs as the others crowded around me. John-Joe flicked out more of the needles and ran his fingers along the gold thread. No one moved. We all stared at the thin glimmering line of gold as the fury of the pines swirled around us.

"Okay, okay. No need to get all excited," broke in Eric. "Now we know for sure. Question is, how do we stop it?"

"And we can't fail," I replied. "Look up and tell me what you see."

As one, we all raised our eyes to the long graceful branches swaying in the wind far above our heads. So high were the arms of these giants that they seemed to be within grasp of *kije manido*.

"If the gold is mined, what do you think will happen to them?" I walked towards a nearby giant. Wanting to feel its living, breathing soul, I ran my hand over the time-ravaged bark and dipped my fingers into a sticky dribble of sap. I breathed deeply the life-giving aroma. "It'll destroy what the ancients fought for."

"You got it lady, and a pile of money it'll make us too." hissed a voice from behind the tree. A pale mass stepped out from the shadows. My heart stopped.

"Thought I told you to stay away." Charlie Cardinal's threatening scowl glared down at me. He held a rifle, pointed downwards to the ground. "If you know what's good for you, you'll go back to where you belong in the white man's shit-hole. Now get out of my way."

He swatted me aside, as if I were a mosquito. I stumbled but didn't fall. Frozen with shock, I watched him walk towards Eric, John-Joe and the others. A sound of heavy breathing, thumping footsteps and six men brushed past me. They flanked Charlie Cardinal. Two of them carried rifles. One held a large logging ax. None wore bright yellow.

Eric stood firm. His white scar glowed. John-Joe, feet apart, arms crossed over his chest, stood beside him. The other three ranged behind them. They formed a solid barrier.

Charlie stopped about twenty feet from them. The fringe of his pale buckskin flirted with the wind.

"Eric, I knew you couldn't keep away," Charlie sneered.

Eric didn't move, didn't answer. I watched his gaze coldly appraise Charlie, then settle on the long black and white feather attached to his braid.

"You're sure tempting the anger of the spirits by wearing that eagle feather, Charlie," Eric said.

Charlie's hand jerked towards the feather on his shoulder.

I was confused by Eric's remark. Surely if Charlie were an elder, he could wear the sacred feather.

From the inside of his jacket, Eric brought out the black and white feather discovered on the beach "Sure you don't want to exchange it for this one?"

Charlie stiffened.

What was Eric trying to do? Get Charlie to admit the feather belonged to him and in so doing establish that he was the one who'd pushed the tree on top of me?

"I don't know what you're talking about." Charlie shot back, as he reached once more to the feather tied to his braid. "The Creator gave this eagle feather to me, and as hereditary chief of the Migiskan, I have every right to wear it. Now get your asses off this island."

He resumed walking towards Eric, still holding the gun barrel pointed to the ground. His men spread out behind him. I recognized the shaved eagle haircut of Charlie's mouthpiece from the General Store.

"What right do you have to order us off this land?" Eric challenged.

"The right of CanacGold."

Charlie stopped ten feet from Eric. Eric held his ground. John-Joe uncrossed his arms. The other three moved up beside them. I joined the line.

"This land belongs to our people. We're not going anywhere." Eric's face was stone, his voice steel.

"This ain't Migiskan land. Start moving."

"Should've known your dirty hand was in this, Charlie. What did you do? Try some of Louis's tricks and salt it, eh?"

I started at the mention of Louis's name and realized I didn't know the half of what Louis was all about.

"Shut up!" Charlie growled. "Damn right there's gold here, over a million ounces, and you're not going to see a single ounce of it."

"You've sold out, Charlie, for a few pieces of gold. You've betrayed our people by turning over to the white man the land the Creator left in our keeping."

For a moment, I thought Charlie was going to attack Eric, but instead he slowly brought his rifle up and pointed it directly at him. John-Joe grunted. I stopped breathing.

"Are you threatening us, Charlie?" Eric continued, his voice as emotionless as his weather hardened face.

"I'm just asking you very politely to leave. This land belongs to CanacGold."

For an eternity, no one moved, and then someone scraped a boot over some loose stones.

"Fine, Charlie. We'll leave, but I am not giving in. This land is Anishinabeg land. The band and I are going to fight you and your damn mine all the way."

He stepped forward, inserted the black and white feather into the muzzle of Charlie's rifle, turned around and walked away.

FIFTEEN

The next day I woke up late, much later than I'd planned. After the previous day's gun-toting confrontation, I'd decided the safest way to stop Charlie and the damn mine was to prove that the government did not own Whispers Island. I planned to spend the day searching through every single box, trunk and any other belonging of Aunt Aggie's in the hope, no matter how far-fetched, of finding the proof.

But first, my breakfast. I was starved. However, I'd no sooner sat down to a large plate of scrambled eggs, hash browns and English sausages than Sergei, who was supposed to be sound asleep in the front room, burst into an uproar.

"Be quiet!" I shouted. But he persisted. I prayed it was nothing more than a teasing raccoon. However, after yesterday, I was half expecting to see Charlie Cardinal's threatening mass on my doorstep.

I had no idea what he had against me. Even Eric didn't know, just assumed, like Hélène, that Charlie's intense hatred for him was spilling over onto me. That, and the fact I was also against the gold mine. Moreover, Eric was convinced Charlie was nothing but a harmless bully, full of bluster with no substance. He figured that as long as I stayed out of Charlie's way, he'd leave me alone. Eric did, however, tell me to let him know if Charlie threatened me again.

It was all very well for Eric to say Charlie was no real threat. But with the possibility of Charlie arriving on my doorstep, I wasn't sure if I wanted to test out Eric's theory. I debated pretending I wasn't home but decided that was playing into Charlie's hand. So, determined not to allow my fears to get the better of me, I marched to the front door. But no bull moose stood on my doorstep, or anyone else for that matter. Nor was Sergei in sight. In fact, he had stopped barking.

Before I had a chance to return inside, Sergei bounded over the top stair from the dock. Close behind him strode a tall figure, too lean to be Charlie. I relaxed. It was Eric.

"What's up?" I called out, surprised but faintly pleased by this unexpected visit.

He waited until he reached the porch before replying. Instead of a smile, worry creased his face.

"I wanted to let you know before you heard from anyone else."

"What's happened?" I asked wondering what Charlie had done now. But as I looked more closely at Eric's sombre face, I knew this had nothing to do with Charlie. Cold, numbing dread washed over me. This was about Marie.

"We've found the body of—"

I closed my ears. I didn't want to hear her name. If I hadn't been so drunk, she'd still be alive. I grabbed Aunt Aggie's chair and sat down. Shit. Marie. Dead. Because of me.

"I hope you caught the bastard," I lashed out.

"Who're you talking about?"

"Louis, of course."

"Meg, you aren't listening. It was Louis's body that was found."

"Louis?" I cried out, not quite believing my ears.

"Yes, Louis."

"Not Marie?" I still wasn't entirely convinced.

Eric patiently said no.

"Thank God." I relaxed. Too bad Louis was dead, probably drowned, or maybe his liver had packed it in. What did it matter how he died. Marie was alive. "What about Marie, Eric, is she okay?"

"Don't know. I haven't been able to reach Tommy on my satellite phone, which means he's turned it off."

"Wait a minute, didn't Louis die at his hunting camp?"

"No. Frosty found his body this morning at their homestead."

"What was he doing there? He was supposed to be at the hunting camp with Marie."

"No idea, but I'm sure the police will find out during their investigation."

"Police? Does this mean someone killed him?"

"Looks that way, shot twice."

"Do they know who shot him?" I asked.

"Not yet. Meg, I'm going to have to return to the Council Hall. You going to be okay?"

I nodded yes but didn't feel it.

"What about Marie?" I asked. "Does this mean she didn't go to Louis's camp either?"

"We won't know until we hear from Tommy. For the moment, I'm assuming she's there, and for some reason, Louis returned home."

"I sure hope she's okay," I said and left it at that. I didn't want to voice my real fear—that she'd been killed too, and her body lay hidden waiting to be found.

As if reading my thoughts, Eric answered, "Don't worry, I know it looks bad right now, but she'll come out of this unharmed. Marie's a survivor."

He gave me a pat on the arm and left.

*   *   *

Deciding that Marie had greater priority than the ownership of Whispers Island, I gulped down my food and drove to her cabin to find out more. However, a line of yellow tape and a cop stopped me. Close-lipped, he gestured for me to turn around and go back the way I'd come. I drove instead to the General Store, knowing the rumour mill would be running full throttle.

And I was right. The store was humming with excited voices. Hélène, decked out in a vermilion sweatshirt with I ♥ NY etched in black sequins, perched smugly atop her stool as if she were their reigning queen.

This time, my presence didn't stop the conversation. In fact, no one paid attention to me as I walked up to the coffee counter. They were too busy firing questions at Frosty, my coffee drinking buddy with the missing fingers. Unlike the other day, this group was older, closer to my age, a half dozen men and women from the reserve and a couple of local farmers. I said hi to those I recognized and grabbed a vacant stool. Without my asking, Hélène poured some coffee into her special Harrods mug, placed a thick chocolate doughnut on a china plate and passed them to me. I leaned back and listened.

"Cops say I can't discuss the case, but seeing as how you're my friends, I don't see no harm in it." Frosty's preening voice rose above the crowd. "Sure could use some fuel, though."

Frosty's hand with the missing two fingers passed a coffee cup across the counter towards Hélène. With her eye on me, she laughed, reached under the counter and brought out a half full bottle of rye. She poured a good measure into his cup and quickly returned it to its hiding spot. Another hand with all its fingers slammed a couple of bucks down, which were quickly snatched up by Hélène and hidden away in her pocket.

I stared at her in surprise, then passed my mug over. What did I care if she had a little something going on the side.

"It was them flies," Frosty began. "Crawling all over them logs. I figured something was dead, eh? Sure smelled like it too. But I figured it was a raccoon got caught. So I started moving them logs. Had to anyways, couldn't drive around 'em, eh? Then I sees this hand. Damn near made me piss my pants. I—"

"Excuse me, Frosty," I cut in, suddenly realizing which wood he was talking about. "Are you talking about that pile of firewood in the middle of Louis's drive?"

"Yup, big pile. Anyways, I got rid of more logs. And next I knowed, Louis was staring back at me with those funny blue eyes of his. 'Ccpt thcy was dcad eyes, bulging out of his head."

I shivered. I'd walked by that wood, twice, only yesterday. I'd even noticed the flies.

Frosty stopped, took a careful look around to make sure we were all listening and continued. "Once I seen Louis, I knowed I gotta get the Police Chief. So I hotfooted back to the detachment office. Decontie says I was an important witness, eh? So I had to go back to Louis's with him. He even called in them provincial cops, the SQ, it was that important, eh? I watched them take all them pictures, even do that fingerprinting stuff. Sure a bunch of hocus-pocus, you ask me. Anyone could see weren't nothing there to tell 'em who done it."

"Do the police know when Louis died?" I asked.

"Ain't sayin'," Frosty replied.

Maybe the police didn't know yet, but I had a pretty good idea. It could only be between the time when Louis picked up Marie after her phone call to me and when I saw the log pile the following night.

"Shot in the back he was, eh?" Frosty continued. "Jeez, what a way to go. Probably didn't even know what hit him. Poor sucker. Decontie figured it was a rifle done it, eh? Gotta be a Winchester for sure, since that's the only kind good for killing. Why, my own Winchester can kill a moose from three hundred paces. But weren't no gun there. They even searched them logs. Kinda messy, where Louis was rottin'. Guess he been there awhile."

The timing started me thinking. If, as Eric said, it took a day to hike into Louis's hunting camp, then it was impossible for Louis to go to his camp with Marie that night and return home by the next morning. He must've stayed behind.

"They know who done it?" Hélène asked. She held up the rye bottle. Several cups stretched toward it, including my own.

"Think they got an idea, but they ain't sayin'," Frosty replied.

I prayed that Marie had started out on her own, expecting Louis to catch up later. I didn't want to think of the possibility of her being there when Louis was killed.

"I hear the wood came from Crapper's bush, think he done it?" piped up a squeaky voice.

"Why he wanta kill him? He hardly knowed Louis. Couldn't have done it, anyway. Laid up with back trouble," Frosty answered.

"What's that no-good Louis buying wood for when he got a wood lot full to bursting with deadfall from the ice storm?" someone asked.

"And where'd he get the money to buy it?" another voice added.

But no one was able to answer those questions, not even Frosty.

Another voiced the opinion "Shame to waste all that good wood on Louis, eh? Even a load of manure would've been too good for him."

All nodded in agreement. More cups were passed across the counter. Hélène brought out her bottle, quickly replenished them and added more coffee. She put the money with the rest in her pocket.

"I hear they found a bracelet," she said. All eyes turned towards her. "Clutched in Louis's hand."

"I didn't see no bracelet," Frosty said suspiciously. "Who'd ya hear that from?"

"From one of the cops when they were here earlier. They thought it was Marie's."

"What did it look like?" I asked afraid of the answer.

"Orange beads with black horn and real turquoise. I'm sure you've seen it, Meg. It was the one she bought at last year's Pow Wow."

My heart sank. I knew it too well. I'd even remarked on its fine craftsmanship.

"Did the police say anything else?"

"Nope, but I got the impression they think Marie was there when Louis died."

Shit.

I hesitated, but I had to know. "Do they think she was killed also?" I asked.

Hélène dropped her gaze to the counter. "I don't think that's what they meant."

I looked at her with alarm at where this was leading. "Are you saying they think she killed him?" I asked.

"Can't say. Look, we all know Marie wouldn't do a thing like that, eh?" Hélène looked towards the others, as if seeking agreement. "But, hell, if she did do Louis in, she had good cause, that's for sure."

SIXTEEN

I didn't wait to hear another word. Yelling at Hélène to put it on my tab, I rushed from the store and drove straight to the Council Hall. Fortunately, Eric's Harley was still parked outside, right next to the reserve's police cruiser, which should have made me wary, but didn't. Instead, intent only on sticking up for Marie, I raced through the halls of the large cedar building to Eric's small office tucked into a far back corner.

Without bothering to knock, I burst into his room. "What's this about the police accusing Marie? There's no way she could have killed Louis."

A bemused Eric peered at me from behind a desk littered with papers.

"Slow down, Meg," he said, pointing behind me. "You know Police Chief Decontie, in charge of our police detachment. And this is Sgt. LaFramboise with the Sûreté du Québec."

I gulped and turned around to find both policemen coldly appraising me. They filled the only two chairs in Eric's office. Sgt. LaFramboise sat bolt upright in his impeccable brown SQ uniform with his chair shoved against the back wall. He said a crisp "Bonjour" and turned his long pointed nose back to Eric. Chief Decontie, slouching forward in his chair, seemed less intimidating in the slightly wrinkled navy blue uniform of the Migiskan Police Department. He at least smiled.

Embarrassed, I turned to leave.

"Meg, since you're here, you might as well stay," Eric said. "I was just telling these officers myself that Marie couldn't be involved."

"Madame, you are called Marguerite Harris, *n'est-ce pas?*" Sgt. LaFramboise interjected in his thick Quebecois accent.

Distrustful of his reasons for asking, I hesitated before admitting I was.

"*Bon.* I believe you are the last person to speak to Madame Whiteduck?"

"Not exactly. She left a message on my voice mail."

"You have not—how you say—removed this message?"

"No."

"Bon. Do not remove it, *s'il vous plaît.* You will wait at your house. Chief Decontie, and I will come when we finish with Chief Odjik."

I glanced back at Eric to see if he knew what Sgt. LaFramboise wanted. But Eric just shrugged his shoulders and with a slight nod suggested that I should probably leave.

"Okay, I'll go home, but I'd like to know how long you'll be."

"When we finish here," LaFramboise replied, and as a final dismissal, turned his focus back to Eric.

Annoyed by his arrogance, I shot back, "You should be looking for Marie, instead of wasting your time on me. For all you know, Louis's murderer may have killed her too."

Chief Decontie looked thoughtful, while Sgt. LaFramboise glared back at me and said, "Madame, do not concern yourself with the business of the police." And standing up, he showed me to the door.

My immediate reaction was to dig in my heels, but a quick look at Eric told me there was no point. I'd have to wait until we were both finished with the police before I'd learn what was really going on.

*　*　*

Despite what I'd said to LaFramboise, I didn't really believe Marie was dead. Nor could I ever accept that she had killed Louis. Instead, as my truck bumped over the rutted roads towards home, I came to the conclusion that Marie had fled to the hunting camp because she feared she'd be killed after witnessing Louis's murder.

I figured that as long as she was hidden deep in the bush she was safe, not only from the killer but also the police. With Tommy, her lawyer son at her side, she'd be even safer. He'd quickly quash any snap police conclusions and ensure the real story behind Louis's killing was told.

By the time I parked my truck in front of the house, I was feeling more confident that Marie would come through this unharmed. Therefore, with an hour or two to kill before the police arrived, I decided to resume my search for any documents that might resolve the ownership of Whispers Island.

The previous evening, while Eric and I had sat in the bar of the Fishing Camp unwinding after our confrontation with Charlie Cardinal, Eric had told me about an old survey map of railway right-of-ways that he'd found in a box of old files. Although it wasn't dated, he believed it was made in the early 1870s, when railways were mapping the area.

Even though the map's printed boundaries for the reserve did not include Whispers Island, there was a pencilled-in circle around the island with an arrow drawn towards the reserve and the date 1935. From this, Eric concluded that although the island was not part of the original territory establishment under the Act of 1851, it did become part of it in 1935.

And, he said, more importantly, there was clear evidence that Agatha Harris had been involved, for the initials "A.H."

were written over Whispers Island. While I wasn't convinced that this meant Aunt Aggie owned the island, I did promise Eric to continue my search through her records. He in turn intended to present this map to Indian Affairs as evidence the island belonged to the reserve.

And a fat lot of good that'd do, I thought as I headed up the stairs to the attic. Those damn bureaucrats in Ottawa cared more about keeping tax paying miners happy than a bunch of tax consuming Indians.

Halfway up the stairs, the phone rang. I raced back down in time to catch my notary on the other end of the line.

"Please, François, tell me this call means you have good news," I said.

"*Oui et non,* Madame Harris," he replied. "Which would you like first?"

"The good news, I need something to cheer me up."

"*Bon.* Although it is not completely good news, it is—how you call—promising. I am almost certain this island is not government land. It is not listed in any of the official government land registries."

"But why would Indian Affairs lie about it?"

"The Migiskan Reserve was established many years ago, when the government preferred to keep the exact boundaries of these reserves fuzzy, as you English say. It is possible that the *ministère* does not know the true boundaries and is using this confusion for their own purpose."

I told him about the survey map Eric had found and finished by asking "Can't we use this map to challenge CanacGold's legal title to the mining rights?"

"Sadly, the pencil notations will not be considered official," François replied. "It would require a long legal fight, and I do not believe you have such time."

"Then what do we do?"

"It would be best if we could prove this land is privately owned."

"Do you think there is a possibility, no matter how remote, that Aunt Aggie did own the island in 1935? I know it's not part of the Three Deer Point property, but maybe she owned it separately and sixty-five years ago gave it to the Migiskans. Can't you search the records for that time period?"

"A very good suggestion, madame, and we are indeed searching the files, but unfortunately, we have encountered a most curious problem."

"I guess this is the bad news, eh?"

"Sadly, madame. We have discovered that many of the files for the properties on Echo Lake are missing, including your own."

"But how can that happen?"

"It is possible they have been incorrectly filed. However, the registry clerk believes someone has taken them."

"Seems unlikely. Are you sure he's not just trying to cover up his own incompetence?"

"I think not. It seems that we are not the only people interested in the Echo Lake properties. Someone else conducted a title search a few months ago. The clerk believed all files were returned. Now he is not so certain."

"Does he know who it was?"

"Unhappily, he remembers only that it was a woman who spoke very bad French. She did not leave her name or that of the notaire she is working for."

"With no municipal record, how can we determine the real owner of Whispers Island?"

"The deed will tell us the owner. But, unfortunately, we must find the owner to find the deed."

"Perhaps, if we are lucky, I will find it buried in Aunt

Aggie's belongings."

"*Bon.* My clerk will also conduct a thorough search of the registry to ensure the record was not misplaced and to look at other municipal records, such as tax rolls for mention of this tract of land."

"Kind of fishy, isn't it"

"*Excusez,* madame, fishy?"

"Sorry, I meant it's very suspicious that these files are missing at the same time as this gold discovery. I'm willing to bet CanacGold has a hand in this."

"A good word, this fishy."

"Please let me know, François, the minute you discover something, okay?"

"Of course, madame. Probably by the end of next week."

"Not sooner?"

"Unfortunately, the registry office is closed for the weekend."

"What happens if we don't find anything?" I asked.

"As you English say, we will cross this bridge when we come to it."

SEVENTEEN

I slowly hung up the phone, as an icy tingle of apprehension crept under my skin. François had reminded me that today was Friday. In two days it would be Sunday, the day Gareth was coming.

What a fool I'd been to give into Gareth. And for what? A stupid painting. Sure, I wanted it. But it was hardly a good enough reason to let him invade my new life at Three Deer Point. Nothing could be. Not even his supposedly renewed interest. And I believed that as much as I believed we could return to our good times.

So why had I said yes? Stupid idiot, that was me. You'd think I'd have learned by now. But the sound of his voice on the phone had taken me back to the early years of our marriage, when we'd been like any young couple in love. It had made me want to see him one last time, if only for the few minutes it took to retrieve the painting from his car. After all, for fifteen years he'd been a major force in my life. For that matter, still was, if my confused feelings were anything to go by.

Hell, what confusion. I really did want to see him, to touch him, even laugh with him again. But I was afraid, too afraid of where it would lead. They say history repeats itself. Renewal of our relationship would only lead to the disastrous ending it had already once reached. I found it impossible to believe that the Gareth of today could return to the man I'd fallen in love with and married. Too much time had passed. Too much had happened. And as if in confirmation, my arm began to throb.

If only I could shove these conflicting emotions back to where I'd managed to hide them over the course of three years. But it was too late. Gareth's phone call had re-opened the door. Still, there was one remedy I knew that would help dull the pain, so I clamped a lid on Eric's warning and poured myself a good measure of vodka.

Then, fortified with the glass, I resumed what I'd set out to do before the interruption of François' phone call, the continuing search through Aunt Aggie's belongings for any connection with Whispers Island. This too would help to take my mind off Sunday, and maybe, if the gods were on my side, I might even discover the deed.

The only remaining items in the attic offering promise were a couple of wooden boxes shoved under one of the eaves. Unfortunately, they were both nailed shut. So rather than trekking back down two flights of stairs to get a hammer, then up again, I struggled down to the main floor with the lightest of the heavy boxes and hoped I wasn't wrenching my back for nothing.

I placed it on the carpet in what was once Aunt Aggie's favourite room, the octagonal turret room, where the late afternoon sun was flooding through the five windowed sides. It lit up the words stamped on the box, Highland Malt Whiskey, the only brand Aunt Aggie would drink. Although I wasn't following exactly in her footsteps, I at least was keeping up the Harris drinking tradition started by Great-grandpa Joe.

A hammer and large screwdriver soon revealed a box crammed with loose papers and envelopes, all with the brittle yellow texture that comes with age. On the first envelope I picked-up, the address, Miss Agatha Harris, Three Deer Point, Echo Lake, Quebec, confirmed the box did belong to Aunt Aggie. And the cancellation date of July 13, 1910 on the

George V stamp told me I was far enough back in time.

I slid the thin sheets of paper from the envelope and eagerly unfolded them. But a quick read told me I wasn't going to be lucky enough to find mention of Whispers Island in the first letter. Filled with girlish chatter about friends and annoying siblings, it was a letter from a friend called Edith.

I discovered more letters to Agatha from Edith who, judging from their gushing tone and almost daily frequency, must have been her best bosom buddy. While the soul-baring contents reminded me of my own childhood friendships, it was obvious that islands and land holdings didn't even enter the periphery of her girlish concerns.

I scooped out several more layers of papers and discovered a few ancient photographs. From one grinned Great-grandpa Joe, who stood with one arm embracing his rifle and the other resting on the shoulder of a much shorter Indian man, probably his guide. Next to them hung three large deer carcasses, which were strung up by their feet from a beam of the easily recognizable Three Deer Point verandah. Their trophy-size antlers made me wonder if this wasn't the memorable hunt that gave my property its name.

When I reached into the box to extract more papers, my fingers encountered a strange object wedged into a corner. It felt smooth and hard and oddly warm, with a smokiness that made my nostrils tingle. When extracted, I realized the smell came from the soot-coated metal interior of the bowl of a well-used Indian peace pipe. The end of the reed-like wooden stem was also charred, suggesting the pipe might have been partially consumed by a fire.

I found it a strange item for Aunt Aggie to keep and wondered if there was a story behind it, but decided when I retrieved the next items from the box that the pipe, like these postcards, was merely a memento from her close ties with the people of the Migiskan Band. While the postcards confirmed

Aunt Aggie's grand tour of Europe, they also revealed she had a friend among the Algonquin by the name of Snow Flower.

Several of the postcards mentioned "beaux", as she called them, which made me think that if I didn't find anything related to Whispers Island, I might at least discover the answer to her secret marriage.

The rest of the box was filled with more of the same, loose letters, postcards, a few pictures and a thick packet of letters tied with a purple ribbon. Intrigued by the packet, I untied the bow. A folded slip of paper slid onto the floor.

Dearest Agatha,

I am returning your letters. Given how events have turned out, I thought you would want to keep them yourself. While I have found them most enjoyable, I am sure you will take greater pleasure in their memories. You might even someday want to pass them on to your daughter. Oh dear, did I say daughter. I still am unable to imagine either of us as mothers.

Love,
Edith

At the word daughter, I almost choked. First, there was this unknown husband, now it seemed Aunt Aggie might have had a child. I ripped the ribbon from the packet and settled down to read the first letter.

Paris
September 15, 1913

Dearest Edith
You know how we've always talked about meeting the man

of our dreams. Well, I've finally met him, and he is much, much more than I ever dreamed of. Tall, very tall, taller than Father, wavy brown hair with deep, deep blue eyes and a wonderful smile. And oh, he is so charming and correct. He has even tamed Father, and you know how difficult Father can be.

We were introduced a month ago at the Comte de Montigny's Ball. He asked me no less than five times to dance. I was so surprised that such an aristocratic gentleman would pay such attention to plain boring me, that you can imagine my greater surprise when he asked me to dance seven times at the Duc du Bois Ball, three nights later. Since that evening, he has been in constant attention. He even asked Father if he could call on me.

Oh, Edith, I am so excited. Imagine, a German baron actually being interested in little old me. Oh dear, I can see I've forgotten to tell you his name. Baron Johann von Wichtenstein. Isn't that such a wonderfully elegant name?

I had better close this letter. Mimi just knocked on the door to say Johann has arrived. Yes dear, I even call him by his first name. I will write you as soon as I can.

Love,
Your very best friend,
Agatha

I wondered if Baron von Wichtenstein could be the mystery husband. His name at least started with a "W", although it was hardly a simple English name. His description, tall with brown hair, fit the man in the wedding picture. And he was German. So, if Eric's theory was right, this Baron von Wichtenstein might have had a duelling scar too, like the man in the photo.

Several letters later, the possibility became more promising.

Gasthaus Lindenhof, Berlin
December 18, 1913

Dearest Edith

As you can see, we have finally arrived in Berlin. It took us more than a month to travel from Paris, one long, lonely month without Johann. I was dying from impatience, but Father insisted on taking his time, saying he wanted to experience the German countryside. But it was hardly countryside we toured, more like every factory from the French border to Berlin. They were filthy and dreadfully boring. But I shouldn't complain, now that I am with my Johann. And he was even waiting for us at the railroad station with his new horseless carriage. What a treat. I donned veils and sat fearless in the back with Father.

Oh, Edith, it was wonderful to see him again, and it was very difficult to remain perfectly correct in front of Father and the servants. I wanted to fling my arms around him. In two days time, we travel to his castle, Schloss Grünwald, where we will spend Christmas. I hope we can find someplace in this castle to escape from our parents.

I am very nervous about meeting his parents. Whatever will they think of me, a commoner from an uncivilized land? Johann says not to be frightened of them. They look much sterner than they are. He says that I only need smile and be my usual charming self, and they will be won over as he has been won over. Dear, dear Johann.

Unfortunately, our timing doesn't appear to be good. The Germans and the British are going through one of those periods when they don't like each other. In fact, Father is worried that it may develop into something more serious than a diplomatic spat.

So if we are going to get married, it must be soon.

Just imagine marrying Johann and staying with him forever and ever, here in Germany. I know I would miss you and Three Deer Point terribly, but I would miss Johann more if I couldn't be with him. Edith, pray that his parents approve of me and my family. He needs their approval before he will formally ask my father for my hand. I don't know what we will do if they don't give it.

Love,
Your very best friend,
Agatha

To this point, Aunt Aggie had written her dear friend Edith every two weeks, if not more frequently. With this last letter, she suddenly stopped. The next and final letter was written four months later.

Villa Bencista, Fiesole
April 3, 1914

Dearest Edith

Thank you so much for your letters. They have been like a ray of sunshine in this dark hole I've been buried in. Whenever I felt I couldn't continue, I would reread them and feel so comforted.

I apologize for being such a poor writer, but I know you understand. It has been most difficult these past months, but I think now I can even say his name, Johann, without falling into a pit of black despair. The penetrating Italian sun has helped and, of course, your letters.

We are coming home. Father has booked passage on the H.M.S. Lusitania, leaving Southampton on the 31st of May. I am so looking forward to returning to you and all that is familiar and comforting. It will be wonderful to hear your sweet voice again and to see your smiling face. You must come with me to Three Deer Point. I hunger for its cleansing wildness and isolation from all that has gone so terribly wrong.

Johann has written many times, even came to the villa, but I refused to see him or even read the letters. It is over. I cannot forgive him for what he has done.

Love,
Your sad but much wiser friend,
Agatha

I mentally scratched out Baron Johann von Wichtenstein's name from my very short list of candidates for secret husband. Poor Aunt Aggie, she wasn't any better at keeping her men than I was.

Unfortunately, it left me with Mother's disreputable gentleman with a short English name, beginning with "W", and so far I'd not come across a name like that in these letters.

But it was Edith's mention of a daughter that confused me the most. Aunt Aggie with a daughter was even more implausible than a husband. A husband you could pretend never happened if the marriage ended quickly, but a child was an entirely different matter. Unless, of course, the child had died. Still, this would be something my family would know about, not something to hide.

Poor Aunt Aggie. I could still picture her on lazy summer afternoons, sunk into her rocking chair deep within the shade of the verandah, glass in hand, the pale liquid flowing with the rhythm of the rocking. "Me medicine," she used to call it.

Well, it never did her any harm, I thought as I refilled my vodka glass. No reason why it should me. And as the numbing warmth of the tonic crept over me, my anxieties over Gareth retreated further.

EIGHTEEN

Eric shoved a mug against my lips. "Meg, for god's sake, drink it."

I clamped my mouth shut, grunted "No!" and jerked my head away. "I'm not drinking any more of that shit."

"Well, at least you're talking in intelligible sentences," Eric replied.

My head swirled. "I'm going to be sick." And I vomited into the bucket Eric shoved under my chin. "God, I feel awful."

"I'm sure you do."

I opened my eyes. Eric's concerned face swam into view. I snapped them shut. "I'm going to be sick again," I said, and retched once more into the bucket. Mortified, I wished I could disappear into the bucket myself.

I felt my body warm to the weight of his hand on my shoulder. I opened my eyes. His face didn't swim any more. "I'm okay now." He left his hand for a second longer on my shoulder, then he took the bucket away.

"What happened?" I looked around, amazed to see the morning sun streaming through the kitchen window. It was the next day.

"Isn't it obvious? You passed out." Eric held up an empty vodka bottle. "Do you remember how full it was?"

I lied. "I think there was only about a third left." It was more like three-quarters. No wonder I'd passed out.

"Meg, when are you going to stop fooling yourself and face up to the fact you have a drinking problem?"

"Yeah, yeah," I muttered. I didn't have a problem. I could stop any time I wanted.

"How did you get in here?" I asked to change the subject.

"Through your unlocked door."

I swore. I'd been too drunk to lock the doors. Would've served me right if the guy in yellow had walked in.

"Meg, you can't keep avoiding it. The sooner you face up to it, the sooner you'll get cured."

"Look, Eric, I really appreciate your being here. But I'm sure you've got better things to do, so if you don't mind, I'd like to be alone." I got up from the kitchen chair and would have fallen, if Eric hadn't been standing next to me. "Whoops…guess I'm still a bit dizzy."

Eric sat me back down into the chair like I was some kind of a china doll and passed me the mug of coffee. "Here, drink more of this, and take these." He passed me a couple of Tylenol. "Some food will help. I'll make you breakfast."

With two hands, I raised the trembling mug to my lips. The warm liquid felt good. My head pounded.

I set the mug down and watched Eric move around with the ease of someone very familiar with the workings of a kitchen. "I didn't know you could cook."

Eric threw some chopped dill into a bowl of eggs, smiled and said, "Just one of my many talents." He whisked them into a fluffy golden liquid and poured the mixture into a sizzling pan. He shook the pan back and forth over the burner. "Want some cheese with your omelet?"

"Sounds good." I tried to sound cheerful but felt more like

burying myself six feet under. "Look, I'm sorry to put you through this. It's not very pleasant."

"Meg, you aren't the first drunk I've dealt with, and you certainly won't be the last."

He called me a drunk. Is that what he thought of me? I took a gulp of hot coffee and almost burnt my mouth.

"You usually seem to know your limit, Meg. What got you going this time?" He placed the perfect omelet on the table in front of me and sat down. Today, with his thick black hair tied behind his head in a ponytail, his face appeared more open and, I suddenly realized, more careworn. Obviously, he had more important problems on his mind than my piddling ones. "Something's bothering you, Meg. I think it's been a worry for some time. Tell me, if it will help."

I took a bite of omelet. "Delicious." I took another bite. I'd never told him about Gareth.

Eric drank his coffee in silence. I patted Sergei and looked out the window then turned back to Eric. His soft grey eyes were still focused on me. My arm throbbed, but I tried not to rub it. He smiled with a twisted smile that seemed to say, "Take your time. I'll be here when you need me."

I hesitated, then blurted out, "My ex is coming tomorrow."

He raised his eyebrows in question. "Tell me about him." And I did.

At the end he said, "I think you should call and tell him not to come."

"I can't. I need to see him. I need to firmly close the door and lock it."

"Do you want me to be with you?"

I looked at his sympathetic but strongly masculine face, and thought not. "Thanks, I appreciate the offer, but I need to deal with Gareth on my own."

"Everything's okay, Meg. You can stop rubbing your arm."

I looked down at my hand moving slowly back and forth. I hadn't even realized I was doing it.

"Don't worry, Meg, I'll make sure nothing happens." Eric placed his hand gently over my hand and held it tight.

For a long moment, I sat absorbing the comforting warmth, then pulled my hand free. I didn't want this. I didn't need it. Not now.

Eric gave me a searching glance, then nodded his head as if to say, "I'll go your speed," and got up to retrieve the coffee pot. He filled my mug and poured himself some.

"Did the police come by yesterday?" he asked.

I searched through yesterday's fog, but couldn't remember. What if they had come? "Why do you ask?"

"I want to know what they said to you about Marie."

I took a deep sip of coffee. "Nothing."

Eric stared at me, his expression signalling that he didn't believe me.

"Okay, okay. I don't remember. I was too damn drunk. Is that what you want to hear?"

I jumped out of my chair and stomped to the fridge to get Sergei's food. I'd probably forgotten about him, too. Although, judging by his non-committal state on the floor, I'd say I did manage to do at least that much.

"You're lucky. They probably didn't have the time before they went into the bush to get Tommy and Marie," Eric said.

"Oh, dear, that means they'll arrest Marie."

"If they find her. Turns out she wasn't at Louis's camp."

"But...she left a note saying she was going there."

"The police think she ran away. They're searching the woods around the camp as we speak."

"Why? She has no reason to run away from the police. And

with Tommy by her side, even less reason."

"I know it doesn't make sense. I tried to tell the police as much, but that damn LaFramboise is so focused on her being Louis's killer that he's convinced she's trying to evade capture."

"Come on, Eric. Do you believe she killed Louis?"

Eric got up from his chair and walked over to the window. He stood, his back to me, facing the distant shore of Whispers Island. "It doesn't matter what I think."

He continued looking out towards the island, then he turned around. "What matters is the evidence points in that direction. The bracelet, her being seen with Louis before he died and, of course, the fact she's missing."

"Maybe the killer shot her at the same time and hid her body. Anyone think of that?"

"Yeah, I had Decontie search the grounds around their place. He found nothing. Want some more coffee?" Without waiting for an answer, he returned to the table with the coffee pot in hand.

"Eric, can't we assume that whoever killed Louis used a truck to dump those logs on top of his body? If so, then Marie couldn't have done it. She doesn't drive."

"I had the same question. But that SQ SOB brushed it off by saying under stress anyone can do anything."

"Where's the damn truck, then? Find the truck, and you've found the murderer."

"Yeah, that's the most damning piece of evidence. The police found Louis's pickup near the start of the trail to his camp. Still had some logs in the back, and worst of all, Marie's fingerprints were all over it."

"What would they expect? She's in the damn thing as much as Louis," I said in exasperation.

"I know it's hard to accept. We all like Marie and have

certainly sympathized with her over the years. But it's not the first time one of my people has retaliated when pushed to the wall by an abusive relationship, and I know it won't be the last."

I sat back down on the chair feeling very deflated. If Eric was thinking Marie could have done it, what about others? "Is that what most people in the reserve think?"

Eric nodded.

I persisted. "But Louis wasn't exactly your upstanding citizen. There's got to be someone else who wanted him dead more than Marie?"

"Although quick with his fists, Louis was basically harmless. No one took him seriously," Eric replied.

"Like Charlie Cardinal?"

"Meg, one thing you should realize. This isn't the city. The only crime that ever happens around here is domestic. My people are basically good. They just sometimes have problems dealing with the tough conditions they live in."

Maybe Eric was right. He knew his people. I didn't. Still, he could also be too close to his people. Maybe his judgment in this instance was blinded by his desire to protect them. Maybe there really was a bad apple in the reserve.

"What's Tommy saying?" I asked.

"Not much, he's as shocked as the rest of us."

"What happens if the police don't find her? Can she survive for long alone in the bush?"

"For a while. My guess is she has Louis's missing rifle, so she can hunt for food. Don't worry, Meg, I'll make sure Marie is okay."

I started to ask how, but from the shuttered look on Eric's face, I knew he wouldn't answer. I got up to make more coffee.

We continued talking as the sun gradually filled the kitchen with healing warmth, while the pounding in my head slowly diminished to a dull ache. Eric, whose dirt threshold was obviously lower than mine, insisted on doing not only the breakfast dishes, but also the food-encrusted stack from the last few days. Embarrassed by my lax housekeeping habits, I insisted on doing what I thought was the worst job, the wash-up.

After he left, I went to bed. I figured an hour's sleep would completely cure me, then I'd be fit to face Tommy with some as yet unanswered questions.

*   *   *

A couple of hours later, feeling somewhat more human, I turned my truck into the Whiteduck drive. Marie's home looked as dismal as ever. The only brightness was the yellow security tape fluttering from several trees. I tried not to visualize Louis's battered body as I drove past the firewood now neatly stacked at the side of the drive. At least the flies had gone.

My knock rang hollowly through the dark and silent shack. I knocked again and finally saw Tommy's dishevelled figure approaching through the door's tiny window. He was clad only in an old pair of jeans. Glowering at me, he opened the door a crack.

"What do you want?" he said rubbing his eyes.

"Sorry, I didn't mean to wake you, but I want to know about your mother. And, Tommy, I'm sorry about your father."

He pushed his thick black hair from his forehead and replied, "Yeah, well…it had to happen sometime, too bad this way."

"You know the police think your mother did it."

"I don't know what to think."

We stared uncertainly at each other until I asked, "Do you mind if I come in?"

Tommy looked back into the room, then opened the door a fraction wider. "Excuse the mess, I had some visitors."

142

I pushed it open and followed him into the room.

He was right. It was worse than the mess that was growing exponentially at my place. Clothes and newspapers were strewn across the floor. The chesterfield, pushed onto its back, revealed a split in the underside where the stuffing squeezed out. Empty beer bottles littered the Arborite table.

"Wow, some party," I said.

Tommy glared at me. "Party? I wish. Nope, someone broke in while I was gone."

With my eye on the beer bottles, I decided not to challenge him and instead asked "Anything taken?"

"So far the only thing I've discovered is a broken window out back. I haven't had a chance to check if anything was stolen. Though I did notice my great-grandparents' picture is gone from top the TV. But it's probably just buried somewhere under this mess."

"What did the police say?"

"Nothing. I'm not going to involve them."

"But don't you want to find out who did it?"

"I'm sure it's just kids from the rez high on something looking for a thrill. Who else would be dumb enough to think there was something worth stealing from this hole?"

He did have a point.

Now that I was face-to-face with Tommy, I hesitated asking my question. I wasn't sure what his reaction would be, and of course, I could be completely wrong. But Eric's protective stance towards his people had started me wondering, and I wanted more than Eric's non-committal "don't worry" to satisfy myself that Marie was safe.

I drew a deep breath and asked, "Tommy, I know Marie wasn't at your father's hunting camp when the police arrived, but was she there when you arrived?"

His body tensed. "Are you saying I lied to the police?"

"I think you would to protect your mother."

He relaxed. "You're right, I would. The old man had it coming. But—" He stopped, looked me directly in the eye and said, "She was not at the camp, and as far as I could tell, had never been there."

"Why are the police searching the area, then?"

"That's their prerogative."

"Why would she leave the note and then not go?"

He shrugged his shoulders. "Must have changed her mind."

"Where would she go then?"

"How should I know?"

"Don't you care about your mother?

He shot me a look of blazing blue. "For Chrissake's, get off my back."

Tommy walked through the mess to the front door and opened it.

But I didn't budge. I'd failed Marie twice before. I wasn't going to fail her again. "Tommy, I won't leave until you satisfy me that she's okay. I promise I won't tell the police. I only want to know that someone is looking after her. I don't care whether it's you or someone else in the reserve. I just want to know she's safe."

"You think someone's hiding her? No way. But even if someone was, it's none of your business, okay?"

"Damn right it's my business. She's my friend, and I want to help."

He stood stone-faced at the door. He didn't intend to give any indication that I was on the right track. And if he were anything like his mother, he wouldn't budge, no matter how hard I pressed him. So I started picking my way over the

144

clothes lying in my path to the door and promptly stubbed my toe on something very hard and unyielding hidden under a ragged lumberman's jacket. Annoyed, I flung the jacket away.

"Whose is this? Yours?" I gasped, suddenly alert. I tapped my foot against the red tackle box last seen in the boat belonging to the guy in yellow.

"Papa's. Who the hell cares?"

"Does he own a yellow jacket?"

"How should I know. I'm not his keeper."

"Marie's an elder, isn't she? Would she give her eagle feather to Louis?"

"Not a chance. She uses it only for ceremonies. What the hell you asking all these questions for?"

"Could you please check to see if the feather is where she normally keeps it?"

He gave me a suspicious scowl, then grudgingly headed to a back room and returned within seconds. "No, it's not there. What's this all about?"

"I'm not sure. Would your father have taken the feather?"

"I doubt it. He doesn't believe in Indian hocus-pocus, as he calls it. What's so important about Mooti's feather?"

I told him about Whispers Island and the feather. I finished by asking if he thought his father could have pushed the tree over the cliff.

Tommy shrugged his shoulders. "I suppose if he were drunk, maybe. But what's this got to do with Mooti?"

"Nothing, I hope. Do you know of any reason why your father would be on Whispers Island?"

He gave me a hooded look, then quickly transferred his gaze to the view out the window.

Wondering what Tommy was hiding, I tried a possibility. "Could he have been working for CanacGold?"

145

"Papa work for someone? That's a joke."

Perhaps there was another reason. "Do you know anything about the two Algonquins buried on Whispers Island?"

He continued to look out the window. Finally, he said, "Ancestors."

"Ancestors, yes but whose?"

"How should I know?"

And remembering Marie's mention of ancestors the day the planes came, I asked, "Does your mother know?"

"What's with you? All these damn questions. You never stop. Leave us alone, okay?" Tommy wheeled around and stalked to the back of the house.

I stood for a few seconds longer, wondering what nerve I'd hit, and if it was the same nerve I'd struck with Marie.

*   *   *

As I drove away, I felt more confusion than anger. Despite Tommy's non-answers, I was fairly certain he had hidden Marie away in a safe place deep within the bush, well out of reach of police searchlights and sniffing dogs.

But was running in her best interests? If she had killed Louis, she had had every right. A good lawyer—and I'd make sure she had one—should be able to successfully argue self-defense. In fact I was surprised Tommy, fresh out of law school, hadn't thought of this. Surely it would be better for her to go through the short-lived agony of a trial than to be on the run for the rest of her life.

Tommy had definitely made it clear that it had nothing to do with me. As far as he was concerned, my only role was to keep my mouth shut. As much as I disliked the position to which I was relegated, it was probably for the best. Better to let Tommy and his people look out for Marie. They knew what they were doing. I didn't.

I turned into my driveway and thought about Louis being the guy in yellow. It didn't compute. Although I might not have been all smiles towards him, it was hardly a reason to attack me. And I agreed with Tommy, he wasn't the kind of guy CanacGold would hire to protect their interests. Besides, it looked as if Charlie had taken on that job.

Unless the attack was related to the crosses. When Marie had feared that the men from the planes would anger the ancestors, I'd assumed she meant Anishinabeg ancestors in general. Now with Tommy's angry reaction to my question I was wondering if Two Face Sky and Summer Wind weren't in fact her relatives. Maybe Louis was only trying to prevent me from disturbing sacred ground. But what a way to do it. A simple yell would've worked just as well.

The smaller footprints I'd seen on the beach could have been made by someone Marie's size. Though I doubted short, wiry Louis had made the other much larger tracks. They were more Tommy's size. But he was away when those footprints were left in the sand. At least, that's what he'd told me.

I was so caught up in my thoughts that I failed to notice the car parked in my driveway until I found myself swerving to avoid its gleaming bumper. A newly minted black Porsche, the kind of car that shouldn't be driven within a hundred miles of these dirt roads.

NINETEEN

I puzzled over the identity of my visitor until I saw the all too familiar oil painting propped against the bottom verandah stair. Gareth. He was here. A day early. My stomach lurched. I had half a mind to drive away and return in a couple of hours when I was sure, given his low patience threshold, that he would be gone.

Before I had a chance to decide, Gareth stepped down from the verandah. He sauntered towards me, his brown eyes alert, his cinnamon hair marred by only a few streaks of grey. The weight he'd put on from too many client lunches had been shed. His body had returned to the firm slimness of his youth. He looked good, too good. Something deep inside me twisted.

"Oh, hell," I muttered to myself.

He stopped several metres away and gave me one of those smiles that used to make my knees weak.

"Megs, it's great to see you," he said.

Determined to end this quickly, I ignored his opening words and said, "Thanks for the painting. I appreciate you coming all this way, but I think it best if you get back into your car and leave."

"Please Megs, can't we at least spend a few minutes together," he said, "for old times sake." He made no attempt to move closer, as if sensing that one step nearer could very well send me fleeing back to the safety of my truck.

"I don't think it's a good idea. "

He ran his fingers through his wavy hair. "Sure you want it this way?"

I could hear Sergei barking in the house and wondered what would happen if I let him out. During the short time Sergei and Gareth had lived together in Toronto, the two of them had waged a war. From the moment I brought the squirming ball of black fluff home to our condo, Gareth had refused to have anything to do with him. In fact, Sergei had been the cause of several arguments, most notably the time I caught Gareth kicking him after Sergei, full of puppy excitement, had peed on his dress pants. Perhaps I could use the dog as further incentive in getting Gareth to leave.

A sudden gust of wind ruffled Gareth's hair and loosened a shower of pine needles from the branches high above. Several landed on his designer sports jacket and in his hair. He flicked one or two off but didn't bother with the rest.

"We had so many good times together," he said. "Surely you can't pretend they never happened."

My heart thumped at the kaleidoscope of memories that came flooding in with his words. I tried to thrust them back. "It's too late."

He looked at me with the kind of longing I'd not seen since our early years together. "Okay," he said. "I'm sorry you feel this way, but I'll accept your decision."

I felt my eyebrows rise in surprise with his last words. This was out of character. Gareth did not admit defeat so easily, especially to me. I searched for the sarcasm that would invariably lurk behind his eyes and saw none. Maybe our last terrifying argument had scared him as much as it had scared me and had caused him to have a good hard look at the kind of man he'd become.

He seemed at a loss, unsure what to say or do next. He cast a bleak glance at the painting and said, "Enjoy it." Then, with a wan smile, he walked towards his car.

It was the dejected slump to his shoulders that did it. I began to feel sorry for him. Maybe I was being too harsh. After all, it was partly my fault things had gone so disastrously wrong at the end. "Okay," I called out, "come in for a drink."

"You're sure? I wouldn't want to push you into anything you didn't want."

"Yes, I'm sure," I replied, reaching for the painting. This wasn't turning out to be the traumatic confrontation I'd feared for the last three years.

He followed me into the house, where he confronted his old nemesis, Sergei. But amazingly, after a few threatening growls, the dog quieted down, even condescending to receive a few pats.

"I thought you were coming tomorrow," I said as I poured us both some lemon vodka, the drink he'd introduced me to.

"Last minute change in plans." He glanced around the large kitchen. "I see you've made a few improvements since my last visit."

"Aunt Aggie may have been able to cook in a turn-of-the century kitchen, but I couldn't. I had the new cabinets and appliances installed last year shortly after I moved in. The only remaining fix-up is the repainting of the chairs. What do you think?"

"Looks good. Not too modern. Blends nicely with the age of the house. Do you mind if I take a look at the other rooms?"

So with Sergei bringing up the rear, we started in the large dining room, where Gareth ran his hands over the antique patina of the mahogany table and suggested that the wall above the buffet would be the perfect spot for the Chaki painting. Next we wandered into the small room I'd converted into my television room and disregarded another small room still jammed with the empty packing crates from the move. Then we crossed the hall to the largest room on the ground floor, the living room spanning the entire lake side of the house. But Gareth ignored this room and walked across to the turret that occupied the front corner.

"Best room in the house," he said, surveying the octagonal walls with their long floor to ceiling windows. His eyes drifted over the antique desk and oriental carpet and fell upon Aunt Aggie's old wooden box, but he made no comment. Thank goodness I'd returned all the letters and replaced the lid. I wouldn't want him asking awkward questions.

Returning to the living room, Gareth looked appreciatively over the massive stone fireplace. "Boy, they sure don't make them like this any more."

"Hey, isn't that your aunt?" he said, picking up the wedding picture. "Sure was a looker in her day, just like you." And he ran his eyes over my spreading middle-aged body, stopping to focus on the too-tight sweater I'd mistakenly put on this morning. "You look terrific. The wilds must agree with you."

Embarrassed, I muttered some sort of a reply and suggested we go out onto the verandah to finish our drinks, where Gareth immediately installed himself in Aunt Aggie's old rocker. I started to protest, then decided I shouldn't be so set in my ways. I sat down in the wicker chair, which was really just as comfortable. Sergei slumped his large, curly haired body down on the wooden floor between us.

Mumbling about something digging into him, Gareth extracted his cell phone and his key chain from his jeans' pocket and placed them on the table beside his drink. He took a long sip and said, "I'd forgotten what a fantastic view you have of the lake from here." He lit up a cigarette.

"I see you're still doing your best to become another lung cancer statistic," I said.

He laughed. "And you're still nagging me about it." He attempted to blow the smoke into my face, but it scattered with the breeze. He continued, "Got a good view of the island too. What's it called?"

"Whispers Island, or Minitig Kà-ishpàkweyàg as the Algonquins call it, Island Where the Big Trees stand. Majestic, isn't it?" I was about to mention the threat of the gold mine but stopped, figuring best not to bore Gareth with my environmental woes.

"You still the only one on the lake? No cottages or farms?" he asked.

"Nope, mine's the sole private holding on this lake, and it occupies the only accessible shore. The other shorelines are too steep. Probably why the government has never sold off the land. Of course, there's the Migiskan Reserve on the north side of the lake."

He dragged deeply on his cigarette and blew the smoke out in one forceful stream. "Yeah, the Indians, forgot about them. You don't have much to do with them, do you?"

"Well, we are neighbours," I said and left it at that. His faintly derogatory tone told me he wouldn't welcome my close relationship with Marie and especially Eric, whom he'd probably view as a threat. Gareth always did have a nasty streak of jealousy. He used to get quite upset when I spent what he considered too much time talking to another male.

His face softened. His eyes shone with a forgotten tenderness. "Remember that trip we took to Waterton Lakes? This place has the same quiet, peaceful feel to it." He paused, then continued, "Boy, we had some wonderful moments together, didn't we, Megs?"

With a few more words, he plunged me back into the happy years of our marriage when we were two young people very much in love. As the afternoon sun gradually spread its warmth into the verandah, we laughed and smiled over shared memories of exploratory trips to out-of-the-way places, of lingering afternoons lying in bed, of candlelight dinners and other special moments. Once in a while, the words would fade, as each of us became lost in our own private memories.

After one long pause, Gareth said, "Don't you think we could go back to those days?"

Lulled by the memories, the soothing afternoon sun, I said, "Perhaps."

He reached for my hand lying beside my glass. For a second, I enjoyed the soft caress, then like an electric shock, the painful memory of his last touch flooded back. I jerked my hand away.

"Hey, what gives? I didn't hurt you, did I?" he said.

I shook my head, too stunned by the force of my reaction to come up with a good excuse.

But it looked as if Gareth knew the cause. "I wasn't going to say anything, Megs. I thought you wouldn't want to drag up old dirt. But look, if it means anything, I'm sorry, really sorry I hurt you. I never meant to. I don't know what got into me that day."

I took a long slow sip of vodka to try to still the trembling that had returned. "You're right, I'd just as soon not drag up the old dirt. Why don't you tell me about that new job of yours?"

He turned a startled look towards me. "How do you know that?"

"I called your old office number. Who did you go with? Anyone I know?"

"No, you wouldn't know them. Great job, though. Came after me and made an offer I couldn't refuse."

"Enough to eat into your usual hefty credit card balances?"

He laughed, "You sure know me, don't you? Yeah, I like the high life, why not? And with the bonus I'll get when I deliver on this special project, I should be on easy street."

"Oh, what's that all about?"

He lit up another cigarette, sipped his drink, then replied, "Nothing much, it would only bore you. Hey, what do you think about my new car?"

"Great," I said absentmindedly, while I thought about the special project that he didn't want to divulge.

"Company car. Didn't have to spend a cent of my own." He glanced quickly at his watch and continued, "What about yourself? Like living in the wilds?"

"It suits me," I said.

"Do you think you'd ever move back to Toronto?"

"In time perhaps, but not now."

"Well, you do have a special place here, Megs," he said. "Not many like it. I know people who'd pay a fortune to stay at a place like this. Ever think of converting it into a lodge?" he asked.

"No, why would I?"

"Just a thought. How are you for finances these days, now that you're no longer working?"

"Aunt Aggie's money provides me with enough. Besides, living here doesn't cost much," I replied, beginning to wonder why he was asking me these questions.

"Must cost a bundle to maintain this old building, though?"

I nodded. I'd just finished writing out a cheque for five thousand dollars to pay for the drilling of a new well.

"Ever think of selling it?"

My antenna went on alert. "Of course not."

Gareth rocked back and forth in Aunt Aggie's chair. He

puffed on his cigarette, then took a drink. I waited.

Finally he said, "Look, I might as well not beat about the bush any longer. I've got this client who's looking for a property exactly like yours to develop a resort. I know I could arrange it so you'd get top dollar."

"Now the truth comes out," I said, trying to keep from shouting. But before I had a chance to really blast him, a loud pounding from the other side of the house cut me off.

Half-hoping it might be Eric, I went to answer it. As I turned the corner of the verandah, I said, "Hi Eric, glad—" and stopped. Instead of Eric standing at the front door, it was the grinning mass of Charlie Cardinal.

Too startled for words, I could only gape.

"Expecting your boyfriend, eh? Whatever would your husband think? Tell Mr. Patterson I'm here."

"You never mentioned a boyfriend, Megs," sounded Gareth's voice at my ear. "He this guy Eric you called me on the phone? Never mind, we can talk about him later. Go inside while I see what this guy wants."

Gareth brushed past me and down the verandah stairs with Charlie Cardinal in tow and a barking Sergei not far behind. I remained rooted, trying to fathom why Charlie Cardinal was here, let alone how he knew Gareth.

I watched Gareth march towards his car, abruptly turn around and jab his finger into Charlie's chest. Charlie just stood there and took the full force of Gareth's anger. For a second, I almost felt for Charlie, for I knew too well how it felt to be pummelled into the ground by Gareth's scathing words. I strained to hear, but caught only the familiar condescending tone of his voice. I moved closer.

"I told you not to come here," Gareth hissed. "If you screw up this deal, Charlie, I'll kill you."

His face twisted in anger, he finally noticed me. "Get inside, Meg. This has nothing to do with you."

Old habits die hard. I started to do his bidding, then I woke up. "The only person leaving is you…and your henchman," I shouted.

"Now, Megs, no need to get yourself worked up. You've got it all wrong." Gareth tried to erase his anger with a conciliatory smile. But it didn't work. The glint of sarcasm had returned to his eyes.

And I was suddenly back to where we'd been three years ago. Gareth standing over me, saying those exact words in that same patronizing tone after I'd finally mustered up my courage to confront him about Janice. His words hadn't stopped me. Determined to find out the truth, I'd believed that once he admitted to the affair that that would end it, and we'd go back to being the loving couple we were supposed to be. How stupid. All I got was a trip to the hospital after he'd slammed me against the kitchen counter.

This time I wasn't going to be a fool. I was going to do what I should have done then.

I turned around and walked back to the verandah, where not five minutes ago we'd almost been old friends. I grabbed his keys and cell phone, went inside and locked the door behind me. I locked all the other outside doors. Then I stomped back to the front door. I wrenched it open, threw his stuff as far as I could and shouted. "Gareth, it's over. If you're not gone in five minutes, I'm calling the police."

I returned inside and double locked the door. I held my breath and waited. Silence reigned. Even Sergei had stopped barking. I peeked out the side window. Where minutes before tenderness had gazed out of clear brown eyes, now only anger flashed.

He walked towards the stairs. "Megs, listen to me," he shouted. "You've got it all wrong. Let me in, and I'll tell you the whole truth."

I stepped away from the door. He started hammering on it. "Damn you, let me in!" I heard Sergei's muffled growls. "Get away, you damn dog!" Gareth snarled.

"Keep at it, dog," I whispered and retreated into the living room.

The pounding filled the room, filled my head. What was I going to do? I was miles from help. I stood frozen, emotions whirling, afraid to move. A sudden yelp from Sergei woke me up.

"Leave the dog alone!" I cried.

I ran to the kitchen, grabbed the phone and a butcher knife. I dialled Eric's number and got only his voice mail. I called the provincial police and was told it would take at least twenty minutes. I tried the Migiskan Police, but they were tied up on another call.

I'd have to deal with Gareth myself.

I took a deep breath, clutched the knife firmly and walked steadily to the front door. The hammering had stopped. I waited. I strained my ears, expecting to hear Gareth's ragged breathing behind the door. Nothing. Total silence.

And then I heard the sound of engines firing up. By the time I got to the window, Gareth's company car was roaring down the drive with Charlie's red Yukon in hot pursuit. A yapping Sergei chased after them as I collapsed into Aunt Aggie's rocker.

TWENTY

The sound of their engines was still reverberating through the hills when rage took over. And it was rage directed not at Gareth, but at myself. Sure, he'd betrayed me, but he was only being the bastard he'd always been. He hadn't changed. Why should he?

And I hadn't changed either. Despite all my efforts to escape his controlling grip, I'd still been sucked in. Like a dewy-eyed bitch, I'd fallen for his phony line. He didn't need to do more than smile, bat his puppy eyes, and I was hooked. Just like every other time.

"God damn it!" I shouted to the walls. I kicked at the chesterfield and threw the cushions to the floor. I pounded on the coffee table and almost broke my hand. Then I saw the Chaki painting still leaning against the wall where I'd dropped it.

With single-minded purpose, I walked over, picked it up and marched outside to the overhanging bulge in the verandah. I leaned over the railing as far as I could and flung it into the air. It soared down the cliff wall like a flying saucer, then a sudden gust of wind picked it up and deposited it in the twisted crown of a pine growing out of the rock. I couldn't even do that right.

I marched into my bedroom, put on some outdoor clothes and hiking boots and stomped outside. I needed to get out of there. This time, vodka wouldn't do the trick. I needed to drown myself in the wilds.

I stomped along the trail towards the Lookout, through Aunt Aggie's now defunct sugar bush. I kicked my anger out on the fallen leaves, creating a mini bow wave of shifting gold. As if knowing better than to stay near me, Sergei raced up the trail and was soon lost behind the converging trunks of the maple trees.

I cursed myself with every forward step. I was an idiot and a fool. All the things Gareth had called me at one time or another. Well, I wasn't going to be a fool any longer. It was clear Gareth would never be the man I'd thought I'd married. He was a selfish, controlling bastard, always had been and always would be. It was high time I accepted it. I had my own life now. I didn't need him any more.

Around the next bend in the trail, the remains of Aunt Aggie's maple sugar operation loomed into view, and with them came the muffled barks of Sergei. It was a sorry-looking collection of log shacks that had once housed the huge iron cauldrons Aunt Aggie used to boil the clear maple sap down to the super sweet brown syrup. Only one of the shacks remained standing, with its roof still intact. The others were jumbles of rotting squared timbers, broken planks and rusted metal roofing.

From under the shack emerged Sergei's black hind quarters, his tail wagging vigorously. As I approached, he backed out, shook the dirt from his fur, emitted one shrill bark then resumed digging. Praying it wasn't a skunk he'd found, I hurried past and started the slow weaving climb up the steep hill to the Lookout.

"Gareth is gone. Gareth is gone," I vowed with every step. From this point onwards, Gareth was out of my life, never to return. And as I hiked up the hill, the anger gradually dissipated, leaving in its wake a sense of peace. I said the word "Gareth" and felt nothing. I felt the tension flow from my shoulders, down my arms and out my fingertips. This time he was gone, forever.

I breathed in deeply the fresh forest smell and stopped to listen to the honking of geese flying overhead. Around the next bend, I found myself staring into startled brown eyes, then with a flash of its white tail, a deer disappeared through a wall of gold.

I continued walking. This time I kicked the leaves in play, not in anger.

I reached the smooth granite knoll of the Lookout feeling invigorated and not out of breath, as was my usual state after climbing the hill. I perched atop Aunt Aggie's rickety bench. Two feet away, the granite plunged a hundred feet to the vibrant canopy of the maples below. Through gaps left by fallen leaves, I could see rusty sections of the remaining sugar shack's roof.

I reached down to pick up a piece of birch bark wedged in a crack and discovered instead a cigarette butt. I started to get annoyed at the thought of trespassers but decided there was no harm in others taking advantage of this unique view. I hoped it was the same person I'd spied from Eric's boat the day we went to Whispers Island. I didn't want too many people invading my private retreat.

I held out my arms and embraced the magnificent unfettered view of my world, a world that would never contain Gareth. I breathed the crisp clear air, air that would never smell of Gareth. The sparkling waters of Echo Lake winked back at me as if to say "I'm with you, gal." Even Three Deer Point seemed to be passing opinion on Gareth with its long finger-like point.

The lake was surprisingly busy for so late in the afternoon. Several boats were speeding towards Forgotten Bay Fishing

Camp, while others were racing away. I could just see the tip of the camp's dock, where an unusually large crowd congregated. I assumed it was a large fishing party getting ready for some dusk time trawling. But sporadic flashes through the trees of something large and red moving towards the Camp made me wonder if something else wasn't going on.

When I looked out towards Whispers Island and saw a line of boats cluttering the northern spit, I wondered if this activity didn't have something to do with CanacGold. A thought re-enforced by the frequent bursts of light coming from the island's backbone, where we'd discovered CanacGold's mining claim.

It also made me wonder if this wasn't the real reason behind Gareth's visit. For when Charlie had suddenly appeared on my doorstep, it had taken me less than a second to jump to the obvious conclusion. Gareth's new employer was CanacGold.

But why would a mining company hire Gareth? He was a criminal lawyer. The only thing he knew about gold was how to buy it; gold cufflinks, gold bracelet, even a gold Rolex watch, all in the interests of looking successful. Unless CanacGold's only requirement for a lawyer was sleaze, of which Gareth had plenty.

Still, it didn't answer the question of why Gareth wanted my land. Or should I really say CanacGold? Was it possible there was gold on my land too? Was I Gareth's special project? Get me to sell my land, and he got the big bucks?

Damn that double-dealing bastard. I'd better get to the Fishing Camp and try to find out what he was up to.

*   *   *

From my canoe, I heard the echo of angry shouts across the water long before I saw the tense crowd of people at the

Camp's boat launch. They were watching Eric and Charlie Cardinal standing face to face, shouting at each other. Some of the onlookers were positioned behind one or the other of the antagonists, while others stood further back, as if reluctant to show sides. And lurking behind them like a giant lizard waiting to pounce was the red object I'd seen from the Lookout, a huge transport trailer with letters emblazoned in gold along its side that spelled out the word "CanacGold".

I beached my canoe on the shore, not far from the action. Although a few watchers cast angry glances in my direction, most eyes were fixed on the shouters.

"For the last time, tell the driver to haul that damn truck back to where it came from," yelled Eric, the scar beneath his eye a searing white.

"Like hell I will. He has every right to be here," came the angry retort from Charlie Cardinal.

They were both standing feet planted apart, arms crossed, faces locked in stubborn refusal. A faint breeze nudged the eagle feather attached to Charlie's braid, while Eric held his own feather ramrod straight in his left hand.

I searched for Gareth and found him where I expected, standing by his car waiting for events to unfold. Never one to get his hands dirty, Gareth let others do it for him. Under the full force of his glare, I turned away and determinedly aligned myself behind Eric's solid back.

"Charlie," Eric shouted, "you know damn well, that truck has no right to be on our land without band permission. I'll charge the driver and all his friends with trespassing if they don't leave immediately."

At a nod from Charlie, a man who looked like a retiree from the Hells Angels walked towards the cab of the transport trailer. A line of men in red CanacGold windbreakers held their ground beside the truck.

"As hereditary tribal chief, I give him the right," Charlie retorted.

From his groupies rose sporadic cries of "That's right Charlie", "Give him hell".

"You don't have the authority," Eric replied.

"Damn right I do," Charlie yelled. "My ancestors were chiefs of the Migiskan when yours were Mohawk slaves. Now get the hell out of the way, or this truck'll run you down."

And to emphasize his challenge, the truck let off one piercing peal of its horn, which throbbed against the bordering cliffs until it dissipated into the bay. Gareth remained by his car, watching and waiting.

But the threat only made Eric stand firmer. "Charlie, you're only making things worse for yourself. Only the band council has the authority, and we voted earlier this afternoon not to permit CanacGold the use of band lands. So tell the driver to leave, and we won't bring the police into it."

"Yeah, that's right Charlie, we don't want them bastards here," came a shout from one of Eric's supporters.

"Knock it off, Charlie", "Forget it" came others.

But the CanacGold response was a dull clank as the truck's gears shifted into drive and slowly moved towards us, only to stop as it met our line of silent, determined faces. The truck inched forward again. I gulped, not sure how far I wanted to take this. Some of the men gave way, I with them, but John-Joe stood his ground. The truck's gleaming bumper nudged John-Joe's chest, causing him to lurch backwards and fall. The truck stopped. John-Joe picked himself up and planted his feet in front of the waiting truck. I walked over, stood beside him and heard the shuffle as others joined our line.

Finally, Gareth made his move. "Enough, Charlie," he shouted.

For a moment it looked as if Charlie were going to hit Eric, then he turned abruptly on his heels and strode away, forcing a path through the men who blocked his way to the truck. He wrenched the door open and climbed into the cab beside the driver.

Gareth, his face a mask of professional calm, stalked over to Eric. "Sorry about this misunderstanding, Chief Odjik," he said with barely disguised contempt. "We won't disturb you again. We'll bring our supplies in another way." And cupping his hands to his mouth shouted, "Okay guys! Everyone in your trucks, we're leaving."

The CanacGold men jumped into several shiny pickups and a couple of nondescript rentals. Gareth turned to leave, then as if changing his mind he walked over to me and spat out, "Indian lover, I wouldn't touch you with a ten foot pole…" he turned towards Eric, "…now."

Infuriated not only by the insult to me, but to my friends, I threw a handful of stones after him and grinned when he wheeled around, rubbing his head. And since Gareth had to have the final say, he jerked his finger at me with a gesture that needed no translation, then turned back to his car.

With a groan, the truck slowly backed away from the boat launch, past the timber lodge, with its windows filled with cheering onlookers. The spasmodic beep of the back-up horn echoed off the watching hills. The driver didn't dare attempt to turn the massive vehicle around in the limited space. He just continued reversing down the narrow winding Camp road towards the main road, more than a mile away. Close on his front bumper followed the cavalcade, with a dusty Porsche in the lead.

A war whoop erupted, accompanied by shouts of "Hurray, we did it!" There were even a few steps of the warrior's dance I'd seen at the last Pow Wow.

Grinning broadly, Eric shouted, "Thanks, men, but show's over. Back to work!" With more war whoops, they dispersed.

"Hi, Meg. See you caught the fun." Eric walked chuckling towards me.

"Congrats. Round one to the good guys." I laughed, luxuriating in this minor victory.

"Might as well enjoy it. Not sure how many more we'll have," Eric replied, suddenly looking serious. "They need to get that equipment over to the island to start the drilling. You heard that guy, they'll find another way."

"That guy was Gareth," I said. "As you saw, he's one of them."

"I'm sorry, Meg. Sorry for you that he had to turn up like this." He searched my face as if seeking answers. Finally, he asked, "How are you feeling?"

"Okay now." I sat down on a nearby picnic table and motioned Eric to join me. "I've made many mistakes in my life, Eric, and will no doubt continue to do so, but he's one I won't make again. So tell me, what's this about CanacGold drilling?"

"They want to start exploratory drilling next week to confirm the size of the deposit."

"There goes our theory about nothing happening until next spring. What are we going to do?"

"I think we can still buy ourselves some time. As long as we deny them access."

I thought his tactic made sense. The Fishing Camp offered the only truck access to the lake. Most of the Echo Lake shoreline was either too far from a road or too steep to permit the off-loading of heavy mining equipment.

And then I understood why Gareth wanted to buy my land. My property had the only other possible access point, a low marshy area that stretched from the main road to Echo

Lake, which could easily be filled in to make a road wide enough for truck access.

Damn him. The nerve of him to think I would so easily do his bidding. But he was right. The old me would've eventually sold it to him. Well, he'd shot his bolt, so to speak. From this point onwards, I wouldn't even let him and his CanacGold buddies breathe on my land, let alone run their trucks over it.

Eric and I sat for a few more minutes, discussing what more we could do to stop CanacGold. Other than continuing to pursue the island's ownership, we decided some lobbying of politicians was in order. Eric knew some people he could call upon. I had Carrie, an old school friend, now a parliamentarian in Ottawa. I promised to phone her the minute I returned home.

We were about to go our separate ways, when John-Joe approached, looking worried.

"Eric, what do you want me to do about Louis's boat?" he asked, pulling the brim of his orange cap further down his forehead. He flashed me a Tom Cruise smile, which seemed to say I was okay.

"Nothing that I'm aware of. Can't we just leave it for Tommy to take it away?"

"That's the problem. Tommy said he can't get to it for a couple of days. I can't wait that long. It's in the way."

"Move it then."

"Can't. Tommy locked it to the dock with a chain."

Curious at the mention of Tommy's name, I asked, "When was that?"

John-Joe replied, "Can't say exactly. Boat's been there almost a week. I suppose it was last Tuesday or Wednesday."

"Are you sure?" I asked, surprised by his answer. Last Thursday, the day Tommy caught me peering through the windows of his house looking for his mother, he told me he was just returning home from a trip.

John-Joe repositioned his hat, bringing the brim down till it almost covered his eyes, then he answered. "Yup, had to be. Caused me a shit load of problems with that big fishing party we had Wednesday morning, eh?"

So Tommy had been lying to me from the beginning to protect his mother. He'd used the boat to take her to some isolated location on Echo Lake. She would be well hidden anywhere on the uninhabited shore, but still within easy reach of food and supplies. Whispers Island was even a possibility. That would explain the footprints on the beach, two sets arriving, only one leaving. But with CanacGold intent on moving in, would the island remain such a good hiding place?

I turned to Eric to ask if he or Tommy had already thought of this, but he was fast disappearing into the main lodge. Just as well, I thought. I wasn't sure how to bring this up delicately, without revealing that I knew where they were hiding Marie. Besides, it probably wasn't a real concern, as long as we could stop CanacGold from moving their equipment onto the island.

Deciding it could wait, I shoved my canoe into the water and headed towards the cliffs of Three Deer Point. When I reached home, I phoned Carrie, who didn't hesitate to offer to help stop CanacGold. She suggested that if I didn't mind the long drive to Ottawa, I could meet her on Monday at her parliamentary office.

TWENTY-ONE

The Peace Tower clock on Parliament Hill was striking noon when I entered Carrie's suite of tiny offices tucked into a back corner of the West Block. Cramped and narrow, her office looked more like a broom closet, which it probably once was when the number of people required to govern the country was considerably less than today. Since Carrie was still tied up in a committee meeting, her assistant gave me a security badge and told me to wait for her at the parliamentary restaurant.

Carrie Zbrowski, a good friend since university days, had gone the political route after graduation and was now a full-fledged Member of Parliament. Although she didn't represent my specific electoral riding, she did represent another Quebec riding, and a powerful one at that. I figured she would know someone who could make CanacGold's pursuit difficult, if not stop them altogether.

I made my way through the throngs of gawking tourists towards the Gothic arches of the Centre Block's main entrance. After flashing my badge at the guards, I headed along the stone corridor towards the House of Commons, past the watching eyes of yesterdays' Prime Ministers, and was stopped by a loud and blinding media scrum intent on cornering the current Prime Minister in the Commons foyer. With a few forceful elbow jabs, I squeezed my way past, climbed up several flights of stairs, to where the restaurant was hidden far from public view above the House of Commons.

I quickly scanned the long and very full room for Carrie's familiar face, but the marble columns, which support a line of Paladin dome ceilings, obstructed much of my view. The House had obviously broken early for lunch. Crammed with assorted politicians, journalists and various hangers-on, the restaurant was a bustle of craning necks, planted smiles and waving hands. A few I recognized as people I'd met through Carrie, but most were faces seen through the glare of television lights or peering out from black and white print. All the treasured alcoves were occupied, their inhabitants engrossed in tête-à-tête conversations.

Thankfully, Carrie's assistant had made a reservation. The maitre d' led me through the congestion to an empty table next to one of the marble columns supporting the domed ceiling. While I waited for Carrie, I immersed myself in the pulse of the current rulers. Today it was a low rumble of muted conversations and clattering dishes. There was an undercurrent of tense anticipation, perhaps a reflection of some key vote that was scheduled in the House for later today.

Signalled by a turning of heads, Carrie arrived. Looking every inch the sober politician, she was dressed in a dark grey worsted suit, the pale yellow of her silk blouse providing a softening contrast to her deep brown hair. The life of the parliamentarian obviously suited her. She had a confident, in-control manner that blended well with the friendly, outgoing aura of her personality.

With her life extremely busy and mine in retreat, we had not been together since the night we'd celebrated my divorce. Deciding I wouldn't bore her with my woes over Gareth, I plunged into the subject of CanacGold the minute we finished greeting each other.

"So, Carrie, can you stop them?" I asked optimistically.

"Well, Meg, as I told you on the phone, CanacGold's in bed with almost every politician in this city." she replied, glancing over the menu infamous for its country club meals at luncheon counter prices.

"Hopefully not with you," I conjectured.

"What? Me? Get out of here. But, now that you mention it, the CanacGold CEO does have potential."

"He could only be a sleaze ball. I thought you had better taste than that?"

"Well, a man's a man" she replied, rolling her eyes, at which point the waiter minced towards us for our orders, and we both burst out laughing.

Continuing in a more serious vein, Carrie said, "It's going to be very tough to stop CanacGold. Not only are they firmly entrenched in Ottawa, but they also have strong connections in Quebec City. In fact I discovered that the CEO's sister is married to the Quebec politician whose ministry hands out the mineral rights."

"Shit, I should have expected something like that. We can't fight that."

"Don't be so hasty. There's plenty we can do."

"Like what?"

"I've pointed the environmental watchdogs in their direction."

"Tell me more. I like the sound of this," I replied with my eyes glued to the thick slice of filet mignon being placed before me. Fine cuts of beef rarely made their way to the Migiskan General Store. I glanced at Carrie's lobster salad. No wonder she retained her slim girlish figure while I kept adding inches.

Carrie cut herself a small slice of the lobster, then continued, "It seems Quebec's Environment Minister didn't know that CanacGold had screwed up royally in the Territories with their gold extraction process. Now he knows. Apparently they weren't careful with the tailings. And the arsenic that has been leaking for years is now causing a major environmental disaster."

"This will help? Sounds like Echo Lake's death knell to me," I groaned.

"Trust me, Meg. It's good news. When the Minister was informed, he vowed that he would tie CanacGold up so tight in regs that they wouldn't be able to fart without his permission. Seems that there is a little matter of a long-running feud between the two ministers, so this guy has jumped on the chance to screw one of his opponent's darling projects."

"Do you think he can stop them?" I asked, looking around. Many of the diners were starting to leave.

"Perhaps not immediately. But give him time. I am sure he will think of a way."

Out of the corner of my eye, I saw two men across the room leave one of the alcoves. With a shock, I recognized one of them.

"Quick, Carrie. See those two men walking towards the door. Who is the one on the right?"

"Why, that's Senator Canelli. He's got his nose into everything around here. Wait a minute. Isn't that your ex with him?"

"Right on. Now what do you think Gareth is doing with the Senator?"

"Well, coincidental to our discussion, Canelli is one of the big power brokers around here for mining interests. Would that concern Gareth?" She asked, peering at me through her wire-rim glasses.

"You bet," I replied and proceeded to tell her the latest on Gareth.

When I'd finished, she said, "That explains it. I saw the two of them a few weeks ago, deep in conversation at one of the party fundraisers. Although I was surprised to see your ex so far from his home ground, I assumed he was just keeping up his contacts with the government in power. Obviously, he was lobbying for CanacGold."

"How much influence does Canelli have?" I asked.

"Unfortunately, a lot, but I can counteract with my own influence," Carrie said with a confident smile. "Still, the senator isn't above underhanded dealings. He has a reputation for doing whatever is necessary to further his and his friends' interests. The RCMP have investigated him a couple of times but have never found enough evidence to charge him."

"Well, given the kind of man Gareth's become, I'd say he'd go right along with whatever Canelli proposes. What can we do about it?"

"Leave it to me. I'll put the right people in the know about his link to this new mine. They'll know what to do." Carrie brought out her pager. "Drat, the call I've been expecting. Sorry, Meg, I'm going to have to cut our lunch short. I hate to do this, but look, I'll make it up to you by doing all I can to stop this disastrous mine of yours."

After settling the bill, Carrie raced off, leaving me to make my way to the rotunda, where I escaped back into the normal world. I headed towards my truck, which was parked around the back of the Parliament Buildings, close to the flying buttresses of the Parliamentary Library. For an extra measure of luck, I made a quick detour to rub the glossy tail of Queen Victoria's regal lion sitting at the base of her stolid bronze statue.

I needed all the luck I could get. Maybe Carrie's feuding

minister could make life very difficult for CanacGold and eventually stop the mine, but he wouldn't be able to achieve anything by next week, or even next month. I was convinced that by the time he got the slow wheels of government rolling it would be too late, the ancients' forest would be gone. Moreover, I didn't trust party politics. Despite Carrie's best intentions, I had no doubt that the party hierarchy would close ranks around Senator Canelli and do little more than issue a cautionary warning.

I'd almost reached my truck when I recognized a car I'd seen only two days ago tearing down my road. Gareth stood beside the black Porsche, his back to me. He was engrossed in a conversation on his cell phone.

Thinking it might be useful to listen in, I snuck up behind him.

"Canelli said to destroy those files, so there'll be no—" He turned around and saw me. "Do it," he said and snapped his phone shut.

He glared at me, then attempted a crooked smile. "Well, well, well. Small world, isn't it."

"What files?" I asked.

"Nothing that concerns you."

"Must be bad news for CanacGold, if you want to get rid of them."

"Look Meg, I don't know where you think you're going with this. I'm just talking about a brief I put together for the senator that's no longer valid."

"Anything to do with your special project...that failed?" His smile turned to a thin grim line. "No Three Deer Point, no big bonus, eh?"

Gareth's response was an angry scowl and the slam of his door as he jumped into his car. He was gone before I remembered the missing registry files for another significant property.

I ran to my truck and drove to the nearest phone to call François. Although my notary was disgusted by the possibility of a fellow lawyer stealing legal records, he viewed it as another indication that the land wasn't crown-owned. Unfortunately, until he had actual proof that the land was privately held, there was nothing he could do to stop CanacGold. Meanwhile, his clerk was continuing her search through the municipal records.

TWENTY-TWO

I reached the turnoff to Three Deer Point in the failing light. The deluge, which had been threatening from the moment I left Ottawa, let loose as my truck turned off the main road. With wipers on overdrive, I drove up the long twisting lane to my cottage and came to a stop as close to the side entrance as possible. I flung open the door and scrambled up the stairs to the protective cover of the verandah.

The screen door banged in the wind. Sergei emerged from the trees on the other side of the driveway. Yelping wildly, he raced through the rain towards me. All my nerve endings went into high alert.

I'd left him locked in the house.

He crashed up the stairs and flung himself at me, whining and yelping, a turmoil of flying water and black fur. I placed a firm hand on his wet back to try to calm him down.

How in hell did he get out?

With racing heart, I tiptoed along the porch towards the kitchen door with Sergei glued to my side. The door swung open at my touch. The dog started to growl. I carefully pushed the door further open and walked gingerly into the kitchen. Everything looked normal. Exactly the way I'd left it that morning, dishes stacked at the sink, newspapers scattered on the table.

Sergei growled louder, ears flat against his head. Suddenly, he pounced snarling into the living room. In the uproar, I almost missed the tinkling sound of breakage.

I raced into the room only to see the front door slam, the dog yelping furiously in its wake. Stumbling over him, I managed to pull the door open just in time to see a figure in brilliant yellow disappearing through the rain down the stairs to the dock.

Without thinking, I ran after the intruder, but by the time I reached the top of the stairs, it was too late. From below came the roar of a high-speed motor. Through the streaming curtain, I watched the retreating boat speed towards Forgotten Bay, the yellow figure a blur in the vanishing stern.

I slapped the railing in anger, then reality set in. What was I doing? This could've been the guy who'd tried to kill me on Whispers Island. What if I'd caught up to him?

Preferring not to dwell on the answer, I headed back through the rain to the cottage. Still, it would've been helpful to see his face. And then I realized there was a safer way to discover who he was. I raced inside and phoned the Fishing Camp.

John-Joe answered, and judging by the noise level in the background, he was in the bar.

I shouted above the din, "Could you please look out your window and tell me if you see anyone at the dock or approaching in a fast boat?"

"Hang on while I take a look."

Several minutes passed. I impatiently brushed the dripping water from my eyes while I tried to ignore the growing puddle on the floor. A soggy Sergei clung to my side like a frightened child. I gave him a comforting squeeze.

Finally, John-Joe returned. "Meg. You still there? Yeah, number of guys on the dock. A big fishing party just come in. That help?"

"Did you recognize anyone?"

"Sure did. Eric and Tommy. And some suit, probably from

that mining company, standing by a real cool car. Boy, what I'd give to own one of those. Oh yeah, and there was another guy tying up a boat, but I couldn't tell who it was."

"Quick, go see who it is."

Cool car? Must be Gareth. I wondered what brought him back here so quickly.

"Hi again. Sorry, the guy's gone."

"Damn. Was anyone wearing yellow?"

"Sure were, most of the guys. They've got the Camp's rain gear on."

Of course. How could I have been so stupid not to remember the yellow rain slickers? Even Eric had forgotten about them. But I supposed it was human nature not to focus on the obvious. And what could be more obvious? The lake was sprinkled with yellow dots whenever it rained.

And that was the problem. Everyone had access to the Camp's rain gear. I'd even borrowed a jacket once or twice myself. So although I now knew the guy was probably wearing the camp's rain gear, the knowledge wouldn't lead me to him.

But I could probably eliminate Louis as my attacker on Whispers Island, unless the guy tonight was a completely different person, which seemed unlikely.

*   *   *

While I waited for the police to drive from Somerset, I seethed at the damage this thief had done to my pride and joy. Perhaps it wasn't much by city standards, but it was enough to get me vowing I'd never let anyone invade my privacy again.

If the guy had rifled the kitchen drawers, I might not have been so upset, but he had invaded what was most personal, my bedroom. It seemed as if every item of clothing I owned, including my underpants and bras, lay scattered on the floor with the overturned drawers on top. Even my bed hadn't been immune to his invasive search. The bedclothes were ripped off and the mattress dragged partially from the bed frame.

But these seemed to be the only things he touched. The pictures were still hanging on the walls, even the Tom Thomson cigar box sketch, though I supposed only an art connoisseur would know its real value.

Although my jewel box had been moved, a quick glance revealed my aunt's diamond butterfly brooch and my wedding rings were still inside. The brooch, however, wasn't in its usual spot, which suggested the intruder had actually looked at it. But since I hadn't worn it for some time, I could easily have forgotten where I'd last placed it.

As for the living room, I could only describe it as my worst nightmare. Chairs were overturned. Stuffing oozed from slashed sofa cushions. Chips of blue paisley porcelain lay scattered over the stone hearth, which probably explained the tinkling sound I'd heard. A set of whiskers and a glaring eye stared back at me from one of the larger pieces. At least Sergei would be happy to discover his stalking china cat was no more.

Nor did the intruder leave my desk alone. He'd dumped the contents of every drawer onto the floor. He'd even forced the lock of the one drawer I thought secure. And from the way my correspondence and financial statements were strewn across the desk, I'd say he went through the documents one by one. Thankfully, nothing appeared to be missing, although I decided I'd call my banker first thing in the morning. I did, however, say a silent prayer to François, who'd recommended that I secure all the really important documents, such as bonds and the Three Deer Point deed, in a safety deposit box.

A quick search that revealed no other rooms had been

touched and everything of value, like my stereo and computer, even Aunt Aggie's silver, was still in its place. It was obvious that this guy was no ordinary thief. But when the police finally arrived, they jumped to the same conclusion that Tommy had when his place was broken into. They assumed it was someone from the reserve looking for a few thrills.

But I refused to believe that. Thrill seekers didn't take the time to go through personal files. Nor were they likely to go after the same person twice. Nope. This guy wanted something from me. But what?

And though it looked as if his motive on the island was to keep me from trespassing, tonight he was the trespasser. So what was he after? I could only hope that tonight's attempt was enough to convince him that, whatever it was, it wasn't here.

Later, as I swept up the shattered cat, I did discover one missing item, of no value except to me.

Aunt Aggie's wedding picture was gone.

TWENTY-THREE

I set out to master my growing fear as dusk slid into night. I figured since I'd managed to make it through the night after my first encounter with the guy in yellow, there was no reason why I couldn't do it again.

But tonight it proved impossible. He had invaded my home. I twitched and jumped at every creak and rustle in the empty house. Convinced the guy was out there waiting to make his move, I scanned the outdoors continuously, but in the downpour the flood lights acted more like a curtain than a window. Still, I vowed I wouldn't go crawling for male protection.

And I was almost winning, when the storm did me in.

For several tense minutes, the cottage throbbed with strobe lightning and rumbling thunder. Waves of rain hammered against the windows. The pines moaned in wind-whipped fury. And then, with a final eye-searing flash and ear-splitting crack, the storm ended. But it wasn't completely over. With an agonized screech, a giant pine snapped and crashed to the ground. It landed with a resounding thud, which shook the house from top to bottom, leaving in its wake an empty eerie silence and blinding darkness. The power had gone off. Terrified, I stumbled through the pitch black for my keys, my coat and the dog and fled to my truck.

Next I knew, I was hammering at Eric's door, and he was

standing in front of me, calm and secure, wrapping a blanket around my trembling body. He sat me in front of the hot crackling fire where I collapsed from nervous exhaustion and remained for the rest of the night, cloaked in a cocoon of warmth with Sergei curled on the floor beside me.

In the morning, feeling very foolish for having given in to such a silly fear and very embarrassed for intruding so rudely, I attempted to leave without waking either him or, as I'd discovered much to my consternation, his female companion. But Eric stopped me before I reached the door, insisting that his friend didn't mind, and he didn't want me to leave without my breakfast.

She was rather nice about it all and kept saying between mouthfuls of Eric's delicious pancakes, that it was so nice to have such a strong brave man like Eric for protection and hinted that maybe I should find my own. In response, Eric winked at me and served me another pancake, which went a long way towards making me feel less like a third wheel.

Angered by the break-in, Eric phoned the provincial police to ensure they gave it their full attention and Police Chief Decontie to have him pursue it from the reserve end. Then Eric insisted on coming to double check that everything was safe at Three Deer Point. I didn't try to dissuade him, even though his lady friend looked none too pleased.

Feeling considerably rejuvenated, I set out for home with Sergei, who'd been equally well fed with some leftover steak. With his chainsaw lying securely strapped down in the back of my truck, Eric followed on his motorbike. As for his lady friend, she departed back to Ottawa without saying goodbye, which raised my spirits even further. Maybe that was the end of her.

At home, everything looked as I'd left it. No one lurked in the shadows, nor was there evidence of the intruder's return. While the mess from the break-in looked worse in the daylight, I could clean it up later. The fallen pine was another matter. It needed Eric and his chainsaw.

"You were very lucky," Eric said as the two of us stood before the once mighty tree. "*Kije manido* must have been watching over you when the lightning struck."

I could only nod in stunned agreement. The massive trunk, which had cut a swath through the surrounding trees, had missed my home by what seemed inches. Another few feet, and it would have destroyed the entire back end of the hundred year old building. The only damage had come from the branches. One monster limb had carved a deep gouge in the timber wall, and another had shattered a kitchen window. I said a silent prayer to Eric's *kije manido* and thought for one brief second that it was too bad the guy in yellow hadn't been under it.

Eric sparked his chainsaw into life and began slicing through the thick branches. As I watched the dismemberment, I couldn't help but feel sad. I'd grown up with this tree. In fact, Aunt Aggie would've grown up with this tree. Even Great-grandpa Joe. Now it was gone. Felled by an arbitrary strike of nature. But at least man didn't cause its death, which would be the fate of the pines on Whispers Island if we didn't stop CanacGold.

However, I didn't want to worry about the gold mine just then. I just wanted to enjoy the crisp fall day and Eric's company. I breathed deeply the invigorating smell of freshly cut pine and watched Eric. He expertly severed one branch after another from the trunk. His body flowed with the rhythm like a fencer's as he jabbed and thrust the whirring blade through the wood. In a single fluid motion, he cut the long branches into short manageable lengths. I felt tempted to reach out and touch him.

As if sensing my staring, he glanced up at me through his

goggles. "This ain't no side-show, gal. Grab a branch and start hauling."

Embarrassed, I bent down to pick up one of the cut lengths and started dragging it towards the clearing behind the woodshed. "Get a hold of yourself," I muttered under my breath. He was just helping out to be nice. Besides it appeared he was already taken.

Behind me, Eric chuckled and said, as if reading my mind, "Don't pay any attention to Josée. She likes to think she still owns me, but she doesn't."

Yeah sure, I thought to myself. I'd heard that one before. I threw the branch to the ground and stomped back for another. Stupid. What was I getting upset for?

Soon we had a good working rhythm established, and before I knew it, half the branches were removed. My back also knew it, and my arms and my legs. They screamed for a break. Eric, however, looked as if he could keep at it all day. I was debating whether I should admit the need for a rest when the ringing of my phone saved me. Hoping it might be François with more news about the island, I ran inside only to discover the call was for Eric.

While Eric talked with his caller, I started up the wood stove to heat up some soup for lunch, then headed outside to Aunt Aggie's rocker.

"Boy, it sure feels good to sit down," he said, flopping into the wicker chair beside me.

I remained non-committal but smiled inwardly.

"That was Decontie," he continued. "He said Marie has been sighted."

I received the news with dread. "Have they arrested her?" I asked.

"Nope, this was a few days ago. Hasn't been seen since."

"Where was she?"

"Somewhere near Somerset."

"But I thought she was hiding on Whispers Island."

"What gave you that idea?"

"Tommy's actions."

He gave me a dismissive look, then told me that one of Hélène's customers, a passing hunter, mentioned to her that he'd seen an Indian woman about fifty or so hitch-hiking early one morning on the highway near Somerset. Further questioning had convinced Hélène it was Marie. Unfortunately, by the time the police arrived, the man had gone, saying he didn't want to get involved. The police, armed with an arrest warrant, were now searching the Somerset area and beyond.

"It doesn't make sense," I replied. "Marie hasn't left this area for over thirty years. Why would she leave the only place where she would expect to find help?"

"I know, but Decontie is fairly certain that the description matches Marie. Tommy has even gone to Somerset to look for her."

Unconvinced, I persisted. "Are you sure Tommy isn't going there just to keep the police from searching this area?"

"Forget it, Meg. Tommy isn't hiding Marie. Besides, I'd be against such action. If she killed Louis, she did it in self-defense. The entire band will support her. She's better off going to trial."

Still doubting, I looked into Eric's eyes and saw the open honesty I'd come to know was him. And I saw something else.

"Okay, I believe you. But her running away won't help her cause, will it?" I asked quickly, afraid to trust the hint of affection.

"She's like a scared rabbit right now," Eric answered. Then he smiled and patted the back of my hand, "Please, don't worry, Tommy will bring her back." The pat merged into a lingering caress.

I jumped up as all thought of Marie fled from my mind. "Time to get back to work," I said and slipped my work glove over my burning hand.

Eric gave me a searching look, then said, "It's okay, Meg, I understand, I'll go slow."

I didn't know what to say, so I said nothing and walked back to the pile of sawed branches. Maybe Marie wasn't the only scared rabbit.

I grabbed a branch and dragged it along the well-worn path to the woodshed, while behind me Eric's chainsaw leapt into life.

TWENTY-FOUR

After removing all the branches from the trunk, Eric and I tackled the broken ones scattered along the fall line of the giant tree. By this time, my back was complaining in earnest over the constant bending and pulling. I decided it was time for lunch, and no sooner did I have the words out than Eric, rubbing his own back, had his saw turned off and was lying on the ground. I wasn't such a wimp after all.

"Meg, you missed one hell of a day yesterday," Eric mused a little later as he sipped a steaming hot mug of soup.

We sat with our backs against a sun-warmed timber wall, out of the wind that the storm's demise had ushered in.

Drawing an obvious conclusion, I asked, "What's CanacGold up to now?" I cupped my hands around my mug to keep them warm.

"Get a pair of binoculars and have a look at the northern tip of Whispers Island," Eric replied grimly.

With the naked eye, I could only see a line of dots, but with the aid of the binoculars, a military camp sprang into view. Except in this case it was a mining camp with a large red and gold flag flapping from a pole and a row of neatly staked white tents, which covered a strip of land where yesterday trees had stood.

"How did they get there?" I shot back in dismay. "I thought we'd blocked CanacGold's access to the island."

"That's all they managed to get onto the island," he replied. "And then we stopped them." Two dimples erupted as he began telling the story.

"I was checking out one of the fishing sites early yesterday morning, when this plane landed so close to me it almost capsized my boat. Once I saw the name CanacGold, I knew something was up, so I followed it to Whispers Island. While I waited to see what was going on, another one landed and taxied up beside the first.

"Soon they had a couple of Zodiacs running back and forth to the island carrying what looked to be equipment and supplies. By the time I was heading back to the camp to see how I could stop them, another plane landed. Looks like your ex didn't waste any time in coming up with another solution, eh?"

"Yeah, well…what can I say. But since I don't see any planes today, it looks as if you did succeed in stopping them."

"That we did, but not the way you think." Eric chuckled in that deep-throated manner I was beginning to realize was his way of facing life's challenges. "It was John-Joe's idea. Keep the buggers from landing. And that's when the fun began.

"Figuring what did we have to lose, John-Joe and I and several others spread out across the lake to wait for the planes' return. I wasn't quite sure how we were going to do it, but when the first plane began its descent, John-Joe put his boat directly in its path. Next, all of us were buzzing over the water in ten different directions in an attempt to scare the pilot from landing. We circled around and around, going back and forth, almost hitting each other."

Laughing, Eric flung his arms around to show the motion. I laughed with him.

"And we succeeded. The plane didn't get within a hundred feet of the water before the pilot climbed back into the sky. He tried again, and so did the other plane, but each time they chickened out. It was very exhilarating, especially for an old guy like me. I haven't had so much fun in years."

"Nothing like trying to get yourselves killed," I hazarded, thinking no one could pay me enough to be out there in a tiny boat with several tons of plane zooming towards me.

"John-Joe almost did," Eric continued. "The pontoons of one of the planes barely missed his head when the pilot changed his mind at the last minute. It was touch and go whether the guy was going to keep the plane in the air, but he succeeded. The CanacGold guys tried to chase us away in their Zodiacs. But they only made it worse. Just added more boats to the fray. After that, the planes gave up and flew away."

"Terrific! But what about today, and the next, and the next? Gareth won't give up that easily," I said.

The sound of a chainsaw drifted on the wind. I looked towards its source and saw a tree tumble close to the tents on Whispers Island. The rape had begun.

Eric turned his gaze in the same direction and nodded grimly. "Yeah, I see it. Hopefully they don't have enough supplies to keep that up for long. We're going to live on that damn lake. The moment a plane tries to land, we'll do what we did yesterday. I've got five boats on the lake right now. If I need more, I'll bring in more. See, there's one of them now."

He pointed to a large aluminum outboard emerging from behind the cliffs of Indian Point. I noticed two others in the middle of the lake, one with John-Joe's bright orange cap. But, thankfully, there was no droning speck on the horizon to gear them into action.

"And where was Charlie Cardinal while all this was happening?" I asked.

Eric shrugged his shoulders. "Haven't heard a peep from

him, but I did get a nasty call from your ex. He threatened to send in the police, if we didn't let them land their planes."

"Sounds like his approach, call in heavies to do his dirty work."

"Up to a little action, Meg? Why not join us tomorrow?"

"You've got to be kidding?"

"Why not? As dangerous as it might look, I'm convinced it's safe. This is like the Oka blockade. If CanacGold injures or even kills one of us, the company would have a bigger problem on its hands than just trying to get supplies in."

"You don't know Gareth."

"Sure I do, he's like Charlie, a bully. Call his bluff, and he runs. So what do you say?"

"Okay," I said, thinking I'd even pay to see him run again. "And speaking of Gareth, he's got something else up his sleeve." I told Eric about seeing Gareth with Senator Cannelli and the words I'd overheard in the parking lot.

"My instinct tells me these documents he mentioned are the missing registry files. And the fact they want to destroy them says they're bad news for CanacGold. I see this as further evidence Whispers Island isn't owned by the government. As for Aunt Aggie owning it, I've found nothing that points in that direction. Still, with all the secrets I'm discovering about her past you never can tell."

"Just get a move on it, Meg. I don't need to tell you we're running out of time."

I watched another tree topple. Within a week, they'd be approaching the giant pines.

"You know Eric, I'm confused about the motive for last night's break-in when the only item taken was Aunt Aggie's wedding picture."

Eric turned his grey gaze back towards me. Frowning, he said, "Are you sure?"

"Yeah. He was searching for something too, something I might keep in my personal files or tucked away in my bedroom. He even checked under the mattress."

"Any idea what it could be?"

"Not really. But I guess I'm beginning to realize that you aren't the only person who thinks Aunt Aggie owned Whispers Island."

Eric nodded. "Possibly. I'm sure I'm not the only one of my people to remember your aunt's link to the island. Leave it with me. I'll check it out."

A sudden thought came to mind. "Charlie Cardinal wouldn't happen to be one of those people, would he?"

Eric chuckled. "First person on my list."

"There's another interesting aspect to last night. Gareth was at the Fishing Camp about the time of the break-in. I wouldn't be the least surprised to discover he had something to do with it. Especially if the guy last night turns out to be Charlie Cardinal."

"Take care, Meg."

"Strange. I don't fear Gareth any more. You said it. He's a bully. He lost his power to terrorize me the moment I finally I stood up to him." And it was true. The feeling of tightness had gone.

*   *   *

We finished dismantling the tree by mid-afternoon. The trunk, far too heavy to move, I left for the local mill owner to cut up and take away. After helping me remove the broken glass and board up the kitchen window, Eric left, promising to return later to cook me a sumptuous dinner with one of the lake trout he was keeping for just such an occasion. I wasn't sure what he meant by this latter statement but decided I'd leave tonight in the hands of the gods.

Despite my sore back, I couldn't leave my vandalized cottage in its current state of confusion. I started with my bedroom. Not having Marie to goad me into folding my clothes neatly, I just jammed them back into the drawers. I'd worry about tidiness later. After replacing the mattress, I arranged the bedding as neatly as I could, even going so far as to fluff up the duvet and the pillows. I didn't want to give a bad impression.

I then moved into the living room, which had suffered the worst damage. I wasn't sure what to do about the sofa cushions. The size of the slashes suggested total replacement. I stacked them in the corner along with the damaged chair. I gathered up the scattered documents and shoved them back in the desk drawers.

As I cleaned, swept and put things back in their place, the outrage I'd felt last night returned. Outrage that someone had dared to break into my home, invade my privacy and scare me away. I cursed even louder when I saw the damage that he'd done to one of Aunt Aggie's treasured antique end tables. The splintered mahogany fretwork and the cracked top suggested the intruder had just kicked it aside in his haste to leave.

While I was sweeping under one of the wing-backed chairs by the fireplace, I discovered a square of folded paper wedged underneath one of the curved wooden legs. Bending down to pick it up, I realized it might be the object I'd seen fall from behind Aunt Aggie's wedding picture, the night it had shattered on the hearth.

I carefully unfolded the thin sheet of brittle paper and spread it out on the coffee table. It contained a letter written in thick ink now faded to a soft sepia. The sharpness of the creases suggested she'd re-read it many times.

At the top right-hand corner was the word Berlin and underneath 4 May, 1914. The rest of the letter filled the page.

My Dearest Agatha

Or as I prefer to call you, Liebchen, in the language of my birth. I cannot bear to have you leave me. Please, I desire you to be my wife. I was very wrong to insist you accept what is common practice in my country. I beg again for your forgiveness and ask only that you forget what is a distant past. We could have such a wonderful future together. Please, I will go wherever you wish, even to your wonderful wild country.

Please forgive me. I want only to be with you.

dein Johann

Embossed at the bottom of the page was a family crest with the name, Baron von Wichtenstein, written in a fancy German script.

I almost yelled out "Eureka". I could only assume that Aunt Aggie had ended up marrying the wayward baron, for there could be no other reason for her to have kept his proposal letter tucked securely behind her wedding photo. So even if she had been left in the lurch, as Mother had said, by the man with the short English name beginning with "w", she'd obviously not suffered for long. It also supported Eric's suggestion that the angry scar on the groom's face might have been the result of a sabre duel.

Still, I was no further ahead in discovering what had happened to Baron von Wichtenstein or why Aunt Aggie had kept her marriage to him a secret to the end.

At which point my musing was interrupted by Eric's arrival, to the accompaniment of Sergei's ecstatic yelps. Soon the kitchen was a swirl of enticing aromas, sizzling sounds and our laughing faces. And before I knew it, the evening was over and Eric gone, but not without a lot of misgivings on my part. True to his word, Eric hadn't attempted to move faster than I was prepared to go. And I knew I wasn't ready yet.

TWENTY-FIVE

The next day, with some trepidation, I ventured onto the lake in Aunt Aggie's old wooden motor boat with an ancient fishing rod lying along the length of the boat's bottom and a Styrofoam container of worms tucked under the stern seat. By the time the sun rose above the Lookout, Eric, John-Joe and three others from the Fishing Camp had joined me. We'd been patrolling for a couple of hours when the planes arrived, glimmering silver with the words CanacGold emblazoned in gold. The six of us were crisscrossing the only area of the lake large enough to handle their landing. Each of us had a section to patrol. Mine was the far one, which was supposed to be the least dangerous.

So far the planes had made five attempts to land, each time more daring than the last. The pilots were losing patience, becoming angrier and more willing to call our bluff.

Our constant circling was working. The water was well-stirred, the wind adding to the height of the chop. "Planes prefer to land in calm, flat water," I was told. "Make it good and soupy!" We tried to time it so that there was no clear landing path.

"Ready! Here they come again!" Eric shouted from his boat, his voice a hoarse croak above the noise of the wind and racing engines.

I looked up to see the silver flash of a plane swoop over the distant hill towards us. The boats closest to the plane leapt into action, churning up the water in its path. But the pilot continued his descent and zoomed over their heads towards Eric and me. I revved up the engine and swerved my boat across the path of the landing plane.

"No, Meg! Not that way! Keep to the right, to the ri…ight!" Eric shouted.

I pushed the tiller hard over, but the boat wouldn't respond. Something was wrong. Frantic, I leaned over the stern to see what was preventing it from turning. The motor coughed, sputtered and died. In desperation, I yanked the engine cord. No response.

"Oh my God, he's almost down…get out of the way!!"

I looked behind and saw nothing but my damn hair. I shoved it aside. Shit! He was flying straight towards me. The pontoons edged closer to the water. Splash! They touched down! The whirling propellers raced towards me…

I yanked the engine cord again. "Come on, you stupid boat, start!"

I turned back towards the plane. The pilot glared at me, eyeball to eyeball. I stopped breathing. I was about to dive into the water, when with a roar he swerved back into the air. I felt the rush of his passing what seemed inches above my head. Icy drops sprinkled over my face, my clothes and trickled down my neck. Slowly, I released the air from my lungs and gulped deeply. That was way too close! John-Joe may like the thrill of a near miss, but I sure didn't. I pulled the cord again, and this time the engine started.

I zoomed over to Eric and yelled, "Damn you, I thought you said it was safe!"

He, looking equally angry, yelled back, "Why in the hell didn't you—" and was cut off by John-Joe's shout.

"We did it! The bastards are going!" John-Joe cried and

194

threw his orange cap into the air. It promptly fell into the water. John-Joe scrambled to the side of his boat almost capsizing it, but managed to pull his dripping cap out. He stuck the soggy mess back on his head.

I watched the two fading specks head north over the brow of the distant hills. Out of sight their drone continued, roared louder and suddenly stopped, putting an immediate end to our victory celebration. They'd not flown away in surrender, but had landed on a neighbouring lake to regroup.

Glad for the respite, no matter how brief, each of us relaxed, slowed our engines to a crawl and continued a more leisurely patrol. Unfortunately, the reprieve was soon over.

"Hey, guys! Look! Isn't that a police car?" shouted John-Joe, pointing to the distant dock of the Fishing Camp, where red and blue lights flickered like electrical sparks from the end of Forgotten Bay.

"Whadda we do now?" someone else yelled.

"Nothing!" shouted back Eric. "We have every right to be on this lake. So get out your rods and fish!"

I pulled up the rod from the bottom of the boat that was filled with several inches of water. Even though my feet were soaked, the bottom of my jeans dripped, and my heart still pounded from my near miss, I found it exhilarating. Eric was right. I hadn't had this much fun in years. I pulled out the container of worms. Unfortunately, fishing had never been one of my loves. Particularly the part where you pulled this writhing glob of goo out of the container and held it while attempting to pierce and then thread it onto the hook two or three times until the bait was securely attached.

But, in the interests of stopping CanacGold, I persevered, jammed the yucky thing onto my hook and cast the line over the side of the boat. Then, deciding to take advantage of the interlude, I grabbed the bucket and started bailing. A glance at the others revealed they were doing likewise.

When the policeman finally reached us, he was met by a sedate group of fisherman slowly trolling the water, intent on catching the big one. Eric had even managed to catch a large silvery bass.

The officer, his back towards us, sat squeezed into the narrow bow seat of a large green motor boat. His brown uniform was liberally sprinkled with dark wet blotches. At the helm sat Charlie Cardinal, encased in a dripping yellow Camp rain slicker, an Ottawa Senators cap clamped down over his brow and a smug grin on his round, glistening face.

And in the middle of the boat, his designer suede jacket splattered, his knuckles white against the dark green boat gunnels, glowered Gareth, who just happened to be afraid of water. Served him right, I laughed to myself.

"Bonjour, messieurs-dames!" shouted the policeman, who turned out to be Sgt. LaFramboise, his nose as arrogantly pointed as the day I'd met him in Eric's office. Today it appeared he'd forgotten his English.

And a good day to you too, I thought. I felt something tug at my line. I jerked it up, but it fell slack.

"Une journée formidable pour la pêche, n'est-ce pas?"

Yes, this clear sun-filled windy morning was perfect for fishing. Couldn't he see the big one Eric was holding up?

"Vos permis, s'il vous plaît."

Uh-oh. I never thought I'd need a fishing licence. I didn't have one, and it was a three hundred dollar fine.

Charlie, his bulging stomach propped against the side of the boat, steered the officer from one boat to the next, as each of the "fishermen" showed him their permit. Balancing a clipboard on his knees, Gareth took down the names.

"Et vous, madame. Est-ce que je peux voir votre permis, s'il vous plaît?"

He'd finally reached me. I feigned ignorance. "What is he saying, Eric?" I mumbled, stalling for time.

"Sorry, I can't hear you, Meg. Speak louder," Eric replied, as his dimples created tiny puckers on either cheek. Gareth gave him a scathing look.

I tried again "What does he—"

At that moment, the loud roar of plane engines burst over the trees. From the shore of Whispers Island, a fleet of Zodiacs sped towards us.

"Ah excusez-moi, messieurs-dames. Il faut que nous reculions pour permettre aux avions d'atterrir." Sgt. LaFramboise motioned us to move towards shore, away from where the planes would be landing. Charlie sat in the stern, beaming, while Gareth lips creased into a smug smile. In his hand, he held what looked to be a radio transmitter.

The Zodiacs arrived. Cutting their engines to a crawl, they drifted to either side of Charlie's green boat. Then the boats, like a set of grasping pincers, advanced toward us and slowly began to push us to the shore. We were caught like a school of helpless fish.

I glanced at Eric, who shook his head. "We don't have a choice, guys. We'd better move out of the way," he said reluctantly.

"Too bad, guys," Gareth shouted. "Better luck next time."

I ignored him and so did Eric. But Charlie responded with a loud guffaw.

Gradually, we were herded closer to shore, while overhead the two planes slowly circled.

We had almost reached the shore when Gareth lifted the radio and spoke several sharp words into it, after which one of the planes started its descent. Suddenly, John-Joe burst from the pack and roared back into the middle of the lake. Close on his stern, another boat followed, its powerful Mercedes engine throwing a stream of water into the air. The Zodiacs leapt after them. In their wake lumbered Charlie and the police officer, with Gareth clinging to the sides of the boat. The plane arched upwards and back into the air.

"I order you to halt!" shouted Sgt. LaFramboise through a megaphone. Now the English came out.

Shouting "Stay out of this, Meg!", Eric turned his boat and raced after the others, his black mane flying like a flag of defiance.

The lake became a swirling churning mass of boats and spray. It was like a pack of sharks fighting over prey. Above the roar, I heard intermittent shouts of *"Halte-là!", "Attention!", "Arrêtez, arrêtez!"*

Without warning, a loud thud rent the air. In the middle of the chaos, a green hull reared skyward, hung there for one long heart stopping moment, then crashed back to the lake, its contents tumbling into the cold, frothy water. All movement stopped.

A single silver hull sped to the spot where the officer, Charlie and Gareth had fallen in. Next, Eric was hauling the three bedraggled shapes, one after the other, over the side of his boat.

By the time I reached Eric's boat, Charlie and the policeman had managed to shake off much of the excess water. With his brown uniform looking as if it had been through a wringer washer, Sgt. LaFramboise gesticulated and shouted at Eric. Charlie, looking massive in a clinging purple T-shirt, continued shaking his yellow jacket over the side. Gareth, in ruined suede, just sat there glaring, as water dribbled down his face. He made no attempt to wring himself dry.

The drowned rat look suits you, I thought to myself.

Charlie's boat was floating hull up a short distance away. Next to it drifted John-Joe's aluminum boat with the bow staved in. He sat in the stern bailing, while a couple of the others tried to right Charlie's boat. But they soon gave up and tied a thick yellow towrope through the bow ring.

And all the while, the fleet of Zodiacs slowly circled us. They made no move to help out. Now that they had us trapped, they wanted to ensure none of us broke loose. But they needn't have worried. With John-Joe out of action and Eric trying to placate LaFramboise, none of us had the heart to resume the action.

With tails between our legs, we returned in single file, at funereal speed, to the now crowded dock of the Fishing Camp.

My heart thudded as the planes landed. One after the other, they skidded across the puckered surface of the lake as the Zodiacs turned back to meet them.

What would we do now?

TWENTY-SIX

With a warning that it would be jail if we tried to prevent the planes from landing again, Sgt. LaFramboise told all of us to leave the Fishing Camp and go home, except for John-Joe. Insisting that John-Joe had rammed Charlie's boat intentionally, LaFramboise threatened to charge him with assaulting a policeman. When Eric tried to intervene, the SQ officer threatened to charge him too. Some of the surrounding angry crowd started to move in, which ignited an angrier response from the CanacGold men standing next to a soaking Charlie and Gareth.

However, before things could go too far, Eric stopped them.

"Relax, everyone," he said. "We don't want to make matters worse. I suggest you all leave, while I work things out with Sgt. LaFramboise."

For a moment the crowd hesitated, then in ones and twos they backed off. Some hopped into their cars; others retreated to the Fishing Camp bar. Deciding to wait for Eric, I joined the throng headed for the bar.

The pine-panelled room quickly filled with angry and frustrated voices. Two of Charlie's supporters were dumb enough to follow and were resoundingly booed away.

As I waited in line at the bar, I found myself staring into the dead eyes of a large muskie mounted on the wall. Scanning the rest of the mounted trophy fish, I wondered whether this collection would grow any larger if CanacGold did succeed in developing the mine.

With beer in hand, I searched around for a familiar face and surprisingly spied Hélène's strong-jawed face above a group of heads at the far end of the bar. Intending to kid her about having the nerve to leave the General Store in some else's hands, I made my way towards her. However, by the time I pushed through the crowd, she'd vanished. A quick question revealed she'd just upped and left without even saying goodbye.

Deciding I wasn't really up to making small talk, I escaped outside with my beer to a picnic table near the dock. Eric and Sgt. LaFramboise sat talking in the front seat of the nearby police cruiser. John-Joe's orange cap glowed through its back window. I smiled at the thought of LaFramboise sitting clammy and sodden while the two people he was trying to arrest sat comfortably dry.

I looked for Gareth and found him beside his Porsche, gloating with Charlie. While Gareth had somehow managed to change into a dry set of Eddy Bauer chic, Charlie still dripped. The eagle feather hanging from his braid appeared to be the only item that had dried. Several of Charlie's supporters were bailing out the green boat, while the guy with the eagle-shaved head was attempting to start the motor.

Overhead, a plane droned. I watched it land on the lake just off the shore from Three Deer Point. It taxied in the direction of Whispers Island, but it was lost from view when it disappeared behind the head of land that marks the beginning of Forgotten Bay. The far hills echoed with clamouring engines that sputtered and died, only to be replaced by the buzzing whine of boat motors.

Radio static made me look around to see Gareth walking towards the dock with his transmitter in hand. Charlie Cardinal squelched behind him. Gareth glanced in my direction, then as if making a decision, he headed towards me. I tensed and waited.

"You thought your little lobbying scheme with Carrie was going to work wonders," he hissed into my face. "Well, I've got news for you. The Premier is about to announce a change in the Environment Ministry. Your man's out, ours is in."

Damn, he'd found out. "Don't count your chickens yet," I spat in return. Then, wondering if I could make him run, I said, "Your mineral rights deal is about to collapse."

His body recoiled as if I'd hit a bull's eye. "So you did find—" he blurted out, then stopped and glared at me. "Your claim can't touch us," he sneered. "Our leasing rights are solid." And turned on his heels back towards Charlie's boat.

Gotcha, I said to myself. I was right. Gareth was behind the break-in. But the irony was he thought I'd already found whatever he'd sent his henchman after. However, judging by his dismissive tone, it couldn't be the deed to Whispers Island, otherwise he'd be sweating. Still, I'd better have it in my possession before Gareth discovered I was only bluffing and sent Charlie back in.

Deciding I'd better return home to continue my search through Aunt Aggie's papers, I started for my boat. As I reached it, I heard Eric call out, "Gareth, go to your planes if you want, but your car's parked on private property. If it's not gone in five minutes, I'll have it towed away."

Atta boy, Eric, I said to myself, sock it to him.

I turned back to see Gareth waver, half in half out of Charlie's boat. I knew Eric's challenge was awfully tempting to him, but my bet was on the car. He took too much pride in it.

He wouldn't want to see it damaged. Charlie tried to claim that Gareth was his guest, but Eric refused to accept it. With a few quick words to Charlie, Gareth stalked over to his car and with an "up yours" gesture, he drove off.

Meanwhile, Charlie and a couple of his groupies clambered back into his boat and roared out of the bay towards Whispers Island, but not before I noticed a chainsaw blade sticking above the side of the boat.

I walked over to where Eric stood, looking tired. Beside him slouched a very subdued John-Joe, who seemed more intent on ensuring the brim of his baseball cap was bent into proper shape than on being contrite. There was no sign of the sergeant or his cruiser.

"What did you do? Promise LaFramboise a free fishing trip?" I asked, surprised the SQ officer had relented.

"I wish it had been that easy," he replied. "While he refused to concede that the ramming was accidental, he did at least agree to our own police handling the investigation. Meanwhile, I'm to act as surety for John-Joe. So I guess it's single rations and cold showers for you, eh guy?" Eric pulled the brim of John-Joe's cap completely over his eyes.

Pushing the cap back, John-Joe smiled weakly, shrugged his shoulders, then with a quick "Thanks, Eric," walked towards the entrance to the bar, where he was greeted with slaps and loud guffaws.

"You okay, Meg?" Eric asked, turning a concerned glance towards me. "I shouldn't have involved you."

"I wouldn't have missed it for the world. Except it now appears we probably didn't have to go that far." And I proceeded to tell Eric about my latest confrontation with Gareth.

While we talked, another CanacGold plane landed on the lake. It ploughed through the whitecaps towards Whispers

Island. A strong gust sent a shower of golden leaves skittering across my line of sight and brought the sound of chainsaws.

A boat suddenly appeared around the headland and raced towards us. Eric and I stopped talking and watched its approach. I felt uneasy. There was something about its haste that suggested this was not a carrier of good news, which was further reinforced by the grim look on the messenger's face as he docked the boat.

"What's up?" Eric shouted.

"We've gotta do something, Chief," the messenger cried. "They're gonna start cutting tomorrow."

"Cutting what?" Eric shouted back.

"The ancients' trees," came the answer as a shiver of dread ran down my spine.

"It's time to do something drastic, like chaining ourselves to trees," I said.

Eric nodded. "Or more effectively, tree spiking. Unfortunately, it has one major drawback. It can kill a man."

Eric explained how the blade of a chain saw would jump and possibly shatter when it encountered metal spikes hammered into the trunk of a tree. The only way to prevent injury was to discourage the loggers from cutting the trees. The best way to do this was to inform them of the danger by posting signs. It was assumed that, armed with this knowledge, the logger would rather go against company orders than risk losing a leg or an arm.

Eric finished by saying, "But I'm not ready yet to go this far. I don't want a man's death or his maiming on my conscience if he chooses to ignore our warnings."

"Nor do I, but do we have a choice? We need to stall CanacGold while I try to find documents that can stop them," I countered. "Despite appearances, Gareth isn't completely bad. I'm sure he wouldn't risk men's lives if he knew trees were spiked."

Eric smiled wanly. "I hope you're right. I'll let you know our plans once I talk to the band council."

*   *   *

As I motored home through the rising chop, a plane took off, only to be replaced by another landing. After tying up my boat, I remained on the dock and watched as the Zodiacs ferried the new load back and forth to the island. Partway up the island's backbone, the top of a tall fir tree wavered, then fell through the yellow canopy of surrounding birch. Another dozen trees, and they'd be cutting the ancients' forest.

Not feeling very optimistic, I climbed the stairs to my cottage and headed to the attic to retrieve the other wooden box. For the rest of the afternoon I sifted through its contents. At first, my hopes were raised when I read 1935 on one of the documents but were slowly dashed as each successive document proved useless. Not a word about owning Whispers Island, not even an acknowledgement of its existence, although I did see several references to the selling of a parcel of land along the main road.

The mishmash of documents did, however, tell me how lonely and isolated Aunt Aggie's life was. None of them contained anything the least bit personal. No treasured letter from Edith or other friend; no memento photo of Aunt Aggie or her constant companion Whispering Pine, let alone one of a visitor. Rather, they represented a lifetime of caring for Three Deer Point; bills for supplies, taxes and the like, correspondence to lawyers, and a very detailed account of her maple sugar operation.

And they revealed her generosity. There was a letter from a grateful neighbour thanking Aunt Aggie for the loan of a fairly significant amount of money and the promise to repay it as soon as times were better. And an itemized list of other loans she'd made.

Occasionally, the roar of engines would send me to the window, and I watched with increasing dread as another plane took off while one landed. And as the afternoon progressed, the yawning gap in the island's profile grew larger.

The last plane was flying into the orange ball of the setting sun when Eric called.

"Any luck?" he asked.

"No," was my frustrated reply.

"Chin up, it was an outside chance you'd find proof this quickly. We've decided to begin the spiking tonight. Come to the Fishing Camp dock at midnight. Wear dark clothing and bring your canoe and a hatchet or large hammer."

I hung up feeling hopeful this would buy us some time, but also anxious over where it could lead.

TWENTY-SEVEN

The murmuring chants of a smudging ceremony came to greet me as I silently paddled through the black water of Forgotten Bay towards a growing circle of light. The breeze carried the faint scent of burning sweetgrass.

As I tied my canoe to the Fishing Camp dock, a voice whispered from the shadows, "Here, Meg. Put this on." John-Joe passed me a container of a dark, greasy substance. "To blacken your face. We're calling this our Oka war paint."

I then noticed the others, ghost shadows against the lake's shimmer, their black faces invisible in the veiled light of a waning moon, their eyes lit by the low flame of the burning sweetgrass. About twenty were sitting in a circle around a chanting elder, whom I recognized to be Eric under his camouflage.

Eric motioned me to where he sat in its centre with a container of burning sweetgrass. With his eagle feather, he washed the smoke over me, while I rinsed myself with its pungent odour, the way he'd taught me. He then gestured for me to join the ceremonial circle by entering it in the clockwise direction, he, as its elder, had set. We sat in silence while Eric chanted. With the container in hand, he slowly walked around the circle, stopping to cleanse each of us in turn.

"This will give you strength," he said, as the smoke gently flowed around me.

When he was finished, he sat for several minutes in quiet contemplation, then he reached over to a pile of long iron spikes and began passing them out. Afterwards, he told us the plan.

Each canoe was to work as an independent unit spiking every fourth tree in a designated part of the ancients' forest. The idea was to spread the spiking throughout the old growth stand, making it impossible for CanacGold to clear-cut. He and John-Joe would post the warning signs. Although the sound of hammering would eventually alert the CanacGold men staying on the island's north end, Eric felt we'd be able to spike enough trees before they reached us on the ridge.

He finished by saying, "Remember, the word is quiet. I do not want to hear a single squeak out of you as we approach the island, not a splash or a whisper. If they hear us coming, it's game over. So be quiet. Don't even breathe!"

As we loaded ourselves very silently into the canoes, two people to a boat, John-Joe passed each of us a long slender hawk feather, intended to give us the eyesight and lightning strike of a hawk.

I stuck mine into the side of my black toque, pointing its tip skyward. I imagined myself an ancient Anishinabeg warrior about to descend upon an unsuspecting camp of squatters, which CanacGold was, as far as I was concerned.

My fellow warrior was Tommy, which surprised me, since Eric had told me he was in Somerset looking for his mother.

"Did you find her already?" I asked, crawling into the stern of my canoe. "Or was it the police?"

His eyes glared back at me like two glittering orbs from his blackened face. "What do you care? You won't believe me anyway." He clambered into the bow with such force that he almost tipped us over.

"Easy," I said. "Look, I'm sorry, it was a mistake, okay? I wanted to believe you were hiding her. Tell me, how's she doing?"

"No idea. I haven't found her yet, and I don't think the police have either. I'm only here because Eric needed me. I'm going back first thing tomorrow." He thrust his paddle deep into the water and shot us towards the other canoes.

"But how can I completely believe you, if you don't always tell the truth?" I asked. "It turns out you were at the Fishing Camp the day your mother disappeared. Why did you lie to me?"

He turned around and gave me another angry glare. "None of your damn business." And he jabbed his paddle into the water with such force that it propelled us to the head of the line.

"Shush…keep it quiet," hissed someone from behind us, which put an immediate stop to further questioning.

Twisting my paddle into a j-stroke, I turned us towards the opening of Forgotten Bay. Under the dome of the midnight sky, we followed what Eric called *ke'taksoo wowcht,* the spirits road of the stars, towards the invisible island. We slipped through the black shimmering water like a ghost armada, propelled by a chorus line of silent paddles.

Tommy and I followed the knife-edged trail of Eric's canoe, which, like the rest of the flotilla, merged with the wavering shadows of the shifting ripples. We were all but invisible to each other and hopefully to any watchers. The only indication of our presence was the sound of the bow waves slapping against the moving hulls.

The wind had died, leaving a breathless air, heavy with the pungent smell of northern woods and nervous sweat. It was a night when even the merest brush of a paddle on the gunnel would be heard on the distant shore. From behind us came the quiet plop of a jumping fish while the haunting call of a barred owl drifted from another shore.

Before long, the solid mass of Whispers Island loomed into sight. All was still as we stole past the shrouded shore. The only sign of life was the limp flutter of the CanacGold flag under the harsh brilliance of a floodlight. I trusted Charlie and his men were back in the village and the CanacGold men sound asleep in their tents.

Further along, John-Joe turned inshore, where he and his partner were to wait for sounds of our activity before beginning the task of placing the warning signs. I could hear the gentle roll of gravel as they pulled the canoe up onto the land. We slid past, our destination an indentation in the rocks around the point, which thankfully was at the opposite end from the CanacGold camp.

With only a few scrapes, I managed to manoeuver the canoe through partially submerged boulders towards a flat sandy wedge. Using our paddles for support, Tommy and I stepped one after the other onto rocks. And with a final heave, we hauled the dripping hull onto the low bushes skirting the bottom of a cliff wall. Several canoes swooped in behind us.

Our target was the group of pines towering high above the ridge. The way up the cliff face looked impassable, but Tommy knew of an ancient hunter's trail that would lead us to the top, hence the need for his involvement. Like mountain goats, we crept single file upward along the narrow ledge of rocks that formed a path considerably more treacherous than the one Eric and I had used as our exit from the infamous beach. The footing was slippery and precarious, with only an occasional shrub for support. Several times, I almost slipped and was only saved by firm hands from behind.

We were almost to the top when a sudden clang shattered the stillness. We froze and waited. Dead silence, then a hoarse whisper drifted from below, "It's okay guys, only me." We waited several breathless minutes, before regaining enough confidence to resume our slow inching skyward.

Tommy was the first to reach the top. He stopped, signalled us to do likewise and waited. I strained my ears for anything out of the ordinary, an abrupt movement, an alien sound. Nothing, only the soft muttering of the pines above my laboured breathing and the chilling howl of a lone timber wolf from a distant hill. We continued our crawl upwards and over the ledge.

The terrain was a covert warrior's dream. Flat with a centuries' thick carpet of pine needles to deaden all sound and clear of crackling underbrush to warn possible watchers of our arrival. But it was dark, so dark I could barely discern a path around the massive tree trunks as I attempted to follow Tommy to our designated part of the forest. The thick canopy of pines blocked all but a few stray strands of dying moonlight, which twinkled off the metal clips on Tommy's backpack.

The muffled footfalls of a nearby group of ghost warriors mingled with the soft murmurs of the waiting forest. The sharp clink of metal against metal rang out from somewhere deeper in the forest. Someone had begun to spike a tree.

After another five minutes of walking, Tommy stopped and gestured for me to do likewise. We stood at the base of a large craggy veteran. I dropped the heavy pack, which landed with a faint clanking sound on the ground.

"Shush," hissed Tommy.

I slowly unclipped the top of the pack and carefully extracted one long, cold spike. Tommy reached for his axe.

Suddenly, the night erupted with screeching howls and piercing whistles. A dozen shapes sprang from behind nearby trunks. Night burst into day as they leapt towards us, spraying shafts of blinding brilliance.

"Run for it!' shouted Tommy as he flung the axe in their direction. It landed with a thud. For one long paralyzing minute it was as if the VCR were on pause. And then it surged forward.

I turned and raced away from the crashing forms and

searching lights. I heard the grunt of someone being tackled, followed by the thump of a body landing on the ground. I ran down the slope, towards what I hoped was the water. I was a strong swimmer. If I made it, I could escape to the distant shore.

Close behind, the panting of someone gaining. "Go left...go left!" a man shouted. It was Tommy. Further back, the quickening pace of many feet. I raced in and out of the trees towards the growing brightness of open space.

The trees were thinning, the underbrush thickening. Suddenly, they disappeared and with them the ground. A ten foot drop fell before me. I stopped, uncertain what to do.

"Jump!" shouted Tommy. I jumped and landed on a soft mound of sand. Tommy landed beside me. Springing up, I started to race towards the sound of lapping waves, but the way was blocked by a mass of roots. I looked around, searching for a gap through the tangled mess. Above my head, thundering feet were fast approaching.

"This way!" hissed Tommy, pointing to the water.

But I knew where we were. "No! this way!" I cried as I started to shove my way through the snarled roots. Overhead, the din of snapping branches and strained breathing grew louder. I stopped. The pitch-black cave entrance yawned before me. From it drifted the remembered odour, which had grown to a putrid, cloying, nostril clenching stench.

"No! Not in there!" hissed Tommy. "Our chances will be better in the water."

The running footsteps stopped. "Where did they go?" a harsh voice rang out.

"Too late, Tommy." I knocked the brittle roots aside, stooped down and plunged into the blinding darkness. Tommy stood silently for another second, then followed me in.

The smell was unbelievable. Even through clenched

nostrils, I could smell the rancid odor of decay. I wasn't sure how much further into the blinding depths I wanted to go. Outside, feet thudded on the wet sand.

"You wanted it, you might as well go all the way," whispered Tommy.

"Do you think the bear or whatever is gone?" I feebly asked.

"Bear? Sure. He'd be letting us know by now, if he weren't," was the reply, mixed with a brittle laugh.

I dropped down onto all fours and crawled into the dank darkness of the cave. At my heels, Tommy did likewise. I crawled a few more feet to ensure we were well away from the entrance and stopped. The stench was unbearable.

"God, this is awful," I whispered.

From behind me came a low singsong murmuring.

"Are you crazy, Tommy? They'll hear us," I hissed.

The chanting stopped, then continued barely above the sound of my panting.

I tried to peer through the gloom, but saw only a wall of pitch black. Outside, I heard the dull thump of someone else landing on the sand.

"Do you see or hear them?" shouted someone outside. Tommy and I inched further into the cave.

"No, I don't hear a thing," was the reply almost at the cave entrance. "They must be hidin'. I'll look around here. You check the shore."

I crawled further inside. The abominable odour crowded out all other senses. At this point, I felt more than saw the cave widen, but in the impenetrable black it was impossible to tell. I could no longer see even the faint outline of Tommy's bent form behind me. From the depths of the cave came the intermittent tapping of dripping water.

I ran my hand along the ground in front of me. The earth

felt damp and cold, but clear of any barriers. I inched deeper into the putrid tunnel. The stench permeated every pore in my body. It was as if I'd become the smell. I stopped, almost gagging. I wasn't sure if I could go any further. Tommy hissed at me to continue on.

I moved my hand forward, but instead of feeling hard firm ground, I touched something soft and pliant, like a piece of clammy rubber. Startled, I jerked my hand away, then curious to know what it was, swept my hand back over the ground directly in front of me.

Encountering only damp earth, I thought my imagination had overreacted, but then my hand brushed over something soft and fibrous that moved with my touch. Steeling myself, I followed the shifting tendrils until I felt the cold and clammy object once again. I ran my quivering fingers lightly over the surface, which felt smooth and round, like boiled sausage.

Abruptly the texture changed to a rough fabric. For a moment I stopped, then with bated breath, I moved my fingers along the fabric until I felt a strange stiffness. And then something slimy crawled onto my hand. "Yuuuk!" I screamed and reared backwards.

A bright light suddenly shone into my eyes. "Who's there!" came a harsh cry from behind the light. "Don't move!"

I looked away from the blinding dazzle, back towards the interior of the cave. On the ground a short distance from my knees lay long tendrils of black hair, bloated fingers of an outstretched hand, and a writhing jumble of blue and gleaming yellow pierced by broken sticks of white.

"Oh, my God! It's Mooti!" Tommy groaned. And I vomited.

TWENTY-EIGHT

We were a chastened group of would-be warriors who sat on the cold hard rocks of the beach, waiting for the police. Tommy remained inside the cave with his mother's body, or what was left of it.

I tried to block out the last dreadful image of my friend — and failed. Her body had probably lain there rotting since my first visit to the beach more than two weeks ago. More than enough time for the animals to feast.

It looked as if I'd failed her again. Not once, but twice, I'd noticed this stench of decay; when I'd first discovered the isolated beach and later with Eric. Both times, instead of investigating the cave, I'd turned away. If I'd only had the smarts to question the smell's source, I would have discovered Marie's body sooner and prevented this final insult. I looked to where Eric stood at the edge of the lake and wondered if he was thinking the same.

He was here along with several others from our raiding party. On hearing my horrified screams, they'd quickly joined us. The moment Eric realized what had happened, he cleared us from the cave. Her death was clearly questionable, and he was the only one with sense enough to recognize the need to preserve whatever evidence might still remain. The rest of us were too dazed to do more than meekly follow his orders.

He sent John-Joe for the police and told the rest of us to stay put. The waiting group included the men who'd ambushed us. Not surprisingly, they were Charlie Cardinal and his groupies.

It appeared Gareth had warned Charlie to be on the lookout for trespassers. But the island was large and his men few, so whether it was coincidence they were in the pine forest at the time we began spiking or whether it was because of prior knowledge, Charlie wasn't saying, nor was Eric asking. For the moment, the battle between them was on hold.

We waited in the growing dawn, each person immersed in his or her own thoughts, some trying to wipe off the black war paint, others just staring into the empty cold lake. No one was feeling particularly triumphant. An unspoken truce had settled. The reserve was a small community. All had known Marie. Everyone had liked her.

I found myself sitting next to Charlie on a large flat rock within sight of the ruined crosses of Two Face Sky and Summer Wind. At this point, I didn't care whether he was the guy in yellow. After Marie's tragic death, my scrimmages seemed trivial. We both stared across at the far shore and watched the rising sun's light creep down the night-shrouded hillside. From behind us drifted the same singsong murmurs Tommy had chanted when we'd entered the cave.

Curious, I asked, "What is Tommy chanting?"

"The traditional chant of the dead," Charlie replied, and closing his eyes, joined Tommy in the chant.

While I sat absorbing the hypnotic rhythm, I contemplated the troubling implications of what he'd just told me. However, not wishing to interrupt, I waited until Charlie stopped, to ask my question. "Don't you find it curious that Tommy began chanting before we knew his mother's body was in the cave?"

"No. This cave belongs to the ancestors," replied Charlie, pointing to the remains of the crosses. "A warrior must ask their permission to walk on sacred ground."

His answer left me feeling not only relieved but a little sheepish for even thinking that Tommy had known his mother lay dead in the cave. It also meant I didn't have to contemplate the more troublesome question of how Tommy knew.

As if voicing his inner thoughts, Charlie started talking, his face a carved statue in the spreading light. "We grow up together, Marie and me. Our fathers were sons of Mishomis, my grandfather. They trapped the line together. In winter, when they were in the bush checking the lines, Marie and her mother, Whispering Pine, moved to my mother's hearth to share food and fire.

"When Marie's dad got killed huntin', they stayed. Whispering Pine had no parents. My father said we look after them. It is our destiny, *Mí enendagozidj*. And now I fail. Marie's dead."

He walked to the edge of the lake, threw his half-smoked cigarette fizzling into the water, bent down and picked up a large round rock and flung it as well. He picked up another and threw it in, then another...

"What happened to Whispering Pine's family?" I asked.

"They died when Whispering Pine was a small baby." Charlie lowered his heavy body slowly back down onto the flat rock beside me. "They died in a fire. Mishomis saved Whispering Pine and took her to his mother's hearth. Whispering Pine lived with my grandparents until she married my uncle, the first son of Mishomis."

He got up and paced along the beach, kicking the rocks and bits of driftwood that were in the way, while the whine of several motor boats drew nearer.

He returned and sat down again. "Marie is of my clan. Like a sister. I never wanted her hurt. I only wanted what was good for her. And now this!" He flung another rock into the water.

I asked the question, which had been waiting since he first mentioned the word ancestors: "Do these crosses on the beach belong to—"

Before I could finish, he closed his eyes and started chanting again.

I let my question die in the cold morning breeze. I shivered and moved over to warm my hands at the small fire someone had started with some deadfall, which I noticed with a wry smile just happened to be from my notorious spruce. I searched for Eric to ask him my question, but he was talking with one of his men. From the cave, Tommy's soft chanting continued.

I felt numb, not fully believing Marie was dead, that those lifeless bones had once been my living, breathing friend. I shivered again, but not from the cold. I was certain there was only one cause. Someone had killed her. I glanced at the others waiting on the desolate beach and wondered who.

A sudden loud roar of engines ended the waiting. Three boats rounded the point, raced towards us and beached on the cold wet sand. Several policemen, including Chief Decontie and Sgt. LaFramboise, swarmed onto the beach.

*   *   *

The sun had turned the beach into day by the time the police finished questioning everyone but Tommy, Charlie and me. Since we were the only ones who'd actually seen Marie's body, I figured we were in for some intensive questioning. As the police began ferrying the others back to their canoes, Sgt. LaFramboise started his interrogation of Charlie beyond hearing range at the other end of the beach.

I remained seated on my flat rock and watched Chief

Decontie and the other Migiskan police search the beach. A useless exercise, since we'd already trampled over most of it. From inside the cave came the strobe flashes of a camera. Another boat arrived with the coroner, or so I assumed from the official looking medical bag. Decontie led him into the cave.

And while this activity went on around him, Tommy stood on guard near the cave entrance, his face a frozen mask, his eyes closed. Next to him stood Eric, a worried look on his partially smeared face, the hawk feather drooping from his hatband.

I had a sudden feeling of being watched and looked up to see the raven perched at the top of the pine where I'd first seen him. His black, beady eyes glared back at me. He burped a low hoarse croak, ruffled his feathers as if trying to gain a more comfortable perch, then sat still. From time to time his head moved as if he were watching and listening to the scene unfolding below him.

This was the third time I'd seen him here on this beach. Eric had said his people consider the raven a spirit messenger. Maybe he had witnessed Marie's death? Too bad he couldn't talk.

When Sgt. LaFramboise finished with Charlie Cardinal, he began my interrogation. He adopted the same high-handed, arrogant manner he'd used in Eric's office. Needless to say, this did not predispose me to be helpful. I answered only the questions he asked. Maybe it was irresponsible of me not to tell him about the two sets of footprints I'd seen on the beach and my suspicions. But I wanted to confirm how Marie had died before raising awkward questions. And for the moment, LaFramboise either didn't know or wasn't saying what had caused her death.

The questioning was just finishing when one of the SQ policeman emerged from the cave carrying a fluorescent orange object in one hand and a rifle in the other. He held up the rifle. *"C'est à quelqu'un?* Anyone know this?"

It just looked like one of the many beat-up guns I'd seen in the hands of local hunters, but Tommy stiffened at its sight, so did Eric.

Next, the policeman held up a hunter's orange cap, crushed and filthy, with the earflaps turned up and a band of green and blue beading.

"Goddamn it!" shouted Tommy and plunged into the lake. Without hesitation, Eric dove after him. Within two brisk strokes, he reached the flailing form and grabbed Tommy's collar. Arms flinging, water flying, Tommy tried to fight him off. Chief Decontie waded in to help. Together they pulled a sodden but subdued Tommy to shore.

"A qui appartient ce casque, cette carabine? You tell me!" ordered LaFramboise thrusting the crumpled cap into Tommy's dripping face, as Decontie held his arms behind his back. *"C'est à vous?* Belongs to you, eh?"

"No!" shouted Tommy through clenched teeth. He looked at Eric, who nodded imperceptibly. "It's Papa's." He finished, his eyes downcast, his mouth tight in grim resignation.

"Yes, that's Louis's gun. I'd know his *p'tit gars* anywhere," confirmed Charlie.

"Eh bien, for sure, this gun kill Louis Vert," LaFramboise announced.

TWENTY-NINE

I'd no sooner arrived home than clouds blackened the sky, and the rain came down. For the next four days, it poured almost as if Marie's *kije manido* were mourning her senseless death, until the day of her burial, when the sun finally shoved the low clouds away.

And through these cold, wet days, I waited in dread of the phone call that would confirm what the cave's evidence so clearly pointed towards, Marie had shot Louis and then herself. But it was too easy a verdict, one I didn't want to accept. I even tried to steer Sgt. LaFramboise away from the obvious by finally telling him my suspicions about the two sets of footprints on the beach the morning after Marie died and Tommy's use of a boat that same morning.

Early that morning, the phone call finally came, from Eric. Murder-suicide. Louis's *p'tit gars* the weapon. Case closed. It looked as if LaFramboise had paid as much attention to my evidence as he would to a mosquito. Even Eric felt the verdict was fair. Maybe it was. I wasn't sure. But I was an outsider. My evidence could tear the band apart, so I hadn't told Eric what I suspected.

Instead, I retreated as I usually did to Aunt Aggie's rocker on the verandah with a tumbler of vodka clutched in my hand. I tried to wash away my uncertainties with the usual tonic of rhythmic rocking, the hypnotic view of Echo Lake, and of course the mind-numbing vodka.

Except after a few sips, I put the glass down. Eric was right. I didn't need this stuff. In fact, I hadn't felt the need to drown myself in it since my confrontation with Gareth. It looked as if fear of him had been the motivation behind my drinking. Once that fear was gone, I no longer needed the crutch.

I continued rocking and thinking about Marie. Reluctantly, I came to accept that murder-suicide was the only plausible verdict. After years of abuse from Louis, she had finally snapped. When she realized she'd killed him, she had fled to the island, where, in a state of remorse, she'd killed herself. The footprints were purely coincidental, made by other people who just happened to be visiting the beach around the same time. As for Tommy and the boat, there was obviously another explanation. I would ask him at the first opportunity.

And this was how I felt as I drove to Marie's healing ceremony in the early afternoon. Originally, I'd decided not to go. It was a traditional Algonquin ceremony intended to ease the pain of the death of one of their own. As an outsider, I felt it wasn't my place to attend. Besides, I didn't want to create any discord should Tommy or other band members object to my presence. Instead, I would only attend her funeral service, which was to follow afterwards in the Migiskan Church.

But a quick call from Eric wanting me to explain my absence convinced me otherwise. He said I was no less affected by Marie's death. I too could benefit from the healing process. And if anyone objected to my presence, he'd deal with them. Swayed but still fearful of causing a disturbance, I agonized a few more minutes before deciding. By the time I arrived at the low cedar strip building of the Ceremonial Hall, the ceremony had started.

I almost turned back at the sound of chanting. But deciding that Marie was more important than my discomfort,

I entered the already crowded room. The chanting stopped. Every face turned towards me. Embarrassed, I stopped. And then the elder sitting at the circle's entrance, an older woman I didn't know, turned towards me and smiled.

Although I didn't understand her Algonquin words, the meaning was clear: "Please, enter the circle." She indicated its clockwise direction. Thankfully I knew enough to honour the circle, otherwise I would not only have embarrassed myself further by walking in the wrong direction, but would also have angered the spirits.

I searched for a place to sit, but Marie's friends had already filled in the circle. Those not early enough to get a seat on the surrounding cedar benches sat cross-legged on the floor a respectable distance from the centre. Eric smiled from the far end and pointed to a few spots on the floor where I might squeeze in. However, before I reached these, John-Joe, acknowledging my presence with a sombre nod, vacated his seat on a bench and took one of the free spots on the floor. I gratefully accepted his offer.

I smiled hi to the few people I knew, Marie's friend Dorothy, dressed soberly in black, my coffee drinking buddy Frosty in a clean shirt. Not far from Dorothy sat Charlie Cardinal, beside a fat downtrodden looking woman, probably his wife. I even nodded at him, figuring he wasn't totally bad, given his special bond with Marie.

Tommy sat cross-legged near Eric. He didn't so much as glance in my direction, let alone acknowledge my presence. From the closed-in look on his face, I didn't think he was paying too much attention to anyone.

Kneeling before a small pottery bowl of burning smudge, the elder resumed her quiet chanting. She placed bits of dried sweetgrass and cedar into the bowl and fanned it with her brown-speckled eagle feather. Her clothes were simple, a plain cotton skirt and a black turtleneck sweater covered by a fringed deerskin vest. Over her grey-streaked hair she wore a band of pink and blue beads. But it was the expression on her heavily lined face I found the most remarkable, a look of serenity that bespoke of someone wholly at peace.

Although I'd never been to a healing ceremony before, I recognized, from the smudging ceremonies I'd attended, the traditional elder's medicine bundle lying in the centre of the circle. Its sacred objects were scattered over a well-used piece of deerskin with its four corners marked in turn by a traditional yellow, black, white or red flag. Though these four colours have many different meanings, the one I preferred equated them to the races of mankind, and because the circle provided equality, no one race was placed higher than the other on the circle.

This elder's sacred objects were an odd assortment of natural and man-made; a fine piece of jade next to a small crystal vase, black mussel shells sprinkled over what looked to be a shocking pink velvet shawl. While none were what I'd call medicinal, all would have sacred meaning to this elder. Perhaps a special person had given her the vase, or she'd found the shells on sacred ground. Even the unusual pink colour must have significance, for in addition to the shawl and her headband, there was a dyed pink ostrich feather and choker of pink beads.

With the smoking smudge pot in her hand, the elder walked slowly around the circle, stopping at participants to allow them to cleanse themselves with its sweet smelling smoke. The first time I'd attended a ceremony, I'd felt a bit ridiculous performing the motions of the ritual washing. Now, with a few more ceremonies under my belt, I found myself wafting the smoke over my body twice to ensure I was cleansed enough to open the path to Marie's spirit.

I'd expected the mood of the ceremony to be sombre and sad. Instead, people smiled and talked quietly amongst themselves as the elder moved from participant to participant. I found myself liking this relaxed, friendly mood, a sharp contrast to the religious restraint I was used to.

When the elder had finished, she returned to her seat at the circle's entrance and began chanting in Algonquin. Then she switched to English, the one language she could be assured of all band members understanding. She talked of Marie and the sadness of her untimely death. She didn't mention how Marie had died, but I could see in others' eyes that it was foremost in their minds. Then she invited the circle to share their memories of Marie.

Charlie Cardinal was the first to take up the offer. "You people know Marie and me were like brother and sister. We grew up together at my mother's hearth. Times were hard. Food scarce, but we were happy. In summer, we lived in the bush. Marie cleaned my first deer. I killed her first fish. We followed the cry of the loon to a secret lake, where I had my vision quest. Then, one day it was all gone, forever."

He moved his glance deliberately around the circle, then directed his angry eyes at me. "Fuckin' residential school!" he spat out. "Destroyed our way of life."

A hushed silence followed. The elder admonished him quietly, saying this was a time for healing, not angry confrontation.

Nonetheless, I squirmed inwardly as every pair of eyes turned to me. While I was no stranger to the damage inflicted by the Church-run residential schools on the Indian nations, I felt now was not the moment to do anything other than murmur some kind of apology and keep my eyes downcast.

I also knew what the school had done to Marie. She had told

me one day last summer. So as Charlie continued with his memories of Marie, I remembered my own conversation with her.

"I was just a little thing, not eight years old, when they told me I gotta leave my Mooti," Marie had said in her quiet matter-of-fact tone, with no hint of accusation. "I cried many days. The sisters yell at me to stop, forget my people. They say our ways no good. I gotta do things the way they do things. But it was very hard. They hit me many times. I run away. They find me and bring me back. Hit me again. I run away. Again they find me and hit me. Again I run away. But this time I hide. They don't find me.

"I go to the big city. I live on street, no money, no trees, no song of laughing bird. It was very hard. I wanna go home, back to my Mooti, but didn't know how. Finally, Dorothy's mother find me and bring me home. I never leave my people again."

By the end of her story, I was feeling no little amount of shame and wondering how I could make up for my own people's misguided ethnocentrism.

Marie did it for me by simply saying, "For long time I angry with the sisters and the white man. I also want my Mooti to stop working for Miz Agatta. But Miz Agatta change me. She teach me not every white man bad. She show me the good in the white man's ways can work with the good in my people's ways. So now I just feel sorry for the sisters. Their eyes were blinded."

As I remembered Marie's words, I realized the depth of inner strength they revealed, an inner strength that probably helped her to face other hurdles in her life, like Louis.

An elderly woman in a purple dream scarf took over from Charlie. She began by saying, "Marie so young, so pretty when she come home. But she was cursed." And that set the tone for her continuation of Marie's story.

After Marie's return from the streets of Montreal, she had

226

moved in with her mother into the small cabin, which Whispering Pine shared with Charlie's family. But there were too many people and too few rooms. Fights were frequent.

"And some mens were bad." The woman turned to Charlie, who offhandedly shrugged his shoulders.

So Marie had moved in with Dorothy's family. For a time, everything went well. She found work, was able to bring a bit of money into the household. And then tragedy struck. Someone left some socks to dry on the wood stove overnight. They caught fire and ignited nearby curtains. Within minutes the house was gone. Marie was forced to move back with her mother and the Cardinal family.

"Terrible time she had," said the woman, sadly shaking her head. "I told her come live with me all alone in my small cabin, but she say she can't. Poor girl."

A deer skin covered arm slapped Charlie on the back, while another face snickered.

The elder, shaking her head, glanced in their direction. The smiles disappeared from the men's faces. Their gaze dropped to the floor.

Eric continued, "Snake Woman's right. What happened was wrong. Still is. I was only a boy at the time, ten or eleven, but I haven't forgotten the snickering. 'Marie had better keep her legs clamped shut,' many whispered. 'Old Man Cardinal is trying his damnedest to pry them open.' We thought it funny, not caring how it hurt Marie. We forgot that in Marie's eyes, Charlie's father was her father too."

The smirk on Charlie's face changed to stone. "So my old man wouldn't leave her alone, but I never touched her, never. What about you? Don't say you never wanted a go at her."

I could almost see the blushing under Eric's tan. "Okay, I admit, as a boy I had a crush on her too," he said. "She was one gorgeous chick. In fact, my friends and I used to follow her through the village. But it was innocent fun. She'd laugh and throw stones to chase us away, and then she'd signal us to come join her, play tag, go fishing. But in the end, you know what happened."

He paused to look at the now still faces around the circle, then he continued, "She ran to Louis because we wouldn't leave her alone."

No one smirked. Several nodded sadly.

"Remember how he arrived twenty-five years ago? Right after *kije nòdin*, the great wind, which destroyed half the village," Eric said. "I can still feel the terror of that shrieking wind which uprooted trees and sent our homes flying into the air. We were cleaning up the mess when Louis arrived one day from the south.

"Remember his shiny new red Chev? The kind of car few of us had ever seen, much less owned. He said he'd help us, make us rich. We believed him. In fact, we made him our administrator. How naïvely stupid we were. We gave him the keys to the kitty and never once thought it might be at risk.

"And I'm sure those of you old enough can recall the riches he promised." Eric paused.

Some grizzled heads nodded knowingly. A few turned their glances towards Charlie, who puffed his chest out and said, "Okay, so Louis said there was gold on our land. But that was different."

"Only difference this time, Charlie," replied a small, wizened man with his eagle feather attached to his headband, "us elders are a lot smarter. We learned good. So don't bring your little white rocks with gold in 'em like Louis done and ask for money to get your mine goin', 'cause we ain't givin' ya one red cent."

"I don't need your money," growled Charlie. "Whether you like it, or not, this mine's going to happen. This time there really is gold. I seen it."

"Enough," Eric said. "For now we're talking about Marie. I don't blame her for being deceived as much as the rest of us. Louis was sure one cool customer back then, before drink got to him, especially with those white man eyes. And I supposed she probably thought of him as a means of getting out of here. But it didn't happen. By the time Louis's fraud was discovered, she was pregnant and the money gone. She once told me that she moved in with Louis because she wanted her child to grow up with its real father."

All eyes turned towards Tommy, but his gaze remained fixed on the elder's medicine bundle in the centre of the circle.

"Not the best choice in husbands," Dorothy added. "All loving sweetness until she moved in with him. Then she started sporting black eyes and swollen cheeks. I ignored it at first, thinking the abuse wasn't that different from the other relationships I knew. But then it got serious. She turned up at my house, clutching her arm. It was broken in three places. Marie told me she'd fallen from a chair while cleaning windows. This time I didn't believe her. Eventually, she owned up that Louis had come home angry and drunk."

Dorothy brushed a tear from her cheek. "I tried, as I tried on several later occasions, to convince her to leave him. But she refused to listen. Said she loved him, couldn't leave him to fend for himself. Besides, she believed he didn't mean to hurt her. He loved her. It was only the drink that had taken over.

"Maybe it was, but she sure put up with more living hell than blissful love, right up until her bitter end. If only I'd been more forceful, maybe she'd still be alive today." And the tears began coursing down Dorothy's chiselled face.

A large woman with a kindly smile wrapped her arm around Dorothy, while another said, "Don't blame yourself, *widigik*. We all knew, and none of us did a thing about it."

I silently agreed as I thought of the time, only days before her death, when I had meekly let Louis drag Marie away.

Wiping the tears from her face, Dorothy said, "But despite all the years of abuse, I never thought it would end this way. I find it very hard to believe she finally turned on Louis and killed him. Why? You know she was a gentle person. Not once did I ever see her respond in anger to Louis's abuse. She just accepted it as her lot in life, as she did anything else, good or bad. In fact, Louis had calmed down in recent years, more shouting than actual physical abuse."

Dorothy ran her eyes over the cheerless faces and asked, "So why now? What did Louis do that was so terrible Marie could no longer endure it?"

A hushed silence ensued as each person pondered the implications of her question.

The elder answered for us. "Marie was a good woman. She endured much hardship with little complaint. Now she is with the spirits. They will know if she killed him for good reason. If not, she will answer to their anger."

She paused and scanned the waiting faces. "But I think, if she killed Louis, she had good reason, very good reason."

As the elder continued in Algonquin, I considered the door she'd left open with her words, "If Marie killed Louis".

I thought over the many examples I'd just heard of the uncomplaining resolve with which Marie had faced life. They helped to finally convince me that she would never have killed Louis, no matter how hard she was pressed. And because Marie was a survivor, she would never have ended her own life. So I promised myself I would find her killer, no matter how disruptive it might be to the band.

THIRTY

Marie's simple Christian burial service was in keeping with her wishes to be buried as her mother had been buried. And it was short. It seemed we'd barely sat down in the small clapboard church of the Migiskan Reserve before we were filing out again, behind her coffin. Tommy, Eric, Charlie and the other pallbearers slowly carried the plain casket of freshly honed white pine through the open doors into the late afternoon sun. In contrast to the heightened emotion of the healing ceremony, a sense of futility and dejection hung in the air. Faces closed, eyes down, we followed her body to the small weed-ravaged cemetery next to the church.

The hole was waiting, a yawning black gap in the dead autumn grass. Gold needles from nearby tamaracks rasped the smooth surface of the coffin. With a few more hushed prayers, and some quiet tears, Marie was assigned to her final resting place, beside her mother, Whispering Pine.

Directly behind, I noticed two white marble headstones, considerably larger and more elaborate than others in the small cemetery. They leaned towards each other, almost as if they sought to undo the separation brought by death. On one of the headstones, etched in black lichen, were the words "Two Face Sky 1893 to 1925". On the other, "Summer Wind 1904 to 1925".

"Her grandparents," Dorothy murmured into my ear. "They died in a fire on Whisper Island."

And so my question was finally answered. But it left me feeling discouraged. It meant Marie and I hadn't been as close as I'd believed. I thought we'd bridged the gulf dividing us. I was wrong. She didn't trust me enough to tell me that the ancestors on Whispers Island were her own. Even Dorothy was surprised I didn't know. She'd assumed Marie had told me what was general knowledge within the band.

I became even more dejected when Dorothy told me something else I should've known. Aunt Aggie was the person who'd rescued Marie's mother from the fire. Apparently my aunt, after spying the flames from Three Deer Point on that winter day long ago, had skied across to the island. She'd risked her life to snatch the tiny Whispering Pine from the burning lodge seconds before the roof collapsed, consuming her parents and baby brother. I thought of her unexplained scars and knew this fire had been their cause.

* * *

Dusk was falling by the time I returned home. Sergei was waiting at the door, tail wagging, happy to see me. His devotion was nice, but it wasn't enough. I would miss Marie's friendship. She'd been a welcome interruption in this life of solitude I'd adopted.

After feeding Sergei, I retreated to the lake, where I hoped my dragging spirits would be uplifted by the boundless evening sky. Wrapped in Aunt Aggie's ancient lynx coat, I sat at the dock's edge with Sergei curled against my side and listened to the lapping waves below. Daylight's sharp relief had melded into the flat opaque veil of twilight. The only defining point was the CanacGold light, which marked a path across the lake from their island camp to my feet.

Despite the light's hint of life, I knew it shone over a silent and empty camp, the only upside in the sad tragedy of Marie's death. Sgt. LaFramboise, for once doing something right, had stopped the mining company from further activity on the island until his investigation was completed. Unfortunately, with the case now closed, it probably meant that CanacGold would soon resume cutting the ancients' forest. Needless to say, coming up with another means of stopping CanacGold had been the furthest thing from my thoughts or Eric's.

We'd hit rock bottom in our fight with the mining company. We'd lost the battle to prevent them bringing in supplies and equipment. We'd failed in our spiking attempt to stop further logging. The day before, Carrie had confirmed what Gareth had threatened. The environmental watchdog had become a pussycat and wouldn't interfere. And I'd all but given up on Whispers Island belonging to anyone other than the crown. Aunt Aggie's records had so far revealed nothing, and it looked as if my notary's search through the municipal records was proving to be a waste of time and money.

It appeared with each passing day that the power of CanacGold was growing, while ours steadily sank. According to Carrie, even the provincial Premier had gold glittering in his eyes. Economic votes were far more important than environmental woes, particularly those expressed by a handful of Indians and backwoods hicks.

I was beginning to wonder if I shouldn't do what Gareth wanted, sell my land and leave. I was sure CanacGold would pay a king's ransom for good access to the lake. With the money, I'd buy another much larger property further north, deeper into the forest, far from any mining or logging operation or their threat. It would certainly be the easier path to take. To sit helplessly on the sidelines and watch

CanacGold destroy this northern paradise would destroy me.

My depression deepened when I realized it wasn't yet five o'clock, and already the long, empty, black nights of the coming winter had begun. But at least no clouds hid the Star Trek splendour hovering above my head; Jupiter and its moons, the Big Dipper, Orion and the star-cluttered swath of the Milky Way. And for one brilliant blink, a shooting star streaked and vanished as if it never were. Maybe it was Marie setting out on her journey.

Through the silent gloom, I heard my telephone. It rang three times, then stopped when my voice mail clicked in. I decided it was time to go inside, put a fire on and try to think more cheerful thoughts.

Sergei raced up the stairs. As he bounded over the top, the sound of retreating hoofs burst through the silence, only to be further shattered by the dog's loud barking pursuit. A deer. Another innocent being whose peace had just been destroyed.

The message on my answering message was short and to the point. "Mme. Harris, call me immediately. I have news," spoke the clipped voice of my notary.

With trembling fingers, I quickly dialled his number.

"Please, François, make my day!" I burst in when he answered.

"Slow down, Mme. Harris. *C'est la douche écossaise,* how we Québécois say, good news, bad news."

"Tell me the good, first. I need it."

"It is the information you are wanting. I have confirmed that CanacGold has no legal access to the mineral rights of Whispers Island."

"Hallelujah. You found the missing file," I said, thinking I'd been wrong in suspecting Gareth of stealing the land registry file for Whispers Island.

"Unfortunately, it is still missing. But, my clerk learns from the municipal tax rolls that the taxes are being paid every year since the property was acquired in 1920."

"Fine, but what does this have to do with ownership?"

"It is very easy. The Whisper Island property cannot belong to the crown or the Migiskan Reserve, because the government and Indian reserves do not pay taxes on their land holdings. This means the island is privately owned. In fact, there was a name listed on the tax rolls."

I held my breath. "Aunt Aggie?"

"I am sorry. The property is listed under the trusteeship of a law firm, Bingham, McLeod and Tetro. When I contacted Mr. Wilson McLeod, he can only give me the name of the owner, nothing more."

"What do you mean?"

"It is impossible to contact the owner. Mr. McLeod has no current address. He does not know if the owner is alive, since there has been no contact since 1935."

"That's over sixty-five years ago. Why would the lawyer still be paying the taxes?

"Apparently his law firm was given a significant amount of money to be invested and used for taxes and of course their legal fees."

"It must've been a very large amount of money."

"Perhaps, or the firm made good investments."

"Surely the lawyer tried to contact the owner at some point in time?"

"He tells me that his firm tried to contact the owner in 1958, but was not successful.'

"So where does this leave us?"

"At this moment, it is not necessary to contact the owner. Now that we have evidence to prove the land is privately held, we can file a stop work injunction against CanacGold without the owner's permission. However, when the owner is made aware of this gold discovery, it is possible he will sell the land to CanacGold."

"That means we've got to get to him before CanacGold. But we may already be too late," I said and reminded François of my suspicions of Gareth's possible involvement in the missing land registry file.

François replied, "*Oui,* Madame. You are right to worry. Mr. McLeod has confirmed that a lawyer recently requested the same information about the ownership of this island. Although he did not tell me his name, Mr. McLeod said this lawyer was representing a mining company. I think, madame, you know the identity of this man."

The two-faced liar, I thought. He knew all along, even when he was trying to get me to sell my land by saying he still loved me. Well, he would never make a fool of me, ever again.

"Okay, François, I'm going to stop this guy from selling his land to CanacGold. How do I find him?"

"Madame, it will not be a simple task. Much time has passed. This man is probably dead. There will be heirs. Finding them will be difficult. But, I think if it is difficult for you, it is also difficult for your former husband, *non?* I do not believe he finds this owner yet. However you must begin immediately. I suggest you begin by asking people who live in your area. I will also ask my clerk to search the municipal records."

"Okay, sounds good to me. By the way, what is the owner's name?"

"Watson, William J. Watson."

On first hearing the name, it meant nothing to me, but I'd no sooner hung up the phone than I remembered Mother's mention of Aunt Aggie's jilting lover with a short English name starting with "w".

I quickly phoned my mother. However, my hopes were immediately quashed when she admitted that although the name could be Watson, it could just as easily be White or Waters. Furthermore, she insisted that even if it was Watson, since he was supposed to have been a fortune hunter, it wasn't likely he'd had any money to buy land, particularly land in the middle of nowhere. A point I was inclined to agree with.

She promised to search through Grandpa's papers for any reference to the name of Watson. I thought of going to Toronto to do it myself but decided I couldn't afford to be away. I was in a race with Gareth to find the present owner. While Mother was looking through Grandpa's files, I could be searching around here. Besides, I wanted to be here for Gareth's next move.

THIRTY-ONE

I made some tea and plunged right into my search for the owner of Whispers Island. I tried the only three listings for "Watson" in the local phone book and came up empty. Two were recent arrivals to the area, and the third said that if he had inherited an island, he'd be living on it. However, the calls weren't a total failure. From the last guy, I learned that Gareth wasn't too far out in front. He'd only contacted this Mr. Watson three days ago.

I called all the farmers whose families had been living in the area for at least seventy years. None of them remembered mention of any Watson living in or around the Echo Lake area. Although one farmer, too young to know for sure, promised to ask his Uncle Jim, (who made it his business to know everyone's business), first thing in the morning when the old guy woke-up.

Gareth had also contacted most of them. But since he appeared to be only one step in front of me, I wasn't completely worried, not yet. I also had access to a source totally unknown to him, Aunt Aggie's old papers. What a joke on Gareth if it turned out "William J. Watson" really was Aunt Aggie's jilting lover. I returned to the turret room where I'd left her wooden boxes and started going through them again, this time looking for the specific name.

I carefully re-read all letters between young Agatha and her bosom buddy Edith, hoping to find some reference to a boy or a man with the name Bill, Will or any other variation of William. I sifted through the boring correspondence with lawyers, accountants, and stores, thinking that maybe he was someone Aunt Aggie had done business with.

At one point, my heart jumped when I saw the name Willie, but it was soon stilled when I finally found a reference to his full name, Willie Miller. In none of them did I discover the name William J. Watson.

As for mention of boyfriends of any name, the Baron Johann von Wichtenstein was the only male admirer gushed over by the two friends. I was beginning to wonder if the lover had ever existed.

Not yet willing to declare defeat, I returned to the attic to see if there were other likely hiding places for old papers and discovered several large cookie tins tied with string. I took these back down to the turret room to continue my search.

In one box, I was surprised to discover several letters from Great-grandpa Joe to his son John, my grandpa, dating from the late 1920s. Thinking there might be a good reason for my great-aunt having saved them, I read them thoroughly. However, there was nothing of importance, at least not to me, other than a few admonitions for John to watch out for his sister, and a query about when Agatha would be finally leaving the sanatorium, which supported Mother's comment on the state of Aunt Aggie's mental health.

Underneath lay some loose photographs of the Harris family at play against the backdrop of Three Deer Point. I got a kick out of seeing my grandfather being pushed into the water by a very small version of my father. Even Aunt Aggie was smiling in some of these pictures. From the style of the clothes and the Bonnie and Clyde car, these dated from the 1930s. In none of them was there an unknown gentleman who might have been William Watson.

The next item I pulled from the box finally confirmed that Baron Johann von Wichtenstein was the key man in Aunt Aggie's life. It was a photo album, whose black felt-paper pages were crammed with smiling, frolicking pictures of Agatha and the tall light-eyed stranger of the wedding picture, the man with the terrible facial scar. Like the others, these had been taken at Three Deer Point. And from the ankle length of Aunt Aggie's skirts, I guessed they were taken towards the end of the First World War.

This was an Agatha I would liked to have known: Agatha laughing on the Forgotten Bay beach with Johann, the two of them encased in the shapeless sacking that served for bathing suits at that time; Agatha giggling behind a large birthday cake covered with tiny candles, how many I couldn't count; Agatha and Johann in a canoe, shading their eyes from a hot summer sun; and the two of them sitting on a picnic table, Johann's arm around Agatha, her head on his shoulder, eyes blissfully closed.

I chuckled at a picture of Johann, the Hunter, that was almost a photocopy of the one of Great-grandpa Joe with his trophy deer. Decked out in a worsted jacket, laced knee-high boots with a porkpie on his head, a triumphant Baron stood, exactly as Great-grandpa Joe had stood, leaning on a rifle barrel in front of the verandah of Three Deer Point with an Indian guide at his side. But instead of three dead deer hanging from the verandah hooks, there were four. It made me wonder if the Baron wasn't trying to outdo his father-in-law, something which, given my great-grandfather's legendary ego, would have only put him in Great-grandpa Joe's bad books.

There was nothing of value or interest in the remaining

contents of the cookie tin, so I turned to the next one. A top layer of more useless letters, but underneath lay a promising collection of small leather-bound books. My hopes jumped when I read the word "Diary" embossed on the cover of the top book. If William J. Watson had ever been Aunt Aggie's lover, then surely she'd have written about it in her diary.

I easily unlocked its brass clasp after a few well placed prods with a nail file and with bated breath opened the stiff cover. But it was with mixed emotions that I read the words written on the inside leaf: Diary of Baroness Agatha von Wichtenstein.

Although it finally confirmed beyond a doubt the identity of Aunt Aggie's husband, I thought it unlikely my great-aunt would write about former lovers after she'd married. Still, William J. Watson might have been a friend of the Baron's. And I was very curious to know what had caused the end of their marriage. So, with the tin of diaries in hand, I retreated to the living room, threw another log on the fire and sank into the chesterfield.

It took me until the early hours of the morning to read the collection of five journals, one for each year of their short marriage. In the end I knew the tragedy, which no doubt shaped the remainder of my great-aunt's long life, a tragedy that began without warning.

June 3, 1915, Montreal
Today is the happiest day of my life. What a common statement, but it fits my mood perfectly, for today I married Johann, my sweet wonderful Johann. At last I can say I am the Baroness von Wichtenstein, although Father says I shouldn't use it because of the war. While Father is still not reconciled to Johann being German, he kept it to himself. He was as polite and friendly as any father of the

bride should be to his new son-in-law. Life is truly wonderful. I thank God for giving me the strength to forgive Johann. And I bless Johann for his perseverance. If he had not blocked my way onto the ship, I never would have discovered how much he truly loves me. How silly I was to rip up his last letter without reading its tender loving words. But he rewrote them on our wedding day, and I've hidden them away in a secret place so they will never be lost to me again.

And Johann's words had remained safe until the day I'd dropped the wedding picture.

July 21, 1915, Three Deer Point

At last all our baggage has arrived. I thought travelling around Europe with a carriage load of trunks was difficult enough. Little did I know how difficult it would be to move to Three Deer Point. Our goods have taken a month to travel from Montreal. The railroad lost them for a time, the wagon bringing them from Somerset broke an axle on the Mountain road which then took a week to repair. While it was fun to wear Snow Flower's Indian dresses, I will be so glad to return to my finery. Johann, on the other hand, quite enjoyed playing Indian. I think it is with some regret that he has returned to his civilized suits. I'm so glad Johann has fallen in love with this wild country. I was worried he wouldn't.

At first, I assumed that the newly married couple, following the Harris tradition of spending summers at Three Deer Point, would return to my great-aunt's hometown of Toronto with the onset of fall. But I was wrong. As autumn moved into winter, they stayed, and there they remained as the years unfolded.

February 12, 1916

I never thought Three Deer Point could be so beautiful. We are locked in a land of snow and ice, completely cut off from all civilized life, including the precious letters from my family and friends. Our neighbour Dieter says it will be late April before the roads are passable again. In the meantime, Johann has become the hunter of the family. Sometimes I join him, but usually he spends his days with Rushing Bear trekking through the deep snow on snow shoes, searching for dinner. I have come to quite enjoy venison steaks and stewed hare.

April 3, 1916

I will be glad when the roads are finally passable, and we can have visitors. It has been a long winter and a lonely one, with Johann gone most of the day. One of the first things we will do is raise cattle. With our own source of meat, Johann won't have to devote so much time to hunting. I thought and hoped I was with child, but this morning put an end to our desires. Thank goodness I kept my hopes to myself. This would have hurt Johann terribly.

July 5, 1916

We had a wonderful picnic on the big island today on an absolutely perfect summer day. It took five boat loads to ferry over everything, including our guests, Edith, brother John in his new uniform, and the Vogts with their beautiful baby boy. Such a marvellous change having people around after the long, lonely winter. But with so many friends fighting in France, our visitors are few. Snow Flower brought her youngest sister, Summer Wind, to help out. Snow Flower would like me to hire her sister, but I have no need of another servant at the moment. Still, she is very sweet, so I think I will keep her in mind for when Johann and I have our child. I pray to God it happens soon. Johann is getting impatient. Must ensure the continuity of the von Wichtensteins, you know.

December 18, 1917

I believe I can now safely say I am with child. It is three months since my monthlies stopped. Johann is ecstatic. He is so concerned about my health that he spends every waking moment by my side. I'm loving it. He's not paid this much attention since the first year of our marriage. But I really don't blame him. There is much to do in keeping Three Deer Point thriving, and of course the lure of the wild hinterland is hard to ignore. Johann can't say no to the next bend in the river, but must follow it until he has reached the end. Unfortunately, the end sometimes takes weeks before he finally remembers to return to me. I hope with this child he will remain closer to home.

March 19, 1918

I threw that harlot out of the house today. I don't care if it's still winter. I can't take another minute of that Irish Jezebel. How dare she think she can have Johann. Edith warned me to watch out. She said that when men like Johann succumb to their animal instincts as he did with that servant in Germany, they will be tempted to transgress again. I won't allow it. Even if I am heavy with child. To punish him, I will close my door to him till after the birth.

Now I will have to find a replacement for Beth. Pity, she was such a good servant.

April 3, 1918

I can't find my child. I don't know where he's gone, such a beautiful little boy. Johann says he's gone away, but Johann's lying. That hussy took him. My baby will come back to me. I am his mother.

June 30, 1918

I can finally say it—my baby's dead, poor little Johann. These past months have been so dreadful. Without Johann's calm and caring presence I never would have made it. I love him dearly. He is my life. We are young. We are healthy. Children will come.

April 21, 1919

Today we have been blessed, Johann and I, with the birth of a beautiful little girl. She is whole. She is gorgeous. Johann says she looks just like me, but I know that is his way of saying I love you. We are both so very pleased and relieved that there was no mishap. Now we must find the perfect name for such an enchanting child. We have both decided that at least one of her names must be Summer Wind, for she has been a godsend during my long months of confinement. And if our daughter were to be as sweet and beautiful as Summer Wind we could not ask for more.

October 21, 1920

My child is dead. My husband is dead. I can live no more.

And as I read this last entry, my heart broke as Aunt Aggie's must have broken. So this was the true story at last. At least Johann hadn't deserted her. Instead, he'd stuck by her, even in her madness. It was death that took him away, and not only him, but also their small daughter. And they must have been horrific deaths for Aunt Aggie to lock them away. I had little doubt that this was the tragedy that had sent her reeling into madness.

Mother was wrong. Agatha's terrible tragedy had nothing to do with the betrayal of a lover. And it looked as if Mother was also wrong about the name. None of Aunt Aggie's diaries mentioned a Watson or any other English name starting with a W, nor did I find any reference to such a person in the remaining papers.

I did, however, find one faint glimmer of hope. It was a childhood letter to Grandpa from a Billy. Although it was unlikely that this person became the owner of Whispers Island, it still offered a faint possibility that Mother might have better success with Grandpa's papers.

I smiled at the references to Marie's grandmother, Summer Wind, in several of the diaries' entries. It seemed she was as important to Aunt Aggie as her daughter Whispering Pine later became.

During my search of the last cookie tin, I discovered one more interesting item, actually two; they were small pieces of quartz with a minute thread of gold. They looked exactly like the rock that had lit up our eyes on the granite ridge of Whispers Island. It would appear that Aunt Aggie had also known about the gold.

THIRTY-TWO

D amn you!" blasted the phone receiver. The clock said 6:05. Outside it was still pitch black and sounded like rain. "How dare you serve us with an injunction."

"Who in hell is this?" I fired back as I struggled to get my mind into gear. "Gareth? And how dare you speak to me like this? Of all—"

"Shut up, Meg. Listen and listen hard, I'm only going to say this once. If you don't have the stop work on CanacGold removed within the hour, we'll sue the pants off you and take you for all you're worth, including Three Deer Point."

"Gareth, *you* shut up," I shot back. "I'm not sure who should be suing who. I can just as easily charge you with misrepresenting the facts, even theft. You knew damn well Whispers Island wasn't crown land. And you stole the official registration to prevent us from finding out. Do you honestly think I'm that stupid I'd never twig to your little scheme?"

I heard him suck in his breath on the other end of the line. Then he switched to that patronizing tone that made my teeth grind. "Now calm down, Meg," he said. "No need to get upset. I understand how confusing this is for you. I'll talk to your notary, and we'll straighten this little matter out."

"Cut the song and dance."

"You don't know what you're talking about."

"Damn right I do!"

"Stop interrupting and let me explain the facts of life.

Number one, CanacGold has clear title to those mineral rights. Number two, who said anything about crown land? I said the Indians had no rights to the island, as Tom… I mean Eric kept insisting."

"Liar! Who does it belong to then?" I retorted, trying to trick him into revealing what he knew. It was only later that I realized the significance of the name he'd let slip.

"You don't—" he said and stopped. Then, after a moment's hesitation, he continued, "I'm not at liberty to say. Client/lawyer privilege. But I can tell you this. I'm about to close the sale to CanacGold. So Meg, you don't have a case. Remove the injunction immediately, or else you lose Three Deer Point."

"Not before you show me and my notary legal evidence of your title. And Gareth, don't you ever call me like this again." I slammed down the phone.

Damn. He'd found William Watson or his heir and convinced him to sell the island to CanacGold.

In a panic, I called François's office and left a message. Two hours later, he called back.

"Calm down, Mme Harris," he said. "The threat of a lawsuit is a scare tactic. According to the law, there is sufficient confusion over the ownership of this land to justify the stop work order. Until CanacGold is able to prove full legal title to the mineral rights, the injunction stands. So please do not concern yourself, madame. It is not possible they find this William Watson this fast. It will take much searching to find a man with no address, whose last known contact was over sixty-five years ago."

While François did manage to lower my temperature a degree or two, I was still smarting from Gareth's attack. He'd dared to threaten me. The bastard. I'd show him. I'd call his bluff. I'd hunt down William Watson or his heir, make damn sure he knew what Gareth and CanacGold were all about and stop the sale.

But it was a lot easier said than done. Although I'd finally learned the truth about Aunt Aggie's tragic past, I was still no further ahead in finding William J. Watson.

I quickly dressed and returned to the attic to see if there were any more containers to search, but there was nothing left other than a stack of old newspapers. I was about to dismiss these as useless when a quick glance at the top one changed my mind. *Somerset Weekly* shouted from the top of the yellowed page. Underneath, I read December 31, 1919.

I picked up the heavy bundle and went back downstairs, figuring that if William J. Watson had lived in this area in the 1920s, then maybe, just maybe I'd find a reference to him somewhere in these ancient pages. They were filthy with the grime of eighty years. By the time I'd finished poring over every word on every page of every edition, I was covered with a thin film of black dirt. But it was worth it. I was almost to the end, when I spied the name in a small discreet notice in the Local Briefs column of the November 28, 1920 edition.

We have been informed that Echo Lake resident, Mr. Wm. J. Watson, has passed away suddenly from gun shot wounds inflicted in a hunting accident. It is requested that any outstanding matters be directed to Mr. John Harris at 359 Old Forest Road in Toronto.

Finally, evidence that William J. Watson had actually lived around here. But there was a catch. He was long dead. In fact, a good fifteen years before he was supposed to have contacted those lawyers. So who set up the tax trust? Watson's heir or someone else? Either way, it was obvious that whoever had become the new owner didn't want it known that the title to the land had changed hands. Why?

I had one possible source for answers, a source Gareth didn't have, William J. Watson's contact, Mr. John Harris, my grandfather. It looked as if I'd been searching in the wrong place. Watson had been a friend of my grandfather, not my great-aunt. Maybe he really was Grandpa's childhood friend Billy.

I quickly phoned Mother, not caring if the call woke her up, and cursed when I got her answering machine. Assuming she was still sound asleep, I tried again, but again without success, which meant she'd probably gone to an early morning golf game. The nerve of her, when she had more important things to do, like searching Grandpa's papers. So I left her a message to get on with it and call me the minute she found anything related to William or Billy Watson. I also decided to drive to Toronto and go through the papers myself if I didn't hear from her by that night.

In the meantime, there was another matter just as pressing, finding out the truth behind Marie's death. For her sake, I felt I should give Tommy a chance to explain his actions before I took my suspicions to Eric. I hoped I would be proved wrong, but with Gareth's accidental mention of Tommy's name, they were only deepened. The two men had talked. The reason why could only have something to do with CanacGold.

A quick glance outside revealed that the early morning darkness had lightened to a soggy grey as water poured from the sky. With no thought for breakfast, I grabbed my rain slicker, ran to my truck and drove to what was no longer Marie's but now Tommy's home.

Through the flicking wipers, the collection of shacks looked even more dismal and forlorn. Remnants of police tape clung to drenched trees. Louis's logs had been re-stacked neatly against the wall of an already full woodshed. But the windows that greeted me were empty and black. The driveway was likewise empty.

Hoping Tommy's car was parked behind the house, I dashed through the rain to the overhang at the front door and knocked. The house remained silent and dark. I hammered again and waited. It was still relatively early, a little after nine. Tommy could still be asleep, like last time. I pounded again. But no lights came on nor did a sleep filled face come to the door.

I stood under the overhang trying to decide if I should forget Tommy and take my concerns directly to Eric. I was worried about the impact my suspicions would have on Eric and his people, particularly when coming from an outsider. It was easy for them to accept that Marie had killed Louis in retaliation for his years of abuse. It would be much more difficult for them to accept that a son could kill his own parents, especially a son whose achievements were a source of pride within the small community.

It was the footprints that finally decided me. I noticed them embedded in a dry patch of soil by the front stairs. The last time I'd seen this same tread with the elongated "y" trademark was in the sand near the cave where I later found Marie's body.

I didn't hesitate any longer but returned to my truck and drove as fast as I could to Eric's office.

THIRTY-THREE

Y ou're way offside with this, Meg." Eric's half-closed eyes bored into mine from a face which had become granite. His breakfast of fried eggs sat ignored on the table while its heat escaped into the cold damp air of the Council Hall's small kitchen. "For the sake of our friendship, I don't want you to say another word."

"But I think you have to consider—"

"Please, not another word."

I'd made the mistake of diving straight in with my suspicions about Tommy without any preamble and hit the feared roadblock. While I considered another tactic, I took a sip of the steaming liquid Eric had offered on my arrival. Although he called it coffee, it tasted more like the rain splatters smearing the dirty window.

I tried again. "Why are you so convinced Marie did it? You heard the attributions yesterday at the healing ceremony. You yourself even alluded to Marie's resolve to keep going no matter how tough it was. So tell me, after putting up with Louis's abuse all these years, why would Marie suddenly snap? Surely if it was in the cards for her to kill him, she would've done it years ago, when he broke her arm."

"Maybe, but we had a similar case just last year, when a wife of twenty years shot her husband after an all-night drinking binge."

"Sounds like alcohol caused that. Don't forget, Marie didn't drink."

He nodded in acknowledgment and leaned back into his chair, but his face still wore a look of stubborn refusal.

I persisted, "How do you explain the fact there were two sets of footprints, one large, one small, on the beach the morning she died? Innocent passers-by? I doubt it, particularly when one of them knelt in front of the crosses. You and I both know there's only one person with reason to pay homage to Two Face Sky and Summer Wind."

I looked for a reaction from Eric, and seeing none asked, "Why didn't you tell me they were Marie's grandparents?"

"I'm sorry, but figured since you didn't know, then Marie and your aunt had their reasons for not telling. But you're right about it probably being Marie. Dorothy told me she was in the habit of going there a couple of times a year."

"So, Eric, if the smaller set of tracks was made by Marie, then she wasn't alone when she arrived on the beach. And since only the larger set left the beach, don't you think we can assume she was dead when that guy left?"

"Yeah, and the next thing you'll say is Marie wouldn't kill herself in front of an audience, therefore she was killed by this other person."

"Exactly."

"Now, what were you saying about the tread? Run it by me again," he said, finally digging his fork into what now looked to be a very cold and greasy fried egg.

At last I was getting through to him. It just needed the right approach. I took him patiently through the description of the elongated "y" footprint and the sighting of this same track at Tommy's place. But this time, rather than freezing me out, Eric listened.

"And this makes you think Tommy is involved?"

"Yes, this plus other anomalies."

So I told him about John-Joe seeing Tommy on the lake the morning she died, about Tommy's lying to me over the timing of his return from his trip, his chanting as we entered the cave, almost as if he knew his mother's body lay inside, and a possible CanacGold link between Gareth and Tommy.

When I finally laid all the pieces out into the open, they unfortunately pointed in only one direction. Tommy had killed his mother and probably his father.

"I hate what you're telling me, Meg." Eric ran his hands through his thick hair. "It'll tear the band apart. Everyone sees Tommy and a few others like him as the key to our future. He's one of our first lawyers. A big hero to many of the kids. He gives them hope and courage that maybe they too can make it out there in that big and scary world beyond the trees.

"I still say there's no motive," he continued. "You haven't given me one."

"But Eric, when you think about it, what motive would anyone really have for killing Marie? Enemies? She had none. She was just a simple, kind-hearted soul who didn't get in anyone's way. Killed for her money? Hardly. That only leaves what the police call "crime of passion" and isn't that usually done by someone close to the victim such as a family member?"

"Yeah, but I'd be prepared to swear on the bones of my ancestors that Tommy wouldn't harm a hair on his mother's head. I could see him killing his father in a fit of rage, but his mother?"

"Say Tommy did shoot Louis and Marie somehow got in the way, whatever..." I suggested. "Maybe it was an accident...? I don't know..."

"Yes, I suppose anything is possible..." Eric stopped

talking and turned his glance to the rain streaked window. I contemplated another slurp of the thin coffee, but decided it wasn't worth it. He might be a good cook, but he sure couldn't make coffee. I waited for Eric. Only the rain tapping against the pane broke the silence.

Finally, he turned back to me. "There might be a motive." He paused.

Knowing this was difficult for Eric, I said nothing.

"I don't think it's enough to kill someone for, but who knows. Tommy's been away at school for the last ten years... Maybe he's not the same person who grew up here."

He shook his head sadly and continued, "Marie came to me a little over a month ago, upset over Tommy. She was worried he'd gotten involved in some shady dealings. He was coming and going at odd hours. Refused to tell her what he was up to. And he had money. Gave her a thousand dollars, which she refused to accept because he wouldn't tell her its source. I gather they had quite a fight over that."

Remembering Marie's words of concern a few days before she died, I nodded. "Yeah, she told me something about it too."

"Christ, if he's working for CanacGold, I'll kill the bastard."

"Maybe Marie found out?" I suggested. "And challenged him. Maybe she threatened to tell you, and he tried to stop her?"

"He does have a temper, just like his father. But this doesn't explain Louis's death."

"Maybe Louis discovered the killing?"

"Christ. This will tear my people apart."

I sat for a few minutes more, waiting for Eric to continue, and when he didn't, I asked, "So where do we go from here?"

"I'll talk to Tommy."

"Not the police?"

"Not yet, I want to give him a chance to explain. Could be we've read this all wrong."

"You may be too late. He may have already fled." And I explained about Tommy's empty house.

"Possibly, but leave this to me," he said, getting out of his chair.

After rinsing off his dirty plate, he grabbed his motorcycle helmet and moved towards the kitchen door. I followed, debating if I shouldn't go to the police myself.

As if reading my thoughts, Eric said, "Look Meg, I know you're right in wanting to go to the police, but I guess I'm still clinging to the hope Tommy didn't do it. And I suppose what's swaying me is his mother's amulet."

"How so?"

"It's missing, wasn't on her body. And it was Tommy who told me about it. He was quite upset. Wanted to bury it with his mother."

"How does this help Tommy?"

"She always wore it."

"Like her red dream scarf?"

He nodded. "The fact the amulet wasn't on her body means it was probably taken at the time of her death."

"I can confirm she had it shortly before she died," I added and told him about Marie's visit with Dorothy the day she disappeared, when she almost revealed its contents to Dorothy.

"Then her killer took it," he said. "Now supposing you're the killer. Would you make a big fuss about it being missing, especially when no one else had noticed?"

"Maybe not, unless you're devious enough to use this as a means of diverting attention away from yourself," I countered.

"Yeah, maybe. To tell you the truth, I've been puzzling over why someone would steal it. Sure it has sacred value, but only for Marie."

Outside, the rain had stopped. A few rays of sun were trying to break through the dense cloud. Securing the helmet on his head, Eric walked over to his motorcycle.

"I'll call you as soon as I talk to Tommy," he said. "It might take a while to catch up to him, so please, don't get impatient and go to the police before I call, okay?"

I reluctantly agreed but gave him until lunchtime. If he didn't contact me by then, I would notify Decontie. No telling how desperate Marie's son might become when finally cornered.

"Be careful," I said.

Eric nodded grimly and kicked his Harley into life.

THIRTY-FOUR

The second I placed my key in the front door, the phone started ringing. Convinced it was Eric calling to say he'd already found Tommy, I flung open the door and managed to reach the phone before the messaging system kicked in.

But instead of Eric's deep resonant voice, I heard a high pitched one with a slight lisp, which asked, "Miss Margaret Harris?"

"Who's calling please?"

"Wilson McLeod here. Sorry to bother you, but I have an important matter I'd like to discuss."

The name sounded familiar. "Excuse me, but do I know you?"

"Sorry, my apologies for not introducing myself. I'm the trustee for the Watson property. François Gauthier gave me your phone number."

Of course, William J. Watson's lawyer. But, why would he be calling me?

"Miss Harris, I'd like to ask you a question, if you don't mind?"

"Go ahead."

"Are you related to a Miss Agatha Harris, formerly of Three Deer Point?"

Not another one of Aunt Aggie's surprises. "What's this about?" I asked.

"Please answer my question. Are you Miss Agatha Harris's beneficiary?"

258

"Of course, it's why I'm living here. I'm her great-niece and her heir. Why do you want to know?"

"Do you have documentation to substantiate that?"

"What kind?"

"Notarized copies of your aunt's will, the deed to Three Deer Point and of course your own identity papers."

What's going on? Is this another devious ploy of Gareth's to get something from me? "Sorry, I won't give you anything until I am satisfied you are Wilson McLeod."

"My apologies. I should explain. I have an envelope that was given to my father by the late Miss Agatha Harris a number of years ago. Her instructions were to pass it to the heir of her Three Deer Point property. Before I can give this to you, I am required to establish your legitimacy as her heir."

"Why didn't you contact me when she died ten years ago?"

"Her instructions were very precise. We were to hand over this envelope only if approached on the matter of the ownership of the property you know as Whispers Island."

"Whispers Island? What's Aunt Aggie got to do with it?"

"I'm afraid I'm not in a position to answer your question. The contents were sealed before my time and are only to be opened by Miss Harris's heir. When would be a convenient time to come to my office?"

Could Gareth really be behind this? "Are you trying to tell me Aunt Aggie owns the island?"

"Not to my knowledge. Our records have Mr. Watson as the sole owner."

"Even though he's dead?"

"Yes, miss, but keep in mind that the ownership is under the trusteeship of my firm Bingham, McLeod and Tetro. It will remain in effect until his death is officially confirmed. Would a week from today be convenient for you to come to my offices? This will give you sufficient time to verify that I am indeed Wilson McLeod, a respected member of the Bar."

Maybe this guy really was on the up and up. And if so, I needed to know what Aunt Aggie had placed inside that envelope now, not a week from now. "You're in Ottawa, aren't you? I can be there within a couple of hours."

"Unfortunately, I will be out of town for the rest of the week."

I tried to convince him to courier Aunt Aggie's envelope to me or have one of his partners give it to me directly, once satisfied of my identity, but he ruled out both options, so I was forced into accepting his first available time slot, which turned out to be the following Monday, in six days. I hoped it wouldn't be too late.

Mr. McLeod did, however, allay my biggest fear, when I asked my last question. "You didn't happen to tell Gareth Patterson about this envelope?"

"Please, miss," he replied in a voice bristling with indignation. "I am a well-respected lawyer. I would never step beyond the bounds of client-solicitor confidentiality."

I immediately phoned François to tell him about the new development. He saw no difficulty in waiting a week, since the injunction with CanacGold would be in force until the ownership was resolved to the satisfaction of the courts. He also removed the last of my suspicions by confirming that Wilson McLeod did indeed speak with a lisp. He finished the conversation by saying in a somewhat sour tone that he doubted that the envelope contained documents related to the ownership of Whispers Island, since Agatha Harris, a most valued client, would never have consider employing another firm for her property transactions.

At this point, I didn't know what to believe. At the first

threat of the gold mine, Eric had said that Aunt Aggie might have owned Whispers Island. François had said it was impossible. And I hadn't found any connection, not even a hint that my great-aunt had considered the large island as more than a nice place to picnic. That is, until McLeod's call. Maybe, contrary to François' misguided belief, this long hidden envelope would finally reveal that she really had acquired it from William J. Watson.

Unfortunately, I wouldn't know the truth for six days.

* * *

While I waited for Eric's promised call about Tommy, I did some much-needed house cleaning. By the time noon struck, I might have had a much cleaner ground floor, but I'd heard no word from Eric. I waited another half-hour then phoned the Council Hall and was told he was out. I got no answer at his house. Eric could be persistent. I knew he wouldn't give up on Tommy until he was convinced he'd done everything possible to give Marie's son a chance to explain. I also didn't think Tommy would harm Eric, his friend and mentor. So I decided to give Eric until one-thirty, then I'd call Decontie.

I was washing up my lunch dishes when Eric finally arrived on his bike. He looked discouraged. I invited him inside, but he refused, saying he'd only come to tell me the news, what little there was. Tommy was nowhere to be found on the reserve. Someone remembered seeing him take off in his car shortly after his mother's funeral. He'd not been seen since, nor did he leave word of where he was going. And to make matters worse, Eric's questioning had begun to arouse suspicions within the band.

"I hate to say it," Eric said. "but it looks as if you were right. I'll notify Decontie."

"I'm sorry, Eric, truly sorry, not only for your sake but also for Marie's," I replied. "Maybe I should've left well enough alone. Everyone was satisfied with the murder-suicide verdict. And I'm sure Marie would be resting easier in her grave. But I can't accept it. I'm sorry. If Tommy killed his parents, he should be held accountable."

"I'm with you on this. I just find it hard to accept that he could betray the hope and pride of our people," he replied, angrily snapping his helmet back on. He kicked his bike back into action.

"Don't go yet," I shouted above the noise. "I want to tell you about a very interesting phone call."

He turned off the engine. His smile got broader and broader, the more I revealed about my conversation with Wilson McLeod. However, when I mentioned Gareth, he frowned.

"Meg, don't dismiss Gareth too quickly," he said. "Remember, you thought he was behind your break-in."

"Are you suggesting that Gareth somehow found out about the envelope and sent Charlie to steal it?"

"Maybe not the envelope per se, but its contents."

"But how would he know? Even I don't."

"From Charlie. His grandfather was chief in the thirties. As a result, Charlie probably knows as much if not more than me about your great-aunt's connection to Whispers Island."

"Damn the sneaky bastard. Playing lovey-dovey with me while knowing all the time. He was probably waiting for the right moment to search my house and had to resort to Charlie after I kicked him out."

Eric's brow creased in worry. "To be on the safe side, Meg, I suggest you tell no one about that phone call."

I agreed, knowing it wouldn't be difficult. With Marie gone, I'd already told the only other person close enough to confide in, Eric.

With my promise to join him later for a drink at the Fishing Camp, Eric roared off on his bike, while I returned to my housecleaning.

THIRTY-FIVE

L ate afternoon shadows were creeping across Three Deer Point by the time I finished cleaning the second floor of my too-large cottage. Although it didn't quite meet Marie's high standards for cleanliness, I felt very proud of my efforts. But once was enough. I'd have to begin the search for a new housekeeper soon.

When I entered the kitchen to return the cleaning paraphernalia to the pantry, I found Sergei whining to go outside. He raced off through the opened door and disappeared into the trees, yelping shrilly, which meant deer in sight. I hoped he wouldn't go far. I was more than ready to relax with Eric at the Fishing Camp.

Deciding hunger would soon bring the dog back, I placed his food bowl outside. I showered, then changed into a more presentable set of clothes. When I was ready to leave, Sergei still hadn't returned, nor had his bowl been touched. I called his name. A muffled bark answered. I waited a few seconds, but he didn't come.

I called again. Another bark, but no dog. I cursed. I wanted to go, but I was afraid to leave him outside in case he met up with the wrong kind of animal, like a porcupine. I used the whistle he'd been trained to respond to and got only a barking response.

I groaned in frustration. A cornered animal was the one thing that would keep Sergei from his food. Unfortunately, the only method of extrication was to forcibly drag him away by his collar. I tried to catch a glimpse of him through the trees, but it was impossible to distinguish his black body from the deepening shadows. Besides, his muffled barking suggested he was further into the forest.

With leash in hand and dog bribes in my pocket, I walked quickly towards the sound, which seemed to be coming from the direction of Aunt Aggie's sugar shacks. While I could still see the web of overhead branches against a sunset sky, I could barely see my feet on the path. I figured I had about ten minutes, fifteen at the most, before it became too dark. I debated returning to the house for a flashlight but didn't want to waste any more time. I quickened my pace instead.

Sergei's barking drew nearer, then abruptly stopped. Worried, I called out and was answered by the rustling of leaves. He's finally coming, I thought, and walked on, expecting to see Sergei's dark shape bounding towards me, but reached the sugar shacks without even a glimpse of him.

I blew his whistle. This time only dusk's stillness answered. Where was the damn dog? Half annoyed, half worried, I felt my fear of darkness rise. I frantically pushed it down. Now was not the time to run panicking back home.

I searched the ground for signs and found a number of tracks in the mud near the door of the main shack. Unfortunately, in the fading light it was impossible to tell if a dog had made them. I peered through the surrounding forest, searching for Sergei's darker mass and saw only the converging shadows of night. Frantic, I called again, several times, each time more shrilly as I fought my rising panic.

All of a sudden, the rustling started again. It was coming towards me. I froze. Every nerve ending in my body tingled as I strained to see through the dark.

"Sergei?" I whispered.

I waited. The rustling drew nearer. I edged towards the shack door with the idea of escaping inside. Before I reached it, a black mass suddenly lunged towards me and knocked me to the ground. A wet nose jabbed my face, followed by the sandpaper lick of a dog's tongue.

"You stupid animal!" I cried out in exasperated relief, and gave him a big hug to show that I was more than glad to see him. Then as I stood up, I noticed another dog, almost as large but lighter in colour.

A voice cut the silence, "Meg, that you?"

My nerves spiked. This person knew me. Footsteps slowly approached.

"Who's that?" I gingerly called back. I unlatched the shack door with the intention of barricading myself inside.

"Hélène. You got my bitch with you?"

"God, did you scare me. What in the world are you doing here?"

The glowing tip of a cigarette moved towards me and stopped a few feet in front. I could just make out her tall, lanky shape. Her face loomed into view as she sucked on her cigarette. Her eyes sparked with its fire, then went black.

For a moment she remained silent, then she said, almost as a challenge, "I was at the Lookout. That okay with you?"

"Sure, no problem," I said, then remembering my last trip to the rock outcrop, I asked, "You go there often?"

Her cigarette glowed brighter as she took a deep drag. I heard the slow release of air when she answered, "Why do you ask?"

"Saw some butts on top. Another time, when I was on the lake, I saw a figure in purple close to the cliff edge."

"Yeah, that was me. Look, I know it belongs to you, but that rock has special meaning to my people, kind of religious like, eh? Your aunt used to let us visit."

"Be my guest," I answered, while wondering why Eric had never mentioned the Lookout's sacred properties.

"Do you always go there so late in the day?"

The cigarette glowed again, then she answered, "I guess I kinda lost track of time. And your dog came." She laughed. "Could be your dog's gonna be a daddy."

I groaned. "Don't tell me your dog's in heat. No wonder Sergei refused to come when I called. Come on, let's get out of here."

*   *   *

I didn't completely relax until we finally reached the security of the light surrounding my cottage. Holding Sergei's food bowl inches from his nose, I managed to lure him away from his new friend and lock him inside the house. With a last glance at the building to ensure everything was secure, I headed towards my pickup.

Knowing Hélène would have a very long and dark walk home through the woods, I offered her a ride as far as the turn-off to the Fishing Camp. She gratefully accepted and put her dog, now revealed to be a nice looking golden retriever, into the back of the truck and jumped into the cab beside me. She sat with her long, angular body folded into itself, staring out the windshield while I started up the truck. Under the overhead cab light, her face appeared strained and tired.

"You must be working too hard?" I asked. Shifting the truck into gear, I headed down the drive.

She sat as if she hadn't heard me, then turned a bleak stare towards me and answered, "Just a few things hitting me right now, but nothing I can't solve."

"Want to tell me about it?" I asked, not sure if I really wanted to delve into her personal life. I felt I had enough problems of my own to deal with at the moment.

But she saved me from having to battle my conscience by answering "Ain't much. Only bore you." And continued staring at the beam of light bouncing in front of us.

To lighten the mood, I said, "Nice retriever you got there."

She sat silent for a moment, then answered, "Not mine, Charlie's."

"You mean Charlie Cardinal?" I asked in surprise. Somehow a rottweiler seemed more his type of dog.

She grunted "Yup" and hunched further forward.

Unsure of what else to say, I drove on in silence and quickly reached the end of the Three Deer Point road. I turned onto the main road towards Migiskan Village. Night surrounded us in an impenetrable blackness as we pursued the moving tunnel of light. Occasionally, a stray object would flash into life, then die as the headlight beam pushed forward. I felt as if my entire world was reduced to this barely lit cab of a broken-down truck with Hélène and me its sole inhabitants.

"Too bad about Marie," I said.

Hélène sighed. I felt the back of the truck seat move as she leant against it. "Yeah, a real shame," she replied. "But if a woman puts up with a man beating her up all the time, she's gonna fight back, eh? Might even kill him."

I decided not to challenge her. Better to let the real story of Marie's murder come from Eric or Police Chief Decontie. Instead, I made some benign comment about Marie's funeral.

Hélène continued talking as if she hadn't heard. "I tell ya, I woulda left the bastard years ago. Any man lays a finger on me, wham, I hit him right back. Jeez, no way I take that guff."

I heard her zip up her jacket with one long forceful yank.

"Now me and Charlie, we got an understanding," she continued.

"Are you saying you and Charlie Cardinal are more than just friends?"

"Yeah, well him and me, we have a thing, see," she replied, turning quickly in my direction and then back to the front of the truck. "I guess ya could say we connect. I'm good for him. He and that bitch of a wife don't get along. In fact, he's gonna leave her."

She turned her gaze back to me. "Now, Meg, I'm telling ya this on the q.t.... I don't want ya blabbing this around, eh?"

"I won't say a word. But you surprise me. I thought you kept pretty much to yourself."

"Yeah, that's what I want people to think. Keeps them from sticking their nose in where it don't belong. Ya know once the word gets out, it'll be game over. Me and Charlie have been real secret like. We have a secret place we go to, eh?" She glanced at me. "Anyways, by the time they find out, we'll be long gone."

"You're leaving?" I asked, even more surprised by this additional news.

"Yeah…sometime… Soon as Charlie gets his affairs in order. Then we're outta here. Now don't ya be telling nobody."

"But I thought you loved your job at the store?"

"Yeah…I do. But I gotta get out of this hole. I ain't never seen nothin'. Charlie's gonna change all that. Him and me, we're gonna see the world." Her voice shook with defiance.

"I suppose if you've never lived anywhere else, this place can get to you. Where do you plan to go?"

"I don't know. Somewhere with lots of lights and glitter. Toronto, New York, maybe even Paris, you know the big city in France, where all them painters hang out. I saw some of them pictures in a book once. They were real pretty, that's for sure."

"Sounds exciting, but won't this require a bit of money? Why not settle for Toronto? It's cheaper and would have just as much action as the other two cities."

"Like I said. Me and Charlie got plans. And maybe, just maybe these plans include getting a few bucks. And then maybe they don't."

I didn't bother to ask where the money was coming from. I knew it was courtesy of CanacGold. And judging by Charlie's fancy new Yukon, they were paying him a bundle. No wonder Charlie didn't care about preserving the island. He wasn't going to be around when the mine finally got going.

Out of the darkness, a pinprick of light suddenly loomed into view. Worried it might be a reflection from the eyes of an animal, I slowed the truck down. As I got closer, the white dot was joined by a red one, and rather than remaining stationary the way a deer would when startled by oncoming headlights, the lights wove from side to side across the road.

"Jeez, not another damn drunk," Hélène muttered, voicing my own thoughts.

I slowed my truck to a crawl and wondered how I was going to get around the car without getting hit. I blasted the driver with my horn, hoping to convince him to remain on one side while I attempted to pass on the other. No such luck. The car suddenly swerved across my path. I jammed my foot on the brakes. My truck slid over the loose gravel and came to a stop, inches from the car's bumper.

However, the car, one I recognized with unease, continued its slow aimless course, like a wind-up toy winding down. It bumped along the shallow ditch, lurched over a boulder protruding from the side the road, narrowly missed a tree before wobbling back across the road. Finally, it came to rest against a hydro pole. For one long second everything froze, and then the horn began emitting one loud continuous blast.

With anger overriding all caution, I jumped out of my truck, yelling, "Hey! What in the hell do you think you're doing?" A dark shape slumped over the steering wheel. In the glare of headlights, I saw Tommy.

THIRTY-SIX

L ike father, like son, I thought as I shook him. "Hey, Tommy! Wake up! This is no place to sleep it off!"

Slowly, his body slipped from the steering wheel and slid through the open car door towards the ground. I grabbed for his arm, his shirt, anything to break his fall, but, too heavy, he collapsed in a heap on the road. The horn stopped. Tommy didn't move. It was quiet, almost too quiet.

I slapped his face. No response. Worried this was more than a drunken coma, I checked his pulse and thankfully felt life. I reached around his chest and tried to prop him against the car. I almost had him upright when I felt something sticky and wet. Startled, I loosened my grip and saw a dark stain spreading across his tattered flannel shirt. Covering the back of the driver's seat was a similar stain, glistening red in the light.

"Hélène! Come here! Quick! I need your help!" I called out, expecting her to be right behind me. But the answering silence told me she'd vanished as suddenly as she'd appeared this night. No doubt she was tired of dealing with drunks.

Not knowing what else to do, I frantically tried Tommy's pulse again. He was still alive. Then his eyelids fluttered. With a painful groan, he opened his eyes. Unfocussed blue looked out at me. Across his forehead stretched a dark angry welt.

"Tommy? You have to try and help me get you into my truck."

But his only reply was a faint twitching of his lips. He tried to raise his trembling hand to his face, but it fell back with a thud to his side. I attempted once more to raise his body into an upright position, so I could half-carry, half-walk him to my truck. Impossible. He weighed a ton.

I ran back to my truck and drove it closer. Straining to keep his upper body off the ground, I slowly dragged him towards the passenger side. His boots left two shallow creases in the dirt. Between them dribbled a line of blood.

Finally, I manoeuvered him into the front seat through a combination of pushing and pulling with some feeble assistance on his part. I covered him with the dirty blanket used to protect the seat from muddy paws.

"Tommy? I'm going to take you into the hospital in Somerset. Can you hang in?"

The blue eyes opened. "Yes...I'll...try..." And closed again.

I drove as fast as I dared while trying to minimize the jolts in the road. I had no idea what the injury was or what had caused it. I only knew he was still losing blood, a significant amount judging by the growing patch on the blanket.

Except for his ragged breathing, he was quiet the entire trip. He cried out only once, when the truck was jolted by an unseen bump in the road. Normally a thirty minute trip to Somerset, this time it took me just under twenty minutes to reach the emergency entrance of the town's hospital.

While the hospital staff was transferring him to the stretcher, he opened his eyes and looked directly into mine. "Found the money," he whispered and closed them again.

Before I had a chance to ask "What money?", he was whisked beyond a set of doors that proclaimed "No admittance".

I phoned Eric, who promised to come immediately. Then I got myself a strong cup of coffee and sat down to begin the agonizing wait to learn if he would survive. Within the hour, Eric joined me. We waited several tense hours in the sterile waiting room, before the doctor finally came out. "He's going to live," she announced with a smile.

Thank God, I thought, and smiled at Eric who obviously felt the same. And then I felt my hand squeezed, and realized with surprise that he'd been holding it. I squeezed back.

The doctor continued, "Although he has lost a significant amount of blood, the wound is not life-threatening. Fortunately, the bullet didn't lodge in his body but passed through cleanly, missing vital organs. He was very fortunate. Usually a bullet entering the upper thorax of the back is fatal."

I felt Eric stiffen beside me as I too thought over the implications of what she'd just said. But neither of us interrupted the doctor.

"The wound on his forehead is probably from falling on a hard object after being shot. As a result, he has a concussion. It will be some time before he is fully conscious and able to talk."

When she finished, Eric asked, "Are you saying that Tommy was shot in the back?"

"Yes," she replied grimly. "I've called in the police."

Neither Eric nor I said anything. But we both knew what this meant. I'd made a terrible mistake. Tommy hadn't killed his parents. In fact, their killer had probably just tried to kill him. And if I hadn't been so cocksure that my evidence pointed to Tommy, he would be lying safe in his bed with the police hot on the trail of the real killer. Instead, he was lying here in this hospital with a bullet hole though his back.

I hastily apologized to Eric, but he brushed it aside, saying that in light of my evidence, he had suspected Tommy too. Nevertheless, I still felt very guilty for having thought that

Marie's son could have been her murderer.

For the next couple of hours, I found myself closeted with my old buddy Sgt. LaFramboise. His manner was no less arrogant than in our previous confrontations. In fact, when he glowered at me and said, "Not again" in his surly French, I received the distinct impression he was adding me to his list of possible suspects. However, despite his insolence, I told him everything. That is, except for my suspicions about Tommy. I was too embarrassed.

Once finished with the policeman, I then had to take on Eric, who was now concerned for my safety. He reasoned that with a killer on the loose, remaining alone at Three Deer Point might not be healthy. He insisted I stay at the Fishing Camp. But I quickly quashed his concern by emphasizing that the killings were directed towards Tommy's family and had nothing to do with me.

Eventually, he relented and I headed to Three Deer Point. By the time I reached home, day was fully underway. Thinking only of sleep, I dragged my tired body to bed, where I was greeted by the message light flashing on my bedroom phone.

"Hi, dear. It's your mother calling. Sorry I've missed you, but I've found William Watson. And I was right. Well, dear, since you're not home, I'll put it in the mail right away. Ta."

THIRTY-SEVEN

I frantically dialled Mother's number only to hear: "Sorry I'm not at home to take your call, but please—"

Frustrated, I slammed the receiver down. I waited a couple of minutes, tried again and got the same insipid greeting. With my eyes swimming from exhaustion, I decided a couple of hours sleep was required. Perhaps by the time I woke up, Mother would finally be home. However, when I woke up midway through the morning, feeling somewhat revitalized, I failed to reach her again. This time I left her a message to phone me immediately.

I had slightly better success with the hospital. A talkative nurse told me that although Tommy was steadily improving, he was under heavy sedation. Unfortunately, she anticipated it would be at least another day, if not two, before he would be able to talk.

I received this news with mixed emotions. Although very glad he was improving, I worried that any delay in Tommy's identification of his assailant would be too late. This would-be killer, who I strongly suspected was the murderer of Marie and Louis, would be halfway across the continent by the time Tommy woke up.

Tommy had almost died because of me. When I'd seen the elongated "y" footprint of Marie's killer by Tommy's doorstep,

I should've gone straight to Decontie. Unlike me, he wouldn't have jumped to a knee-jerk accusation. He would've recognized the possibility that the killer was after Tommy and kept him safe.

I felt I had to do something to help, but I didn't know what. I knew I couldn't just sit there and wait. So I decided to drive to Tommy's house, where I assumed the police were carrying out their investigation. As I'd told LaFramboise early that morning, since Tommy's car was only a short distance beyond the driveway when I found him, it was likely he'd been shot at home.

Although I was surprised to see Tommy's car still parked at the side of the main road where I'd left it the night before, I figured Sgt. LaFramboise had decided to investigate the site of the shooting first. However, to my dismay and disgust, I didn't find any police vehicles parked out in front of the shack, nor was there indication they'd even checked it out. I felt my temperature rise at the thought of LaFramboise's blinkered arrogance. He'd probably decided there was no hurry to find the would-be killer of an Indian.

I was on the verge of turning my truck around to track Chief Decontie down at the Migiskan Police station when I caught sight of a large patch of what looked to be blood on the dirt drive. I jumped out to have a closer look and saw a trail of dark blotches leading towards the side of the house. I followed them, stepping carefully to avoid destroying possible police evidence.

At the corner of the house, the trail of blood disappeared into a tangle of weeds and low brush. Although Louis had managed over the years to hack a clearing out of the dense bush at the front of the house, he'd never attempted to do so elsewhere. Sun-starved balsam and poplar crowded against the side wall of the shack, making it appear impassable. However, a faint gap in the vegetation seemed to lead towards the back of the house. I followed it.

Once out of the wind, the sudden eerie stillness made me think twice about venturing into these woods. Surely the gunman had taken off after the shooting. I glanced nervously around. But in dense bush, where every tree was a potential hiding place, it was impossible to know if you were completely alone.

Within a few feet, I found a pool of blood partially congealed in the hollow of a large rock. A trail of broken twigs and crushed weeds led further into the dark woods, away from the cabin. I hesitated. But curiosity overcame my remaining fears and I crept deeper into the gloom.

From the zigzag line of Tommy's track, it was obvious that he had been weak and confused. Several well-trampled spots suggested he might have stumbled and fallen. And where his track intersected an established path, he'd lain for a period of time. The dirt and surrounding rock were sticky with his blood, the earth scoured from his attempts to get up. I could almost feel Tommy's desperation to keep from dying alone in these woods, miles from help. I was surprised the gunman hadn't finished him off, but perhaps Tommy had remained still, possibly unconscious, for so long, the guy had assumed he was dead.

I jumped at a sudden loud bang and jerked around to see the plank door of a small roughly built shed swing open. Another gust of wind sent it slamming back against the doorframe. From under the roofline of the outhouse, two holes, shaped like eyes, stared back at me smugly as if saying, "I know something you don't." On the ground, directly in front of the door, I found more of Tommy's blood. Then I spied a perfectly round hole amongst the irregular knotholes of the door. Curious, I ran my fingers over it and felt metal.

The shiny end of what was probably a bullet stared back at me. Tommy had been shot here.

I scanned the nearby underbrush in an attempt to learn more and noticed a gleam of black. I reached down and pulled up a metal box. Its lid swung open, and out floated two brand new twenty dollar bills. And a few feet from the box I finally found the link to Marie's killer. The exact replica of the elongated "y" footprint I'd seen on the beach where Marie had died. I knew Tommy hadn't made it. Last night he'd been wearing Kodiacs.

And embedded in the track was a crushed cigarette. So Marie's killer smoked. But since a lot of people smoked, I doubted it would provide much of a clue.

At that moment, I heard what I thought was a car door slam. I froze, then relaxed with the thought that the police had finally arrived. I debated returning to show them what I'd found, but figured they could follow the trail of blood as easily as I. Besides, LaFramboise would make me leave before I learned all I could about Marie's killer.

I continued my search and found a small packet of new twenties lying on the ground. Was this the money Tommy had mentioned last night?

A faint glimmer caught my eye. Thinking it was more money, maybe some coins, I reached into the underbrush and laughed out loud when I pulled up a man's gold link bracelet. A clue, I thought, a real clue to this killer.

"Hi Megs, what are you doing?" a voice suddenly said from behind me.

They say sudden shock can add years to your life. This one sure did.

"Good God, Gareth," I said, slowly turning around, my heart pounding. "What are you doing here?"

I stared at the cigarette in his hand, not sure if I wanted to draw the obvious conclusion.

"I heard a noise, I came to check."

"I mean this house, this property. Why are you here? How do you even know about it?" I started to back up, wondering when the police would finally arrive.

"Maybe I should ask the same of you?"

As I stepped back, my elbow knocked against a tree. A glimmer of gold slid from my hand and dropped to the ground. I reached down to pick the bracelet up and stopped.

Staring back at me was the initial "G", engraved on the band.

THIRTY-EIGHT

Good. You found my gold bracelet," Gareth said, looking smug in Polo tweed.

Amazed by his ready claim of ownership, I held up the heavy links with the damning letter. "You admit this is yours?"

"Of course. Give it to me."

Gareth grabbed it. We tugged at the slippery links, then with one firm yank, I ripped it from his grasp and zipped it into my pocket.

"No way you're having this. It's evidence," I said and regretted the words the minute they were spoken.

Deciding I'd better put some distance between Gareth and myself, I started walking towards the front of the house to where my truck was parked.

"What do you mean, evidence?" he said, catching up to me.

"You should know." I quickened my pace. Was he bluffing, or did he really not know the meaning of this bracelet?

"Hey, hold on a minute. Know what?" He grabbed my arm and whirled me around.

I struggled to escape, but his hold was too strong. And suddenly I was plunged back three years to when he had held me just as tightly. It had ended when, in a fit of rage, partly as a result of my goading, he had thrown me against the kitchen counter and broken my arm.

This time I took a deep breath and very calmly said, "Gareth, let go of me."

It worked. I felt his grip loosen.

"Not until you tell me what's going on," he said.

I scanned his face looking for signs and saw the bully I now knew was Gareth. But was it the face of a killer?

"Tommy Whiteduck's been shot," I said and slipped from his grasp. I turned and continued heading towards my truck, not quite sure if I wouldn't be feeling the same kind of slug that had ripped through Tommy.

For a few seconds, the only sound was my beating heart and then, "Meg, stop!"

By this time I was running, desperate to reach the safety of my truck. I could hear his footsteps gaining. I raced along the side of the house, around the corner and almost tripped over a piece of one of Louis's discards. I caught myself and sped towards my truck. Gareth's import was parked a good distance behind. He grabbed me within arm reach of the truck door.

"Release my arm, Gareth."

He glared back at me, then let go. "You saying I had something to do with this shooting?"

"The bracelet says you were here when Tommy was shot." I placed my hand on the door handle.

"Wasn't me. Someone ripped it off me a couple of days ago."

"You expect me to believe that? Or the police?"

I opened the truck's door. But before I could spring inside, Gareth slammed it shut.

"Hand it over. No way you're going to incriminate me," he said.

"Never," I retorted, straining to hear the sounds that would tell me the police were finally coming to investigate Tommy's shooting. I stared into his angry eyes and dared him to hurt me.

But he crossed his arms and leaned back on his heels. "I had nothing to do with Tommy's shooting," he said. "I just don't want to get involved."

"Afraid it'll tarnish your oh-so-squeaky clean image?"

"Give me the bracelet, Meg."

"If you're so bloody innocent, why are you here?"

From his jacket pocket, he ripped out an envelope and threw it at me. It was addressed to Mr. Thomas Whiteduck. "Go on, open it," he said. "It's a job offer."

"What did you do? Offer him thirty pieces of silver to betray his people?"

"I don't know why you believe the mine will hurt those damn Indians. If anything, they'll have more jobs than they'll know what to do with."

"Yeah, I've heard that one before."

"Tommy's father thought it was a good thing. He was the one who told us about gold. He and his partner."

So I was right. Louis had been involved, and it probably explained the money Tommy'd found and the reason for Marie's anger with Louis. Then I remembered what Eric had said about Louis' involvement in a fake gold discovery some years ago and smiled inwardly. Wouldn't it be a joke on Gareth and CanacGold if Louis had done it again?

"Who was his partner? Charlie Cardinal?"

Gareth picked up Tommy's letter from the ground and returned it to his jacket pocket. "Nope," he replied.

I was about to retort "liar", when I realized his self-satisfied grin was telling me otherwise. Instead, I decided to knock the grin off his face.

"This partner could be a killer," I said. "Might have decided he didn't want to share the winnings with Louis."

At which point, a torrent of rain began to fall. But Gareth

didn't move. Neither did I. Nor did I bother to flip my jacket hood over my head.

"Could be he shot Tommy too and killed Marie," I continued.

He remained still, with his eyes riveted on me. The rain flattened his hair, coursed down his face and onto his crossed arms. He ignored it. Finally, he said, "You don't know what you're talking about."

"You could be mixed up with a killer."

His eyes sparked. "Pile of crap."

My ear caught the sound of a car splashing up the Whiteduck drive. I saw with relief the white paint of a police cruiser flashing through the trees. "You can tell that to the police," I said.

The SQ police cruiser drove past Gareth's car and came to a stop next to us. Out stepped the rigid form of Sgt. LaFramboise, joined by his partner.

LaFramboise cast a suspicious scowl in my direction. *"Eh bien,* madame. Curious, how you are always at the scene of crime, non?"

He turned his pointed nose to Gareth. "And you, *monsieur,* why you are here?"

Gareth smiled confidently and held the envelope so the officer could read the addressee, then returned it to his pocket. "I was just delivering this offer of employment to Tommy Whiteduck, when I ran into Miss Harris. She tells me, however, that the unfortunate man has had an accident. So if you don't mind, I'll get out of your hair and deliver this to him at the Somerset Hospital, which is where I assume he is. It'll help to take his mind off his injuries."

At that moment, Chief Decontie's 4x4 cruiser crunched to a stop behind LaFramboise's vehicle. He hopped out and saunteredy towards us, with another Migiskan police officer trailing behind him. He nodded in my direction. LaFramboise said something to his partner in French, which I took to be an order to begin the search, for the cop motioned for the other cop to join him and the two of them walked towards the front door of the Whiteduck shack.

"No, not there," I shouted. "Tommy was shot around back."

LaFramboise peered at me. "And how know you this, madame?"

"I found blood and the bullet holes," I blurted out guiltily. His tone made me feel as if I were the criminal.

"Show me," he said. And we started to walk towards the back of the house. With this downpour, I doubted that much remained of the blood or the elongated "y" footprints.

It was at this point that I suddenly realized Gareth was no longer with us. I looked up in time to see the back end of his black sports car disappearing down the drive.

"Quick, after him," I yelled. "I found his bracelet lying on the ground where Tommy was shot." I held it up.

LaFramboise shouted something at his partner, who ran to the cruiser and with a jet of wet gravel and dirt sped after Gareth. Then, he turned his attention to the bracelet, "Why do you remove it, madame? It is no more good evidence. I do not know if it is true. I only know because you tell me."

I started to get indignant at his implied accusation, then realized he was right. I should've left it exactly where I'd found it. I hastily apologized, then took him and Decontie around to the back of the house to show them the bullet holes in the outhouse door and the metal box where the twenty dollar bills now lay in a puddle of water.

For the next half hour, while the other policeman from the

reserve took pictures of the site, LaFramboise and Decontie drilled me on what I'd found. Thankfully, we sat in the police cruiser, though to be truthful, remaining in the rain wouldn't have made me any wetter.

By the time we were finished, the cop had returned without Gareth. His car had vanished before the chase had even begun, and although the officer had searched the area, he'd found no trace of Gareth. Infuriated, LaFramboise immediately radioed what I took to be a message alerting other police to be on the lookout for Gareth's vehicle.

"And don't forget the hospital," I said in my halting French, which LaFramboise acknowledged with a curt nod.

Good, that should get him, I thought. Let's see him try to brush off the police as easily as he did me. He'll be forced to admit to his involvement in this whole sordid affair and identify the probable killer, Louis's partner.

With a final word of warning not to leave the area, LaFramboise let me go. When I reached home, I found, much to my surprise a voice message from Tommy wanting me to visit him in the hospital. A call to the nursing station confirmed that he had gained consciousness sooner than expected, and although the doctor was with him at the moment, he should be free by the time I arrived.

THIRTY-NINE

At the door to Tommy's hospital room, I was reassured by the presence of a cop standing, or more correctly sitting, on guard. Moreover, he was able to assure me that no one fitting the description of Gareth had visited Tommy's room, from which I could safely conclude that the police had nabbed him.

Tommy lay propped against the raised back of his bed. A large white bandage covered his head wound. A stiff white sheet hid the rest of his body. Judging by the rigid way he held it, he was either firmly bandaged or still in considerable pain. Probably both. Two sets of tubes, one clear, the other red ran from his arms up to the plastic bags dangling from the metal stand at the side of his bed. Considering the amount of blood he'd left behind, the sight of the blood transfusion came as no surprise.

His opened his eyes as I approached his bed. He smiled weakly. "You came…" he whispered and closed his eyes as he winced in pain.

Watching him catch his breath, I realized I'd been too hasty. "I think I should come back later when you're feeling better."

"No, Miss Harris, don't leave. It's all right… I think they've given me some kind of pain killer. It really doesn't hurt me that much… Just the bandages are kind of tight." He struggled to move his body into a more comfortable position.

I reached out to help him. "Please, forget the Miss Harris nonsense. After what we've been through, I think I deserve to be called Meg," I said.

"I've been a jerk, Miss...I mean Meg. I want to apologize—" A fit of coughing stopped him in mid-sentence.

"Don't say anything more. I should be the one to apologize," I replied. "I thought you killed your parents."

He held his eyes closed, then directed their blue brilliance towards me. "I gave you plenty of reason."

"No, I should've trusted Marie's son."

"Please...I gave you no reason to trust me. I behaved badly. I spurned your offer of help, and I lied to you." He stopped and took a few shallow breaths, then continued in a stronger voice.

"And it was for the most selfish of reasons, stupid Anishinabeg pride. All my life I've resented your family, your money and your white skin. I swear from the day I was born, there wasn't a moment when Mooti didn't think the sun rose and shone on Miss Agatta.

"I hate to say it, but I was glad when your aunt died. No more interfering...and then you moved in... I tried to prevent Mooti from going to work for you, but she refused to listen. She tried to tell me that our two families...were like a beaver and a stream, but her analogy only made me hate your family's influence even more..."

Tommy stopped to catch his breath, then continued. "I thought she meant our destiny was to serve you, like the beaver who spends his entire life working to make the stream into a big pond. But I was wrong...

"It took a bullet to make me realize that in her own simple way she was trying to say that our families need each other to survive and prosper. Much...much in the same way the beaver needs to dam the stream to provide food and protection for his family. The stream in turn needs the beaver to make it into a pond, so it can provide a home for plants and other animals."

He coughed. Groaning from pain, he struggled to reach the

water glass on the bedside table. I hastily picked it up and held the bent straw to his lips.

"You know, she was right," I said, mulling over Marie's simple imagery. "We do need each other. And it started with your great-grandmother, Summer Wind. She helped my great-aunt with a difficult pregnancy. Aunt Aggie in turn saved your grandmother's life. And I'm sure you know that Aunt Aggie would never have survived her years of isolation and bouts of madness without the dedicated care of Whispering Pine."

Tommy nodded thoughtfully and added, "And the money your aunt gave us. Sure, I resented its hold, but it did help my mother gain some independence from my father, and of course, I couldn't have become a lawyer without it."

Thinking back on what Marie had done for me, I added, "Without your mother's friendship I'm not sure how I would've overcome my first lonely year at Three Deer Point."

Tommy smiled. "And the circle continues... The doctor says that if you hadn't found me, I wouldn't be here talking to you right now. Mooti was right, our destinies are linked, like the beaver and the stream."

Tommy caught his breath as if in pain, then smiling weakly he continued, "In the language of my people, I want to say *chi-migwech,* many thanks. And I'm sorry I was such a bastard."

"Please, no apologies. I was a bitch too."

At this point, a rotund nurse in floral polyester and pink Hush Puppies whisked into the room, checked his intravenous and thrust two pills into his hand. She held the glass of water to his lips, while he gulped the pills down.

Glancing in my direction, she said, "Mustn't overtire the patient, dear."

Muttering "Of course not," I started to leave, but Tommy

stopped me by saying, "Please...not yet. I want to explain my actions, that's partly why I asked you to come."

The nurse, shaking her head, gave Tommy one last check before leaving the room.

As she closed the door behind her, I asked, "Does it have anything to do with Gareth Patterson?"

Tommy's startled blue eyes looked towards me. "How do you know about him?"

"He told me. He's my ex."

"You were married to that bastard?"

I nodded yes. "But if it's any excuse, he wasn't a bastard when I married him. He only became one later."

"Well, he sure suckered me. I was convinced he was offering me the job of a lifetime, assistant legal council for this big multi-national mining company. And then Eric told me all about CanacGold and Gareth Patterson. Shit, was I mad. I felt like a damn fool for being sucked in again by white man's snake oil.

"And I should've known better when he made me sneak around like a Mohawk weasel. But my eyes could only see the money he promised. And of course, I was convinced this was my chance, me, a poor Algonquin, to make it big in the white man's world."

"If it's any consolation," I said, "it's taken me almost twenty years to become immune to Gareth's snake oil. This sneaking around you mentioned, does it explain why you lied to me about your return the day I was at your place looking for your mother?"

"Yeah, that's part of it. He didn't want anyone to know we were meeting, so I felt I had to pretend I was just getting home. He also kept grilling me about my family, which should have made me suspicious too."

"What kind of questions?"

"Mostly about my grandmother and great-grandparents,

nothing that related to getting a job. I was naïve enough to think he wanted to learn about my people's ways. But when I finally learned of his involvement in the gold mine, I realized his only interest was furthering the interests of CanacGold."

"No doubt. But what does your family have to do with the mine?"

"Mr. Patterson knew about the death of my great-grandparents on the island. I think he was trying to get me on his side to quell any concerns my people might have about the mine desecrating sacred ancestral grounds."

"Even so, it wouldn't stop him," I said, remembering Marie's stark concern the first time we saw the miners trespassing on the island. "You visited the island with Gareth the morning after your mother was killed, didn't you?"

Tommy's eyes opened wide in shock. He tried to fight back the tears, but a couple escaped. "To think I was that close and didn't know."

"Please, don't blame yourself. By then she was beyond help."

"I know," he said with a deep sigh. "How did you know I was there?"

"I saw your boat on the north beach that morning."

"Couldn't have been mine. We were on the south shore, where my great-grandparents once lived."

"Are you sure? The boat I saw had the exact same red tackle box as the one I saw at your place."

"So that's why you grilled me about Papa's box. No, it wasn't his. Besides, a few others in the band have the same box."

"Like who?"

"Eric."

"I know about his, anyone else?"

"John-Joe, and I think Charlie Cardinal might own one."

Bingo, I thought to myself. I could believe Charlie would push a tree over to try to scare me away from the island.

"You didn't happen to see anyone on the island, while you were there, someone wearing one of the Fishing Camp's yellow rain jackets?"

"Nope, didn't see anyone."

He stopped talking and lay quiet for a few minutes. I glanced at the rain-streaked window and wondered how much longer the downpour was going to last. Tommy was obviously tired. And if this rain didn't let up soon, I could find myself rowing home rather than driving.

I started to get up, when Tommy said, "Meg, your mentioning a yellow jacket reminds me of something. I forgot all about it when the police were questioning me. But I remember it clearly now. A few seconds before I felt the gun shot, I saw something yellow. It could have come from one of those jackets."

A sudden chill went up my spine. "Did you see who it was?"

He shook his head sadly.

"Too bad. I guess he was after that money you found."

"Yeah, the money… I found it hidden in the outhouse. It was inside the hole, on a small shelf Papa must've built years ago. Funny I never noticed it before. Maybe this was where Papa hid his hooch from Mooti." Tommy chuckled quietly. "It was a lot too, at least twenty bundles of new twenties. Wonder where Papa got money like that?"

"I think the money was payment from CanacGold for the gold discovery on Whispers Island."

"No shit. After all the years he'd tried prospecting, he actually found something."

Yeah, rather convenient, I thought to myself. I wondered

what prompted him to prospect on Whispers Island after so many years of living almost next to it.

Wincing, Tommy reached for his glass of water with the straw which I held to his lips. When he'd finished, he said, "Police haven't told me whether the money's still where I dropped it."

"Sorry, most of it's gone, but hopefully when the police catch your gunman, they'll find the rest of it. Gareth said Louis had a partner. Any idea who that could be?"

"Papa, a partner, as in business partner? You've got to be kidding. He didn't trust anybody, not even his own kin."

In case Gareth was lying, I decided to ask. "Could it have been Charlie Cardinal?"

"No way. Charlie wouldn't give Papa the time of day. Too caught up in his noble Algonquin heritage. Thought non-status half-breeds like Papa were dirt."

Tommy closed his eyes and lay quiet. Realizing I'd stayed far too long, I hastily wished him well and left. Outside, the rain had fortunately diminished to a Scotch mist, which would make the long drive home a lot easier.

As I drove away from the hospital, I started worrying over the implications of Tommy's evidence. It seemed unlikely that there was more than one attacker wearing yellow. So the man who'd shot Tommy and probably killed his parents and the man who'd tried to kill me on Whispers Island and vandalized my home were no doubt one and the same.

But his motive for going after both of us eluded me. There was no common thread other than it probably had something to do with the gold. Moreover, while I was sure Charlie, under direction from Gareth, had broken into my home and was a good candidate for tree pusher, I found it difficult to believe that he would kill Marie, a person he'd cared for like a sister.

FORTY

When I arrived home, I found a Priority Post envelope sandwiched between the screen door and the front door. Mother had actually come through. She'd even had the smarts to courier the information. If her message about finding William Watson was accurate, this should finally lead me to the real owner of Whispers Island.

I immediately opened the package and extracted a small envelope, only to discover Mother had securely enclosed it with layers of scotch tape. I hastened to the kitchen for a knife, slid it through the thick tape, opened the envelope and pulled out two pieces of folded paper. They appeared to be letters written on tissue-thin paper.

I was in the process of unfolding one of them when the doorbell rang. With the letters firmly clenched in my hand, I opened the front door. My heart stopped when I saw Gareth encased in dripping yellow.

"What are you doing here?" I gasped, shoving the letters deep into my jeans' pocket. I narrowed the opening of the door. "You're supposed to be with the police."

"Police?"

"Yeah, didn't they find you at the hospital?"

"I didn't go. Got tied up. Besides, why would they want me?"

Annoyed by his continuing pretense of innocence, I just glared back at him.

"Christ, you told them about the bracelet. I told you I had nothing to do with the shooting."

"Why did you run away then?" I locked the screen door in his face.

"Let me in, Megs," Gareth said through the screen. "I came to warn you that you might be in some kind of danger."

"My only danger is from you," I replied.

"I'm serious. I did some sniffing around after our little fracas this morning and discovered a few things I don't like. I think you should get away from here until things settle down."

"You must think I'm really stupid to believe anything you say."

"I'm telling the truth. Things have gone further than I wanted them to."

"Yeah, like me refusing to do your bidding."

His face reddened with anger. "Forget it," he said. "Just don't blame me when you get hurt." He turned on his heels and left.

I watched him get into his car. He'd lied to me one too many times. No way it could be a real threat. He didn't care what happened to me. He only cared about protecting his own hide. Besides, why would this mysterious partner—if that's who it was —be after me? No, in all probability, it was a ploy to get me away from my property, so the bastard could resume the search for whatever it was he'd sent Charlie after in the first place.

Then I saw Gareth's last glance as he drove away and almost changed my mind. For an eye-blink, a sincere concern looked back at me from the man I had once loved, then it vanished into the careless indifference that had become Gareth. I stood for a while longer, wondering what to do, leave or stay, but remained undecided. At least, I could keep him occupied with

LaFramboise. I placed a call to the SQ to let them know that Gareth was still in the area.

Afterwards, I returned to the two letters in my pocket. Both were written over eighty years ago, and both were addressed to Grandpa Harris.

The first was from Aunt Aggie; a long letter written in the thin, spidery handwriting I'd come to know well. Dated June 4, 1915, it confirmed what I'd already learned from her diary, her marriage to Baron Johann von Wichtenstein. And like her diary, she was bubbling over with happiness and looking forward to her new life with the man of her dreams.

As I reached the end of the long letter, I wondered why Mother had found it important, for it provided no additional information beyond what I already knew. Discouraged, I was about to set it aside when I realized that more writing covered the back of the last page.

P.S. John, I almost forgot to tell you what my new name will be. As much as you teased me about joining the high and mighty, you won't be able to call me the Baroness von Wichtenstein. Rather you will just have to settle for plain old boring Mrs. William Watson.

Father advises, and Johann agrees, that until the war is over, he should not use his very German name. So he has settled on Watson. Heaven knows how he came up with that. He says it was the name of a character in some English novel his nanny read to him as a boy. And William is the English version of one of his names.

It seemed just too impossible. Aunt Aggie's husband was William Watson, who died in 1920. When he died, she would have inherited, and since I was Aunt Aggie's heir, I was now the owner of Whispers Island. Eric had been right all along.

I let out a war whoop. Gareth, I've got you now! And then I went cold. Someone had discovered I was the real owner of Whispers Island, and it couldn't be Gareth. If he knew, he wouldn't be issuing warnings. He'd be sitting back waiting for the inevitable to happen. Unless. Unless, somewhere under his calcified hide, he still held a vestige of the love he'd once felt for me. And if this were true, then I should heed his warning and not stay in this isolated house any longer.

The second letter rustled in my hand. I debated leaving it for later but decided it must be equally important for Mother to have included it. This one was from my Great-grandpa Joe. And as I read it, the floor seemed to open beneath me.

Toronto
November 12, 1920

Dear Son

Have you seen your sister yet? How is she taking it? I never did like that damn Hun she brought into the family. I never trusted him, too damn smarmy with his fancy manners, if you ask me. Why, that bastard didn't even have the guts to fight for his country. He had to hide behind Aggie's skirts.

And now that damn bastard has gone and left her. Enough that Aggie had to deal with the death of wee Edi, now she has to contend with this. Probably some skirt involved. Didn't he have some wandering dick trouble in Germany? Good riddance is what I say, but Aggie won't see it that way. She only had eyes for him.

I'm too busy right now, so I can't go, but you go to Three Deer Point and see what you can do to help your sister.

For Aggie's sake, I think we should keep this to ourselves.

Lucky we kept the marriage quiet, what with the war and all. No reason why we can't keep this a secret too. And for the few people that do know about the marriage, just put a notice in the local paper announcing the death of William Watson. It'll save Aggie having to do any explaining and force him to use his German name.

Write after you've seen Aggie, and if you see the bastard, shoot him.

Your father Joe

The last of my euphoria had drained away by the end of the letter. My inheritance of the island was no longer secure. Now it was clogged with ifs. If my great-aunt had divorced the bastard, if he had remarried, if he had children, then I could not be the owner of Whispers Island.

I received some satisfaction from the realization that this was the kind of inheritance squabble that would take years to resolve in the courts. It would spell the end of any quick money for CanacGold, which in turn could kill their interest in developing the mine.

But it was also the kind of squabble that would disappear with the destruction of key documents.

I glanced down at the fragile letters and knew I was looking at the reason for the break-in. Charlie Cardinal had known about Aunt Aggie's connection to Whispers Island. Maybe he'd also known about William Watson. Suspecting that documents like these existed, he'd searched my house with the intention of removing them before I found them. And he'd taken the wedding picture, the one readily available piece of evidence that could show Aunt Aggie's link to William Watson. What would Charlie and Gareth do if they knew I now had the proof of Watson's identity?

FORTY-ONE

I buttoned the two key letters securely into the back pocket of my jeans. Wherever I went, they would go too. I glanced nervously at the clock and realized it would be dark in another hour. I knew I didn't want to spend the night alone at Three Deer Point, miles from police help. I placed a call to Eric, the one person I could trust. He proposed that Sergei and I spend the night at his place, a safe block away from the Migiskan detachment. With a promise to meet at the Fishing Camp within the half-hour, I hung up feeling considerably more secure.

After putting the dog out, I went to my bedroom to pack a few clothes. I automatically grabbed my flannel nightgown, then noticed wedged into the corner of the drawer the soft silky one Mother had given me after Gareth had left. It was still wrapped in the original tissue. I picked it up, shook the wrinkles out of it and thought, why not tempt the gods. I carefully laid it on top of the other packed items.

I checked the house to ensure all windows were securely bolted and doors locked. Then, with suitcase in hand, I headed outside to my truck. Although the rain had finally stopped, the heavy cloud cover suggested it wasn't completely over. Patches of mist hovered in the recesses of the forest, making it difficult to see much beyond its edge. The wet, dripping silence was only broken by the raucous noise of squabbling birds, probably ravens, coming from the direction of the sugar bush.

I threw my bag into the truck, then set out to look for the dog. I found him cavorting near the woodshed with a strange looking object clenched between his teeth. He barked in greeting, dropped it to do so, then snatched it back up. But not before I recognized with disgust the bottom portion of a deer leg, complete with fur and hoof. He'd found a deer kill, which explained the quarrelling ravens.

Very pleased with himself, Sergei bounded down the trail to the sugar bush with his prize, looking backwards to see if I was playing his game of catch-me-if-you-can. In frustration, I yelled after him, but other than a quick backward glance, he ignored me and disappeared into the mist.

I'd never get him now. The last time he'd run off with a bone, it had taken an hour to finally coax him to drop the bone and come. Today I didn't have an hour.

Sergei was hungry. His dinner might be the lure. So I placed his bowl brimming with dog food beside the truck, called him and waited. The raven's cackling continued. But no sign of Sergei. Damn him. He'd done it to me again. I was angry enough to abandon him but knew I couldn't leave him alone and unprotected. As much as I feared delaying my departure, I had no choice but to go after him.

I figured he'd most likely returned to the dead deer, which shouldn't be difficult to locate. I'd follow the sound of the ravens quarrelling over the carcass. The problem was the noise seemed to be coming from further into the sugar bush than I cared to go, possibly as far as Aunt Aggie's abandoned sugar shacks a quarter mile away. So before my nerves had a chance to dissuade me, I took a deep breath and headed towards the racket.

I walked along the trail thick with wet leaves and called the Sergei's name in the futile hope that he would come. The reverberating cackles grew louder, as I neared the shacks.

When I finally rounded the last bend, the ravens scattered in an uproar of flapping black and angry shrieks. Several flew to the top branches of nearby maples, while one landed on the metal roof of the main shack, where he emitted a loud croak, as if in warning.

What remained of the deer lay only a few yards from the trail, not far, I nervously realized, from my encounter last night. Just as well it had been Hélène. I didn't want to think what would've happened if I'd met up with the wolves instead.

Although Sergei was nowhere in sight, I wasn't completely disheartened. I counted four hoofs with femur attached amongst the blood-splattered bones and chunks of fur. Three lay tangled in the rib cage. The fourth, the one Sergei must've had, was propped against the starkly staring head of the deer. It was enough to tell me Sergei had returned.

Praying he hadn't wandered far, I called out. The raven sitting on the shack's roof answered with a hoarse chortle. And, miraculously, from inside the timber shack came a muffled bark and the sound of scratching.

I ran to the door, wondering how he'd managed to open the latched door and was brought up short by the sight of the latch still in place. He must have squeezed through a hole in the back. But then again, why didn't he escape back through this same hole?

Warily, I opened the door. Sergei rushed out to me, whimpering, squirming. "It's okay, boy," I said, patting his head. "We're outta here, dog." I snapped the leash to his collar.

I was about to close the door when I realized it had become quiet. The noisy ravens had disappeared from the trees. Only the large one sitting on the roof remained. He gave me a black beady stare, croaked as if wanting to tell me something, then unfolded his wings and lifted into the air.

He'd no sooner vanished then I smelled stale cigarette smoke from inside the shack. I froze, all nerve endings on full alert. The nail securing the latch to the doorframe was shiny and new, not old and rusty like the other nail-heads. Someone had been here. Was this what the raven had tried to tell me?

Sergei strained at the leash to go in. I hesitated. Half of me wanted to get out of there as fast as I could. The other half wanted to find out what was going on. Finally, curiosity took over. I stepped gingerly into the dark interior.

The smell of cigarette ash was strong, and so was the odour of kerosene. I stood a few feet inside and waited for my eyes to adjust to the dim light. Gradually, shapes that had no right to be there emerged from the greyness; a couple of white plastic chairs, a table with an oilcloth covering. A mattress draped in a ragged Hudson's Bay blanket was shoved against a side wall. I was dumbfounded and scared. Someone had moved in. Who?

Sergei continued pulling. With one vigorous tug, his leash slipped through my fingers, and he vanished into the back of the room. I strained to see where he'd gone, but the light was too dim. However, I noticed a kerosene lamp on the table, so I lit it with a match from a nearby box.

Is this some kind of hideout? I asked myself, as I surveyed the room. Another chair, a couple of glasses beside a half-empty bottle of rye, even a rusty camp stove. A can of kerosene stood under the table next to an overturned garbage can whose rotting contents were strewn across the floor. I spied Sergei gnawing on what looked to be a chicken bone. Annoyed, I yanked him away and forced him to lie next to me.

My heart stopped at the sight of an ashtray overflowing with butts, but before I had a chance to absorb its warning, my attention was jerked to a noise outside. I waited. Silence except for water dripping onto the metal roof. Sergei still continued to lie unconcerned with his head flopped between his paws.

Suddenly, his head went up. He looked towards the back of the hut. Was someone out there? I peeked nervously out the back window but saw only a still and misty sugar bush.

As my gaze turned back inside, a glint of light caught my eye, and I found myself staring at Aunt Aggie's wedding picture. It was wedged into the opening of a canvas sack, a sack filled with packets of twenties. I'd found Tommy's stolen money.

Sergei began to growl. Terrified of making my presence known, I blew out the kerosene lamp and held the dog quiet. I remained rigid, barely breathing, while he squirmed under my hold. I waited. The dog relaxed.

It seemed a lifetime, but it probably wasn't more than five minutes before I felt confident enough to admit my nerves had got the better of me. No one was outside. Just an animal stepping on a branch.

I took it as a warning, grabbed the sack and the dog and headed towards the door, but I'd stepped only a few feet outside when I felt a sudden whoosh of air against my ear, followed by a soft thwack in the nearby tree. Then the gun explosion filled my head. I fell to the ground as another shot boomed through the trees.

Sergei barked frantically at a spot of brilliant yellow about a hundred yards to the right. My worst nightmare! I bolted towards the open door as another shot bit into the timber wall. I flung the sack over my shoulder, scrambled inside with the dog and slammed the door behind us.

But the gaps in the log walls told me I was no safer there. This place was a sieve. As if to prove my point, a shot exploded through a window and sent shards of glass in every direction. Another tore a hole in the fragile caulking. I lay flat against the floor and searched frantically for something solid to hide behind. Another shot slammed against the outside wall. I didn't know whether to force him to come get me or surrender now before Sergei or I got shot.

Suddenly a crashing thud echoed through the walls, followed by what sounded like a man's voice hissing "Damn!" He'd fallen, no doubt tripped on some slippery deadfall. I took my chance, grabbed the sack and ran, letting the dog run free. The door banged behind me.

I sped deeper into the sugar bush. I thought my chances would be greater lost in the clutter of trees than racing down the open trail in the direct line of a bullet. I scrambled through the underbrush, weaving in and out of the thick protective trunks.

I almost tripped over a hidden stump but caught myself in time. Several yards later, I stumbled over a large branch and collapsed. For long agonizing seconds, I lay on the wet ground, gasping for breath. Surprisingly, the dog wasn't with me. Then I heard through the mist the sound of shuffling leaves coming in my direction. Praying it was Sergei, I pushed myself up and without a backward glance raced deeper into the sugar bush.

A solid wall of spears stopped me. I'd reached the beginning of a spruce forest. The weather-honed tips of the interlocking branches prevented me from going forward. I had to turn. The problem was, in which direction?

Until now, my only concern had been to get out of firing range. Now I had to decide where to go. I knew my best chance for escape was my truck parked in front of the cottage. But I had no idea in which direction it lay.

I stared back the way I'd come. Nothing moved in the mist, but the swish of leaves grew louder. In my gut, I knew it wasn't Sergei. I tried to remember if I had heard a gunshot after I'd run, but couldn't. While my heart wanted me to return to the shack for Sergei, logic told me I'd be crazy.

Branches snapped. Running feet pounded on the ground. A dark shape loomed. I turned and ran.

I raced over the uneven terrain along the edge of the spruce forest. Jumped over fallen debris. Scrambled over rocks. The pounding behind me grew louder. I expected at any moment to hear a rifle ring out.

A shape lunged towards me! He'd found me! The brown shape leapt across my path. I stopped. It continued on its course. It took me several quaking seconds to acknowledge what my eyes had told me. A deer. I paused to catch my breath.

I tensed as I caught the sound of metal against metal. Thwap! Boom! The branch beside me broke. This time he'd found me! I turned, unsure of where next. Through the tangle of dead branches, I saw a retreating white tail. The deer! It was following a track through the spruce forest. I crashed through the thin break in the black web of branches and raced after it.

I scrambled along the narrow path, through a deer-wide tunnel of broken branches. A pointed end reached out to stab me. I smashed it with my arm. Another took me by surprise and I felt the pain of a scratch on my cheek. I held the money sack in front for protection and used it like a battering ram.

I glanced down at my red jacket and cursed. It made a perfect target. I wrenched it off and threw it to the ground. I continued along the tunnel, skidding over moss-covered rocks and decaying needles, dodged jutting spears. I could see no further than the next web of branches. Soon I realized I was going downhill. I hoped this meant I was heading toward the familiar beaver swamp. Once at the swamp, I could find my way to safety.

I'd no sooner raised my hopes than the crash of breaking branches dashed them. I glanced backwards. No sign of him. The pounding on the ground, however, told me he was closing in. I picked up my pace.

I tripped and lay crumpled in a clearing of moss. Branches snapped. The thud of running feet closed in. My time had run out. I looked around in desperation. The massive remains of a downed, rotting tree stretched along one side of the clearing.

Suddenly it was quiet. He'd stopped. A flash of red through the branches told me he'd found my jacket. I inched slowly towards the fallen tree. The footsteps started up again, this time more slowly. I watched yellow legs move towards me.

I jumped up and over the deadfall. I landed at the bottom of a narrow trench concealed by a tangle of ferns and roots. I heard the sound of laboured breathing. I held my breath.

"Christ! Where is she?" came a hoarse whisper. The footsteps stopped. I sank further into the ditch. I didn't dare look up. Something scrapped along the ground. Clunk! The rifle barrel rattled against a rock. A thump against the rotting trunk, which quadrupled the rate of my already racing heart. "She can't be far from here!"

Suddenly a muffled crash sounded from the direction of the beaver swamp. My pursuer's footsteps retreated towards the sound. But I kept my relief in check and remained in my hiding place, terrified he would return. A shot rang out, silence, and then another.

FORTY-TWO

I waited in the gloom of the dripping forest, my senses on full alert for the gunman's return. I started at a small animal scurrying over twigs. I jumped at a bird's flutter. I waited while twilight closed around me. With the memory of the gunshots still ringing in my ears, I prayed Sergei hadn't been the target.

I couldn't remain here much longer. I had to find my dog. I had to warn the police that the man who'd shot Tommy and probably killed his parents was hiding out in my sugar shack. I hoped with his hideout discovered, he wouldn't be back. But as I touched the sack containing Aunt Aggie's wedding picture and Tommy's money, I knew it wasn't true. He wouldn't leave without this money. Who was he? Charlie Cardinal? Louis's partner? Or were they one and the same? And what about Gareth? Where did he fit in?

I waited a few more minutes in the silence, then grabbed the sack, scrambled out of the trench and headed back the way I'd come, away from the gunman. Using the sack as a shield against sharp branches, I felt more than saw my way through the deer tunnel. Although the dying day still managed to outline the top branches, at ground level everything blended into opaque night.

Afraid of betraying my presence, I trod as silently as I could over the needle packed ground. Instead of smashing branches aside, I gently pushed them away. At one point a twig snapped and sent a shattering message through the listening forest. I held my breath and waited. Empty silence. I continued.

Gradually, very gradually, branches began to take shape against a brightening background of grey light. I was reaching the end of the spruce. Next moment, I stepped with relief into the more visible expanse of the sugar bush. Although this wasn't where I'd entered the spruce forest, I knew my location. The light flickering through the trees had to be coming from my cottage.

I walked towards the light, stopping frequently to listen to the night noises. But other than a startled bird, which sent my heart racing, stillness reigned. I could feel the tension slowly easing as I neared home. Soon I'd be safe inside, locked behind solid doors with the police on their way.

A dog began barking angrily. Sergei! Thank God. He was alive. And then he stopped. My telephone rang. It too abruptly stopped. The gunman was in my house, waiting, waiting for me to return with his money.

I inched slowly forward, trying to decide what to do. Escape via truck was out. Stupidly, I'd forgotten my keys in the pocket of my red jacket now lying abandoned in the spruce forest, and the spare was inside the house. That left me the option of either walking the half mile to the main road in hope of flagging one of the few passing cars, or of taking my motor boat and fleeing to the Fishing Camp, a short ten minute ride away. I opted for my boat.

However, once made, the decision didn't remove me completely from danger. I still had to pass close to the house in order to get to the safety of my boat. Unfortunately, the path to the lake stairs would take me into the glare of the floodlights at the front of the house. I decided instead to skirt behind the woodshed at the back of the house where there was less light. I would then use the cover of the pine forest to reach the stairs.

I continued walking towards the cottage, trying to keep the sound of my passage through the wet leaves to a whisper.

Within minutes, I was standing in the shadow of a large maple, looking onto the side yard drenched in yellow light. Beyond the brilliance loomed the darkened house. He'd extinguished all the indoor lights.

How dumb! If he were trying to ambush me, he should have kept everything the way it was. On the other hand, maybe the blackened house was intended to provide a better view of my arrival. And then again, maybe it was intended to hide his actual position.

I peered into the darkness beyond the light's perimeter, searching for a faint movement or the black outline of a waiting presence. I strained to hear unusual sounds above my nervous breathing. Leaves rustled. An owl hooted. The distant putt-putt of a boat's motor sharpened the air.

Willing myself to silence, I walked towards the woodshed. Staying well outside the circle of light, I inched my way slowly towards the back wall. When a twig snapped underfoot, I stopped and let the silence erase the sound, then inched forward again.

Cigarette smoke! He was close by! I stopped with one foot in mid-step. Another whiff of smoke. I held my breath and waited.

A chair scraped against the wooden floor of the verandah. He was waiting for me around the corner, out of sight. I slowly let out my breath, picked up my pace and reached the woodshed with little more than a whisper's disturbance of air.

Taking the stairs to my boat had suddenly become too dangerous. I would be in full view of the waiting gunman on the verandah. Instead I would have to take the longer, more precarious route that skirted the shoreline beneath the cliffs of Three Deer Point.

Anxious to reach my boat before his patience ran out, I hurried towards the little-used track that would take me away from the cliffs to a more accessible part of the shoreline. In the growing night I felt more than saw the darker outline of the trail. And when I stubbed my toe on a large rock, I cursed myself once again for not bringing a flashlight.

I was within earshot of the restless lake when I stumbled across a large inert hump on the path. It gave with a soft, all too familiar pliancy that I recognized with dread. I knew because Marie's body had felt the same way.

My immediate fear was for Sergei. But it couldn't be him. I'd just heard his bark. No. This killing had been caused by those last gunshots fired after the gunman had failed to find me in the spruce forest.

Dreading that it was some poor person who'd got in the killer's way, I gingerly reached towards the dark mass and touched something that felt like stone, but wasn't. I stretched my fingers and felt fur, then brushed over the sinewy hardness of a slender leg.

He'd killed a deer, probably the deer that had saved my life by showing me the trail through the spruce forest. I sadly patted the still-warm fur. I could even detect a faint murmur. And then with one final shudder, the body relaxed as blood dribbled onto my fingers. I whispered a brief homage to *kije manido*, praying that this useless death would be avenged, like the other two deaths.

From this point, it was a short descent to the shoreline. Any faint hope I had of finding rescue from a passing boat was quickly dashed by the silence of the dark empty lake.

I continued along the shore towards the rising cliffs at the end of the point. Fortunately, numerous rock falls had provided a narrow, boulder-strewn passage between the rock wall and the edge of the water. With one hand clutching the sack of money and the other the wall, I picked my way carefully over the slippery granite.

Partway along, my head knocked against an object jutting from a break in the rock. Thinking it was a piece of deadfall, I reached up to remove it and discovered, much to my amazement, the painting I'd jettisoned in the final act of ridding myself of Gareth. I smiled. Perhaps I should keep it as a reminder of my newfound courage. I tucked it behind a large rock for later retrieval and continued on.

After another hundred yards of scrambling, I finally rounded the point. Before me stretched the dock and the way to safety. Unfortunately, I'd have to walk the entire unprotected length of the dock to where my motor boat was tied up at the end.

For several tense minutes I stood in the shelter of the cliff wall, listening for sounds to tell me if the gunman was watching. But above the cliff edge, only silence and darkness prevailed. I waited until convinced he remained on the verandah. However, a last upward glance before heading to my boat saved me. A sudden flare from a match lit up the railing at the top of the stairs and then went out. He was there!

I squashed myself against the cliff wall, knowing safety lay in its shadow. I was prepared to wait there all night. But it took only a few minutes before I heard his footsteps retreat towards the house. I waited a few minutes longer, then crept along the wooden dock to my boat.

Fearful the least noise would bring him back, I silently lowered the sack and myself into the old wooden boat. I untied the boat, gave it a forceful shove to let it drift as far as possible from land before I signalled my escape with the start of the engine. It moved sluggishly with the current as the aura from the cottage lights rose behind the black cliff face.

Without warning, the boat's hull suddenly scraped over a

sunken rock with a teeth grinding noise. It came to a sickening halt. Feet clattered down wooden stairs. I frantically stabbed the oar into the water and shoved as hard as I could. With a last shattering screech, the boat sprang free. I yanked the engine cord. Nothing! Not again! I yanked again. I heard a rifle bolt hammer home. Engine, if ever there was a time to behave, now was it. I yanked again. With a husky roar, it caught.

I aimed the boat towards the Fishing Camp. With an alarming thud, a bullet slammed into the side of the boat. I ducked. I twisted the throttle completely open. But the fifteen horsepower motor couldn't get me away fast enough. Frantic, I rocked back and forth, willing the boat to move faster. A flash of orange erupted from mid-way down the cliff an eye-blink before the bullet ripped through the water behind me. I waited for the next, but there were no more. I was out of range.

I raced down Forgotten Bay to Eric, frequently checking behind to make sure the gunman wasn't coming after me. I kicked at the sack in the bottom of the boat and considered its implications. I blew on my freezing hands in an attempt to warm them. Unsuccessful, I stuck them in my pockets and felt something other than tissue in one of my pockets.

I pulled out a rock. It was caught in a strip of what looked to be a piece of nylon fabric. For a moment I was puzzled, then laughed perhaps a little too shrilly when I remembered where I'd picked up this piece of flotsam. Returning it to my pocket, I looked up just as my boat was about to ram the Fishing Camp dock.

FORTY-THREE

Intent on getting the police to Three Deer Point as fast as possible, I jumped out of my boat and raced along the Fishing Camp dock to the bar, where country music blasted through half-lit windows. But that was the only sign of life. The rest of the sprawling timber building lay shrouded in darkness.

It looked as if Eric had given up waiting for me. Only one car stood in the parking lot, and it didn't belong to him. Unless he'd parked his motorbike around the back, it wasn't here either.

I stepped into the dimly lit lounge where the glow from the stone fireplace revealed an empty room. Not even John-Joe stood behind the bar.

"Hey, where is everybody?" I shouted above the blare of the music.

I walked towards the door leading to the main part of the building. But before I reached it, John-Joe came rushing through, his head bare of its orange cap, his brow furrowed in worry.

"Sorry, I—" He started to say and stopped when he saw me. "The damn pump's broken again."

"Eric here?"

John-Joe blinked in puzzlement. "He not with you?"

"Nope, why should he be?"

"How am I suppose to fix this friggin' thing?"

"Did Eric go to my place?"

313

"Yeah, you didn't see him?"

"Shit," was all I could reply. He probably ran right into Marie's killer. "When did he go?"

"I dunno, guess about a half hour ago or so, soon as he got the pump going, eh? Now it's stopped. Christ, our biggest customer is coming—"

I didn't wait for John-Joe to finish but picked up the phone and dialed the Migiskan Police. I quickly told Chief Decontie about the killer and my fear for Eric. Although Three Deer Point was outside his jurisdiction, he and another officer would go immediately. He would also alert LaFramboise. I, on the other hand, was to remain at the Fishing Camp. As soon as he knew anything, he'd call.

"Why did Eric go to my place?" I asked.

"He got tired of waiting. He even called, but when there was no answer he got worried, eh?"

If he was dead because of me…

Unable to sit, I paced back and forth in front of the fire. The seconds stretched into minutes, which seemed to stretch into hours. But probably not more than fifteen minutes had actually passed, before I suddenly realized someone was walking through the outside door.

I glanced up and saw Eric.

For a second I didn't want to trust my eyes, then as the anxiety drained out, I cried, "Why couldn't you wait?"

"Thanks be to the spirits," he said. "I thought you were dead. When I discovered your house empty, you missing with your truck parked out front, I–"

"Wait a minute. You didn't see anyone?"

"No one. Why? He came after you, didn't he?" He shoved his thick mane from his face. "Damn, if only I'd gone sooner."

"Before I tell you what happened, just tell me Sergei's okay."

314

"He isn't with you?"

"You didn't see him?"

"No, and he would've come when I called out for you."

"We've got to go back," I said, starting for the outside door. "The police should be there by now. You probably passed them en route."

"Nope, I came here to call them. Your phone cord was ripped from the wall. Another reason for thinking the worst." His eyes smiled. "But thank the Creator you're very much alive."

And so are you, I said to myself. However, embarrassed by his change in tone, I walked outside. Catching up, he placed a reassuring hand on my shoulder and said, "We'll take my boat, it's faster."

*　　*　　*

Even before we reached my dock, I could see the flashing red and blue lights of several police cruisers through the trees of Three Deer Point. A quick climb up the stairs to my cottage revealed several policemen waving flashlights over the ground and Chief Decontie in consultation with Sgt. LaFramboise. Both were strapped into flak jackets.

LaFramboise quickly confirmed that although there was evidence someone had been in my cottage, the person was gone. And the search thus far had not uncovered Sergei, dead or alive. However, one of the SQ officers had found a spent shell casing on the stairs to the dock, which was viewed as further evidence that I'd been telling the truth. LaFramboise made this last comment with a barely contained curl to his upper lip.

"And now, madame, we will search this sugar hut you call a hideaway. Please acquaint us with its location," LaFramboise said, removing his gun from his holster.

I started to lead the way.

"No madame, tell us where it is. You must remain here. It is possible this man waits for us with his rifle."

But I couldn't wait at the house not knowing about Sergei. I shrugged off Eric's restraining hand and followed behind the line of police officers. Besides, the killer would've fled from the first flash of police lights screaming up my drive.

And I was right. The shack was as I'd left it; the kerosene lamp on the table stood unlit next to the half-empty bottle of rye, the mattress with its filthy Hudson's Bay blanket remained shoved against the wall. And in the back corner the chicken bones lay undisturbed. There was nothing to suggest that the gunman had returned after chasing me. Nor did it look as if Sergei had come back.

I waited until the police had finished searching the surrounding bush before succumbing to Eric's entreaties to return to the house. Along the way I called out Sergei's name, even blew his whistle. But it was as if he'd never bounded through these woods.

"We're only in the way here," Eric said, as we started up the stairs to the verandah. "Grab some things, and we'll go to my place. We'll come back at first light and search for Sergei."

I could see he was right as I watched a woman in a crumpled suit and latex gloves brush powder over an empty glass that sat on the small pine table where I usually placed my glass, except this one wasn't mine.

"My suitcase's already in the truck. In fact, let's drive." I'd had enough boating for one night. I just wanted to retreat into some warm, secure place away from police and guys in yellow firing guns. I'd started to shake as I finally realized how close I'd come to being killed.

"Why would he shoot an innocent dog?" I asked, handing

Eric the spare keys kept in the kitchen. We climbed into my truck, me on the passenger side, Eric driving. I wasn't up to dodging potholes.

"Maybe he took him?" was Eric's thoughtful reply.

I let this idea still my nerves,. By the time we reached Eric's place, I was feeling more optimistic about finding Sergei alive.

*   *   *

"I hope I'm not displacing your friend tonight," I remarked as I walked through the door Eric held open. He chuckled in response, but the pungent smell of male sweat tinged with grilled steak gave me my answer.

I suddenly felt like a sixteen-year-old girl on her first date, which was ridiculous. I was over forty, had been married almost fifteen years. My body had more non-conforming bulges than desired ones. My hair, not quite the colour I was born with, needed a good cut. And my clothes looked as if I'd spent the last week in them, which considering the past hours, was understandable. Besides, Eric was just a friend. That was all.

"Come on in. I'll show you your room," Eric said, not quite meeting my eye, which made me realize I wasn't the only one feeling shy.

Not sure if there really was a separate bedroom, I followed him through the neat but simply furnished living room to a small hallway with several doors. He led me past an open door, which revealed a large queen-sized bed with its blankets hastily thrown over the mattress. As I walked past, I caught the glimpse of a dream-catcher floating above the windowsill.

Eric opened a door at the end of the hall. "It's pretty basic but should give you a good night's sleep," he said as I walked into a small neat room that smelt of fresh paint. The door

317

almost collided with a cot hidden by a billowy duvet draped in a newish looking floral covering. A delicately woven dream-catcher hung from the curtain rod over one of the two large windows. I walked over, softly blew on its long slender feathers and smiled.

Eric smiled back. "To ensure your dreams are peaceful. Look, you've had a rough couple of days, why don't you lie down while I go fix us dinner," he said and retreated.

If I didn't know better, I would say Eric had fixed this room up just for me. But I couldn't quite believe that. No doubt he had lots of visitors, but then again his usual lady friends were probably more inclined to share that larger bed down the hall.

Suddenly feeling very tired, I lay down on the billowy duvet and promptly fell asleep.

FORTY-FOUR

I opened my eyes to the grey light of yet another rainy morning. Although I was firmly tucked under the duvet, I was still fully clothed. My feet, thank goodness, were boot free. A second later, I realized the doorbell was ringing. I waited for Eric to answer. It rang again. Why doesn't Eric get it? Again the bell sounded, this time more persistently. I got up to see what was going on.

Eric wasn't in the house. The bell rang again. Afraid to make my presence known, I furtively peeked out a window overlooking the front stoop. John-Joe stood impatiently at the door. In his hand he held the canvas sack I'd taken from the sugar shack.

Horrified at forgetting Louis's money in my boat, I flung open the door and grabbed it. I hastily thanked John-Joe, closed the door and retreated to the kitchen at the back of the house. I hoped no watching eyes had seen my brief appearance. I tried to reach Eric at the Council Hall and the Fishing Camp but connected only to answering machines. Something important must have come up, I thought. Though it was unlike Eric to forget to leave me a note.

I called Chief Decontie to see if they'd found Sergei, and if they'd caught the gunman but received the unhelpful answer that Chief Decontie would call me when he returned.

Wondering what to do, I threw the sack onto the kitchen table. The top burst open and out spilled packets of twenty dollar bills and Aunt Aggie's stolen wedding picture. I quickly counted twenty-five bills in one bundle and forty bundles in all. Twenty thousand dollars seemed a paltry sum to pay for the discovery of a multi-million dollar gold discovery. Trust Gareth to be cheap. But it was probably more than enough to keep Louis happy.

I looked at the picture of a marriage that had destroyed a life and wondered what use Gareth could've made of it. Even if Charlie did know the identity of Aunt Aggie's bridegroom, the picture contained nothing to link the man to the owner of Whispers Island.

As I gazed at the picture, I realized it was lying on top of another object. Moving it aside, I found myself staring at Marie's sacred amulet, the one given to her by her mother, Whispering Pine, the one missing since her terrible death. It confirmed with icy certainty what I already knew, that the gunman who'd fired at me and kidnapped my dog was indeed Marie's killer.

Curious to know why he would steal it, I loosened the fragile thong enclosing the small deerskin pouch and shook the contents onto the table. Out spilled broken bits of shell, and some small rocks, one, a smooth opaque green, another, a jagged greasy white with a thin gleaming thread running along one edge.

At the sight of this last stone, my pulse quickened. Did this confirm another suspicion? I hastily retrieved the stone discovered last night in my jacket pocket and laid it beside the one from Marie's amulet. Two almost identical pieces of quartz, both with a jagged thread of gold. Since the one from my pocket came from Whispers Island, so must the other. Proof Marie had known there was gold on the island.

However, I was certain that because of the stone's sacred nature, she would never have willingly revealed its existence to anyone, not even to her son or her man, Louis. It probably explained her agitation the night she disappeared. She had learned that Louis had somehow found out about the gold on the island. He had betrayed her ancestors.

The amulet still bulged. I shook it. A cylinder of birch bark fell out and rolled along the table towards me. When I picked it up, a thin gold chain slid onto table. With its fine workmanship in such sharp contrast to the amulet's naturally found objects, I couldn't help but wonder about its significance to Marie or her mother.

I carefully unrolled the paper-thin bark. Written in bold black lettering on the inside speckled surface was the following: "On this day, the 8th of June, 1922, on the occasion of the birth of our child, I, Two Face Sky, bequeath to my one true wife, Summer Wind, Minitg Kà-ishpàkweyàg, my beautiful island."

I leaned back in my chair, stunned. This will was the motive for Marie's murder, probably Louis's and the shooting of Tommy. Louis's money had nothing to do with it. The motive was Minitg Kà-ishpàkweyàg, now called Whispers Island. Because of this will, the killer believed Marie, the granddaughter of Summer Wind, had become its owner.

Except it was a disastrous mistake. Two Face Sky may have lived on the island, but he had no ownership rights to the gold discovery. Only William Watson and his heirs did.

Marie died because of this terrible mistake. What would the killer do when he finally discovered the truth? I started praying Aunt Aggie had divorced her absconding husband.

Infuriated but scared, I paced around Eric's large country kitchen, wishing there were some way I could get in touch with him. Another call to his office and the Fishing Camp didn't locate him. I tried Chief Decontie again and was told that he would be notified of my call.

I checked to ensure all the doors were firmly locked and returned to the strange collection on Eric's table. I could understand the killer stealing Louis's money and Marie's will, but I still couldn't come up with a reason for his taking Aunt Aggie's picture. I even tried to penetrate the cryptic stares of

Aunt Aggie and her bastard of a husband for an answer.

And then I realized the sack wasn't yet completely empty. I shook it and another framed picture fell out. I flipped it over, and knew I had the answer.

I placed the faded newspaper photograph next to Aunt Aggie's wedding photo. Although the two men bore little immediate resemblance to each other—one, an aristocratic German dressed in elegant finery, the other, a defiant Indian garbed in deerskin and feathers—there was no denying the obvious.

I didn't have to read the headline under the photograph to know they were one and the same man. The jagged scar on the left check of both men told me that Aunt Aggie's husband, Baron Johann von Wichtenstein, also known as William Watson, was the man in the faded sepia photograph, the one the newspaper called Two Face Sky.

And in front of the standing Two Face Sky sat a woman in much the same pose as in Aunt Aggie's wedding picture, except she wasn't Aunt Aggie. She was a beautiful young Indian woman dressed in the palest of doeskin. Around her neck was the thin gold chain, which lay on the table in front of me. On her lap nestled a small baby wrapped in furs. She could only be Summer Wind with her daughter Whispering Pine, Marie's mother.

Underneath the photo, the headline confirmed that "German Baron Dies in Tragic Fire."

The killer had made no mistake. Two Face Sky had called Summer Wind his wife, which meant Aunt Aggie had divorced him. Marie was the true heir to William Watson, not I. She would have owned Whispers Island, and she would have stopped the gold mine.

My heart ached for Aunt Aggie. Her cherished Johann had deserted her for Summer Wind, the same sweet girl after whom Aunt Aggie had named her baby girl, the baby girl who had tragically died. I could almost feel the agony she must've suffered, especially when he set up house with his new wife within sight of her once happy home. Every glance across the water would have reminded her of his betrayal. Little wonder she suffered from bouts of mental illness. Still, she could have moved from Three Deer Point. Instead, she spent the rest of her eighty-odd years harnessed to the constant reminder.

I removed the newspaper clipping from the frame and discovered the rest of the article folded underneath. It seemed Baron Johann von Wichtenstein had become enthralled with the northern wilds and had taken on the guise of an Indian chief, calling himself Two Face Sky. He gave up the trappings of the modern world and lived off the land as a native. The only mention of Aunt Aggie was a brief reference that he'd once been married to a lady from one of Toronto's finest families. So even in his death the marriage had been kept secret.

But Charlie had known. He'd probably learned this family secret while growing up with Marie and her mother. So he had come to my place that night looking for proof and found it in Aunt Aggie's wedding picture. After that it was simple. He only had to compare it, like I was doing now, to the picture he'd already stolen from Tommy's place.

Still, could Charlie also be Marie's killer? The presence of her amulet with the two pictures and Louis's money pointed in that direction. And what about Louis's mysterious partner whom Gareth had mentioned? Did he really exist, or was this simply Gareth's way of diverting attention from himself?

The phone rang. Assuming it was Eric, I picked it up and heard a low, raspy voice that wasn't his.

"Meg Harris, you better bring that money, if you want to see your dog alive. If you're not at the sugar shack within fifteen minutes, the dog dies. And he dies if you bring the police."

I was certain the voice belonged to Charlie Cardinal.

FORTY-FIVE

I hung up the phone, knowing I'd just heard the voice of a killer. If it weren't so deadly serious, I could almost laugh at the absurdity of the phone call, which made me feel as if I'd just taken a bit part in a B movie. But two deaths and a shooting were more than enough to convince me that the threat would be carried out if I didn't deliver the money. And to make the fifteen-minute deadline, I had to leave now.

Despite his warning, however, I wasn't about to go into the killer's den without police protection. I quickly called the Migiskan police detachment, explained the situation and told the dispatcher my suspicions about Charlie. She now offered to tell me what was keeping the Chief busy. A stake-out with Sgt. LaFramboise and his men. At Aunt Aggie's sugar shack no less. Had been there since last night.

The dispatcher tried to dissuade me from going by saying it wasn't worth putting myself in danger just for a dog, which only served to reinforce my resolve. So with time fast running out, I told him in no uncertain terms to make sure Decontie was prepared to cover me and nab the killer once I had my dog.

I grabbed the sack, ran through the rain to my truck and drove as fast as the groaning suspension would allow. I reached my house with five minutes to spare, barely enough time to run to the sugar shack.

At first I was surprised not to see police vehicles parked in the drive, but I realized they wouldn't want to advertise their presence. I would have to trust that the dispatcher had managed to alert Decontie.

I jumped out of my truck and slammed the door as hard as I could to warn them of my arrival. Amazed at how empty the woods felt, I felt a moment's hesitation before I started racing down the waterlogged trail to the sugar shack. At least the sound of my splashing pace should give the police sufficient warning of my progress.

I was more than halfway when I heard shouts, one rifle shot followed by another. Surprisingly, it appeared to be coming from as far away as the main road, not from the direction I was headed. What was going on? I debated continuing, when a sharp bark from the sugar shack decided me.

I sprinted the last hundred yards down the trail and stopped when the hut's black shape loomed through the rain. The door was closed, windows dark.

Police radios crackled above the rain's patter. Although the noise was still distant, it convinced me the police were capturing Charlie on his way to the shack.

I called Sergei and was answered by a burst of yapping from inside the shack. I suppose I should have wondered why the dog was inside and his kidnapper some distance away. But I didn't. I was too relieved to find my dog still alive.

I dropped the money sack and ran to the door. I wrenched it open and braced myself for his joyous pounces. But his black body remained beyond the range of the meager light from the windows. I ran to the sound of his yelping, and finding him tied to a post, quickly unclipped his leash. But before my mind had a chance to absorb the fact that someone had done the tying, the room suddenly exploded with light and a guttural voice said, "About time."

I jerked around to see the massive yellow figure of Charlie Cardinal leering behind the kerosene lamp, his moose-like features sculpted into a caricature by the harsh light. He pointed a rifle barrel straight at me.

Too shocked to be afraid, I sputtered, "I thought—"

"Ya liked our little trick, eh? A phone tip to that fool Decontie saying we was at another camp down the road. By the time he clues in, we're long gone. So where's the money?"

As Sergei clung to my side, my heart sank with the realization that I was completely without police protection.

Sergei whimpered. "What did you do to my dog?" I asked.

"More like what he do to my bitch? The horny cur wouldn't leave her alone." Charlie curled his lip as if attempting to smile.

I watched him pull out a cigarette package from inside his yellow slicker.

"You said 'we', Charlie? Who else is involved in your dirty dealings?" I asked. I ran my eyes around the brightly lit room in search of clues as to the identity of this mysterious partner.

Charlie smirked in response.

My eyes caught sight of a familiar tweed jacket thrown over the back of one of the plastic chairs. A jacket I'd seen only yesterday on someone who'd tried to convince me of his innocence. "It's Gareth."

Charlie blew out a stream of smoke. "Whatta joke, him being your ex, eh?"

"Where is he?" I asked.

"Wouldn't you like to know. Now give me my money."

I knew if I told him the money was lying outside, all would be lost. He'd escape the police and I'd be dead. Praying the police would quickly realize their mistake and return, I decided my best option was to stall for time.

"Nice scheme you and Gareth cooked up," I said. "Get rid

of everything that reveals the true owner of Whispers Island, and the gold mine goes ahead."

Charlie started to protest, but remembering I'd seen the results of his theft in the sack, grinned instead. "Knew Marie's grandparents and your aunt had somethin' to do with the island. So figured I was on to somethin' when I nabbed them two pictures."

"But the picture didn't prove Marie owned the land," I said.

"Didn't matter," Charlie replied. "Marie never told nobody she owned the island. Once she was dead, we just had to get rid of anything that said she did. Patterson said that with no living owner, the land goes back to the government, and we get the rest of our money."

"Is that why you killed Marie and tried to shoot Tommy?"

"Kill her? What ya talkin' about? She done herself in after killin' Louis."

"Maybe you didn't, but what about your partner?" I asked, not wanting to believe that the man I'd once loved would actually kill someone to get what he wanted.

A twitch suddenly appeared in the corner of Charlie's right eye. He grunted, then spat on the floor, which made Sergei press harder against my side, causing something sharp to jab into my thigh.

"Where's my money," Charlie hissed.

"Hardly yours. You stole it." I reached into my pocket to remove the sharp object and discovered the piece of quartz I'd noticed last night.

"I don't know what you're talkin' about, lady. It's mine. Now give it to me or else." He walked towards me, rifle pointed.

Sergei growled.

"Shut up, you damn dog."

Sergei lunged forward. Charlie grabbed his collar and dragged the snarling dog across the floor to the door. I tried to stop him but was shoved back against the wall. In the scuffle, I dropped the rock. With a final yelp, the dog was outside. The door was slammed against him. The latch was shoved into place.

Charlie swung the pointed barrel back at me. "Now where's the money?"

"I've got it," spoke a voice from outside. Sergei growled. "Get away," yelled the voice, followed by a loud yelp. "Let me in."

"Run away, dog," I muttered under my breath, as I stared at the piece of purple fabric lying under the quartz on the floor and knew suddenly that Gareth wasn't a killer.

Charlie opened the door to a figure, almost his height, who kicked the sodden sack into the room. Water coursed over the yellow slicker onto the floor. One large, angular hand clutched the wooden stalk of a rifle, while the other shoved the jacket hood aside. With the inevitable cigarette jammed in the corner of her mouth, Hélène's acne-ruined face glowered back at me. "Jeez, Charlie, she still here?"

I wasn't surprised. Hélène herself had told me about her lover Charlie. The piece of fuchsia fabric told me rest.

She dumped the money onto the floor and began counting it. "It's all here. I'll get the rest, and then we're outta here. Police might be back any time now."

She walked over to the mattress on the opposite side of the room and shoved it aside. She nodded in my direction and said, "Do something with her."

Afraid what that something could mean, I glanced nervously at Charlie, who continued to guard the only exit. However, he was more intent on watching his lover remove floorboards. His look of puzzlement suggested he wasn't sure what she was up to.

I glanced over my shoulder at a broken window several feet behind me. Prepared to stop the moment Hélène looked up, I stepped quietly backwards until I felt the wall. The window, its pane shattered by yesterday's bullet, was an arm's length away.

Charlie spoke up, "What's that?" I froze. But he ignored me and walked past to where Hélène was removing a canvas sack, similar to the one I'd taken.

I continued inching towards the window. Hélène and Charlie were too focused on the sack to notice me. As I reached the window, I turned around and braced myself to crash through the window.

"What're you doing?" Hélène yelled. I stopped. The rifle bolt hammered home. "Move back," she said.

Temporarily beaten, but not yet ready to declare defeat, I returned to the middle of the room. I listened for sounds that would tell me the police were coming, but I heard only the rain drumming on the roof.

Charlie dumped the contents of the sack onto the floor. Bundles of money spilled out. A look of amazement washed over his face. "Christ, where'd all this come from?"

Ignoring him, she stepped back and stopped when she had us both within her sights. Her cigarette glowed. Her yellow slicker hung open revealing a fuchsia jacket underneath, the jacket I'd seen from the lake. The jacket gaped where a hole had been torn in the fabric.

"That's Louis's share," I said. "Hélène stole it."

She thrust her chiselled face in my direction, her black eyes coldly appraising, and sneered, "It was my money. I was the only one with the brains to go after CanacGold. But jeez, finding Tommy alive gave me a scare. I figured he was dead for sure when I left him."

I sensed Charlie stiffening behind me. I pointed to the

piece of fuchsia fabric lying on the floor. "But you did kill Marie."

Her unblinking eyes stared back at me. She didn't even attempt to hide the damning tear made when she'd crawled out of the cave after killing Marie.

I heard Charlie grunt.

"And you killed Louis too." I said.

Charlie's feet scraped on the floor. "Hon, tell her it's not true," he pleaded, all his bluster gone.

For a moment, Hélène looked nonplussed, then she screeched, "Oh, shut up! You're so damn dumb, Charlie. I don't know why I put up with you. You thought Louis would lead us to riches. Hah! He was all set to sell us out. He woulda left us with nothin'."

Like a robot, Charlie stared at her with unseeing eyes, while a curtain of dread crept over his face. He reached up and touched the eagle feather hanging from his braid.

"I did it for us, Charlie. I had to. You didn't have the guts to do it." She flung back her shoulders and glared back at her lover. Her fingers tightened around the rifle.

"You shot Marie before she could tell me about the island," I whispered softly.

"Yeah," she replied smugly, almost as if she was proud of what she'd done. "Lucky I overheard her on the store phone. Charlie already told me about Marie's link to the island, so I got suspicious. I offered her a cuppa coffee on the house. Soon she was telling me all about this piece of bark her mama gave her. How this means Whispers Island belonged to her, but she wasn't suppose to tell nobody, 'cause it would only bring trouble."

Hélène stopped to take a deep drag on her cigarette, then continued, "Stupid bitch. Imagine owning an island and doing nothin' about it. She got scared when she heard about the gold on the island and told Louis. Jeez, all he wanted to do was sell the land to CanacGold, eh? She was gonna tell you, Meg, so you could stop the mine."

All this time, she had been glaring at Charlie, as if daring him to challenge her words. Now she turned her gaze back to me. But behind her defiance, I caught a hint of entreaty.

"Well, I couldn't let her do that, could I?" she said. "I needed CanacGold to get that gold. It was my ticket outta here. Once they sized the deposit, I'd get the rest of my money. I tried to talk her out of it, eh? But the stupid bitch wouldn't listen. She gave me no choice. I had to kill her."

Charlie groaned. "How could you?"

But as if she hadn't heard, Hélène took another deep drag. "I knew she went to the island to talk to her ancestors. So I told her we should go there and ask them what to do, eh? I locked up the store and we drove to the Fishin' Camp. She waited in the boat, while I went to get the rifle I keep in the Camp's gear shed. But I seen Louis's *p'tit gars* propped against a wall, where he musta forgot it. So I says to myself, why not. They'd think it was Louis done it, not me. Serve the bastard right, eh!"

Héléne laughed, more like cackled. "When we got to the island, she took me into the cave. Said it was the best place to talk to the spirits. I tried one last time to convince her the mine was okay, but she wouldn't budge, so I shot her."

I looked at Charlie to see how he was taking this. But his face showed little expression beyond the twitch near his eye.

While Hélène was telling her story, her grip had relaxed on the gun barrel. Now it pointed at the floor, not at me. Behind me, I could hear Sergei's quiet whimpers at the door. I decided I'd try for the door. As Hélène continued her story, I shuffled backwards.

"But I had to shut Louis up too. I caught him next morning unloadin' firewood. It was perfect, eh? I shot him and dumped the wood on top of him, then I went back to the island and put the gun with Marie. I figured the way I hid the bodies, no one'd find them for weeks. By then Charlie and I are far away."

I caught the faint crackle of a police radio and glanced quickly at Charlie and Hélène to see if either had heard. But they were too intent on the story, the one telling, the other listening. I continued moving slowly backwards to the door.

"Even had the police runnin' off to Louis's camp with that dumb note, didn't I? Sure had you fooled, eh? But the best was making you all think Marie killed Louis and then herself." She finished with a low throaty cackle.

"This eagle feather, Hélène, the one you gave me when I lost mine. It was Marie's, wasn't it?" Charlie whispered, waking from his trance-like state.

Chanting softly to himself, Charlie carefully detached the long black and white feather from his braid and gently laid it on the table beside him. Turning a stark stare back to Hélène he said, "We have angered the spirits. We must answer to *kije manido.*"

"Jeez, Charlie, ain't you ever gonna quit believin' that guff." She spat the burning cigarette from her mouth and stomped on it.

"Hélène, why? Marie was like a sister. How could you kill her?" He looked at her imploringly, as if trying to fathom her betrayal.

"For the money, ya stupid bastard. That's all it ever was, the money. That's the only reason I put up with your snivellin' ways," she sneered as she aimed her rifle.

"How dare you, you bitch!" screamed Charlie as he lunged towards her, knocking her to the ground. Kicking and screeching, she struggled to raise the gun. A glint of metal as his fist jabbed her chest. With the other hand, he grabbed her rifle.

Suddenly, a violent roar shook the building along with a blinding flash as the bullet smashed through the lamp. Flaming oil flew in every direction, coating the floor in a blaze of fire. Within seconds, the ancient shack was an inferno.

The way out was still clear, but where Charlie and Hélène lay, it was a wall of flames. I saw two pairs of feet and pulled the pair with the boots, not the running shoes with the elongated "y" on the sole. While the fire crackled around me, I strained and pulled and dragged the heavy body out the door, where I left it on the ground and ran back to get the other one.

The roof beams had ignited. Terrified they would cave in, I grabbed the feet with the running shoes and pulled. Suddenly there was a loud explosion, which was the last thing I remembered before finding myself stretched out on the ground with Sergei's rough tongue licking my face.

"Stupid dog," I said and gave him a big grateful hug.

All that remained of Aunt Aggie's sugar shack was a bonfire of blazing timber and red hot metal sizzling in the rain. Soon it would be nothing but a smouldering heap of shattered hopes and dreams gone wrong. A stench of smoke, mixed with an odour I didn't want to identify, hung in the air.

Gareth was standing over me, with his arms crossed. "Good, you're alive."

"How'd I get here?"

"I pulled you out. Couldn't let you fry, could I?" he said with a wry smile.

My head hurt. I reached up and felt singed hair. "I suppose I should say thank you."

He shrugged.

I looked over to where I'd dragged the body. Charlie was painfully raising himself to his feet. His face was streaked in soot, one cheek blistered, his braids gone. But apart from a few burnt patches on his heavy outdoor clothing, the rest of his body was spared.

He stood up, wavered a bit, then turning towards the smoking ruins, his face twisted in anguish, gasped, "She didn't feel the fire. She was already dead. I killed her with my knife. I have answered to *kije manido*."

Eric suddenly appeared from the direction of my cottage. "Meg, you're okay!" he cried, running towards me. Behind him were Decontie and his men.

On a branch high above my head, a black shape slowly unfurled his wings, lifted into the air and disappeared with two mighty sweeps of his wings. His role was over. Marie's messenger had delivered his message.

FORTY-SIX

The tragedy of Whispers Island didn't end with the explosion. Four days later, I discovered Aunt Aggie had one last secret.

It had been a strange day, starting with a heavy morning snowfall that was still falling as dusk darkened into night. It was as if *kije manido* wanted to erase the crimes of this terrible autumn with the innocence of winter's first snow.

I sat on the sofa in the orange warmth of a simmering fire with Sergei curled at my side. Although heavy-hearted, I felt strangely at peace. The uncertainty was finally over.

I found it difficult to believe that only three weeks ago, Marie and I had been laughing in the sun of that fateful Indian Summer day, the day the CanacGold planes had swooped into our northern paradise and triggered the fight over gold. Now Marie was dead, my life set on a different course, and the lives of those lured by its promise of wealth changed forever. Even Whispers Island hadn't come through unscathed. The gap in its profile would be a warning to us all not to violate its sacred shores.

Charlie was in the hospital. He had suffered third degree burns to his hands and face and would require skin grafts. But he wasn't going to jail. It was evident Charlie had nothing to do with the murders of Marie or Louis or the shooting of Tommy. As for his killing of Hélène, it was deemed self-defense.

Although he had broken into my place, shot at me, and was responsible for the tree almost killing me on Whispers

Island, I decided not to press charges. He told me he'd accidentally dislodged the tree when he leaned over the cliff to check out my actions on Marie's beach, and the gun shots were fired only as a warning for me to return his money. At no time did he intend to harm me.

Charlie's only real crime was greed and falling in love with Hélène. For his love of Hélène, he was punished. His wife of twenty years left him, taking their three children back to her own reserve, five hundred miles away.

As for his greed, the money he had earned from CanacGold was smouldering ash. And, more importantly, he'd lost his standing as tribal chief and elder within the band. While the Band Council allowed him to remain on the reserve, he was to undergo a sentencing circle to determine what his punishment should be and to begin the healing process, which, according to Eric, had already begun. Upset over Hélène's role in the killings, Charlie had accepted his responsibility for the deaths, no matter how unwittingly.

As for Hélène, she was dead. No greater punishment could be served on her for the killing of Marie and Louis.

And the gold mining saga was definitely dead. Whispers Island now belonged to Tommy. Well, not quite, but it soon would be in his possession.

At a meeting with William Watson's lawyer, Wilson McLeod, I received a cheque for the remainder of the money that Aunt Aggie had put in his firm's trust in 1925 to handle the taxes for Whispers Island. It was the year I now knew to be the actual date of the death of her husband, Baron von Wichtenstein, alias William Watson, alias Two Face Sky. The lawyer also passed me an envelope she'd left with his firm in 1935.

One document was the transfer of ownership of Whispers Island from crown assets to Mr. William Watson. The second, a request form with "Approved" stamped in red for a name to be changed from Johann von Wichtenstein to William J. Watson. And the final document was the deed to the property.

At last I had the means to stop CanacGold. Even Gareth couldn't fight such concrete proof of ownership.

Although I was furious over his role in this gold mining affair, I owed him one. Because he'd saved my life, I decided not to inform on him. He might be an abusive, controlling bastard intent on feeding his own selfish ambitions, but I believed that deep down inside he still retained a trace of the caring man I thought I'd married. I'd let him make the choice; stop this downward spiral into crime by owning up to his involvement or one day find himself facing a far greater sentence.

After reading Aunt Aggie's letter, written ten years after the deaths of Two Face Sky and Summer Wind, I called François. Following her wishes, I set in motion the transfer of the ownership of Whispers Island to Tommy and his sisters.

I will let you decide, the heir to my lands, what shall become of Minitg Kà-ishpàkweyàg. You have read my story and know of the anguish I have suffered with the death of my husband Johann, the man I would never divorce. While I have promised the band full use of this land, I am unable to complete the full transfer. My destiny has been too closely linked to this island. I cannot give it up. Regardless of how painful, it is the last token I have of Johann, that and his treasured peace pipe I found in the embers. But in the fullness of time, if you, my heir, are able to understand and forgive me, I ask that you give this land to the descendants of Whispering Pine, the tiny daughter of Johann, the child who replaced our own dead daughter.

And also in her letter, she removed whatever temptation Tommy might have had, despite his best intentions, not to develop the gold mine. There was no gold on Whispers Island, at least not enough to justify the high cost of development.

Aunt Aggie wrote that she had discovered what looked to be a seam of gold and brought in experts to determine the extent of the deposit. But the drilling had proved the vein was worthless. No doubt CanacGold would have discovered this, but not before destroying the soul of the ancients' forest.

Whispers Island still had one last secret to reveal, the final tragedy of Agatha Harris, her confession, which once read explained so much.

I killed my husband, Johann. There, I have finally written it down in indelible ink. It has taken me ten years to face up to what I did that dreadful day on Minitg Kà-ishpàkweyàg.

Day in and day out I spied on my husband and that native girl, watching every move of their indecent behaviour. Until one day I could no longer endure it. I took my rifle and skied over to the island.

I surprised them in the act of rutting. Something inside me snapped. Wanting only to wipe out the evil, I fired. In my frenzy, I knocked drying clothes into the hearth fire. Within minutes, the lodge was in flames. I fled outside, but once outside I heard the wail of the small child, the living child for whom Johann had left me. I wanted to rid myself of this evil, too. But I couldn't. Thank goodness my reason returned and I was able to save this tiny daughter of my husband's from the fire.

With the crying child in my burnt arms, I stood and watched the fire consume the lodge and all that was within.